HOUSE OF CATESBY

The Final 4 Novels

SUNNY BROOKS

Text and Illustration Copyright © 2019 by Sunny Brooks

ISBN: 9798637010226 (Large Print)

Publisher
Love Light Faith, LLC
400 NW 7th Avenue, Suite 825
Fort Lauderdale, FL 33302

CONTENTS

BOOK 5: MR. HENRY CATESBY AND THE REBELLIOUS REDHEAD

BOOK 6: DILEMMA OF THE EARL'S HEART

BOOK 7: THE SCANDALOUS DOWAGER COUNTESS

HOUSE OF CATESBY
PROLOGUE

Nothing could have prepared the Catesby clan for the unexpected passing of the family patriarch, Earl Joseph Edward Catesby.

On the day of his death, the lives of one woman and her six grown children changed irrevocably. The matriarch Countess Margaret Lilias Catesby was now a dowager countess; her strength and maternal duty the sole driving force pushing herself through the grief.

Each of the Catesby children has been left to carry on their father's legacy, shown physically through their father's green eyes and spiritually through his impassioned attitude for living.

Eldest son Francis had barely a day to cope with his father's death before the title of Lord

Catesby was immediately thrust upon him. With Francis assuming ownership of the estate and his five siblings left to sort out the pieces, each must now find a way to navigate the world without their dear father's guidance.

WILL SIBLINGS FRANCIS, Emily, Helena, Sophia and the twins, Charles and Henry, be able to move forward into society and proudly carry on the Catesby name? There's only one way to find out…

Welcome to the House of Catesby!

BOOK 4: LADY SOPHIA AND THE PROPER GARDENER

BOOK 4

HOUSE OF CATESBY

Lady Sophia & The Proper Gardener

SUNNY BROOKS

FOREWORD

Always listen to your heart and don't be too quick
to judge others. You never truly know anyone
else's life journey or what they have gone through.
Trust only that you do not know the truths of
others.

Our job as humans is to remember that we all
come from the same place. We were once all
innocent children, we are all fragile inside, and we
all yearn to do our best, despite how we show that
to the world.

Give others the benefit of the doubt and you
might find that someone wonderful lies beneath
an unexpected surface.

~Sunny Brooks

CHAPTER 1

"Sophia, are you quite well?"

The book slipped from her fingers as Sophia rose from the window seat, as she gave her sister a tense smile. "Yes, of course." Her stomach swirled with anxiety as she attempted to lean nonchalantly against the edge of the window, hoping Helena would not come over to speak to her, for then she would be able to see exactly *who* it was Sophia had been watching.

Helena's face softened. "I am concerned for you, Sophia."

"Why?" Sophia asked, frowning slightly. "I am not ill."

"I know that it's just that…." Helena trailed off, walking over to stand beside Sophia. "Even before I went to town, you seemed distant and quiet." She put one gentle hand on Sophia's arm. "I do wish you would tell me what ails you."

Forcing a smile, Sophia shook her head. "I am just missing mama that is all."

"Truly?"

Sophia nodded, knowing in her heart that it was not quite true. Whilst she certainly did miss mama, that was not the only concern on her heart.

Helena sighed. "I do miss mama too, I must say. The house does seem quieter without her."

Their mother had gone to live in the Dower house, even though Francis, the new Lord Catesby, had not yet married. Their mama had said something about the house holding too many memories for her, too many old ghosts of the past. Sophia could understand that, in many ways. Every time she looked into the library or poked her head into the study to talk to Francis, she would half expect to see their father sitting there, surrounded by a cloud of cigar smoke.

For a moment, she wondered what her father would say of her current difficulty, although she could easily guess. Sighing to herself, she leaned into her sister, needing the comfort for a brief moment. She had not spoken to anyone of her heart's torment, and nor would she. It was best for everyone if she kept silent, knowing that there was no way forward. There was simply no way for her to have what her heart desired.

Helena wrapped her arm around her sister's thin shoulders, and the gesture made Sophia want to weep. She felt so alone. Francis was busy taking on all the responsibilities of the estate, their mother had relocated to the Dower house and now her closest sister, Helena, was about to marry Lord Richard Livingstone. Of course, there was Henry, her brother, and Charles' twin, but Sophia never really saw much of him. No-one did, truth be told. He occasionally ate dinner with them all but chose to spend much of his time up at night, studying the stars. Charles and Henry were both of the studious types, whereas she hated the confines of four walls.

Thankfully, her father had understood her desire for the outdoors, the need to have her fingers in the earth. Together, they had planted almost the entire garden, although Sophia had left some of the more difficult areas to the gardeners. Of course, now, her mother had taken almost the entire staff with her to the Dower house, but that meant that the head gardener had left the Catesby estate. Now, there was a new gardener, one who seemed to know what he was doing, but his arrival had caused Sophia a significant amount of turmoil.

Helena squeezed Sophia's shoulders slightly,

before dropping her embrace and turning to face her. "Now, you must be honest with me, Sophia," she said, firmly. "I will not ask for your help with my wedding preparations if you do not wish to. I shall not hold it against you if you would prefer not to be involved. Whatever it is that is ailing you – for I confess that I do not believe it is just mother's absence on your mind – I do not wish for it to worsen for my sake." Helena's eyes searched Sophia's face as she waited for an answer and, for a moment, Sophia was desperate to tell Helena everything.

Instead, she simply nodded.

"You truly wish to help?" Helena murmured, softly.

Managing a wide smile, Sophia patted Helena's hand. "Of course I want to help you. That is what sisters are for, is it not?"

Joy sparkled in Helena's eyes. "It is, and I will be glad of your help. I do hope that, when you are ready, you will tell me the truth about what it is that really is troubling you so. No-one should carry their burdens alone."

Sophia knew that Helena was right, especially because she was marrying Richard who had been living an entirely secret life for a great many years. It had all been for good reason, of course, but Sophia knew that Richard felt a huge relief in being able to share his situation with Helena, even if she had forced the issue. Her heart heavy, Sophia watched Helena walk away, closing the door behind her.

Sighing to herself, Sophia resumed her position in the window seat and picked up the book she had no intention of reading. In truth, she had not read a single word thus far. Resting her head back, she lifted her knees and, ensuring her dress was tucked over her ankles, propped up the book on her lap. At least now she carried the pretense of reading.

Why did she long for this so? She knew that this would come to naught, but still, her foolish heart yearned for it. Just a single look, a single smile. Even yet, she still had not plucked up the courage to venture outside. By now, her garden must be filled with weeds. She was too afraid that she would give herself away, that she would seem entirely ridiculous and would rush back inside with heated cheeks and tears in her eyes.

Her heart caught as she looked down into the garden and, out of the corner of her eye, saw him wander into view once more. He looked to be tidying the bushes, although she was certain she had seen him do just the same yesterday.

You are being foolish, she told herself, somehow unable to take her eyes from him. *He is a gardener.*

Sophia knew that one did not fraternize with the servants. She had heard that some gentlemen liked to take their pleasure with a maid now and again, but that idea had been pronounced as vile by both her father and her brothers. So why then was she longing for a man who worked the grounds? A servant, who was employed by her brother no less!

Even worse, Sophia was more than aware that her attraction to him was based only on his physical appearance, which was utterly shallow. When he had come across her in the gardens and had taken the liberty of introducing himself, she had been entranced by the warmth in his hazel eyes, aware that he was looking at her steadily instead of dropping his gaze as a servant ought. To her embarrassment, she had struggled to find her voice, and so had turned away and walked inside. Since then, she had never dared venture outdoors again.

Without warning, the gardener stopped and looked up at the window, directly at her. Sophia caught her breath, unable to look away. Her breathing became shallow as he remained entirely still, simply looking up at her as though enjoying the view.

Then, he turned his head and walked away, back towards the stables, leaving Sophia feeling entirely bereft.

CHAPTER 2

David snipped ineffectually at a few leaves, wondering about the young lady in the window. There was something mesmerizing about her, to the point that he was unable to stop himself from studying her, even if it had been only briefly.

A small smile played around his lips as he remembered how she'd looked when he'd first met her. Her delicate hands had been encased in gloves as she pruned a rose bush, her eyes focused and mouth firm as she took great care in her task. It was obvious that she had done this before.

He had introduced himself without realizing what he was doing. He had only just managed to stop himself from introducing himself with his full title. He realized too late that he was looking into her eyes, instead of dropping his head as a servant should. She was simply too beautiful for him to look away from.

She had not replied to him, so he had not been allowed the pleasure of hearing her voice. Whether it was from the shock of him introducing himself to her, or from some other unknown reason, she had sped back into the house and had not yet come out to the gardens again.

Sighing to himself, David forced his gaze back to the bushes, even though he had trimmed them the day before. The lady intrigued him. There was a sadness in her eyes that had him wondering, and she so often seemed to be alone. He had caught her watching him from the window on a few occasions now, and wondered what her reasons for doing so could be.

Turning his eyes back to the window, David studied her for a brief moment more before walking back in the direction of the stables. Heat filled him as he realized just how forward he was being – and he was meant to be a gardener in Lord Catesby's employ! He could not continue to behave as he once had, for surely he would then be found out. Remembering his place, that was what he had to do.

"Is that you, Hutton?"

It took David a second to respond, still not

quite used to the name he had chosen. "Yes, it's me."

"Good," the groom replied, walking closer and shielding his eyes from the sun. "Lord Catesby wants to speak to you."

"Oh?" A surge of worry suddenly filled David. "Why?"

The groom shrugged. "I don't rightly know, but I'd not wait to get up there. It's not good to keep the master waiting."

David nodded his thanks and walked directly to the servant's stairs, climbing them two at a time and ignoring the frustrated squeals of the maids. Brushing some dirt from his trousers, he walked to Lord Catesby's study and knocked once.

"Ah, Hutton," Catesby exclaimed, beckoning him in as he bent his head over some paperwork. "Come in, come in."

The man did not sound angry, which was a good sign. Walking in, David remained standing a few feet away from Lord Catesby, holding his cap in his hands.

"You are settling in well, then?"

Surprised at the man's question, David nodded. "Yes, thank you."

"Good, very good. I've heard that your work is exceptional and that you do a marvellous job with the under-gardeners."

David grinned. "They are very hard workers, my lord."

Lord Catesby nodded, his face growing more serious. "I must ask you something – has my sister been outdoors?"

"Your sister, my lord?"

Waving a hand, Lord Catesby sighed. "Yes, my sister. Your response tells me she has not been working in the gardens much recently."

David did not say anything, choosing to let Lord Catesby speak.

"My sister, Miss Sophia Catesby," the man continued. "She loves to spend time in the gardens – not walking there, you understand, but working with the plants and flowers." He shook his head. "It was something she did with our father, and it concerns me that she has not been doing so of late."

Clearing his throat, David shuffled the cap in his hands, remembering to keep his gaze low. "I do hope my presence has not perturbed her, my lord."

There was a short pause. "No, I do not think it is that," came the eventual response. "Although I do intend to encourage her back into her hobby. I wanted to ensure you were aware that I would be doing this so that her presence in the gardens would not surprise you."

David bowed. "Of course, my lord. I would be

more than happy to help her with anything she needs."

"Very good, very good," Lord Catesby replied, waving him towards the door. "Thank you, Hutton."

Aware he was dismissed, David walked to the door and shut it softly behind him before pausing for a moment. Taking a breath, he smiled softly to himself, delighted that Lord Catesby would be encouraging his sister to go back to working in the gardens. Perhaps he might have the opportunity to speak to her, although he had to remember that he was here as the gardener and not as the gentleman he truly was.

"Sophia?"

Starting with surprise, Sophia looked up from her book to see Francis walking into the library with a smile on his face.

"Francis," she smiled, starting to get up. "How nice to see you."

He gestured for her to stay seated, sitting down in the chair opposite. His face took on something of a concerned expression, making her wonder about his reason for seeking her out.

"I have not been much in your company of late, have I?" Francis said, heavily. "I am so caught up with estate business that I often take dinner in my study, never thinking that you would find yourself dining alone so often."

Realising that he must have spoken to the cook, Sophia tried to smile. "It is of little consequence, Francis. I know how hard you are working and Henry is so caught up looking at the stars that I find he is often absent when it comes time for dinner." She laughed quietly. "Even when he does join me, he is so busy thinking about his constellations that I get very little conversation from him!"

Francis joined in her laughter, shaking his head at his brother's lack of social graces. "He is quite something, is Henry."

"He will be a great astronomer one day, I am quite sure of it," Sophia declared, fondly. "In any case, neither of you intend to leave me to dine alone, you are both just caught up with important matters." Her smile grew soft as she saw Francis' brows knot together. "I am quite contented, especially now that Helena is returned."

"Helena is here now, of course," Francis said, as though he had just remembered. "Then she keeps you company."

"When she is not busy with her wedding plans," Sophia chuckled. "But yes, she is. In fact, I am meant to be helping her select the appropriate flowers for the wedding." Her voice drifted into silence as she contemplated the fact that sooner or later, she would have to venture out into the gardens.

"Do you miss mama?" Francis asked, quietly. "I only ask because I too have noticed her absence of late."

Sophia regarded her brother for a moment. "I do," she said, slowly. "But I am beginning to wonder what the reason is behind these questions, Francis." She leaned forward, studying him. "Come now, we have always been straight with one another. What is it that concerns you?"

Francis let out a long breath, a wry smile on his face. "Very perceptive, Sophia. In truth, I am concerned for you." He sat back in his chair. "It was only when I spoke to Cook that I realized just how often you are alone. Then I have heard from Helena that you seem very reluctant to return to your gardens."

Tension crept up Sophia's spine. Surely Francis could not guess about her attraction to the gardener? That would be shameful indeed!

"I know that I have hired new staff," Francis continued. "But I do hope that is not of a concern to you, Sophia. David Hutton is an amiable man who seems to have a way with the flowers and plants, in much the way our old gardener did. You need not fear that he will disapprove of your presence if that is what is holding you back." His gaze was piercing. "Unless there is something else troubling you? Are you lonely, Sophia? Is my absence, as well as Henry's and mother's, making you melancholy?"

Sophia was filled with a mixture of relief and gratitude. "I thank you for your concern, Francis, but truly, I am not melancholy."

"Then why do you not return to the gardens?" he asked, carefully. "Sophia, since father's death, you have not gone more than two days without being in the outdoors, even when there is a thunderstorm, as I recall."

Blushing, Sophia laughed a little self-consciously. "The roses needed to be secured to the trellis. Otherwise, they might have been torn to pieces!"

Francis grinned at the memory. "You looked like a drowned rat, Sophia!" His gaze softened. "Then what is holding you back from what you love?"

Sophia struggled to know what to say. She did not want to reveal to Francis her strange attraction to the new gardener, but at the same time could not find much of an excuse.

"I – I must admit, I was unsure about whether the new gardener would accept my presence there," she stammered, not quite able to meet Francis' eye.

"Then you should have asked me."

"You are busy enough," she exclaimed, truthfully. "I could not disturb you."

At her words, Francis rose and walked to sit next to her, taking her hand in his. "Sophia, you are my sister and under my care. You must never fear disturbing me for whatever reason. I want you to come to me with any concern you might have, no matter how small you think it might be." He searched her face, waiting for her to nod. "You must promise me not to keep such things to yourself any longer."

Touched by his kindness, Sophia nodded. "I will. Thank you, Francis."

"Good," he grinned. "Then I shall expect to see you out in the gardens very soon. I have already told Hutton to expect you."

"Thank you," Sophia murmured, watching as Francis left the room. Sinking back into the soft cushions, she closed her eyes and let out a long, drawn-out breath. It seemed she would have to face the gardener once more, otherwise draw more concern from her brother. Perhaps Hutton would simply leave her to work at the flowers alone, for Sophia was quite sure her throat would close up the moment she saw him.

"David Hutton," she whispered to herself. "Whatever am I to do about you?"

CHAPTER 3

"Good morning."

Sophia smiled as Helena walked into the dining room, ready to break her fast. It was a good deal later than Helena normally arose, but they had spent the previous evening talking long into the night as sisters often do. Sophia and Helena had always been close, and Sophia could barely think of the heartache that would follow when Helena finally married and moved away to live in London.

"Did you sleep well, Helena?"

Stifling a yawn, Helena nodded. Sitting down at the table, she helped herself to a piece of buttered toast and gratefully accepted a cup of tea from Sophia. "Did you?"

"Wonderfully." It was a flat out lie, but Helena

did not need to know that. Were she honest enough to tell her sister, Sophia would have admitted that she had tossed and turned for most of the night, knowing that she would soon have to go out to the gardens and meet the gardener again. Try as she might, she could not stop her heart from quickening whenever she thought of him.

"What do you think?"

Blinking, Sophia realized that Helena had been speaking to her, but she had not heard a word.

"Oh, yes, I quite agree," she mumbled, hoping that Helena would not notice her lack of attention, for she could not exactly explain who she had been thinking of.

"Wonderful!" Helena's face lit up, and she clapped her hands. "Francis did say that he was going to try and encourage you to return to your gardens again, so I am very glad to hear that you are so amenable. I do so love those roses."

Sophia nodded weakly, wondering what exactly it was she had agreed to. Whatever it was involved the gardens and her roses.

"Shall we say in an hour?" Helena asked, excitedly. "Oh, I am so glad you have agreed, Sophia. I am sure that, together, we will make a wonderful wedding bouquet! Now, I must go and speak to Cook about the wedding breakfast before

I forget." Still delighted, Helena picked up the rest of her toast and practically ran from the room.

Closing her eyes, Sophia let out a soft moan. By thinking about David Hutton, she had entirely missed Helena's request to put together a bouquet. She had intended to go out to the gardens in the late afternoon, knowing that the servants often took a short break around that time before the dinner gong sounded, but now it seemed she was to go with her sister in less than an hour.

Getting to her feet, Sophia lifted her chin and set her jaw. She was going to have to stop being so ridiculous and just carry on with her life, regardless of what she felt for the man. It was entirely inappropriate anyway, was it not?

Sophia sighed to herself as she left the room. She had never been in love before since they had never spent much time in London and therefore had very little opportunity to mingle with other members of society. She had never felt the loss, given that she simply adored spending time with her sisters, but now the house was growing quieter and quieter as each sibling found a love of their own. Slowly, Sophia realized that her life in the Catesby estate could not go on as it was. Once Helena married, she would be quite alone in the house, even with her two brothers occupying it. Perhaps she would ask to visit Helena at the height of the season next year, where she might finally meet a man she could care for.

Looking out of the window, Sophia wondered if she would ever feel such a fierce attraction to someone in the same way she did to David Hutton. For heaven's sake, she had never even spoken to the man, but she could barely stop herself from seeking him out every time she drew near one of the many windows in the estate. Her heart would flicker with disappointment if she did not see him, and flare to life if she did.

"You must stop being so ridiculous, Sophia," she told herself, firmly. "You cannot ever marry him, so you must stop feeling this way. Hiding from him is no way to overcome such things. You must simply carry on and, in time, you will get over what is a ridiculous infatuation!"

DAVID HEARD laughter on the wind and lifted his head at once. A broad smile crossed his face as he saw the two Catesby sisters walking across the lawn, arm in arm. He had not yet met Miss Helena Catesby, but he knew that she was the only other lady staying in the house. She was beautiful of course, but his eyes were always drawn to Miss Sophia Catesby. Her eyes were filled with laughter as they approached, the dusky pink in her cheeks making her even look even lovelier. They had not seen him yet, which meant that David allowed himself a few more seconds of simply watching the beautiful Sophia.

"Ah, you must be the new gardener."

"That I am, miss," he said, bowing to Miss Helena. "Are you both out for a stroll this fine morning?"

Helena laughed. "No, not at all. You see, my sister has a love for growing beautiful flowers, and has a special love of roses. She has been growing many different varieties for many years."

His admiration grew. "The rose garden is entirely your handiwork, miss?" he asked, directing his question towards Sophia. "It is beautiful."

He couldn't miss her blush, its duskiness matching the bloom she held.

"I thank you," she murmured, still not quite meeting his eyes. "My father and I spent many years tending them."

"And your efforts have been rewarded," David replied, honestly. They were some of the most beautiful roses he had ever seen, and his admiration for her grew. "I only wish I had some of your skills."

Her blush deepened, and she turned away to walk along the length of the trellis, studying the roses carefully.

"We are to choose some for my bouquet,"

Miss Helena explained. "My wedding is only a few short weeks away."

"My deepest congratulations, miss," he replied, remembering to bow deeply. "If there is anything I can assist you with, then I am entirely at your disposal."

"Thank you, Hutton," she replied, before walking away to join her sister.

David lingered near the two Catesby sisters, although he ensured they were not aware of his presence. He could barely take his eyes from the lovely Miss Sophia, finding her delicate features a pleasure to behold. If only he were not pretending to be a lowly servant, he might have the opportunity to make her acquaintance properly, and then ask to court her. Frowning, his mouth twisted as he thought about his life back in town. Were he to reveal himself, she would discover the truth and then reject him entirely. For the moment, it seemed he was only able to admire her beauty from a distance, knowing that he would never be able to reveal the truth to her.

Presently, he noticed Miss Helena walk away from her sister, holding five roses in her hand, each of a different variety. He wondered if Miss Sophia would follow after her, but to his delight, she remained where she was. His eyebrows rose as he saw the way she pushed her hands into the earth, pulling out weeds and, at times, digging for their roots with a small trowel so that they would not surface again. It was clear that she knew precisely what she was doing.

He had never met anyone like her before, for he knew not a single other lady who would be so willing to dirty her dress and her hands and work in the flower beds. They were all too 'proper' for such things. David winced as he remembered how his own mother had mocked his love for the outdoors, telling him that his title meant he should not enjoy such things. His life was meant to be one of fulfilling other people's expectations. He was meant to find a wife, marry, and produce the heir and the spare before settling down into a life pursuing hedonistic pleasures. It made him nauseous to think about.

No, he much preferred having the wind cool his cheeks and surrounding himself with the beauty of nature. Thankfully, his passion for growing all manner of things had given him the opportunity he needed to escape his mother's conniving ways, in the only way he could think of. If he told Miss Sophia the truth, would she ever be able to understand? Would she keep his secret? Or would her responsibility to her brother have her marching into the house to inform him of his lies?

Suddenly, he realized he had somehow made his way over to Miss Sophia's side, and that she was looking up at him with a slightly confused expression.

"Ah, Miss Sophia," he stammered, completely befuddled. "I was just hoping you might...."

"Might?" she prompted, slowly rising to her feet.

His mind scrambled for an answer. "Might teach me about these roses," he said, inwardly wincing at his poor response. "I confess I know very little about them." He held his breath as she looked at him, hoping she would believe his words. In truth, he would find any excuse just to be in her presence and become better acquainted with her, but only if she would allow him the liberty.

She took a breath. "Of course, Hutton. This way."

CHAPTER 4

S ophia hummed to herself as she pulled on her boots, quite prepared to go into the gardens even though gray clouds were pulling in.

"Sophia!" Helena exclaimed, finding her sister lacing up her boots. "Whatever are you doing?"

"What does it look like, Helena?" Sophia retorted, a smile playing around her mouth.

"But it is cold, and I am sure it is going to rain," Helena objected, sitting down on Sophia's bed. "I was just coming to ask you if you would like a game of cards or some such entertainment. I had not imagined you would wish to go outside in this weather."

Straightening, Sophia got to her feet. "Only last week, you and Francis were both encouraging me to return to the gardens, and now you object to my doing so?" Her eyebrow lifted, challenging her sister.

"Well, of course, but I am simply concerned about the cold," Helena spluttered, realizing she was contradicting herself. "The wedding is very soon, and I should not wish you to catch a cold."

Sophia shook her head. "Helena, I have never caught a cold from being out in the wind, as well you know. If you prefer, I will take a shawl and ensure I have warm gloves."

Helena sighed. "Very well. But you must return the moment it starts to rain."

Sophia did not reply and simply walked from the room, chuckling to herself. She would give no such promises. In truth, she had slowly begun to enjoy her hobby once more, now that she had overcome her fear of speaking to David Hutton. The gardener was both charming and helpful, and the more they had talked, the more she grew to enjoy his company. Unfortunately, that had only heightened her attraction to the man, which was exactly why Helena's concerns would not prevent her from returning to the gardens this afternoon.

"GOOD AFTERNOON, MISS SOPHIA."

Sophia felt a warm glow build up inside as she saw him waiting for her, leaning on his shovel.

"Good afternoon, Hutton," she murmured, glancing away from him. "The roses are looking beautiful today."

He smiled and fell into step beside her. "The rains have been good for the soil."

Sophia did not say another word but simply made her way slowly through the gardens. Her heart was already fluttering simply by being in his presence.

"You are quiet today, Miss Sophia."

She glanced at him, before turning away again. "I must confess, I am preoccupied with my sister's upcoming nuptials."

"I can imagine," he said, with a heaviness to his voice that surprised her. "Weddings are often large occasions."

Sophia threw him another glance, wondering at why he sounded so despondent. "You do not think of weddings as a happy occasion, I gather."

His eyes darted to hers, evidently surprised that he'd given so much of himself away. "I suppose I do not consider matrimony as wonderful as...as some others do," he finished, cautiously.

Narrowing her eyes slightly, Sophia frowned at his words, wondering why he appeared to be so hesitant in his response. It was as if he was hiding something from her, although she had no right to ask him what it was, of course.

"May I be bold enough to ask you something, Miss Sophia?"

She smiled, removing the frustration from her face. "Of course, Hutton. Although, I may be disinclined to answer it, depending on the subject matter."

He grinned at her, as warmth sparked in his eyes. "I quite understand, Miss Sophia." They wandered a little further through the gardens in silence, with Hutton showing no signs of asking his question.

Sophia kept silent, allowing him the time to consider his words. Why she was showing him such consideration, she could not explain, but she found herself keen to know what it was he wished to say.

"Does your sister love her betrothed?" he asked, quietly.

She frowned again, turning to face him as they paused in their steps. "That is a strange question, Hutton."

A deep flush swept into his cheeks. "Forgive me, miss."

Her expression gentled. "It is not impertinent, Hutton, just leaves me questioning why you would ask such a thing." She tipped her head up a little further, to see him better. "For what it is worth, I believe my sister is deeply in love with Lord Livingstone and has been for many years."

"Then you believe they will be happy together," he muttered, taking off his cap and running one hand through his hair. "I am glad for them if that is the case."

Sophia saw his frustrated expression and wondered at it. What was it about Hutton that had him asking such things? Why was matrimony such a terrible prospect for him, as though he hated the very idea of it? *And why do I feel so sorrowful over such a thing?.*

"You do not think matrimony can be a happy state, Hutton?" she asked, softly, beginning to wander away from him. "I am surprised to hear it, I must confess."

She could tell he was following behind her, very conscious of his presence close to her. Her skin prickled with awareness as she heard him sigh heavily.

"Matrimony with love is entirely different from the prospect of matrimony without," he murmured, quietly. "To be forced into such a thing is a terrible prospect."

"I quite agree," Sophia replied, looking up at him with a smile. At the same time, a slight nagging began to work its way into her mind. Hutton did not always speak as a gardener would. At times, when he became distracted, he would slip into a much more refined way of speaking. It was as if he had two sides to his character, and he could only present one at any given time. It gave her pause, realizing that she did not know the man as well as she thought. They had spent many hours together over the last week, discussing the gardens and working the soil, but their conversation had never before turned to such a delicate subject as marriage before. It was apparent that Hutton felt strongly about matrimony, which was something she had not expected.

"I had thought a man such as yourself could marry whomever you chose," she said, thoughtfully. "Unhindered by such things as class, or the need for wealth." Daring a glance at him, she saw him studying the ground with fierce concentration. "Surely you cannot find yourself in a situation where you are being forced into matrimony."

"No," came the quiet reply. "No, of course, I am not in such a situation as that." He cleared his throat, lifting his head to smile at her. "I simply know of such a predicament, and it makes my heart sorry to see it." His voice lowered, his expression softened. "One should not marry without love."

Sophia sensed her face grow warm, growing uncomfortable with the sudden heat in his eyes. Whatever it was she was feeling for this man, she needed to stop herself before it got out of hand.

There could be no future for them. There was no prospect of matrimony, no children, nor a home in the country. He was a working man, lower in class than her by far, and Francis simply would not allow it, regardless of how she felt.

"I should go," she murmured, turning from him. "I – I think it might begin to rain soon."

"Wait, please," he begged, catching her hand and eliciting a gasp from her mouth. "I did not mean to speak out of turn, Miss Sophia. Please accept my apologies."

"You did nothing wrong, Hutton," she replied, her breath catching in her chest as he pressed her hand. "In truth, I am a little chilled, that is all." She gave him a wide smile but could tell that he did not quite believe her.

"You will return again to the gardens?" he asked, his eyes still searching her face.

He is a gardener, Sophia reminded herself, finding herself unable to answer such was the tumult of emotions warring in her heart. "I – I must go," she stammered, pulling her hand from his and stumbling back towards the house.

CHAPTER 5

Sophia pushed her bonnet from her head, catching it in her hands. She set it down gently, smoothing her hand over her hair. She did not want Hutton to see her with perspiration on her brow.

She had run from him before when their conversation had grown too intimate for her. It had been foolishness, of course, for she was quite sure Hutton was merely being kind. Although, she was still surprised at his willingness to be so open with her. His heart was bruised for some reason, although she did not know exactly why that was so.

Leaving her bonnet to one side, she wandered through the gardens, hoping she might catch sight of him. Usually, he would appear within minutes of her being outdoors, but she had not seen him this last hour. Her heart sank. Had her quick departure somehow made him believe that she wanted their acquaintance to be at an end?

Sophia drew in a long, shaky breath, astonished to find that she was so close to tears. She had never before felt such an affection for a gentleman, had never made herself so open and vulnerable with a veritable stranger. Could there ever be any kind of future for them both? Sophia shook her head. Francis would never allow it, of course. But then again, he had never once shown any kind of interest in any woman so he would be entirely unable to understand her own heart. It seemed entirely impossible, yet still, deep in her heart, there was the beginning of a small hope. A hope that, despite their differences in status, there might be a way forward for them both. She did not know how to even suggest such a thing, given that she had no true knowledge of his own depth of feeling, but her heart refused to let go of that dream.

Glancing up, Sophia realized that she had walked farther into the gardens than she had intended. To her left, she saw a small path leading to what looked like an area of wilderness. It must have been left unattended for years since it was at the far end of the gardens. She and her father had been entirely focused on their roses for many years, leaving the rest of the gardens to the hired servants. Perhaps her father had said that this patch could remain as it was since no-one ever came here. It would make sense.

Thinking that perhaps she should have kept her bonnet, Sophia found her feet walking along the small path, interested in what she would find. It was completely overgrown, although the path was at least clear of branches and vines. She wandered through it, finding delight in the wildness of the place. There were flowers of all different types growing wherever they chose, the trees spreading their branches across as though reaching for one another. Ivy climbed along their trunks, adding to the greenery. It was a beautiful sight.

"Oh!"

A small, ivy-covered arbour was just to her left. A small deer rushed away as she approached, making her smile with happiness. There was more life here than she realized, hearing the birds continue their song above her. Ivy covered the roof of the arbour, trailing down over the windows and the door. It was just as well she was not afraid of spiders, for Sophia was quite sure there would be plenty of those creatures within.

Lifting the cover of ivy, she stepped inside, giving her eyes a moment to adjust to the gloom. To her surprise, the arbour held a couple of small benches, which were surprisingly clean. Even more astonishing was the small broom propped up against the wall, which evidently had been used to sweep the floor. Someone else knew of this place. But who? Francis? Was this his place of solitude, a place for him to hide away when the stresses of his title became a little too much?

Sophia did not want to intrude if that was the case. She should not remain here if it were meant for him. A keen sense of disappointment filled her as she slowly sat down on the bench, enjoying the solitude. Perhaps there might be another place she could call her own, a place to escape when she wanted to be out in the world, away from the confines of the house.

A quiet whistling broke into her thoughts, making her stiffen in surprise. Someone was approaching, and she had never known Francis to whistle before. A hand pulled back the ivy before Hutton stepped inside.

Sophia saw him physically start with surprise upon seeing her. "Miss Sophia," he stammered, as the ivy curtain dropped behind him. "Forgive me, I did not know you would be here."

Her skin prickled with awareness of just how close he was to her, and of just how alone they were. It was entirely inappropriate, but she could not bring herself to march past him and down the path.

"Excuse me," he mumbled, dropping a bow before making to turn around.

"Wait!" Sophia cried after him, her voice sounding strangled even to her. "I mean – you do not have to leave on my account. This is clearly a place you have come to often."

He dropped his hand from the ivy and nodded. "Of course, this is your brother's gardens, Miss Sophia. If you wish to come here, then I shall find another place immediately."

She saw him visibly relax as they slipped back into easy conversation. "No, I think not," she replied, quietly. "There is no reason we cannot share this place, is there? I doubt anyone else would come this far into the gardens."

His dark eyes flickered to hers.

"I did not mean to run from you," she continued, softly, aware of her sudden, desperate urge for him to remain in her company. "I was a little overwhelmed with your honesty that is all." She smiled at him, seeing his uncertain look. "Forgive me?"

"There is nothing to forgive, Miss Sophia," he mumbled, shuffling his feet. "I was the one in the wrong."

To her very great relief, he sat down on the small bench to her right, taking off his cap and placing it beside him.

"I do hope you will not stop talking with me,"

she replied, her fingers urging her to reach over and take his hand. "I do appreciate our conversations."

He lifted his eyes and looked at her, his features bathed in shadows in the gloomy arbour. "I thought it best to take some time away from you, Miss Sophia," he said, quietly. "If you are certain you wish to continue our acquaintance, then I would be delighted to do so."

There it was again, that unorthodox way of speaking that reminded her more of a gentleman than a servant. Sitting back, she leaned against the wooden wall of the arbor, disregarding any consideration she might have for cobwebs and spiders. Now that he was here with her, she had nothing more to concern herself with. She was back in his company, and that was all that mattered.

"Perhaps we might come here more often," she murmured, her entire body tightening as she gave him what she knew to be an entirely inappropriate possibility. "It is a beautiful place."

Hutton shifted in his seat. "I would not wish to bring any harm to you by our acquaintance," he said, slowly. "I am just a hired servant after all, and you are a lady."

Sophia tilted her head, regarding him. There was a sparkle in his eyes that excited her, as though he were trying very hard to do the right thing but was struggling not to agree to her suggestions.

"But we are entirely hidden here, are we not?" she murmured, shifting a little closer to him so that their knees were almost touching. "No-one would ever see us. Therefore my reputation will be entirely secure."

His eyes drifted from his hands up to her face, a tormented look in his eyes. "Miss Sophia," he croaked. "Please, I beg you. Don't."

She said nothing, but leaned forward, boldly placing her hand on his thigh. His muscles jumped under her hand, but she did not remove it. She was pushing him, driving their unspoken attraction forward. She could not bear to hide it any longer. She knew what he was asking of her, asking her not to open herself to him to the point that he would be unable to refuse her, but she simply did not care. What she felt was too strong.

"Miss Sophia," he whispered again, his eyes now drifting to her mouth.

In a moment, he was leaning over her, his mouth pressing against hers like a dying man living his last few moments. His hands were on either side of her, pressing down against the bench as he kissed her, sparking a myriad of sensations within her. Sophia locked her arms around his neck, refusing to allow him to step away or break the contact, her entire being coming alive at once.

To her surprise, Hutton put his arms around her waist and stood, pulling her up against him. His kisses did not stop but grew in intensity. Fire shot through her as he deepened the kiss, his fingers now digging into her hair until it began to tumble free of its pins.

"Hutton," she breathed, as he feathered kisses along her jawline. She could not say more, closing her eyes as he retraced his steps, touching her lips once more with his. Her world was alight with new sensations, as Hutton held her in his arms, fulfilling the desire she'd had for so long.

CHAPTER 6

"Miss Sophia."

Warmth spread up through her chest as she turned to see the gardener approach. A knowing look was in his eyes as he bowed to her, feigning interest in the blooms she was studying.

"Are you looking to make a new flower arrangement, Miss Sophia?"

"I am," she replied, loudly enough to ensure that her voice would carry through the gardens to anyone who might be listening. "Might you help me select some roses? I would like them to last."

His mouth curved and Sophia's breath caught in her chest.

"Of course," he said, warmly. "This way, miss."

She followed him through the gardens, knowing exactly where he intended to take her but forced herself to look as though she was simply allowing him to lead the way. Her anticipation and excitement rose with every step, her heart quickening its pace as they walked deeper into the vast gardens of the estate.

"Just this way, miss," he said, over his shoulder. His eyes caught hers, lingering there for a moment before he turned away. Licking her lips, Sophia hastened forward until, finally, they rounded the corner and came to the arbour.

The corner arbour had been their place of solace these last three weeks. The growing ivy still covered the window spaces, and the swinging vines that covered the entrance moved softly in the breeze.

Hutton pulled back the ivy curtain and allowed her to enter before him, following her quickly. The moment the ivy fell back into place, his arms were around her, and she melted into his embrace.

"Tell me that you missed me," he whispered in her ear, as his fingers brushed over her cheek and down her neck.

Sophia closed her eyes, hardly able to form words such was the effect he had on her. "I cannot tell you how much, Hutton." Her hands rested on his chest, feeling the strength beneath. It was entirely improper, of course, to have fallen in love with a gardener, but her heart wanted no-one else.

"Please call me David," he murmured, now stroking the back of her neck with gentle fingers. "Hutton seems so formal, still."

Sliding her hands around his neck, Sophia pressed herself against him, uncaring about whether her gown would become wrinkled or dirty. "David," she murmured, shivering slightly at the sensations he was building in her.

"Are you cold?" he asked, his breath tickling her cheek as he lowered his head.

She gave a tiny shake of her head, unable to form words. His breath mingled with hers, his arms tightening around her waist.

Finally, his lips met hers. Even though it was not the first time he had kissed her, Sophia felt the same explosion of feeling. It was as though the world fell away and all that was left was Hutton holding her in the way he did now. Her entire body burned with fire as he pressed at the seam of her lips, and, as she allowed him entry, she heard him groan.

Her fingers tangled into his hair, holding him fast to her. Her breath came quickly as his lips left her mouth, running along her jawline and towards her ear. Delicate kisses were pressed to her neck, making her gasp with pleasure. His hands made their way up her back, over her shoulders and slowly slid down her arms, until they found her hands.

He stepped back, and Sophia felt the loss immediately.

"Please, David," she begged, not knowing what it was she was asking for. An urgent need was burning in her core, a need that she knew only he could satisfy. "Don't leave me, not yet."

Hutton's eyes were darker than she had ever seen them before, his cheeks flushed with colour. "Sophia," he said, hoarsely, reaching for her hand but refusing to kiss her again. "I – "

He bowed his head and ran a hand over his eyes.

"What is it, David?" she asked, hesitantly. He had never stepped away from her before.

David shook his head. "Sophia, I – I am struggling with what I feel."

His words astonished her, making her heart leap with unexpected pleasure. They had never really discussed such things before, having enjoyed each other's kisses too much to give time for words. Apparently, this time was to be different.

"If you are asking me to confess that I care for you, David, then you should know that I do. Deeply." If she were honest with him – even with herself, she would admit that she was beginning to feel the first stirrings of love in her heart.

"Even though I am a servant? A hired man?"

The bite of his words made her start with surprise, heat leaving her body almost immediately. He dropped her hand and moved away to sit on the small bench in the corner.

Sophia remained where she was, hating that there was sadness in his eyes. She had known from the first moment she'd seen him that he was not the right man for her, but she simply had not been able to stop herself from seeking him out.

"Hutton, I do not care that you are a hired man," she said, quietly. "My feelings for you grow with every passing day." An uneasy feeling swept over her as she realized he had not told her anything of his own emotions. Was she merely a passing fancy for him? Was there nothing deeper? Every time he had looked into her eyes, she had seen something glowing there, but as yet he had never given voice to it.

"It is not right for me to feel this way," he groaned, burying his head in his hands.

"Then, you do care for me?"

His face lifted to hers at once, surprise in his expression. "Of course I do, Sophia. How could I not? You are beauty and grace, kindness and compassion. Your gentleness and tenderness draw me to you, in a way I never expected."

Sophia swallowed, her heart beginning to fill with an overwhelming joy. "I cannot tell you how happy I am to hear you say those words, David."

He sighed, and dropped his head in his hands, covering his face. "Sophia, there can be no future for us."

"Don't say that," she begged. "I know it would be quite unorthodox, but I cannot bear to think of you not in my life." Desperation filled her chest. "Can we not continue with what we have now, and put aside fear or worry about the future?" She stepped forward, closer to him, looking down at his bowed head. The ache in her chest grew as she waited for him to say something.

Hutton did not respond, other than to rest his head against the cushion of her chest, wrapping his arms around her waist once more. Sophia brushed his dark hair with her fingers, wanting desperately to find some kind of solution for them both but struggling to clearly see a way forward.

"I think I must leave you, I must stop this."

His words stunned her, the blood freezing in her veins.

"No, Hutton," she stammered, suddenly terrified. "You must not. Please, I could not bear it!"

"This is not right, Sophia. I can offer you nothing." Slowly, he lifted his head so that he might look into her eyes and she saw there a deep sadness. What was it that he was holding from her? Was he already married? Or was it simply their difference in social status?

Sophia fought the despair mounting in her chest, blinking back hot tears. "I cannot bear it if you were to leave me," she whispered. "What would I do without you?"

His face lifted to hers, and he tugged her down beside him. "I will not pretend that I do not feel the same pain at the thought of leaving your side, Sophia, but what future can there be for us?"

"I will elope with you if you ask it of me," she whispered, her hands grasping onto his shirt as though if she held on tightly enough, he might stay. "What I feel for you now will continue to grow, I am sure of it."

Lifting one hand, he brushed his fingers along her temple, before cupping her chin. "Don't say that, Sophia. I am not worthy of your enduring affection. Not when I...." He dropped his hand and passed it over his eyes, his mouth closed as he held back the rest of his words.

"What is it, David?" she begged, fear mounting in her chest. "You have some great pain that you will not share, and I do not know what to do to get you to share it with me." Tears pricked at her eyes. "If only you would tell me, then I might be able to help!"

He shook his head, as a slight groan came from his mouth.

"If it is simply of your status, then can you not see how little that matters to me?" Sophia whispered, her heart filling with sadness and pain. "But it is more than that, is it not?"

David drew in one long breath, finally dropping his hand so he might look into her eyes. "Yes, it is more than that, Sophia, but I will not speak of it. Do not ask it of me. Already I have done more than I should have with you, but I simply cannot stop myself. Perhaps it would be best if I left this employ altogether, until I know what best to do." His fingers caught her chin once more, his thumb brushing her lips. "I want you to know that my heart belongs to you, Sophia. It is true in its affection for you."

She cried then, unable to accept that he was considering leaving her, disregarding any hope for their future together. It was too painful to even contemplate. His arm moved around her shoulders, pulling her into his chest. Sophia rested her head on his shoulder, her arm encircling his chest and resting around his neck. He held her tightly but did not speak a word to take back what he had already said. Sophia knew it was because of the depths of his affection for her, but that did not lessen the ache she felt, the deep, searing pain that came with the knowledge of the secrets he held back from her. If he would only talk to her of them, then they might forge a way together, but it seemed he was entirely resolute.

Hutton had his own secrets to keep.

CHAPTER 7

David pushed a hand through his hair, growing more and more frustrated with himself. He should not have allowed himself to feel any kind of emotion for the beautiful Miss Sophia but, try as he might, he could not stop his heart from longing for her. However, he had seen neither sight nor sound of her for the last few days.

Lifting the axe high, he struck at the log, slicing it cleanly in two. It was an excellent way to relieve his frustrations, although by now he was sure had chopped more than enough firewood.

He could still remember the taste of her kisses, the softness of her skin against his fingers. How much he wanted to be with her. His fondness for her was more than just a physical desire. It was a true appreciation of her character, as well as a developing affection that, if he did not check it, could easily grow into love. Growling to himself, he picked up the axe again and struck down, hard.

They had spent a lot of time together over the last three weeks, and he had found her company utterly delightful. She did not speak to him as he had expected, given that he was a servant of the house, but he had noticed the kindness in her eyes, the compassion in her character. She was always gentle, as though, by her tender persuasion, the flowers grew into their beautiful blooms. In truth, he had never heard a harsh word leave her lips and she was held in high regard by the rest of his staff.

Momentarily, David wondered what his household staff thought of him. He barely gave them more than a glance, expecting them to do what was asked without question and dismissing them if they did not. He shook his head. This experience had taught him exactly what it meant to be in someone's employ, and he was not sure he particularly liked it. There was always the fear of dismissal, the worry that their work would not be of a high enough standard.

David wondered if perhaps that was merely a concern of the newer staff who had arrived, given that the Dowager had taken the previous household staff with her to the dower house. By all accounts, the new Lord Catesby was a fair and kind man, someone he respected immediately upon first acquaintance. In fact, it had been on his mind more than once to tell Lord Catesby the truth about his situation, which would ultimately mean throwing himself on Catesby's mercy – but surely the man would understand? It would also mean that he might be able to court Sophia one day, but only if she could forgive him for his ruse and his terrible lies.

He had gone back to the arbour only once since the last time they had been together. Memories and regrets had hit him hard, coming thick and fast as he'd sat down on the bench and leaned back against the ivy-covered wall. Sophia wanted him, wanted a future with him, and yet he was forced to push her away. He could not allow her to entertain thoughts of matrimony when he was not truly who she thought he was. David knew he should never have allowed himself to touch her, for that had been the start of his downfall – but he could not get enough of her kisses. Even now, only three days since their last meeting, he was hungering for them again, like a starving man might dream of bread.

Throwing the axe to one side, David sat down on the stump and put his head in his hands. He could not risk it. If Sophia were to discover that he had been hiding the truth from her, that he was actually an engaged gentleman, then he knew he would never be able to speak to her again. The hurt and betrayal would be too great for her to endure. She would turn from him, leaving him to his disgrace and hide away from him. In truth, she would have every right to do such a thing, for what kind of woman would wish to engage herself with a cad and a bounder such as he was?

Groaning, David coupled his hands behind his head. Why was his heart so engaged with the girl? He knew he should not be speaking to her, should not be seeking out her company in order to have her in his arms again, but there was a force him that simply propelled him towards her. Why was fate dealing him such a rough hand? He had been forced to run from London, to run from his conniving mother and supposed fiancée. Only to find someone he might truly come to care for when he was pretending to be nothing more than a gardener.

"Pleased to meet you, Miss Sophia. I am Viscount David Armstrong," he muttered, wishing he could say truly say those words to her but knowing exactly what would happen, was he do to so.

Grimacing, he picked up some of the firewood and began to stack it in the shelter he had built previously. He had to remain here, for as long as he could. To return to London would be disaster itself. His mother would continue trying to force him to wed that ridiculous creature, Lady Viola Ermington.

For a long time, he had simply been enjoying his life and his title, although he ran his estates with care and precision. It allowed him to have a good balance between hard work and enjoying time with his friends at various soirees or other gatherings. Of course, he had known he would have to marry at some stage but had not considered it a pressing matter.

Too late, he had realized, his mother considered it the *only* matter of importance in his life.

He could still smell the overpowering, cloying scent of Lady Ermington's perfume. Unfortunately, when he had been introduced to her, he had taken a breath and practically swallowed the scent, forcing him to cough for a good few minutes. It had only been when he had finally recovered his breath that he had finally been able to bow to the lady. He had thought nothing of it, but soon it became clear that both she and his mother were in cahoots, planning to shackle him to Lady Ermington forever.

It was not simply the case that he did not appreciate his mother's interference in his life, but more that he found Lady Ermington singularly unattractive, in both face and character. She had cold blue eyes that did not warm when she smiled, a perfectly straight nose but a thin mouth that held a hint of cruelty. She wore far too much rouge, and batted her eyelashes once too often, making him almost nauseous in her obvious attention towards him. It was only when he had made it clear that he was not in the least interested that she had wormed her way into his mother's good graces.

Unfortunately for him, his mother had taken to Lady Ermington and, together, they had hatched a plan for his future.

Lady Ermington was respectable enough, but had gone through four seasons and, thus far, not found a single gentleman interested in wedding her. He could understand why, of course, but her interest in him reeked of desperation. Why she had chosen to sink her claws into him specifically, he did not know, but perhaps it was simply because his mother had taken a liking to her. In truth, Lady Ermington and his mother shared much of the same qualities – both were devious, sly, and extremely good at looking down their noses at others in society, regardless of their social standing.

David closed his eyes at the memory, hating that he had fallen so foul of their evil intentions. He had attended a ball celebrating the engagement between a Miss Harlington and his dear friend, Lord Darwent, only to discover that Lady Ermington was also in attendance. His attempts to avoid her had failed and, unfortunately, he had found it increasingly difficult to detach Lady Ermington from his side. At one point, he had been forced to physically remove her hand from his arm, something she had not taken too kindly to him doing. He had seethed inwardly, seeking out the quiet of the gardens for a brief moment in order to keep his temper.

That had been a mistake.

Lady Ermington had, somehow, discovered him in the gardens and had attempted to kiss him. He had been repulsed and pushed her away, only for his mother to appear and ask him, in a shocked tone, what exactly he had been doing with Lady Ermington.

It was only then that he had realized exactly what it was their intentions were. Without a word, he had strode back into the house, picked up his gloves and left, choosing to go to Whites instead of returning home. He had woken up in Whites the following morning, with gritty eyes and a thumping headache, to discover that he was now betrothed to Lady Ermington.

He had found out they had, apparently, been seen that evening in an embrace. His mother had been the one to assure the gossips that he was, in fact, engaged to the Lady but that they had kept their engagement quiet so as not to take attention away from Miss Harlington and Lord Darwent. Society, of course, had lapped it up and the town was now abuzz with the news, despite the fact that David himself had never even agreed to such a thing. So how then, had he woken to discover himself engaged?

HE HAD THROWN himself on the mercy of his friend, Lord Darwent, explaining the situation and seeking a way to extricate himself from Lady Ermington. Unfortunately, Lord Darwent had been of very little help, pointing out that he was duty bound to marry the lady now. Otherwise, he would greatly affect not only his own reputation but hers. David had been uncaring, stating that he would rather society knew that Lady Ermington was something of a conniving witch, but Lord Darwent had then pointed out that Lady Ermington had two younger sisters who were having their first and second season respectively. That had forced David to reconsider. If he broke the engagement, then her sisters would be adversely affected. Their invitations to societal events would slowly decline since they would be tainted by his actions. Slowly, he had sunk into despair, returning home to simply sit in his room, refusing to speak to his mother at all.

Eventually, he had come upon an idea. He had been forced to simply disappear. It was the only solution he could think of. If his mother could not find him, then she could not coerce him into setting a date for his nuptials. David was quite sure Lady Ermington would grow bored of his absence after some time had passed and would move onto another gentleman. She would need to marry soon, so as not to be considered entirely on the shelf. This was better than publicly breaking the engagement, knowing the shame it would bring to both him, his mother and Lady Ermington's family.

The firewood was stacked, and David realized he was completely exhausted. He had worn himself out physically and emotionally, thinking of what it was he was running from. By now, he was sure his mother would be speaking to anyone and everyone she could about her son's disappearance. He was worried that the rumours might spread to the country. Perhaps Lord Catesby would hear of them – but given that the man had only laid eyes on him twice, and barely looked at him since, David was sure that Lord Catesby would not hold any suspicion.

What of Miss Sophia?

That had him pausing in his steps, his eyes turning almost involuntarily, towards the window. Was she there, watching him? Would she guess his true identity, if notice of his disappearance reached the estate?

He had to stay away from her. He could not risk it, not now. His heart quelled at the thought of removing himself from the woman he had begun to care about, but he knew he had to remain hidden, otherwise find himself back in the clutches of his mother and Lady Ermington. He had told her that he might consider leaving the estate altogether, but his heart quailed at the prospect, forcing him to remain for the time being. He would simply have to soak her up in his memory until the time came for him to move on – whether to another estate or back to his true life.

"Hutton?"

Her sweet, soft voice drifted across the wind towards him. Turning, he saw her descend the steps leading into the garden. Pretending he had not heard her, he picked up his axe and, whistling loudly, strode across the gardens away from her. He pretended he did not feel the ache in his heart, the pain slicing through him as she called to him once more.

This was for her best.

CHAPTER 8

Sophia wept hot tears over Hutton's behaviour, aware that he was doing exactly as he had said but still hurt by it nonetheless. She had attempted to approach him, only for him to turn and walk away as though some kind of danger was snapping at his heels. It appeared he would not even talk to her and she felt the loss keenly.

Ever since the first time she had seen him chopping wood, Sophia had tried to approach him on two further occasions, leaving a day in between each, but he had been quiet and apparently uninterested in talking with her. In fact, he was more of a servant than she had ever seen him. He kept his head down, never once glancing at her with those hazel eyes of his. She found herself longing to see them, almost desperate for him to look at her again. Sophia felt as though she could hardly bear it, wishing she had the strength to drag him to the arbour and force him to tell her what it was he was hiding from her.

Wiping her face, Sophia drew in a long breath and tried her best to calm herself. There had to be some sort of solution.

"Sophia?"

Hoping that her face was not overly tear-stained, Sophia turned to see Helena walking towards her, a bundle of ribbons in her hands.

"Oh, my!" she exclaimed, scurrying forward to take them from her sister. "Whatever has happened?"

Helena shook her head. "It is best not to ask." A spot of colour appeared in both her cheeks, making Sophia laugh. Helena could, at times, have something of a fiery temper which pushed her to do the most irregular things, but this was certainly the first time she had ever seen her sister's irritation taken out on ribbons!

"Was there one you were looking for, particularly?"

Glancing up at Sophia, Helena nodded "I could not find it."

"Why are you so upset over that?" Sophia inquired, sitting down with the bundle of ribbons on her lap. "Richard is going to think you beautiful, no matter what you wear."

Richard had returned to town for a short while but was going to be joining them for this evening's dinner. Surely Helena could not be so concerned about her appearance now, not when she was already secure in his affections for her.

"I want to look my best for him," Helena muttered, throwing herself into a chair. "It upsets me when I am apart from him."

"You miss him, then," Sophia replied, calmly. "That is quite normal, I am sure."

Helena's face slowly relaxed. "Yes, I am sure it is, but I am just surprised at the great amount of feeling I have for the man. He is gone for but a few days and I am already desperate to be in his company again!"

Sophia grew uncomfortable, recognizing that her own emotions were very much in tune with what her sister was saying. Licking her lips, she ran her fingers over the ribbons and did not respond.

"I cannot wait to see him again. We have such a bond, such an ease of conversation that I find I cannot have, not even with you," Helena continued, her voice soft. "More than anyone, he understands me. The care and consideration he shows bring joy to my heart. I find that I can barely take my mind off him"

"You think of him often, then?" Sophia mumbled, her own heart beginning to quicken as her mind was filled, once more, with a vision of David Hutton.

"It sounds quite ridiculous, I know when he has only been gone for a few days, but the way he looks at me...." She trailed off, a gentle smile curving her lips. "I hope you will feel the same one day, Sophia."

Swallowing hard, Sophia ducked her head and concentrated on attempting to work her way through the ribbons. She could not be honest with her sister and tell her that she already did feel much the same way over a gardener, but she could at least be truthful with herself. What Helena described was much the same way she was feeling about David Hutton, finding herself almost desperate for his company once more. He spoke to her in such a gentle way that she found herself willing to open up to him, to tell him things that she would not mention to her sister. She remembered how they had once spoken of her sister's upcoming wedding and of her own increasing loneliness. It was, as Helena said, that David seemed to understand her more than anyone else did.

She had to admit that she could not get her mind from him, wondering where he was, what he was doing and why they could not be in conversation together. Warmth crawled up her neck and into her face as she recalled the kisses they had shared.

"There is such a thing as missing the physical affection too," Helena murmured, her fingers still working at the ribbons. "The physical intimacy between husband and wife only increases with matrimony, I have heard it said. Although apparently, mama wishes to talk to me about that." Helena glanced up and laughed on seeing Sophia's hot face. "Come now, Sophia, you cannot let such talk make you so embarrassed! You may as well come with me to talk to mama since I am sure you will be wed next."

Relieved that her sister thought her blushes were over their current topic of conversation, Sophia feigned a laugh. "Nonsense, Helena. I have no intention of marrying anytime soon."

"Nonsense," Helena replied, dismissively. "All you have to do is find a man who looks at you in a certain way, and you will be head over heels in love." She smiled and patted Sophia's hand. "Of course, he must love you in return, but I have no doubt that will happen. In fact!" she exclaimed, her eyes suddenly alight. "Once I return from honeymoon, you shall come to London and stay with me. We shall find you a great number of suitors and then you might have your pick."

Sophia tried to laugh, but the sound stuck in

her throat. "Oh, Helena," she managed to say, unable to hide the break in her voice. "You have such ideas, but I am quite contented here at home."

She saw Helena frown, lines marring her forehead. "There is that melancholy again," her sister murmured, softly. "There is still something on your heart, Sophia." Frustrated, she leaned forward to catch Sophia's eye. "Why do you not tell me, Sophia? Are we not always close? Why now do you hold this from me? I want to help!"

"You cannot!" Sophia exclaimed, tears trickling down her face. "No-one can. It has all turned into such a disaster." Dropping the ribbons, Sophia buried her face in her hands and sobbed.

Helena moved to sit next to her almost at once and wrapped her arm around Sophia's shoulders. Knowing that she was going to tell Helena everything, Sophia leaned into her sister's embrace and let out all the emotion she had been holding back. It came out in a torrent, in a rush, her entire body shaking with sobs.

"My dear Sophia," Helena murmured, evidently upset by her sister's distress. "Whatever has upset you so?"

"My heart is broken," Sophia whispered, her sobs eventually lessening. "I have been so foolish, Helena. Whatever am I to do?"

CHAPTER 9

Once Helena had rung for tea and given Sophia time to compose herself, she sat down next to her sister once more and gave her a sharp look.

"Now, whatever it is that is troubling you, I must ask you to promise that you will not keep things from me any longer. I want to help you, and this is clearly distressing you more than you can bear."

Sophia nodded, knowing that Helena was right. "You will think me entirely foolish when you hear all of it, Helena," she sighed, wondering what Helena would think of her taking up with a servant. "I have fallen hopelessly in love."

Helena gasped, her eyes sparkling with sudden delight. "You have? How wonderful!"

"It is not so wonderful when you hear who it is that has captured my heart," Sophia said, miserably. "It is the gardener."

A stunned silence filled the room as Sophia kept her gaze firmly in her lap, her fingers smoothing minute creases in her gown. The maid arrived with the tea tray, and Sophia waited with trepidation as the maid placed the tea tray down and then exited the room. She dared not look at Helena, sure that there would be some kind of ridicule or exasperation there.

"And, does he return your affection?"

Startled by Helena's question, Sophia stared at her sister. "Helena, did you not hear me just now?"

"I heard you very clearly," her sister replied, softly. "And I do not think it so terrible, Sophia. One cannot help one's heart, of course. Although, it complicates matters if he returns your affection."

"He does," Sophia replied, miserably. "But now he has parted himself from me, and will not return to my side. He has decided that he cannot continue with what we started."

Helena patted Sophia's hand. "Perhaps that is for the best, though," she answered, gently. "He is attempting to do the right thing, Sophia. He is not within your sphere, Sophia, nor can he ever be.

Not unless you.…..” Helena trailed off, her eyes widening. “Pray tell me that you are not considering matrimony!”

Knowing that this was precisely what she had been hoping for, Sophia lied and shook her head. “I know it is quite ridiculous, Helena, but my heart is broken over him.”

“And I well understand that pain,” Helena replied, gently. “For years I believed my love for Richard was not returned, and the agony of it almost broke me.”

“Your love for him continued regardless,” Sophia pointed out, not seeing any solution in her sister’s words. “Which means I have very little chance of recovering from this. I know he is someone who is in the employ of our brother, but I feel as though no other man could compare to him.” She shook her head, hating that tears were falling from her eyes yet again. “I believe that he is holding something back from me, something that, if he were to tell me of it, might open up a way for a future together, but he simply will not trust me.”

Helena drew in a long breath. "Sophia, I love you dearly, but I must warn you that your association with a servant is not a favourable one. I know you love him dearly, but you must put him from your mind and your heart, no matter how long it takes. I am sure that, once you come to London and enjoy a few balls and the attention of various gentlemen, you will slowly forget your gardener."

Sophia shook her head as tears crept from her eyes and began to make their way down her cheeks. "I cannot forget him," she whispered, brokenly. "He understands me like no other, Helena. Not even you." Looking up, she saw the hurt cross Helena's face but did not take her words back. "I do not mean to upset you, my dear sister, but David sees into my soul in a way no one else ever has. Even though we are the closest of sisters and the dearest of friends, there is something different about him."

Helena sighed heavily, although a small smile played around her mouth. "Oh, Sophia. You have truly fallen for this man." She gave her a soft smile. "Your sentiments match with what I feel for Richard."

"Then you can see how much in earnest I am," Sophia replied, quietly. "And see how much my barren my future is without him."

"And you do not think that you might forget him in the whirlwind of London society?" Helena probed, gently.

"I can never forget him," Sophia answered, truthfully. The man she had shared her soul with, the man who had brushed her lips with his, who had shown her what it was to be alive with passion – no, she could not forget him.

"Then you must find out what it is that holds him back," Helena replied, firmly, shocking Sophia entirely.

Blinking back her tears, Sophia wiped her eyes and stared at her sister. "A moment ago, you were encouraging me to forget about him and to find myself another gentleman," she exclaimed, her voice wobbling with emotion. "And now you are telling me to seek him out?"

Helena laughed. "I had not realized just how deeply you were in love with him until just now," she replied, her eyes sparkling. "I must say that I am quite delighted for you, although I feel it my duty to warn you that the future might present many difficulties if you continue your association with him."

"I know," Sophia replied, knowing exactly what Helena was talking about. "But that still does not push me from him."

Nodding, Helena handed Sophia her handkerchief and turned to pour the tea. "Then you must find out what it is that holds him back from you and find a way through it."

"Do you think Francis will be angry?"

"Most likely, yes," Helena replied, practically.

"But that is just Francis' way. After all, you are the youngest of the sisters, so it is not as though your association with a gardener will negatively influence any younger sister. You may marry the stable boy if you wish it."

Sophia could not help but giggle, suddenly filled with relief that not only did her sister understand, but that finally, she had some support in her current predicament.

"I would also suggest that you tell mama," Helena replied, lifting her teacup delicately and taking a small sip. "It may come as something of a shock to her, but I am sure she will understand."

Hardly able to believe what she was hearing, Sophia shook her head to herself and let out a soft laugh, one that was mingled with tears. She had not expected such a reaction from Helena, but her unwavering support meant the world to her.

"Well, what are you waiting for?" Helena asked, giving her a slight dig in the ribs. "Are you going to sit here all afternoon?"

"Helena!" Sophia exclaimed, glancing behind it. "It is storming thunderously outside!"

"No excuses, now," Helena replied, with a slight smile. "And what better reason to be stuck outside in the gardens – hidden away somewhere – than the rain? Should Francis ask where you are, then I shall simply inform him that you have gone out to the gardens but will be sheltering somewhere until the rain stops." Pressing Sophia's hand, her smile gentled. "Take as much time as you need, Sophia. Find out the truth and do not shy away from it. If you love him, then fight for your future together, no matter what it takes."

CHAPTER 10

A raindrop landed on Sophia's forehead and ran down her nose, as she rushed towards the rose beds, glad that she had worn her boots. The clouds were still low, filled with swirls of grey and dark blue as they poured their deluge down on her. She was going to be soaked through if she did not find some shelter soon.

She did not know where to go, nor where David might be. Her heart pushed her towards their hidden arbour, the only place she could think of. If he were not there, she would wait until the rain stopped before searching for him again. Helena was right. She could not give up this time, would not allow him to continue holding her at arm's length. The truth would have to come out so that she would know for certain whether or not there was a future for them.

The ivy was wet and glistening in the rain, the dampness brushing her cheek as she pulled the ivy curtain aside and stepped in. Her heart thundered in her chest as she looked around, only to sink into her shoes as she realized it was entirely empty. Even though she had known it was quite ridiculous, she had hoped that he would know she was searching for him and be in the arbour, waiting for her.

"Foolish," she muttered to herself, removing her bonnet and shaking the water from it. "You are a foolish girl, Sophia."

Sitting down heavily on the bench, Sophia leaned her head back against the wood wall and let her eyes close. Listening to the sound of the rain, she let her mind empty of every thought. She no longer feared about the future, did not need to worry what her mother or brother would think. Helena was right. There was no younger sibling to consider and, whilst her association with a mere servant might be considered a scandal, she was sure it could be kept fairly quiet. Who knew? Perhaps Francis might find it in his heart to bequeath a small sum on her, as well as her dowry so that they would not have to live as paupers.

"Even if we do," she murmured to herself. "I do not think I would mind it so much." Sophia knew the torment she had gone through these last days, having been separated from David. Surely life with love, even without wealth, was better than a life absent of love?

"Sophia!"

"David!"

The ivy curtain had been pulled back suddenly, and Sophia found herself looking into David's face, the astonishment she felt mirrored in his eyes.

"I – I did not expect...." he began, trailing off and beginning to back away. "I do apologize. Forgive me."

There it was again, the way his manner of speaking sounded more like a gentleman than a servant.

"Please, David," she begged, getting to her feet and catching his arm. "Do not leave me again. I have come out to the gardens to wait for you, but I could not find you anywhere."

She saw his eyes flare as he looked at her, water streaming down his cheeks from the rain he had just been walking in.

"Don't leave me," she whispered, her body suddenly coming alive with feeling. "I have been entirely miserable these last few days."

He closed his eyes, although did not pull his arm away. "Do not, I beg you."

"Do what?" she asked, confused.

"I cannot be near you," he replied, his own voice husky. "Sophia, I cannot be near you!"

Tears fell like rain on her cheeks as she found his hand, clinging to it with her own.

"I know you love me," she replied, sobs breaking through her words. "You are tearing yourself away from me, and I do not know why – all I know is that I cannot bear it. I cannot, David! I am bereft, left entirely alone." She swallowed hard, seeing the agony on his face as she spoke. "Please, tell me what it is that keeps you from me, from the future we might have together where we are bound together in love." Lifting one hand, she brushed the raindrops from his cheek, boldly capturing his face in her hands as she inched closer to him. "I have determined that I will not let you escape without the truth," she finished, her tears still falling. "I love you, David. Body and soul, I love you. Tell me that you do not feel the same way."

Her heart pounded in her chest as she looked at him, desperate to hear his answer. She felt him sag, tension leaving his body and he gazed into her eyes, emotions flickering over his face, emotions that she could not quite read.

Then, in an instant, his mouth was on hers – hot and urgent. All of her breath left her body, caught up in his sudden embrace. The tears she had cried mingled with the moisture on his face, her hands digging into his hair as his hands wrapped around her waist. They stumbled back, until Sophia felt her back against the side of the arbour, clinging to David with such a passion that it almost frightened her. She could not give a name to the feelings rising in her chest, and, to her shame, she sobbed against him as his lips left her mouth and trailed down over her cheek.

"Oh, my dear Sophia," David whispered, lifting his head and pulling her into his embrace. "How much I have hurt you."

Sophia tried to reply but could not get the words out, sobs shaking her body. It was tears of relief, she knew, her heart slowly healing as David held her.

"I have found myself almost mad without you," he continued, pouring words of love into her ear. "To see you, to hear your voice, but to have to keep myself at a distance from you…." He pulled back and looked deeply into her eyes. "It has been a torment, unlike anything I have ever known before."

"David," Sophia wept, her voice breaking. "I cannot bear to be parted from you again. My heart is twined with yours."

David rested his forehead against hers, waiting until his own breathing slowed before responding. "Sophia, I want to tell you all, but I am afraid it will push you from me forever."

"It will not," she promised, desperate to know the truth. "Whatever it is you are keeping from me, I know you are only doing so in order to protect me – to protect us." Closing her eyes, she captured his face with her hands, letting her fingers run down his rough cheeks. "Can you not see that there can be nothing for us unless you tell me all?"

For a moment, she thought he might refuse her again, the silence stretching out between them like an impassable gulf. Opening her eyes, Sophia stepped back out of his embrace just a little, so that she might see his face. What she saw there was a face lined with fear and worry, with something like guilt hidden amongst it.

"I will tell you," he said, eventually. "But you will despise me for it, Sophia."

"I will not."

He shook his head. "It must come out in the end, I suppose. But not today."

Sophia's shoulders slumped immediately, her heart sinking into her boots.

"Not because I do not wish to tell you all, but because it is growing dark and you must return to the house," he continued, catching her hands in his. "Your reputation, Sophia. Should you remain outside, there will be concerns raised at the house and perhaps even a search party." A slight smile broke out over his face. "And then what would we do?"

"You might be forced to marry me," Sophia replied, lightly.

He dropped his head, a grim look on his face. Fear lurched in her soul.

"Oh, no," she whispered, attempting to back away from him but finding herself pressed against the arbor wall. "That is what you have been hiding from me? You are married already?" Nausea rolled in her stomach as she thought of what she had shared with him.

"No, no," he exclaimed, his eyes meeting hers so swiftly that she was forced to draw in her breath. "I am not married, Sophia, I swear it." He tried to smile, but she could still see the anxiety behind his eyes. "I am free, I promise you."

Slowly, her shoulders drew down as the tension left her body. She knew he would not lie to her, trusting that what he said was the truth.

"Now go," he said, catching her hands in his once more. "I will find you here come the morrow?"

"The early afternoon, I might think about taking a walk in the gardens," Sophia replied, softly, her eyes sparkling as she saw his slow smile. "I have missed you so very much, David. I cannot tell you how glad I am that you have chosen to share all with me."

"I want a future with you, Sophia," he swore, fervently. "I only pray that you will still be able to see one with me when you know all."

Sophia did not reply but pressed her lips against his in response. Their kiss was smooth and sweet, not frantic and desperate as it had been before. It was difficult to tear herself away from him, but Sophia knew she had to return to the house.

"Tomorrow," she whispered against his lips. "Tomorrow, my love."

"I love you, Sophia," he replied, as she walked to the door. "Never forget that I love you."

CHAPTER 11

"Ah, Sophia!"

Smiling at her brother, Sophia took her place at the dinner table, aware that her hair was still a little damp.

"Helena tells me you were out in the gardens this afternoon. I must confess I was a little worried what with all the torrential rain, but she assured me you would be fine. You have not caught a cold, I hope?"

A little surprised at Francis' concern, Sophia shook her head. "No, I have not caught cold. I was a little chilled, I confess, but a hot bath has set that to rights."

"It was a pleasant walk in the gardens, I hope?" Helena asked, her eyes alight with a hint of mischief.

Sophia attempted nonchalance, although she could feel the heat burning its way up into her cheeks. "Very pleasant, despite the rain. I thank you."

Helena's smile widened. "Good. I am truly glad to hear it."

Sophia, catching Francis' slight frown, dropped her gaze to the table. Henry, of course, was nowhere to be seen. He was probably working on something in his room or in the library. That left herself, Helena and Francis to continue the conversation as dinner progressed. Thankfully for Sophia, the remainder of the dinner passed without further comments on her activities, although Sophia did not miss Helena's inquiring glances. Just as they finished their dessert and about to leave Francis to his port, the butler entered with a note on a silver tray.

"My lord," he murmured, holding the tray out to him with a gloved hand. "This was sent as a matter of urgency."

Sophia made to rise from the table, but Francis waved her back down. "No need to rush away, Sophia. Henry is busy with his own studies, and I do not much like the idea of drinking port on my own. Perhaps tea?" On seeing her answering nod, he looked to one of the footmen. "And a port for myself, as usual."

Sitting back down, Sophia smiled at Helena as

the footmen cleared the tables, soon serving them their own tray of tea each and setting Francis' port down in front of him. It had been some time since they had sat like this together, albeit without Henry. For once, Francis did not seem inclined to rush away, evidently preferring to spend some time with his sisters instead.

"How interesting," Francis murmured, his eyes narrowing as he read the note from town.

"What is it?" Helena asked, as inquisitive as ever. "Nothing bad, I hope?"

Francis threw the letter on the table. "Nothing of importance, no. It seems that Charles has some news from town and has sent a description of the man so that we might keep our eyes open. Although, I will say that a missing Earl is a cause for concern, of course."

"A missing Earl?" Helena repeated, reaching for the letter. "You do not mind if I read it, Francis?"

"Not in the least," he replied, pouring himself some port. "You may read it too if you wish, Sophia."

Sophia saw Helena's eyes suddenly round, her fingers briefly touching her lips as though troubled by what she read. How strange. Was there something about this missing earl that worried Helena? She watched as her sister folded up the letter and placed it to her left, before turning her attention to pouring some more tea.

"May I?" Sophia asked, gesturing for the letter.

"Oh, I do not think that necessary," Helena replied, lightly. "There is nothing of importance there. Francis is quite right."

That in itself made Sophia's concern grow. "Helena," she said, quietly. "The letter." Her eyes narrowed as she saw the desperate look in Helena's eyes, as she searched for a way to continue to keep it from her. When she saw that Sophia was not about to be put off, she handed her the letter with a deep sigh.

"Keep in mind it may not be what you think," she said, softly, then turned to engage Francis in conversation.

Sophia stared at her sister for a brief moment, her heart slowly sinking in her chest. Her fingers began to tremble as she opened the letter and began to read.

'My dear Francis,

I hope you are all well. I am writing to you very briefly to alert you to a concerning situation here in town. It appears that the Earl of Marching, David Armstrong, has disappeared. His mother and fiancée, Lady Viola Ermington, are utterly distraught since they have very little idea of where he has gone. Initially, it was presumed that he had simply taken some time away, but as the weeks have gone on and there has been no word from him, the belief is now that he might have found himself in some kind of nefarious situation. If you do see anyone akin to his description, please do inform me at once. He is a tall man, with light brown hair and brown eyes, I believe. I know that does not narrow it down very much, but I thought it best to inform you regardless.

I will write to you again soon.

Charles.'

Sophia finished reading, but could not lift her eyes from the page. Already, she had come to the same conclusion as Helena, but could not allow her heart to believe it. Had there not always been something about Hutton that had surprised her in the way he spoke, in the manners he displayed? At times, she had thought his behaviour to be more like that of a gentleman than of a gardener….and now it appeared she knew the reason why.

"Sophia?" Helena asked, touching her hand and making Sophia jump. "Are you quite all right?"

"No," Sophia replied, a sob catching in her throat. "I must excuse myself. I have – a sudden headache."

"Let me assist you," Francis replied, getting to his feet and coming around to her. "I must say, you look quite pale, Sophia."

Sophia shook her head, tears burning in her eyes. She could not let them fall, not in front of her brother, for then he would insist on knowing what was wrong and she was already afraid she might tell him.

Helena rose to stand beside them both, knowing exactly what it was that truly troubled Sophia. "I shall take care of her, Francis. Why don't you send up fresh tea trays to us? And perhaps a cool compress?"

Francis peered into Sophia's face, concern evident in his own. "Very well. But do send for me if you need to, Sophia. I am here for you."

"Thank you, Francis," Sophia managed to whisper, wondering if her brother knew just how much his words meant. "I am sure I will be quite recovered come the morning." Giving him a wane smile, she saw Helena quickly fold up Charles' letter and slip it into her pocket before coming to Sophia's side and take her arm.

"Come now," Helena murmured, as they left the room. "Just up to your room, Sophia, then you may weep for as long as you wish."

How Sophia managed to climb the stairs to her room without letting a single tear fall, she was not quite sure. All she could feel was Helena's arm around her waist, guiding her up to the staircase and into the welcoming warmth of her bedchamber.

"Now," Helena said, sitting her down in the chair next to the fire. "What can I do for you, Sophia?"

Sophia opened her mouth to answer, only for tears begin to pour down her cheeks, sobs racking her body. She did not know how long she cried for, only that Helena was right there beside her, murmuring soothing words of sympathy and comfort.

"It may not be him," Helena said when Sophia's sobs eventually abated. "You will have to speak to him, Sophia, to discern the truth."

"How could it not be?" Sophia whispered, recalling the words of the letter. It was as though they were all seared into her soul, tearing strips from her heart. "This tells me why I so often found him more of a gentleman in manner and tone, and why he was unable to give himself to me entirely. His inability to see a future for us, the way he pushed himself from me for a time….it is because he is already engaged." Her voice became nothing more than a whisper, her eyes unseeing as she stared blankly into the flames in the grate.

"I confess that it does seem to be the appropriate conclusion, Sophia, but you know what the *ton* is like.

Rumors abound. Perhaps Charles has, unwittingly, been caught up in some and has only written what he has heard. He might well be mistaken."

"I do not think so," Sophia replied, heavily. "Charles is not like that, and neither is Abigail. I do not think they can be wrong."

A heavy silence wrapped around her for a few moments, her grief and pain almost overwhelming her.

"You will have to speak to him come the morning," Helena said, interrupting the quiet. "I will come with you if you wish it?"

"No," Sophia answered at once. "I need to be alone with him. I will know the truth the moment I tell him of what I have read. I will see it in his face."

"I still have the letter," Helena said, quietly. "Do you wish to have it?"

Considering for a moment, Sophia nodded and accepted the folded note that Helena had previously slipped into her pocket. "Perhaps I shall ask him to read it," she murmured, running her fingers over the paper. "For I do not know if I can find the words to tell him what I know."

Helena gave her a brief smile and got up to pour some tea. "I do not think you shall sleep well tonight, my dear. I will stay with you until you are ready to climb into bed."

Grateful for her sister's kindness, Sophia managed a watery smile. "Thank you, Helena."

"Not at all," her sister replied, handing her a steaming cup of tea. "I will be with you through this, Sophia. You will find a way through, I promise you."

CHAPTER 12

David paced up and down the small arbour, barely able to take more than three steps before having to turn back again. Sophia should have been here by now, for it was well past the hour when she had said she would arrive. Instinct told him that there was something very wrong, that the Sophia of yesterday would not be the Sophia he met with today, should she appear at all. The Sophia of yesterday would have been right on time, if not earlier, desperate for his kisses in the same way that he yearned for her.

He had much to think on the night before, knowing that he was now forced into telling her the truth. Over the last few weeks, he had tried to convince himself that his feelings for her were nothing more than infatuation. That they would pass in time. He had told himself over and over that nothing could come of this, only for him to start hoping that perhaps there might be a future for them. His attempts to separate himself from her had come to naught, for he had been driven almost to the brink of madness in an attempt to stay away from her.

It was only when he had identified the deep love in his heart that he'd finally realized that he could not keep the truth from her any longer. As much as he did not want to tell her of his true identity, of the reasons he had hidden away as a gardener, David knew that he had no other choice. He would throw himself on her mercy and pray that she might understand, forgiving him for his lies and deceit.

"David?"

Turning on his heel, David let out a sigh of relief as Sophia stepped into the arbour, stepping forward to take her into his arms. To his shock, she stepped away, her normally sparkling eyes not able to meet his.

His heart thudded to a stop for a brief moment.

"What is it, my love?"

"How can you call me that?" she replied, her voice barely louder than a whisper, forcing him to strain to hear her words. "When you have someone waiting for you back in London?"

Nausea rolled in his stomach at once, his jaw slackening as he took in the paleness of her cheek, her red-rimmed eyes. Clearly, she had discovered the truth.

"I do not love her," he replied, trying his best to explain. "My mother – "

"Your mother is frantically looking for you," Sophia interrupted, pulling out a note and handing it to him. "I think you had better read this before you say anything else, David."

David took the parchment from her, hating the way she jolted when their fingers brushed. He did not need to ask her what it was she had discovered, for the grief in her eyes told him that she knew everything. Unfolding the parchment, his eyes skimmed the note, feeling anger boil in his stomach.

"I do not have a fiancée," he snarled, scrunching the parchment in his hand. "This is just a scheme of my mother's, Sophia. I am not betrothed, I swear it!"

She did not flinch, her eyes looking at him with an unwavering calm that quite unsettled him. "You are the Earl of Marching, Lord David Armstrong, then?"

David swallowed, his anger evaporating in an instant. "I am."

"And you did not tell me."

"How could I?" he replied, his voice growing louder with each word. "If I had told you from the very beginning, would you not have gone straight to your brother with the news, as you ought to? If I had told you once we had fallen in love, you would have despised me for lying to you and would have left my side." He tried to catch her hand, only for her to tug it away. "I could not lose you, my love."

Sophia turned away, and he saw her shoulders shake. She was crying, and, from the redness of her eyes, had been crying for some time. Even though he told himself that he could not have told her before now, the realization that he had betrayed her began to slice into his heart. She was utterly distraught, robbed of everything she'd thought she knew about him. That cut deep.

"I – I am sorry, Sophia," he whispered, not sure what else to say. "I thought I was doing this for your protection, but perhaps I was wrong."

"You tell me that you are not betrothed," she replied, turning to face him. "But you have kept the truth of your identity from me since the first moment we met."

"I know, but –"

She held up one trembling hand, silencing him. "How can you expect me to believe you now when you tell me you are not betrothed? How can

I trust a single word from your mouth?" Fresh tears filled her eyes as she gazed at him, waiting for his response.

David found that he could not give one, finding nothing to say in answer. She was quite right, he realised. Were he to find himself in her position, there would be nothing he would believe.

"So, you see," Sophia continued, when the silence became too great. "I cannot believe that you are not engaged, *Lord* Armstrong. To think that I gave you my love when you were holding such a great truth back from me, holding back your very self!" She shook her head and swallowed hard. "I think our acquaintance must be at an end, my lord."

David could not accept what she was saying, even though he knew she was being more than fair in her assessment. The thought of being parted from her, never to have her in his arms again, was more punishment than he could bear.

"No, no," he cried, stepping forward and finally catching her in his arms. "You cannot mean it, Sophia. I know I have hidden my true self from you. But nothing I felt, none of the words I spoke to you of love, none of that was a lie, I swear it."

Sophia struggled weakly in his arms, pressing her hands flat against his chest. "I cannot, David. Let me go, I beg of you."

"Sophia," he whispered, loosening his grip but still holding her tightly. "Look at me, please. I beg of you."

She stilled, her face still turned away from him.

"Please, Sophia," David pleaded, struggling against the desperate fear that clutched at his soul. "Please, just look at me. Look into my eyes. See that all the words of love I have told you are true." He could not let her go, not yet. Not until she believed that he loved her and that this revelation did not change anything about how he felt.

"What we had," Sophia said, brokenly. "It is at an end. It does not matter whether you loved me or not, for I could never be with a man who has so willingly hidden his entire past from me, and one who has run from his mother and his responsibilities."

"I have not run," David replied at once. "My mother has pushed this lady upon me, to the point of announcing my betrothal in society papers without my knowledge or consent." His own voice broke as he spoke, still desperate to cling to Sophia. "I have never loved before, Sophia, and I doubt that I will ever love again. My love for you has grown since the very first moment we met and has become so wide and deep that it fills every last part of my heart. It has rooted itself there, ever more to remain. This, I swear, is true."

Sophia looked at him then, her face still pale and eyes filled with such a myriad of emotions that David found he could not begin to decipher what it was she was feeling. He cursed himself for having caused her so much pain, so much distress.

"I should never have hidden my true self from you," he finally admitted, holding her tighter. "Believe me when I say that I struggled to think of a way to tell you the truth. That is why I chose to separate myself from you so that I would not, one day, cause this exact situation." Boldly, he lifted his hand and brushed a loose strand of hair away from her face, relieved that she did not jerk away from him. The harshness of her stance slowly softened as he trailed his finger down her cheek, guilt slicing through him once more. "I could not do anything but return to you," he finished, dropping his head in shame. "Despite knowing that I should stay away from you until my own situation was worked out, my heart would not turn you lose. I can never undo what I have done to you, Sophia, but I only pray that you will consider the love we have shared, and find, in some way, the ability to forgive me."

With bated breath, he looked down into her face, desperate to see some kind of understanding there, some kind of softness. Instead, her expression remained exactly as it was, without even a hint of a smile. Her hands pressed against his chest lightly, but there was no reaction from her. David tightened his arms instinctively, knowing he was trying to hold onto something that was desperate to be let go. Not knowing what else to do, he dropped his head and kissed her full on the mouth.

There was no response.

He lifted his head and pressed his forehead against hers, refusing to accept what he knew was going to happen.

"Goodbye, David," she whispered, putting her hands on his arms and giving them a gentle press so that he would let her go. She did not say a single word, did not give him another look, but simply stepped through the ivy curtain and walked away, walking away from him and out of his life.

CHAPTER 13

"Francis?"

Opening the door, Sophia couldn't help but smile at the sight of Francis, his head propped up on one hand but his eyes firmly closed. Her brother was working so hard that he clearly wasn't getting enough rest. It was unfortunate that she was going to have to wake him, but the truth needed to be revealed.

"Francis?" she said again, stepping further into the room and shutting the door. The click of the door woke him at once. He snorted in surprise as his elbow slipped from the table.

"I'm sorry to wake you when I can see you are quite tired," Sophia continued, moving to sit down opposite him. "But I have something I must tell you." Her heart squeezed with pain as she remembered how, only a few minutes before, she had seen David walk away from the estate, a bag in his hand. Why she had waited for him to leave before approaching Francis, she could not quite say. Perhaps it was because she did not want Francis to tear David limb from limb once he'd discovered the truth. Or perhaps it was, despite everything, she loved him still and had to, for her own good, watch him walk away. Regardless of her reasons, she was here now, knowing she had to tell her brother everything that had gone on.

"Sorry," Francis muttered, rubbing a hand over his eyes. "I've not been sleeping well."

"Something on your mind?" Sophia asked, getting up to ring the bell for tea – of coffee, given how tired her brother looked.

Francis grimaced. "Yes, unfortunately."

"Anything I can help you with?"

He shook his head. "No, although I do thank you for your concern." He smiled at her, although the frustration didn't leave his eyes. "It's unusual for you to come and seek me out. Is something wrong?"

"Yes."

He frowned immediately, leaning forward in his chair. "Please, sit down, Sophia. Whatever's the matter?"

Sophia sat down on a chair beside the fire, waiting until Francis had come round from behind his desk to sit opposite her. She opened her mouth to speak, only for the maid to come in with the tea. The concern over Francis' fate as he waited for the maid to leave made her heart swell with affection for her brother, although she was still worried about what his reaction would be.

"Now," Francis began, the moment the door clicked shut. "Whatever has happened Sophia? I have been concerned for you, of course, but I had thought that your return to the gardens signaled that you were doing much better." He leaned forward, his eyes grave. "Is it mama? Are you missing her? Are you lonely?"

Sophia lifted a hand, stemming his words. "Francis, wait."

"Sorry," he mumbled, realizing he had been talking far too much. "I am just worried, Sophia. You have never come to me like this before."

Drawing in a breath, Sophia reached to pour the tea, trying to think of the right way to tell Francis the truth. Once they both had a cup of tea at their elbow, she folded her hands in her lap and looked directly at her brother. "Do you remember that letter Charles wrote to you? The one you read at the dinner table last evening?"

A slight frown puckered his forehead. "Yes, of course. The missing gentleman."

"The missing Earl," Sophia corrected, her

heart beginning to hammer in her chest. "Well, I am aware of where he is."

Stunned silence met her ears as Francis' mouth dropped open.

"I should have told you this last evening, but I had to confirm it before I came to you," she continued when he said nothing. "And, before you go in search of him, he has returned to town."

"You know who he is?" Francis repeated, spluttering slightly. "Why did I not know of him?"

Now it came to it, the crux of the matter. Sophia's heart was beating so fast she thought she might become ill. The words were on the tip of her tongue, but she could not quite bring herself to say them.

"Sophia," Francis said, a little more sternly. "Who is he?"

She licked her lips. "He is – was – the gardener, Francis."

"The gardener?" he repeated, looking utterly confused. "You mean, *our* gardener is the missing Earl?"

"Yes, that is exactly what I mean," Sophia replied, the pounding of her heart slowly lessening as she managed to tell him the truth. "The Earl of Marching has been here, working as our gardener."

Francis' mouth dropped open, the colour slowly draining from his face.

"You need not worry that you have somehow been in the wrong by hiring him," Sophia continued quickly. "He wanted to be in hiding, and this was the best way for him to do so. He has a natural inclination towards plants and the like, so his hobby became his profession." A swirl of nausea rolled in her stomach, and Francis closed his mouth and ran one hand through his hair. It was more than clear that he had not expected this in the least and a further shock was yet to come.

"How – how did you discover this?" Francis asked, his voice thin with surprise. "And if you knew of his true identity, why did you not say?"

Sophia began to fiddle with her skirts, aware that she was going to have to tell Francis exactly what her relationship with the Earl had been. "I spent a great deal of time in his company, Francis." She saw her brother frown deeply, and was forced to draw in a breath to keep her resolve steady. "He was the gardener after all, and you know how much I adore being outside."

"Your roses," Francis murmured, his frown deepening still. "Pray tell me that nothing untoward was going on between you both."

Licking her lips, Sophia looked helplessly at her brother, knowing that she could not do as Francis asked.

Francis let out a loud groan and ran his hand through his hair before pressing his forehead into his palm. Sophia felt heat rise in her cheeks, suddenly unsure about where to look. Her breath came quickly as Francis simply looked at her, saying nothing. The silence stretched between them, making her more and more uncomfortable.

"I cannot imagine how difficult this has been for you, Sophia," Francis murmured, eventually. "I assume that he did not tell you his true identity from the start?"

Stunned at the sympathy in his voice, Sophia nodded. "No, he did not."

Francis shook his head, his eyes dimming. "Then you must be heartbroken, my dear sister. To discover that, not only was he hiding his true identity from you but also was attached to another...." He sat forward and reached for her hand. "I am deeply sorry for the hurt that you have experienced."

Sophia tried to speak, but the unexpectedness of his kind words to her forced tears to her eyes. She had thought that Francis would be angry with her, furious even. Instead, he had overlooked her impropriety and lack of wisdom and had simply considered how hurt she must be. His kindness was more than she deserved.

As she began to cry, she heard Francis pull his chair closer to hers before putting one arm around her shoulders and pressing his handkerchief into her hand. She was relieved that she had managed to tell Francis the truth, but the pain of watching David walk out of her life, his lies and secrets no longer hidden, had not lost any of its severity.

And yet, Sophia knew she would love him until the day she died.

CHAPTER 14

David's return to his townhouse had spread all around town within a few hours. His mother, still prone to dramatics, had put on a great deal of shock and surprise, which ended with smelling salts being waved under her nose. David was not taken in at all, standing irresolute as his mother sagged in her chair. Once she had fully recovered, he told her curtly that his stay was not to be of a long duration. He was only there to discuss his situation with her and his so-called betrothed.

And so, it was now that he was standing in front of his mother and Lady Viola Ermington who was looking at him with a wide smile on her face.

David glared back at her, but her smile did not

falter. Apparently, she expected that, due to everything that had happened, there was no way for him now to escape her clutches. What with the second announcement in the newspaper over their betrothal, Lady Ermington seemed to believe that she was soon to be his bride. David smiled inwardly. She was about to discover that he was not a man who allowed himself to be told what to do.

"I have returned, as you can see," he began, holding up a hand to still the words of delight that he was sure were going to spill from his mother's mouth. "But that does not mean that I have done so willingly."

"You are not glad to see me?" Lady Ermington cried, sounding quite astonished. "Your betrothed?"

"We are not betrothed, Lady Ermington," David replied, curtly. "As you well know. This is simply a scheme you and my mother have concocted together, and I simply will not be a part of it."

To his surprise, his mother let out a trill of laughter. "Come now, David! You know that the notice has been in society papers at least twice. All of London is talking of your engagement to Lady Ermington. You cannot break such a thing now."

"I can and I will," David replied, firmly. "I

have never asked Lady Ermington for her hand, as you both know."

His mother sniffed. "That is but a small detail, David," she stated, clearly refusing to believe that he was about to break the sham of engagement. "To leave Lady Ermington now would bring shame on both her and you and to our family."

David narrowed his eyes at his mother, knowing that it had been she who had come up with the entire scheme, having found Lady Ermington, a willing partner of course.

"Mother, I am here to tell you that I have fallen in love."

She gasped and clapped her hands, her eyes bright.

"Not with Lady Ermington," he continued, seeing the light in her eyes fade almost at once. "But with another dear lady who has been badly hurt by what has gone on here. She believes me to be engaged and has torn herself from me, despite my declarations of love." He took a breath, remembering how Sophia had looked at him when he'd admitted that she was right in the accusations she'd levelled at him. Pain sliced through his heart. "I have caused her distress by refusing to tell her the truth of who I was, but her pain has doubled because she believes me already engaged. That belief *must* come to an end."

His mother's mouth was ajar as she stared up

at him, whilst Lady Ermington shifted uncomfortably in her chair. David said nothing but looked back at his mother unflinchingly. He was not about to listen to one of her tirades, intended to push him back down under her wing. She had pushed and pushed until she had pushed him too far. David vowed that his mother would never have such an influence over his life again.

"Lady Ermington," he said, turning to the lady in question. "We have never been betrothed, and you are more than aware of that. To continue with such a falsehood is both morally and spiritually wrong." To his surprise, he saw a slight sheen of guilt cross the lady's face. "You know I have never loved you."

"I do not think such a thing matters, my lord," she answered, looking directly at him and giving a slight sniff of disdain. "What your mother says is quite right. We are, by all accounts, engaged."

"Not by my account," David growled, wishing that just one of the two women in front of him would simply accept what he was saying. "I have already sent a retraction to the paper." He had done so that very morning and had been assured that it would be in the paper in two days' time, and would remain there for a week.

Two gasps of shock met his ears, as two pairs of eyes stared at him in astonishment.

"But my reputation!" Lady Ermington cried, her eyes wide. "What of that?"

David shook his head, anger rising in his chest. "Did you really think that you could simply go along with my mother's schemes and have everything go just as planned? That I would simply accept my mother's intentions for me without question? I am not that kind of man, Lady Ermington."

His mother rose to his feet, her hand shaking as she pointed one finger at him. "You are a disgraceful son," she declared, loudly. "You have disappointed me over and over again, and now you are to bring shame on Lady Ermington and on this house! It is almost too much to bear!"

"I quite agree," David replied, calmly. "That is why I have already started preparations to remove you from this house – and from my estate. As I intend to wed soon, it is fitting that you retire to the Dower House."

His mother's face paled at once, her eyes still lingering on him as she collapsed into her seat.

"I have had more than enough of your meddling, mother," David continued, quietly. "And I will not have you near my bride, should she finally accept my proposal. I should have taken a firmer hand in my affairs a long time ago. It is only because of this convoluted and, frankly, disgraceful matter that I have finally seen what I should have done many months ago. And that is to my shame." He lifted his chin and looked down at his mother, feeling no pity for her. "You are to retire to the Dower house and live quietly, mother."

"And if I do not?" she asked, her voice thin and reedy although she glared at him nonetheless.

"Then you will find yourself with a skeleton staff and very little funds at your disposal," David replied, seeing the look of defeat in her eyes. "I do not wish to threaten you mother, but after what you have done, it is no less than you deserve."

"And what of me?" Lady Ermington asked, the fight gone from her also. "I am to have the embarrassment of being a woman who has had her fiancée leave her for another. And you have sent in a retraction without even considering me."

David turned back to Lady Ermington, not feeling even the slightest modicum of sympathy. "May I remind you, Lady Ermington that you agreed to this engagement without consulting me. For the record, I have issued a retraction stating that my *mother* was the one in the wrong," he replied, quietly. "You will carry some of that shame for a time, Lady Ermington, but I am quite sure you will recover. You should never have allowed my mother to embroil you in her schemes."

Lady Ermington opened her mouth as though

she wanted to reply, but could find nothing to say. Instead, she slumped back into her chair, looking utterly despondent.

"If you will excuse me," David finished, giving them both a short bow. "I have somewhere to be." Turning to his mother, he frowned heavily. "And when I return, I expect you to already be at the Dower house, mother. Do not delay in an attempt to force me to feel any sympathy for you. Do not test me." He waited until his mother gave a feeble nod before turning on his heel and stalking from the room.

CHAPTER 15

Sophia was busy with her needlework when she heard Helena draw in a sharp breath, her eyes staring down at the paper she held in her hand.

"What?" she asked, slightly interested. "Is there some more shocking news that I should know of, Helena?" One eyebrow lifted slightly. "I do hope Richard is not embroiled in some kind of dastardly scheme so close to your wedding day!"

To her surprise, Helena closed the paper and gave her a quick smile. "No, not at all. Something did catch my eye, but it is of little importance."

"Then the wedding can go on as planned?" Sophia murmured, softly.

Helena laughed, folding up the paper and

placing it beside the tea tray. "Yes, I believe so. It is tomorrow after all."

Frowning, Sophia studied her sister. There was something forced about Helena's laugh, and the way she had folded up the paper and put it away told Sophia that there was something within that Helena did not want Sophia to see.

"Now," Helena said, changing the subject entirely. "Is everything ready for tomorrow? I must admit, I am more than a little excited."

"Helena," Sophia asked, slowly. "What is it that was in there?" She put her needlework down and frowned at her sister. "Do not hide it from me, sister dear."

Helena's smile became fixed. "Sophia, you are being quite ridiculous." Sophia narrowed her eyes as she saw Helena's gaze flicker towards the newspaper. "Come now, I must ensure that everything is in place for my wedding day."

Sophia settled her shoulders, folding her hands neatly in her lap. "Helena," she said, firmly. "I am quite aware that you are not telling me the truth. You have never been much good at lying. Now, if you do not tell me what it is you have seen, then I shall pick up the paper and scour every page myself until I find whatever it was that has caught your attention." She kept her gaze fixed on her sister who, after a few seconds, shook her head and sighed.

"Very well," Helena said, heavily, her shoulders slumping. "I just do not want you to become distressed, my dear sister. After all, Lord Armstrong has not left your thoughts since he left, has he?"

Wondering what this had to do with David, Sophia pursed her lips but chose not to say anything. It was quite true. She had been unable to forget the man, and the pain over what he had done had not only grown deeper but came tinged with regret over her own actions. She had given him no time to explain, had simply called to an end everything they had shared. Now that a week had passed, Sophia wished that she had given David a little more time to tell her what truly was going on. He had insisted that he was not engaged, but her heart had not wanted to believe him.

Perhaps, if she allowed him to tell her everything, she might understand why he had chosen to do what he did. After all, it was quite a desperate thing to leave one's titled status and pretend to be a servant in another lord's household. To her regret, Sophia began to feel some sympathy for David, even though he was gone from her side. She could not imagine what had driven him to take on such a façade, but realized, in hindsight, that it must have been severe indeed.

"Here it is," Helena murmured, scrunching up her face and peering into the newspaper. "Be prepared, Sophia. This may come as something of a shock to you." And, so saying, Helena laid out the newspaper on the table and pointed at one particular area.

Was she about to discover that David had married? Had she been quite wrong in feeling any kind of sympathy for him? Her eyes lingered on her sister for a moment longer, thinking that perhaps she had made some kind of mistake in insisting that she read whatever it was Helena had been so surprised over.

Drawing in a deep breath, Sophia leaned forward and looked down at the paper, her eyes landing on the article Helena was pointing to.

"Statement of Retraction:," she read aloud. "A previous notice had stated a betrothal between a Lord W. and a Lady E. It seems, however, that this was quite in error and that Lord W. and Lady E. are not engaged. It appears that Lord W.'s mother, in her fright over her son's disappearance, chose to make such an announcement in the hope of encouraging Lord W. to return home. On his return, Lord W. became aware of the erroneous notice in the paper and now seeks to correct it. He hopes that society at large will forgive the error."

Sophia stared down at the notice, her voice growing wispy as she finished reading. David had been telling the truth. He was not engaged, not in the least. Tears blurred her vision as she looked up at her sister, hope beating wildly in her heart.

"I have made such a mess of things," she whispered, an ache in her throat. "I sent him away without giving him the chance to explain why he did such a thing."

"He did hide his true identity from you," Helena reminded her, gently. "You were badly hurt and confused over his behaviour."

"But I should not have ignored his desire to tell me the truth about what had happened," Sophia replied, dashing tears from her eyes. "Oh, Helena, I have been so foolish."

Helena studied her for a moment, frowning hard. "He has written to you, Sophia," she said, quietly. "I had not thought it wise to tell you, and, in truth, I have kept the letters from you for I did not wish to cause you any further pain. Besides, I was not quite sure what you would do with them" A slight smile lifted the corner of her mouth. "You might have burned them and then where would we be?"

Sophia nodded in understanding, knowing that she would, most likely, have thrown them in the fire, unread, such had been her state of mind. "How many are there?" she asked, hardly able to trust her voice. "One? Two?"

Helena's smile was gentle. "He has written to you at least once each day since he left."

"Oh." Sophia swallowed the lump in her throat as yet more tears came to her eyes. He had not left her alone, without any kind of hope. Through his letters, he was proving that his love for her was true. She was not sure what the letters contained, but she knew that they had to be of great importance. Suddenly, Sophia was desperate to read them.

"I'll fetch them at once," Helena said, evidently seeing the emotions on Sophia's face. "I won't be long."

Sophia nodded, her fingers plucking anxiously at the creases in her skirts. Would the letters tell her everything? Explain why he had been forced to hide his true identity from her? Would she get the chance to speak to him again, to apologize for sending him away without allowing him the chance to explain? She could still feel his lips on hers as he'd held her tightly in his arms, but she had been too numb to respond. The agony in his eyes had torn at her soul but, in the end, she had stepped away from him, thinking that she would never see him again. How wrong she had been!

"Here." Helena walked back into the room, her hands carrying a small, ribbon tied bundle. "As I said, there are more than a few."

Sophia could not stop her hands from shaking

as she took the bundle from Helena, pulling gently at the ribbon that kept them together.

"I will leave you in peace for a time," Helena said, softly, pressing Sophia's hand. "You need some time to read these alone, I think. Do come and find me when you are ready. I shall be in the library, I think."

Her hands still on the letters, Sophia looked up at Helena and smiled, her heart lighter than it had been before. "I thank you," she murmured, gently. "It appears there might be hope for me yet."

"Of course there is," Helena replied, bending down to kiss Sophia's cheek. "The man loves you, and you love him. Let that knowledge be your guiding light."

Sophia nodded and smiled, her fingers breaking open the first seal as Helena left the room.

CHAPTER 16

Helena knew that the groom was more than a little surprised when she requested that a horse be saddled for her, but she was not about to go in search of Francis to ask for the carriage. In fact, she could not wait a single moment more.

The letters had held more than she had ever thought possible, her heart squeezing in sympathy for him, as well as with regret for her hasty actions. Now, she could understand why he had left his home and hidden himself away, although she would not agree that it had been the best course of action. Then again, she considered, as she pulled herself up into the saddle, she had never experienced the difficulties of having an entirely overbearing mother.

"Does the master know where you are going?" the groom asked, looking a little concerned. "Not to overstep, miss but…."

"My sister does," Sophia replied, gathering the reins. "I thank you for your concern, however."

Trotting out of the stables, she made her way out of the estate gates and down the road towards the nearby inn.

The letters had spoken of David's love for her in almost every sentence he wrote. He had begged her forgiveness over and over, promising her that the love he carried for her would never be quenched. In fact, even in their parting, it had grown until it had become so much of an ache that he had been forced to return to the estate.

However, he had not come knocking on the front door or sent a calling card to Francis. Instead, he had simply told her that he was staying in the local inn, and would do so for a fortnight, in the hopes that she would send for him. David's final letter had told her that he was about to leave forthwith, and that he was afraid that, in her lack of response to him, he might not have any hope of being reconciled to her again.

Her lack of response was, of course, due to Helena's diligence in keeping his letters from her, believing it to be in her best interests. Sophia could not imagine the agony David was suffering, sending off each and every letter but never receiving a single note in return, not even when he had explained everything to her.

She should have sent for him, of course, but her heart would not allow her to wait. Instead, she had hurriedly told Helena where she was going and, without a moment's hesitation, had left the room. Sophia was quite sure Helena would understand.

Her heart began to beat frantically in her chest as she approached the inn, seeing many people milling around outside. Would he still be here, even though his hope would be fading?

Pulling the horse to a stop, she waited until one of the stable boys took the reins and helped her to dismount before leading the horse away and leaving her entirely alone.

Taking a deep breath, Sophia stepped across the muddy ground towards the front entrance of the inn and, just as she was about to open the door, Lord Armstrong stepped out.

"David," she whispered, as his eyes landed on hers, his face paling slightly. "I – I read your letters."

She saw him swallow, apparently lost for words at the sight of her. He certainly looked different, now dressed in his gentleman's clothes with his hair swept back but he was still as familiar to her as the first day they had met. Sophia twined her fingers together as they stepped back to allow another patron entry to the inn, feeling herself shaking inside.

"I cannot believe you are here," David said, so quietly that she had to strain to hear him. "When I didn't hear from you, I thought…."

"You thought I had decided against you," Sophia finished, seeing him drop his head in shame. "But I have not, I assure you. Helena, my dear sister, kept your letters from me thinking that I was already going through enough." His head lifted, and he looked at her again. "She meant well, for had I received them earlier, I would have tossed them away without a second look. It was only when I read your announcement in the paper that I realized that you had been telling me the truth." She smile trembled somewhat. "You are not engaged." Her words ended in a breathy sob, and David nodded taking her hand in his at once and placed in on his arm.

"Might we walk, my love?" he said, softly. "I believe we have much to speak of."

Sophia nodded, unable to speak as she fought tears that had come all too readily to her eyes of late. She walked beside David for a good few minutes, until the inn was left behind them.

"There is a small bench just there," he said, eventually, nodding to a small wooded area to her right. "We might sit there for a time?"

"You have been here before?" she asked,

looking up at him as they walked.

His smile was tinged with sadness. "I found this the first day I came to the inn and it has become my place of solitude. A place to sit and think, or even to pray." His hand tightened on hers. "How glad I am to be able to share it with you, although it is certainly not as private as our arbor."

The mention of the place where they had shared numerous kisses brought a blush to her cheeks and a warm glow to her heart. The man loved her still, and the memory of their embrace brought gladness to her instead of pain.

"Oh, Sophia," David murmured, the moment she had sat down. "You must know how much I have been longing to see you again." His hand brushed over her shoulder and down her back, before taking her hand again. "Tell me that you have come to save me from my agony."

Frowning, Sophia studied him. "What do you mean?"

"You have not come, I hope, to tell me that all is lost and that I should stop writing to you?" he asked, his eyes searching her face. "I could not bear it if that were so."

A glad smile crossed Sophia's face, and she brought her hand to his cheek, seeing the way his eyes closed in relief. "Of course I have not," she replied, gently. "I love you so, David."

"How can you still love me after what I have done?" he asked, putting his hand over hers. "I should never have treated you so ill."

Sophia, knowing that it was important she was honest with him, set her shoulders. "I will not say that I think your scheme to hide from your mother and faux fiancée was quite ridiculous, but I realize now that you were verging on desperation." Her smile softened. "I cannot imagine what that must have been like for you."

He groaned and looked away. "I was, in truth, utterly desperate. I did not think that my mother would do anything of the like, but it just shows you how manipulative she can be. I realize now that I should have taken her controlling nature in hand some time ago, but never did. Perhaps if I had done so, she might not have behaved as poorly." His eyes met hers, filled with regret. "I must beg your forgiveness, Sophia, for having kept the truth from you. I should not have even come near you, but you drew me to you so that I was unable to do anything but come close to you. Your compassionate nature, your spirit and your beauty of both face and heart have convinced me that I cannot live this life without you by my side."

"When you left, I was broken," Sophia admitted, hating that she had sent him away. "I should have allowed you to speak, David. I should have let you tell me the truth about your engagement."

He shook his head, holding up his hand to stop her. "No, I will not allow you to take any guilt upon yourself when it is not yours to take. Your pain, your grief and sense of betrayal were all of my doing." His fingers lingered on her cheek, running down her jawline and sparking all kinds of sensations. "I am just grateful that you chose to read my letters and believed what was contained within them."

Struggling with her emotions, Sophia gave him a somewhat watery smile. "I have never doubted your love for me, David. Not after what we shared. I realised that your character had never changed, and, now that I understand your reasons for your deception, I find that I can forgive you."

She saw David's eyes close, heard the long breath he let out slowly. Her words had brought him relief, and, that moment, her own heart healed.

"I love you, David," she continued, framing his face with her hands. "Love overcomes, does it not?"

"It does," he whispered, finally opening his eyes to look into her face.

"And our love *has* overcome," Sophia said, smiling gently. "That is how I know our love will last, for even now, it grows with every passing moment."

His lips caught hers, and Sophia could do nothing but return his kiss, running her fingers into his hair. Tears slipped from her cheeks as they had done before, but this time, they were tears of joy.

"Say you will marry me," he begged, hardly drawing his mouth back from hers. "I cannot bear to think of my life without you. I do not want to be parted from you again."

Sophia laughed softly. "You might have to discuss the entire situation with Francis, but yes, of course, I will marry you. A future with you is all I have ever wanted, David."

"Then a future I will give you," he murmured, stroking the back of her neck with gentle fingers. "A future where I will ensure that you always know how grateful I am for you, how much of a delight you are to me. A future where you will know just how much I love you, each and every day."

Thinking that she had never felt so happy in her life before, Sophia rested her forehead against David's, simply resting in his embrace.

"And you shall grow roses," he finished, his lips now brushing hers. "As many roses as you wish."

Sophia smiled. "And perhaps a hidden arbour, where we might go when it rains," she whispered, before pressing her lips to his once more.

BOOK 5: MR. HENRY CATESBY AND THE REBELLIOUS REDHEAD

BOOK 5

HOUSE OF CATESBY

Mr. Henry Catesby & the Rebellious Redhead

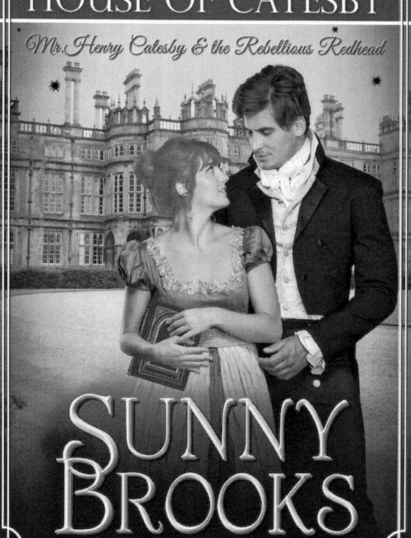

SUNNY BROOKS

FOREWORD

You are courageous, strong and worthy of happiness. Follow your heart, follow your curiosity, and stand up for what you know is best for you. I will be supporting you from afar.

- Sunny Brooks

CHAPTER 1

"Henry, I've decided that it's time for you to marry."

Henry did not immediately react, turning around slowly to view his brother Francis with a somewhat disinterested air.

"Is that so?" he muttered, putting his pencil behind his ear.

"It is," Francis declared, with a firmness that surprised Henry. "You are spending far too much time alone, doing....whatever it is you are doing....and you need a home and a family of your own."

That brought a twinge of worry into Henry's soul. He frowned, his eyes narrowing just a little. "You intend to throw me from your house, is that it?"

Francis, much to Henry's relief, looked horrified. "No, not in the least! This house is your own."

"Then why must I marry?"

"Because, as I have said, you are spending far too much time on your own and, after what happened with Sophie…"

Henry's brows furrowed. "Our dear little sister Sophie fell in love and married."

"Yes, but not without a great deal of confusion and heartbreak, which stemmed from a lack of responsibility on my part," Francis declared, his expression grim. "I will not allow that to happen again. I have a responsibility to care for all of you."

"And you are doing so," Henry replied, gesturing to the house around them which had been given to him by Francis. "You need not concern yourself with me."

"You are by yourself far too much, Henry. I barely see you anymore. You need a wife to bring you back into the real world, to force you to think of something other than your studies. You are missing out on so much already."

Henry bit back a harsh retort. He was quite content with his life, with his solitude. Francis had no need to interfere in order to try and change it.

"And so you intend to force me to wed?" he asked, after a moment.

"Yes."

"What do you think will happen if I do not?" Henry asked, lifting one eyebrow. "That I shall become some kind of hermit, a family secret that everyone must keep hidden?"

Francis looked a little uncomfortable, his gaze drifting away from Henry as he evidently struggled to answer. Apparently, this was exactly what he was worried about.

Henry sighed, shook his head and turned back around to continue with his work. He was not about to become a recluse. The work he was doing was of value. At least he felt it had value, for he was in constant contact with other astrologers and they were making some excellent discoveries about the night sky.

"Henry. I mean it. If you do not start making an effort, then I will find a bride for you. At least attend some social occasion or other. It is not too much to ask, is it?"

"Oh, do go away, Francis," Henry sighed, wanting nothing more than to lose himself in his work. He heard his brother huff, muttering something under his breath but, much to his relief, Francis eventually left Henry's small study and shut the door behind him.

"Thank goodness for that," Henry said aloud, putting his pencil down and sitting back in his chair with a heavy sigh. Whatever was Francis thinking, trying to get Henry to marry? Henry was fond of his own company and therefore had always been a little off-put by the idea of marriage. Not that it was a bad thing, given how happy his parents had been, but Henry knew it was not something he wanted for himself. After all, being the third son – albeit by only a few minutes – he did not need to marry. Charles, Henry's twin brother, was married and settled and Francis, the eldest and the new Mr. Catesby would soon enough find himself a wife and heir. Why he had not done so already was quite beyond Henry, for surely Francis should be most concerned about producing an heir at the earliest opportunity rather than ensuring his brother was wed.

Then again, Henry could not pretend that Francis had not been very good to him. He had, after all, given Henry a smaller house all of his own, where he could work in peace and quiet. It was not Henry's by deed, but Francis had made it quite clear that he was to treat it as his own home. It bordered Francis' larger estate so that Henry was never too far away, yet managed to have a place he could call his own.

The only trouble was, Francis could visit whenever he chose, interrupting Henry's work. Of course, it helped that Henry was busy enjoying the stars and learning as much as he could about them, which meant that during the day, he was often asleep. When he was not asleep, Henry had found he also enjoyed cultivating plants. He was growing a wide variety of new and interesting flowers in his small greenhouse at the back of his home. Francis did not intrude on him there, at least.

Henry liked his solitude and, given that he had a rather large fortune of his own, had very little else to worry him. There was no need for him to find work, nor any need to marry and produce an heir. He was able to just do what he pleased and, instead of throwing himself into pleasures had chosen to take a more studious route. He had truly never had any kind of thoughts on matrimony or the like. The subject simply did not interest him.

"Besides, what kind of lady would accommodate me?" he muttered to himself, writing down the details of his last stargazing study. A lady who would be willing to see very little of her husband and would allow him to work, uninterrupted day or night. Henry doubted that Francis would be able to find any woman suitable for him, despite his threat of practically bringing a bride to his door.

No, there was nothing to worry about. Francis had more than enough to engage his thoughts. Henry was sure his eldest brother would soon forget about his bachelorhood altogether and focus on his own responsibilities instead. Turning his thoughts back to the papers in front of him, Henry let out a small, contented sigh and forgot about the matter entirely.

CHAPTER 2

"Laurie!"

Miss Lauren Davenport shrank back as her father, Viscount Munthorpe, stepped into the library, his dark eyes piercing the gloom.

"Laurie, are you in here, girl?" he shouted, his voice so loud it practically rattled the ornaments on the mantlepiece. "Lord Umbridge is here to see you."

Laurie winced, hoping that the curtain would hide her from his view, even though it was only partially pulled. She did not want to see either her father nor Lord Umbridge and had intentionally hidden in the window seat of the library, book in hand. Thankfully, it was a rather dreary day which had turned the room somewhat gloomy, hiding her presence even further. Laurie was glad she had chosen not to emerge in order to warm herself by the fire, even though her skin prickled with cold.

"Where is that blasted girl?" she heard her father mutter, his footsteps moving towards the door. "Lord Umbridge is a perfect match for her. If only she would see sense." The door closed with a quiet click behind him and Laurie let out a long sigh of relief.

She was more than aware that Lord Umbridge was her father's chosen suitor, but she could not warm to the man. She had met him on more than one occasion and, whilst pleasant enough, there was something about the manner in which he regarded her that sent a wave of nausea right through her. It was as though he saw her as nothing more than a possession, something that belonged to him. Laurie leaned her head back against the dark brown wood of the window seat and let out a soft chuckle. Well, Lord Umbridge would have to learn that she was not about to acquiesce to his demands now or ever. She was quite determined that she would not have him, nor him her.

It was not as though her father was a cruel man but rather that he saw her as she truly was — a red-haired, freckled, curious soul with very few airs and graces, and certainly none of the attributes a young lady of her position ought to have. This was despite the years of training and tutoring, which had brought her no pleasure. Her watercolors were blurry, smudged things, her voice held no graceful tune, and her piano playing made the stable cats yowl in fright. No, Laurie had shunned those things the very moment her tutors had thrown up their hands in frustration – and had refused to do anything of the kind any longer.

Her father despaired after her, and that was the only thing that made Laurie grieve over her lack of accomplishments. How she wished she could prove to her father that she did not need to be able to paint beautifully in order to be seen as a successful young lady but, try as she might, he could not see her that way. He loathed the term 'bluestocking' and quite forbade her from reading any such books that might add to her own knowledge – not that she had listened, of course. She longed to learn more about the world she lived in, to find detailed descriptions of places she had never even heard of before. The only interesting place she'd visited outside of her father's country estate had been London and then only for one rather disastrous Season some three years ago now.

Cringing, Laurie tried not to allow the memories of what had occurred in London to flood her mind, but they could not be stopped. She had been so young and so innocent, entirely unaware of what a gentleman's intentions might truly be. With no mother to speak of – for hers had died in bringing Laurie into the world – she had been given a Miss Stanley as her companion, who spoke very little but watched everything. Being an unmarried spinster, she was around the age Laurie's mother would have been and ensured that Laurie was not allowed to escape her notice in any way. Even now, Laurie could still remember the sharpness of her eyes when she had found Laurie and Lord Longleat in a rather intimate embrace.

Laurie's cheeks burned. She had thought that, when they had been discovered, Lord Longleat would declare his love for her and demand they marry at once. Instead, he had just laughed in her presence, ignored her whispered pleas, and stormed back inside.

Miss Stanley had taken her home and put her to bed, speaking to her quietly and calmly, without any hint of anger or disappointment. That had been the day Laurie had learned to be careful around gentlemen. She had felt ashamed at what she had allowed Lord Longleat to do in taking her to a secluded part of the gardens and kissing her senseless, his hands roving wildly over her body. Being a little more aware of the reality of things now, Laurie concluded that he would have taken her virtue, had she let him, with very little consideration. Apparently, some gentlemen lived for such things and being as innocent as she had been, she had presented no challenge to Lord Longleat.

At least she had learned her lesson before it was too late.

Laurie let the cool air calm her warm cheeks, recalling how she had refused to return to London for another Season. Her father had been both frustrated and relieved, evidently pleased to be able to stay at his estate during the Season. Although, he had informed her that he did not intend for her to remain a spinster for the rest of her days. She would have to find a husband from somewhere.

Laurie had not taken his words with any degree of severity. She needed time to forget what had occurred and had, with great abandon, thrown herself into learning all she could about the world around her. All thoughts of gentlemen were gone from her mind, replaced with something that held a great deal more interest for her. She could not imagine Lord Umbridge allowing her to continue her own personal studies, however. He would be just as her father was, telling her repeatedly that such a thing was not for a lady of her age and inclination. There would be no more reading and studying if she were to marry him.

"Then I shall not," she muttered to herself, putting her book down and wrapping her arms around her knees. "I shall not marry him."

"Then what shall become of you?"

Laurie let out a shriek, clapping one hand over her mouth as the curtain was pulled back to display a rather disgruntled looking Miss Stanley. Her greying hair was pulled back into a tight bun as it usually was, her dark brown eyes a little narrowed as she planted her hands on her hips, clearly irritated with Laurie's behavior.

"Your father has been looking all over for you," she said, rather disapprovingly. "Lord Umbridge wishes to see you."

Frowning, Laurie pulled the curtain back in between herself and Miss Stanley, hiding away again. "I have already made it clear that I do not wish to spend any more time in that man's company," she said, firmly, refusing to listen to Miss Stanley's tut of disapproval. "He wants to marry me and father is apparently delighted by the idea, but they forget that they will need my consent if such an arrangement is to take place. I do not intend to give it to them."

"Then I ask again, what shall become of you?" Miss Stanley asked, her voice a little muffled from behind the thick curtain. "Your father will pass away one day and then where shall you go? It is not as though you have an elder brother who will take you in. In fact, I do not recall if there is any family who would care for you."

Laurie swallowed, her blood running cold. "No, there is not," she answered, truthfully. "I have not considered what I might do."

Miss Stanley slowly pulled the curtain back once more, a rather sympathetic expression on her face. "You must think carefully, Laurie. This is not something to be ignored simply because you do not like Lord Umbridge. This is about your future and what you intend to do with your life."

Laurie's shoulders slumped. "What *can* I do with my life?" she muttered, looking out of the window across the gardens. "I have no prospects other than a rather decrepit gentleman who does not care for me, and all I want to do is to explore and discover and learn!" Shaking her head, she sighed and rested her chin on her knees. "What other gentleman is there that might consider me?"

There was nothing but silence in response. Laurie felt the weight of her future resting on her shoulders and, when she turned to speak to Miss Stanley again, she saw that her companion had left.

Deciding on her future was not something Miss Stanley could help her with, in the same way that her father could not force her to wed Lord Umbridge. These were matters that Laurie had to take into her own hands and figure out for herself.

But what else was there for her to do? She could not run away, for she had no fortune of her own. Her dowry came to her on her wedding day, should that ever happen, which left her with nothing but her pin money – and she could not exactly live on that!

"I don't know," Laurie murmured to herself, leaning her head back against the wall, feeling much more burdened than before. Whatever was she to do?

CHAPTER 3

"Lord Umbridge."

Having been quite unable to remain in hiding for the rest of the afternoon and having heard from her companion that Lord Umbridge was to stay about the house until she made an appearance, Laurie had not had any other choice but to walk to the drawing room to greet him.

Lord Umbridge rose to his feet at once, a lewd smile instantly settling on his somewhat repugnant face. Laurie's face burned as she curtsied, immediately averting her eyes. Lord Umbridge was much too obvious with his thoughts and she found that she disliked that intensely.

"Where have you been, my girl?" her father asked, with a smile on his face but a steely look in his eye. "I have been searching all over this house for you."

"Have you?" She put an innocent grin on her face. "I was reading outdoors in the arbor, father."

His eyes narrowed slightly. "Is that so?" he murmured, throwing a glance towards the window. "I find that most....unlikely."

She did not let her smile slip for even a second. "You know how much I enjoy reading, father."

This comment did not go by unnoticed, for her father's brow furrowed and he said nothing more, although his lips were held in a thin, tight line. It was another reminder to her of just how much he disliked her bluestocking tendencies.

"It does not matter, I assure you," Lord Umbridge said, directing his words towards Lord Munthorpe. "I am *very* glad to see you, Miss Davenport."

Laurie tried not to cringe as he took her hand in his and bowed over it. His palm was rather sweaty, making her want to tug her hand back and wipe it on her handkerchief. Praying that he would not allow his lips to touch her skin, Laurie waited impatiently for the long, lingering bow to end.

Finally, Lord Umbridge released her, allowing her to take her seat opposite both her father and her supposed beau. Her father muttered something about requiring a fresh tea tray and got up to ring the bell, allowing Laurie a few minutes to regard Lord Umbridge with fresh eyes.

She had managed to avoid him for quite some time – and would avoid him again after this particular visit. In looking at him now, she confirmed to herself that he certainly had not improved since the last time she had seen him. Being a good many years elder than she, although she could not be sure of just how many precisely, he was tall and somewhat rotund, with jowls that seemed to move of their own accord any time he spoke. His small, dark eyes were fixed on hers, that leer capturing his lips with a permanency that left her shuddering. She knew precisely what it was he wanted from her and was not about to give it to him. There was no possible way she could accept his court and certainly not his hand in marriage. She would rather be a spinster than have to warm Lord Umbridge's bed!

"My dear Miss Davenport, may I say that you look quite wonderful this afternoon."

His words were dripping with sweetness, but the taste of them made her stomach curl.

"You have such a freshness about you," Lord Umbridge continued, as Viscount Munthorpe came to seat himself again. "A vitality that lights your eyes and gives you such a brightness that one can barely look away!"

I wish you would look away, Laurie thought to herself, somewhat mortified that Lord Umbridge was still refusing to let his gaze drop from her for a single moment. Aware of her father's sharp look in her direction when she did not reply, she finally managed to say, "You are very kind. I thank you."

This seemed to satisfy Lord Umbridge, at least, for he beamed at her in delight, his hands clasped together as they settled over his chest. Apparently by her few simple words, she had somehow given him the impression that there was some sort of hope.

"Where has that tea tray got to?" her father muttered, shaking his head darkly. "I must go in search of it." Rising to his feet again, he shot a quick glance towards Laurie, who immediately felt her heart begin to thunder wildly within her chest, panic stealing away her breath. Surely her father did not intend to leave her here with Lord Umbridge? It was most improper, for one, even if he only intended it to be for a few minutes.

"I quite understand," Lord Umbridge murmured, a dark glint in his eye that made Laurie rise to her feet in fright.

"I can go, father," she stated, quickly, hurrying towards the door. "You need not trouble yourself."

"No, no," Lord Munthorpe grated, pressing one firm hand flat against the door of the drawing room, his eyes glaring at her. "I insist you remain here with Lord Umbridge. I will not be long. After all," he finished, his voice dropping to such a low whisper that she could barely hear it. "After all, you have been avoiding him for such a long time that I have no intention of allowing you another exit."

Laurie's eyes widened but she was forced to step back, knowing that she was to be denied her escape. Her father was pushing her toward Lord Umbridge with a greater urgency than she had expected. Surely he must understand why she did not want to marry Lord Umbridge! Was he truly intending to force her hand in this matter?

"My dear Miss Davenport, you are *very* kind in wishing to aid your father," Lord Umbridge murmured, as she dragged herself back to where she had been sitting. "But you need not worry. He will be back very shortly, I am quite sure."

At least he has left the door open, Laurie thought to herself, as the sound of her father's footsteps echoed down the hallway. Struggling to come up with something to say to the still leering gentleman, Laurie averted her eyes and stared at the fire burning in the fireplace, thinking that it would be best not to give him any further encouragement.

"You cannot be ignorant of my reasons to call upon you, Miss Davenport."

Lord Umbridge's voice was breathy, moving to

the front of his chair as he spoke as though his earnestness would beguile her in some way.

"Indeed, Lord Umbridge, I am quite at a loss," she lied, with a slight shrug. "I thought perhaps you and my father had estate business to discuss."

Lord Umbridge chuckled darkly, apparently not taking offence. "You are much too innocent then, Miss Davenport. No, indeed, it is not business nor your father that has brought me to this house time and again. It is you."

Her stomach twisted, her skin crawling as she threw him a quick glance, trying to hide her repugnance and her fear. "I see," she murmured, not quite sure what else to say.

"I have every hope that you will one day soon become my bride," Lord Umbridge said, with a good deal of satisfaction in his voice. "*Very* soon."

"I am surprised you have such hope," Laurie replied, quickly, refusing to allow him to hold onto this belief. "I have never heard of your intentions thus far and certainly have not had time to consider them."

Lord Umbridge shook his head, his eyes narrowing. "You may play these games with me, Miss Davenport, but you forget that I know the truth already. Your father has made it quite clear that he will induce you towards matrimony and I have every hope of his success."

Before she could say a word, he was out of his chair and bending over her, his hand grasping hers before she could move. Frightened, she shrank back, seeing the fervor in his eyes.

"I *will* have you," he hissed, his face lowering closer and closer to her own. "You must understand, Miss Davenport. I intend to get whatever it is I wish. I have long desired to have you as my wife and very soon, my desires shall be fulfilled. It would be best for you not to refuse me."

Her stomach was twisting this way and that with fright but, lifting her chin, she held his gaze steadily, refusing to allow him to intimidate her.

"I think, Lord Umbridge," she stated, quite calmly. "That you will find yourself denied in this present situation. Whatever my father has said to you, I can assure you that he has not said a word to me as yet. I have no intention of agreeing to any such engagement."

Lord Umbridge's face grew dark. "We will see, Miss Davenport."

It was with great relief that the sound of her father's voice hurrying the maid along the corridor came between them, forcing Lord Umbridge to let her hand go and make his way back to his seat. Her breathing a little ragged, Laurie sat up, her head still held high, her anger beginning to burn.

Lord Umbridge might try to intimidate her, might try to force her into marrying him, but she was not the obedient, weak willed woman he thought her to be. No matter how hard he tried, she was not about to let him hold a hand of fear over her throat. She was stronger than that. She was stronger than both Lord Umbridge and her father.

"We will see, Lord Umbridge," she muttered aloud, as her father walked into the room with a broad smile on his face, acting as though he was doing her a great favor by allowing them time alone. "We will see who will be the victor in all of this. I have very little doubt that it will not be you."

CHAPTER 4

"Oh no, not today!"

Glancing out of his window, Henry saw a rather familiar figure riding towards the house and, without hesitation, grabbed his coat, pulled on his hat, and slipped out of the house using the back door.

Francis was not about to catch him today, only to rabbit on and on about Henry's need for a wife. Over the last sennight, it had become an almost daily occurrence and one that Henry could very well do without. The only time he had managed to quiet Francis had been when he had mentioned the fact that Francis himself was without a wife and should he not be leading by example. On that day, Francis had left Henry's home without another word, only to return the next day with a multitude of reasons as to why his own current matrimonial state had no bearing on Henry's.

The cool air brushed at his cheeks as he hurried outside, hearing the hooves drawing ever closer. Francis would be disappointed today. Moving quickly through the small garden, Henry slipped through the gate and into the trees that lay just beyond it. Moving through the trees carefully, he soon saw Francis slip from his horse and tie the reins to a post before walking purposefully towards Henry's front door. He knocked once, then twice more, before beginning to gesticulate wildly, exclaiming loudly that Henry was being more than a little ridiculous.

"Ha!" he triumphantly exclaimed, a trifle more loudly than he had intended. The sound echoed through the trees, making Henry shrink back into the shadows, hoping that Francis had not heard him.

Apparently, he had not.

Relaxing a little, Henry continued to peer out of the trees towards his brother, seeing Francis try the door handle. Discovering that the house was open, he disappeared inside as Henry chuckled to himself and leaned back against the tree trunk. Francis would soon discover that he was not at home and, in all likelihood, simply return to his own house and try again tomorrow.

"I'm not leaving, Henry!" Francis shouted, his

voice muffled as he strode through the house. "I know you're here somewhere."

A frown appeared on Henry's brow as he waited, wondering what Francis intended. Surely he did not think to wait for Henry to return so that he could simply talk to him again about matrimony. That would be ridiculous.

"I have Miss Smythe and her father calling tomorrow," Francis called again, sticking his head out of the front door and looking all about him. "You are to attend, Henry. I know you are avoiding me, but I will not be so easily put off!" Henry shrank back just as Francis's gaze narrowed, scanning the trees, still unable to locate his brother. "A cup of tea while I wait, mayhap."

Muttering a curse under his breath, Henry took a deep breath and tried not to acknowledge the fact that he would now be separated from his work for a good hour or so. Francis did not look as though he was about to be put off, but Henry had no intention of returning to his house so that his brother would succeed in his intention of giving an invitation to join him when Miss Smythe came to call.

If he was not at home, he would have no knowledge of it. Which, therefore, meant he would not have to attend. However, his plan would only succeed if he was able to avoid Francis and that meant staying away from his home until Francis had given up and gone.

"He will find me more resolute than he expects," Henry muttered to himself, turning away from the house and storming through the trees.

Branches cracked under his feet, the sound echoing through the forest, but Henry did not care. It was a little cold, given that it was the turn of the season and heading quickly towards the autumn, but Henry simply tucked his hands under his arms and continued on his way. He was frustrated with his brother, frustrated at his insistence that Henry find himself a wife when Francis himself was still a bachelor. As far as Henry was concerned, Francis ought to look after his own matters first before bothering Henry!

He did not know where he was going, although the forest was not particularly dense. His irritation slowly began to lessen as he made his way through the trees, kicking at pinecones as he walked. His determination grew as he went further away from home. Francis would not succeed. If he had to wait even until the morning before he could return home, then Henry would do it.

The light began to grow as he walked and, looking up at the branches above, Henry realized that he was drawing near to a clearing. Pausing,

Henry looked out ahead of him, only to see a small, tumbledown shack right in the middle of the woods. The trees had been cleared around it, and there was even a small garden – although it was quite wild at the moment. From the looks of it, no-one had lived here for a rather long time. There was no smoke rising from the chimney, and the front door looked to be a bit rotten.

Henry's heart lifted. Here was a wonderful space where he might escape, where he might come to hide whenever Francis tried to seek him out. Whilst the shack was on Francis' property, Henry was certain his brother would know nothing of it. It was not as though Francis often ventured into the woods. He had far too many other things to keep him busy.

Moving through the trees towards the shack, Henry smiled to himself at the discovery. The sound of rushing leaves surrounded him and a peace crept into his heart, pushing away the frustration and irritation Francis had brought him. Pausing, he listened hard for any signs of life, but all that met his ears were the sounds of the forest.

"Hello?"

His voice echoed softly through the forest, with only the occasional falling leaf rustling to the ground to capture his attention. There did not seem to be anyone else about.

Tentatively, he pushed at the door and, much

to his surprise, it opened without resistance. The musty air tickled at his nose, making him wince as he stepped a little further inside.

There was no-one to be seen. Dust floated in the lazy beams of light that shone from the grubby windows, and everywhere he looked, all he could see was dirt.

His shoulders slumped. This shack needed a great deal of repair, which he did not have the skill to do. And if he were to ask Francis' men for advice, then news would surely get back to Francis, which was entirely what he had intended to avoid.

Sighing, Henry looked all about him, wandering through the three small rooms. They were each as dirty as the next, and it appeared that there were a great many small rodents who had taken up residence. Not that Henry cared about such things, although he did want to ensure that the shack would not fall down around his ears should he decide to come out here again.

Setting his shoulders, Henry drew in a deep breath and tried to regain his focus. A little dirt was not going to dissuade him, was it? Surely, if he set his mind to it, he could have this shack to rights within a week – provided it was safe, of course.

"I could have a desk here," he murmured to himself, moving towards the window that looked out over the clearing. "The natural sunlight would give me enough to see by, and I might even have a view of the stars at night." A small smile settled over his face as he continued to look around the rooms, seeing them all in an entirely new light. It would take a great deal of hard work but, should it come to rights, then it would provide him with a wonderful space all of his own.

"Away from Francis," he murmured, a slow feeling of satisfaction settling over him. "Away from his constant haranguing." Francis was not likely to come into the forest to search for him, he would simply have very little idea of where Henry was. Chuckling to himself, Henry sat down in a rather dusty chair – hoping it would not shatter beneath his weight – and when it held fast, settled back into it.

"Wonderful," he said to himself, closing his eyes as he thought of the many happy days he would spend here in privacy. "It will be simply wonderful."

A sudden thump caught his ear and, as he jerked to attention, he saw the door fly open, and a rather disheveled young lady stagger into the shack. She slammed the door behind her and leaned heavily against it, her eyes closing as she slid down to the floor.

"Good heavens!" Henry exclaimed, getting to his feet. "Whatever is going on here?"

Her eyes widened to stare back at him, dust billowing around her as it caught the gloomy light from the dirty windows.

"Explain yourself!" Henry continued, firmly. "Who are you and what are you doing in my cabin?"

CHAPTER 5

Laurie stared at the gentleman standing inside the run-down old shack, not quite sure what to say. He was clearly rather upset with her sudden entrance but there was a slight uncertainty to his gaze that told her he was not altogether sure of her.

"*Your* cabin?" she puffed, slowly getting to her feet and aware that he was not making an attempt to assist her in any way. "I do not believe that this is your cabin, sir."

He planted his hands firmly on his hips. "Mister Henry Catesby, *if* you don't mind."

Laurie took him in with a little more curiosity. "How good to meet you. Miss Lauren Davenport." She finished with a quick curtsy and slight amusement playing on her lips. "Daughter of Viscount Munthorpe."

She looked at him steadily now, not caring that she was alone with a gentleman in a broken old shack in the middle of the woods. It was not as though anyone would find them, for she had made sure not to be seen. Henry Catesby must be the brother to the new Earl Catesby since these woods were on his grounds. The grounds, however, were large, and so she had not thought that anyone would find her should she trespass onto them.

"Why are you in my cabin, Miss Davenport?"

The question was brought forth from terse lips, punctuated by green eyes that flashed as he spoke. His brows were knotted, his dark hair adding to his wrathful appearance. It was more than clear that he was not happy with her presence.

"My dear Mr. Catesby," Laurie began, brushing down her skirts so that she would not have to meet his gaze. "I was simply exploring, that is all. You see, I find my life so very dull at times, and short of my books, I have to seek ways to make it a little more exciting." She tilted her head and lifted her gaze to his face, seeing confusion slowly replace his anger. "Surely, you can forgive me for that, I think."

His frown deepened. "You appeared to be running from something."

She shrugged. "Just the rain," she explained, just as a thunderous clap rolled across the sky. "I was vastly surprised to see the weather change so abruptly and, just as the first few drops fell, I saw this cabin and hastened towards it."

The frown fell from his face and he hurried towards the windows, evidently searching for evidence that it was now raining. There was no sound of rain on the roof, nor on the windows but, as Laurie watched and waited, she heard another thunderclap followed by the steady beat of a thousand raindrops falling from the sky and hitting the earth.

"Just in time," she declared, coming away from the door and walking towards him. "Although it is about to get rather cold, I think." Shivering a little, Laurie wished to goodness she had thought to bring a coat instead of her flimsy shawl, but it had been very warm and sunny when she had first left the house.

"This is not appropriate," Henry muttered, stepping away from her. "You should not be here."

Lifting one eyebrow, Laurie studied him for a moment. "Do you really intend to throw me out of your little cabin in the middle of a thunderstorm?"

That realization deflated the wind from his

sails a bit. A slightly abashed look crossed his face and he cleared his throat gruffly. "Well, no."

"Good. Then we may as well try to make a fire in the grate, don't you think?"

He cleared his throat again, looking away from her. "No, I don't think that would be wise."

Frowning, Laurie glanced towards the empty grate, only for something strange to catch her eye. With a gasp of surprise, she hurried towards it, realizing just why Mr. Catesby had been so reluctant to allow her to start a fire.

It was filled with nothing but cobwebs, spiders, and dusty old branches that she was sure would be riddled with insects. It was as if there had been birds nesting in the chimney.

A sudden thought struck her and, as she looked around the rest of the old shack, it continued to grow with certainty. The mustiness of the house, the thick layer of dust that lined every surface told her that this place had not been disturbed in a long time.

"You have never been here before, have you?" she said directly, looking at Mr. Catesby in the eye. "Is this your first time here?"

He shuffled his feet uncomfortably. "I do not think that is any of your business since this is still on my land."

"Your *brother's* land," she corrected, not caring

as to whether or not he found her rude or overly blunt. "Does he know this place exists?"

Henry let out a long, frustrated breath before seeming to crumble just a little. "Miss Davenport, I would beg of you to keep this place entirely secret."

Feeling as though she were slowly peeling back a layer of Mr. Catesby's cold manner, Laurie laughed softly and shook her head. "My goodness, Mr. Catesby. If you are going to ask me such a thing, then I'm afraid you are going to have to give me a few more details."

He frowned and shook his head. "No."

"Then I find I have no inclination to keep this place to myself," she replied, airily. "I am sure my father will soon call on the new Earl, and I shall make sure to mention the tumbledown shack in the woods I stumbled across one day." Lifting one eyebrow, she saw Mr. Catesby let out his breath in a hiss, aware that she was riling him but yet finding that she somehow relished holding this particular secret over him. The truth was, she quite liked this place and found Mr. Catesby to be somewhat intriguing, even though it was clear he was very upset with her presence here. After all, had she not been searching for something new for her life, something to push her away from the quiet boredom that had surrounded her for so long?

"It does not matter whether or not I have been in this place for five minutes or five weeks," Henry said after a moment or two of thought. "It is not your property, and therefore, you are trespassing."

Laurie sighed heavily and shook her head, looking up at him with a wry smile. "It appears you are not willing to talk to me, Mr. Catesby." She tilted her head, regarding him carefully. "I shall be honest with you, however."

"If it will make you leave this place, then I beg of you to do so at once," Henry replied heavily. "I enjoy my solitude, Miss Davenport, so I would very much appreciate being left alone just as soon as you are able."

"Then we are very different in that regard," Laurie replied softly, her eyes flitting to the floor. "I am very much on my own, but find myself tired and dull because of it. My father is pushing me to marry a particularly disagreeable gentleman and so, whenever I hear he is to visit, I try my best to leave the house just as soon as I can." She gave a quiet laugh, her heart filling with a certain degree of pain. "It is just as well the weather has turned a little brighter, else I should be stuck within the confines of the house with no way to escape."

Looking up at him, she saw something flicker in his eyes, as though he understood what she meant. Her spirits buoyed just a little, she bit back a sigh and shrugged her shoulders. "It is to be inevitable I suppose, this marriage of mine, but I do so wish to try and escape it for as long as I can."

Henry studied her for a moment or two, his expression blank as he did so. Laurie felt herself being studiously examined, as though she were a puzzle he could not quite figure out.

"I am surprised to find that I understand your predicament," he admitted, after another few moments. "Although, I did not think that a young lady would be so unwilling to marry."

She laughed then, her hands on her hips. "And how would you feel, were the man your father thought you might wed looked at you as just another trophy to add to his collection?" Tugging at one of her red curls, a sad smile stretched across her face. "I know I am not a dazzling beauty, Mr. Catesby, but I am an only child, and my father has bequeathed me a large dowry. I know that this is the only reason Lord Umbridge wishes to marry me and I find myself disinclined towards him because of that."

The glint in Henry's eyes grew. "Indeed, I suppose that is to be considered. I can understand your lack of willingness in that regard."

"Thank you," Laurie replied, carefully. "That is why I am here, you see. I do not want to return home when I know Lord Umbridge is waiting. Can you not take pity on me and allow me to linger for a short time so that I might avoid his company altogether? After all, if I were to return home now, then he might think that I have hastened to meet him, giving him hope which I must then dash." She winced, looking away from him. "It is very difficult having one's life decided for them."

Glancing at Mr. Catesby, she was surprised to see that he was looking back at her with something like compassion and understanding, as though he too felt as she did. Holding her breath, she waited for his judgment to fall.

Henry sighed heavily, passing a hand over his eyes. "Very well, Miss Davenport, you may remain here for a time – although I will say that I do not much like being manipulated into doing so by threats of revealing this place to my brother."

She shrugged, not caring in the least what he thought of her but being rather glad that she was to get her way at least. There would be no need to return home as yet, and she could make the excuse to her father that she had been forced to shelter from the thunderstorm, which would take some of his anger and frustration away over her absence.

"Might I be assured of your silence on this matter?" Henry asked, folding his arms across his chest in what was either a defensive gesture or an attempt to keep himself warm. "Not that I think you will meet my brother any time soon, but still…" He trailed off, lifting one eyebrow and Laurie tried not to laugh.

"Yes, of course, Mr. Catesby. My lips shall not pass a single word about this place to anyone."

Relief etched itself across his features. "Very good, Miss Davenport." She watched him as he wandered across the room, taking in every dusty surface, every cobweb that stretched across the ceiling. It was going to take a good bit of hard work to get this place clean.

She shivered as the rain continued to pour down outside, a draft of air coming in through a crack in the window to wrap itself around her shoulders.

"Here."

She looked up in surprise as Mr. Catesby handed her his coat, leaving him in only his shirt and waistcoat.

"Please, take it," he said, not looking at her as he held it out. "You are cold."

The warmth of the coat was too much to refuse, and so Laurie took it from him and wrapped it around her shoulders at once. The relief from the cold was instantaneous, making her smile to herself as she drew it around herself.

"Thank you, Mr. Catesby, you are very kind," she said, gingerly sitting down in an old, rather dirty looking chair which he had only just now dusted for her. "Do you intend to restore this place? Set it to rights?"

Her golden-green eyes settled on the gentleman as he walked here and there, seemingly inspecting everything. He was intelligent, that was clear, given the sharpness of his eyes and the way he took everything in, considering it all carefully.

"Yes, that is my intention," he said crisply, not even turning around to face her. "Although, I do not know how long it will take."

She paused, an idea flickering in her mind. "I, I could assist you if you wish," she said slowly, seeing him jerk around to face her. "I *can* clean, after all. Although I confess, I am no good at unblocking chimneys."

He shook his head fervently. "No. It is entirely out of the question."

Rolling her eyes at him, Laurie shook her head, refusing to accept his answer. "And why is that, Mr. Catesby?"

"Because I do not want you here," he said, firmly. "Have I not made that quite clear, Miss Davenport?"

Growing a little frustrated with his tone, Laurie let out a long sigh, narrowing her eyes at Mr. Catesby. "Might you at least try to be civil, my lord? I am aware that this is not a situation you much care for but if you could at least discuss the matter with me, then I would appreciate it." She saw his face flush as he turned away from her again and knew she had hit on a weak spot. "Can you not tell that I am troubled with matters at home? Can you not see that this offer of help is not in any way an attempt to be in your company but, in fact, to bring myself a modicum of relief?"

She sighed again, aware that she was being much more frank than she ought to be, but continued on regardless. "If I were able to come here and assist you in the cleaning and restoration of this place, then for a time, it would give me a purpose in life. It would mean that I would not have to endure Lord Umbridge's company in the hope that, perhaps in time, he might give up his pursuit of me." She tilted her head, watching Mr. Catesby as he kept his back to her. "I would not even have to be here at the same time as you if you did not wish to so much as speak to me," she continued, growing desperate in her desire to convince him to let her help. "I can clean just as well with or without your presence."

"Miss Davenport."

Henry turned around sharply, his dark green eyes filled with something like anger.

"Yes, Mr. Catesby?" she asked, her chin lifted as she did all she could not to shirk from his evident frustration.

"Miss Davenport, I have neither a need nor a desire to aid you in any way," he said, firmly.

"Have you never considered that it is I, in fact, who requires a place of solitude? A place where I might escape to also?"

He blew out a long, irritated breath, gesturing wildly as he spoke. "No, you did not. You think solely of yourself and what you might gain from this rundown shack, without considering any of the consequences. What would your father think if he were to find you here? Would he be glad to know that you are spending time alone with a gentleman in the middle of the woods?" A harsh laugh escaped his tight lips. "No, indeed. He would insist that we marry and, Miss Davenport, I have no intention of marrying anyone at the present moment – and that includes young ladies who try to shoehorn me into it."

Anger burst in her like a furious fire, forcing her to her feet.

"How dare you?" she whispered, tugging the coat from her shoulders and throwing it at him. "How dare you think so little of me? It may come as a surprise to you, Mr. Catesby, but not every eligible young lady you run across thinks so highly of you. Not every young lady has a desire to marry, or to manipulate you into such a thing. You barely know me and, whilst I have spoken to you freely about the difficulties I face, it has only been in the hope that you might feel some compassion for my situation. I can see now that your heart is entirely selfish, and that it is wrapped up in thoughts and considerations only for yourself."

Storming away from him, she pulled open the door of the shack, suddenly uncaring about the cold and the rain outside. Mr. Catesby was not the kind of gentleman she wanted to be near, not after how he had spoken to her. Glaring at him, she lifted her chin, ignoring the astonished look that came over his face.

"Good day, Mr. Catesby," she said, narrowing her eyes at him. "I hope we never have the opportunity to meet again. Shame on you for how you have spoken to me."

And with that, she slammed the door hard, bringing a shower of dust down on her head, before hurrying out into the storm.

CHAPTER 6

Henry spent the next five days at the shack, only returning home to eat and to rest. He knew that Francis had been at his house on multiple occasions, having received various notes through his door, but he paid them no attention. In fact, he simply swept them aside, leaving them in a neat stack just outside the front door, held down by a paperweight. He wanted Francis to see them the next time he came calling with some ridiculous invitation for Henry to meet some eligible young lady.

The shack was nothing other than filthy from top to bottom, and Henry knew that his staff was rather astonished to find his usually pristine attire so dirty. He had taken to wearing nothing but an old shirt and pair of breeches whenever he went into the woods, not wanting to ruin any of his good jackets or cravats for the sake of a dusty old chimney.

The only problem was, however, that he could not get the ridiculous Miss Davenport out of his mind. She had left the shack in such a hurry that he had not been able to say a single word to her. He had not meant for his words to chase her out into the storm. Especially when she only had a thin shawl wrapped around herself, and to his frustration, he was concerned for her.

He hoped that she had managed to return home safely and had not taken ill from being caught in the rain. In addition, he regretted his hasty words to her, annoyed that he had refused her request so quickly and without due consideration. The truth was, he had disliked having an unexpected interruption in a place he had only just discovered. His mind had been filled with dreams of what he could do with it, what he could make it and how it could be his own secret hiding place, away from Francis and his constant haranguing.

And then Miss Davenport had appeared, resplendent in her rough beauty. He had been angry with her for disturbing his peace. In addition, he had grown angry with himself for noticing her red curls, for the way her eyes had glinted with flecks of gold as she'd looked at him curiously. He did not want to notice her, nor did he want to continue to think of her. But, yet he found that he could do nothing else. She was there regardless of what he wanted, or what he did not want. He could not get her from his mind, wanting to ensure – for whatever reason – that she was safe and well at home.

"Ah, there you are."

Henry jumped visibly as Francis walked into the room, having appeared out of nowhere. Henry, who had been busy preparing to go to the shack in the woods, ignored his brother entirely. His back remained turned until another voice sounded.

"Miss Davenport, Viscount Munthorpe, this is my brother, Lord Henry Catesby."

"How very good to meet you, Mr. Catesby."

He turned slowly, relieved that he had not, as yet, changed into his old attire to go to the woods. Miss Davenport was standing just in the doorway of his study, her green and golden eyes slightly narrowed with no smile lingering on her face.

"Miss Davenport," he said, slowly, inclining his head, before turning his gaze to the gentleman standing next to her. "And Viscount Munthorpe. Glad to meet you both, of course."

Viscount Munthorpe sniffed, a barely discernable cringe on his face as he let his eyes rove around the room. "So, you are one of those intelligent sorts, are you, Mr. Catesby?"

Henry bristled. "Yes, Lord Munthorpe," he managed to say, aware of Francis' sharp glance. "I suppose that is correct. I particularly enjoy studying the night sky."

"I see." Lord Munthorpe shrugged, clearly disinterested. "It is not really a subject that I find in any way fascinating. Not to judge, but I would much prefer a gentleman do something profitable with his time."

Francis cleared his throat, whilst Henry battled to keep his annoyance under control. "Henry assists me with the running of the estate," he said calmly, sending another glance in Henry's direction to ensure he was remaining as composed as he ought to be. "And he has written some very insightful papers that have been widely received."

Whilst Henry appreciated Francis's support, he saw that it was wasted entirely on Viscount Munthorpe, who now appeared to be bored with the entire discussion. Henry turned his gaze towards Miss Davenport, who had two spots of pink in her cheeks, clearly embarrassed by her father's behavior.

"May I enquire after your health, Miss Davenport?" he asked, hoping that he was not being too abrupt. "There has been a lot of rain this last week, and it has brought a certain chill to the air."

Her eyes remained dim. "I am quite well, I thank you, Mr. Catesby."

Swallowing, he inclined his head. "I am glad to hear it."

Francis was looking at him with a slightly puzzled expression, but Henry ignored him entirely, his mind still fixed on Miss Davenport, and wondering how he might engineer a quiet conversation with her somehow so as to apologize for his previous rudeness.

"Are you returning to the house?" he asked, turning towards Francis, who nodded in reply.

"We are to take tea with Lord Catesby," Miss Davenport said quietly, as Lord Munthorpe turned to leave the house entirely. "Do excuse us."

"Might I join you?"

Henry could see Francis' astonished expression but kept his focus fixed on Miss Davenport and ignored his brother completely.

"Of course you may," Francis replied, slowly. "I am sure Miss Davenport and her father would appreciate the addition to our company."

"Miss Davenport."

Henry offered her his arm at once, aware of the surprise that leapt into her eyes as he did. Much to his relief, she took it anyway. He escorted her out into the fresh air, making sure to leave

Francis to accompany Viscount Munthorpe. As he walked from the house, Henry looked down at the lady on his arm. It appeared that she was doing all she could to turn her sight away from him.

"Miss Davenport, I must apologize to you," he said quietly, letting Francis and Viscount Munthorpe walk past so that he would not be overheard. "I have been thinking of a way to ensure that you are quite well after your excursion in the rain, and I am very glad to see that no harm has come to you."

She sniffed disdainfully and kept her head turned away.

"I know that you must be angry with me for my callous words, and can I assure you now that they were not harshly meant," he continued, hoping that she might at least glance up at him. "I was angry and upset, and I'm afraid that I allowed those emotions to overcome any consideration I should have had for you."

Laurie sighed and sent him a quick glance, her expression troubled. "You were rather rude, were you not, Mr. Catesby?" She sighed again, shaking her head. "And yet, I was also intolerably rude, speaking much too openly in the hope that you might take pity on me." She laughed sadly, her lips twisting as she did so. "Foolishness only, of course. I shall give you my apologies now, Mr. Catesby, in the hope that you might forgive me of such impropriety."

She was so different from how she had been when they had first met. There was none of that tenacity, no sign of the spark she had shown when they had talked. Instead, she was demure and proper, behaving just as an eligible young lady ought.

Henry hated it.

"Miss Davenport, might you wish to return to the shack?" he said suddenly, surprising even himself with such a question. "You indicated before that you might wish to.....spend some more time there, and I – "

"You made it very clear, Mr. Catesby, that I was not to set foot in what you deem 'your property,'" she interrupted firmly. "I must abide by that."

"I was wrong to speak so hastily," Henry countered, his frustration with himself only growing. "Please, Miss Davenport, if you would wish to return and to do what you can to help me in the restoration of the place, then I would be glad to allow that."

He held his breath as she considered his suggestion, not giving him any clear indication either way as to what she was thinking. He could not say why he had been so willing to allow her to return, after being so certain that he did not wish anyone else's presence in the shack, but he could not retract such a statement now. There was also the matter of propriety since they should not be in the shack together without the presence of a maid or some other chaperone, but he supposed that was a question that could be answered much later.

"You are something of a conundrum, Mr. Catesby," Miss Davenport uttered, as they approached the large manor house. "One moment you are ensuring me that you do not wish to so much as lay eyes on me again and the next, you are apologizing for your harsh words and inviting me back again." She turned her head towards him, arching one eyebrow in suspicion. "You have suggested that I am trying to trap you into matrimony by returning to the shack whilst you are present. Are you telling me now that you no longer believe this to be the case?"

Heat crawled up his neck, sending warmth into his face. "I was wrong to speak to you so, Miss Davenport. I can see that this Lord Umbridge – or whoever he may be – may be unsuitable for you and can understand why you seek a way of escape."

A quiet laugh escaped her. "Ah, so it is your first impression of my father that has brought you to such a decision, then?"

Henry considered this for a moment, before shaking his head. "I do not know what it is, Miss

Davenport. Perhaps it is because I can understand what it is like to have the idea of matrimony thrust under your nose with the expectation that you will do just as you are told, or perhaps it is a realization that my behavior was shameful and improper." Looking down at her, he saw that her eyes no longer held the angry suspicion that had been there only moments ago.

"I was in the wrong to speak to you so cruelly and with such a lack of feeling, Miss Davenport. You are welcome to return to the shack whenever you wish, although I should say that perhaps an old, rather worn gown might be suitable if you did wish to return." He wrinkled his nose, recalling just how dusty it had been before. "My staff are having a great deal of trouble getting some stains from my crisp white shirts."

To his surprise, Miss Davenport laughed aloud, a tinkling sound that made the corner of his lips turn up. She smiled at him then, her expression open and free from all anger and frustration.

"Thank you, Mr. Catesby, I think I shall return to the shack. I have been in the doldrums these last few days, what with Lord Umbridge's constant attention and the fact that I have nowhere to escape to."

"You do now," he said, quietly. "Come and go as you please, Miss Davenport. I have taken two men with me to the shack on occasion to aid me with some of the more difficult tasks, but you may wish to bring a maid for propriety's sake, just in case our paths should cross."

Her smile spread, her eyes twinkling up at him. "Indeed, Mr. Catesby. I shall consider doing just that." Her hand tightened on his arm for just a moment. "And thank you, Mr. Catesby, for your kindness and generosity. It is gratefully accepted with true appreciation."

"But of course, Miss Davenport," Henry assured her, finally feeling a good deal more at peace now that he had finally resolved matters between himself and Miss Davenport. Perhaps, working together, they might be able to get the shack in decent order sooner rather than later. Although what she would do after that, remained to be seen.

"Perhaps I might visit tomorrow?" she asked, as Francis stood at the door of the manor house, waiting for them. "In the afternoon?"

He nodded, unable to explain the swirl of excitement that raced through him without warning.

"That would suit me perfectly, Miss Davenport," he agreed, surprised to discover that he was already quite eager at the thought of showing her what improvements had been made at the shack already. "I look forward to it."

CHAPTER 7

Laurie smiled sweetly at Miss Stanley, who looked back at her suspiciously.

"Truly, I do not require your company for a short walk, Miss Stanley," Laurie said again, keeping her face entirely composed. "But I do thank you for your kind offer."

Miss Stanley frowned. "You are aware that Lord Umbridge is coming to afternoon tea with your father, are you not? I would hate to think that you are deliberately avoiding his company."

Realizing that her façade was not working on Miss Stanley in any away, Laurie let out a long, painful sigh and shrugged her shoulders before slumping back in her seat.

"I know you do not care for him, but he will keep you secure in your future," Miss Stanley continued before resuming her embroidery. "Besides which, you know that a lady such as yourself does not always get to do just as she pleases, no matter how much you might wish it."

Aware that her companion was giving her a little bit of a talking to, Laurie felt the old, familiar sense of frustration rising within her. "Be that as it may, Miss Stanley. I am not inclined to marry Lord Umbridge, despite my father's attempts to persuade me. I feel no regard for him and have decided, therefore, to ensure that my company is not often available to him when he visits my father." She lifted her chin, seeing Miss Stanley glance over at her. The older woman's expression showed nothing of surprise, though Laurie could see her thoughts at work as she continued her needlework.

"Miss Stanley," Laurie continued, quickly, "I know it is a great deal to ask of you but might you support me in this? You cannot truly believe that Lord Umbridge is a suitable gentleman for me, given that he is at least twenty years my senior at the very least. You know how he looks at me, how he does not particularly care about what I have to say or think, never showing me any interest whatsoever! I am nothing but a large dowry to him, another fortune he can add to his coffers."

Shaking her head, Laurie drew in another steadying breath. "I swear to you that I shall ensure you are taken care of for the rest of your days when the time comes for me to marry, but I cannot abide the thought of being wed to a man within age of my father." She suppressed a shudder, closing her eyes tightly. "I cannot bring myself to agree to such a union."

"You are not trying to manipulate me, I hope," Miss Stanley uttered, her eyes still sharp as they bored into Laurie. "You know very well that every companion's fear is what will become of them when they are too old to work any longer. But that is not something that you should capitalize on."

Laurie swallowed hard, awash with shame. "I apologize, Miss Stanley, if it appeared to you that I would only care for you should you aid me with Lord Umbridge. That is not the case. No matter what occurs with me, I shall make sure that you have a comfortable home in your elder years, whether that is in Lord Umbridge's home or in another gentleman's home entirely." She looked back at her companion with fondness, despite the embarrassment that still washed over her. "You know very well that I will always care for you, particularly after all you have done for me. Can I not ask for your help in this matter? Or have you grown tired of trying to guide me?"

Miss Stanley sighed heavily and put down her

embroidery, turning to look at Laurie with those perceptive eyes of hers.

"Very well," she said after a moment. "Run along, and I will let your father know that you have gone out for a walk should he come in search of you." She frowned as Laurie let out a small shriek of delight, only for Laurie to clasp her hand over her mouth. "I think you must take a cloak with you, however, if you are not to return from your walk in the state you were in last time."

Laurie got to her feet at once, leaning down to kiss Miss Stanley on the cheek, seeing just a hint of a smile pulling at her companion's mouth.

"Thank you, Miss Stanley," she said, hurrying towards the door. "You are truly wonderful. And yes, of course, I will make sure to take my cloak."

Sometime later, Laurie approached the tumbledown shack in the woods with a degree of trepidation, which she could not quite explain. Was it because Mr. Catesby had been rather confusing the last two occasions she had met him? The first, he had been angry and frustrated with her, only to later apologize for his actions and request the pleasure of her company back at the shack whenever she wished it.

She could not quite figure Mr. Catesby out, although she had to admit that she found his apology both acceptable and well thought out. It was clear he *had* been considering her these last few days and the fact that he had been worried about her since then had to say something about him, did it not?

"Ah, Miss Davenport!"

She looked up as Mr. Catesby stepped out of the front door of the shack, which she realized, had been replaced by a new one.

"Good afternoon, Mr. Catesby," she echoed, carefully stepping over the ruins of what she assumed had once been a wall that had, perhaps, enclosed the house garden. "You have been busy, I see."

He smiled, although it did not quite reach his eyes. Laurie felt her heart drop to her toes, wondering if Mr. Catesby was, underneath it all, still rather displeased at her presence.

"Indeed I have," Mr. Catesby replied, offering to take her hand as she made her way to the front door so that she would not trip over a few large branches that had fallen from the trees above. "Would you like to come in and see?"

Accepting his hand, Laurie was surprised at the spark that shot up her arm, sending her head into a much quicker pace. She let his hand go the moment she was safely at the door, looking all about her as they walked inside.

"I have not managed to achieve a great deal in terms of cleaning the place," Mr. Catesby began, betraying nothing of the moment before. "Rather,

I have been ensuring that the shack itself is quite safe. I am glad to say that it is now perfectly usable."

He gestured to the fireplace, where a small fire now burned in the grate, sending a wave of warmth towards her. "The roof has been fixed, the fireplace mended and cleared, and the windows, shutters, and front door either replaced or secured," he finished with a flourish. "Which is just as well, given that the weather is becoming a little cooler of late."

Laurie managed a small smile, still rather unsure what to make of this gentleman. "It is the autumn, I suppose."

He glanced at her, then smiled. "Yes, indeed. So it is."

They remained like this for a few moments, with neither speaking a word to the other, and Laurie felt her skin prickle with nervous anticipation. She was not certain what to say, still not sure whether or not Mr. Catesby was truly content with her presence here, but just as she opened her mouth to speak, Mr. Catesby cleared his throat and gestured to the room beyond.

"There is a key to the front door waiting for you in the kitchen," he indicated. "I have set it out next to the tea things." Seeing her surprised look, he shrugged, appearing a little abashed. "It made sense to give you a key, in case you should happen to come by and I am not yet here," he explained, his cheeks a little red. "There is a teapot, and everything else you require should you care to make yourself a pot. In addition, one of the men has found a small cellar just to the left of the kitchen, on the floor of what I think must be a pantry of sorts. He is clearing it out at this present moment, and milk can be stored down there if required. I shall bring some fresh each day, however, until it is quite ready."

She nodded slowly, tilting her head to regard Mr. Catesby a little more carefully. "Do you intend to repose here during the day, when it is quite complete?" she asked, curiously. "I know that you are interested in the stars and the like, but surely you cannot see anything much in the middle of the wood!"

He laughed spontaneously and, as he did so, his demeanor changed completely. No longer was he the serious, unsmiling gentleman who had first greeted her the day she had stepped into this place, but instead he was warm, friendly and welcoming, his eyes alight with mirth.

It was a sight that sent a sudden pang of affection deep into her heart.

"Indeed, Miss Davenport, you are quite correct," he said, laughing still. "In truth, I am not yet quite sure what it is I intend to do with this place, although I confess that it holds a great deal of delight for me as it is. To be so far away from any hindrances, any frustrating conversations and interruptions upon my time, that is a welcome thought indeed."

Her own smile faded as she realized that he was a rather solitary gentleman, which meant that once she aided him in cleaning the shack from top to bottom, then, most likely, she would not be welcome back again.

That is what you suggested, Laurie, she told herself, trying to smile at Mr. Henry Catesby. *You asked to come here in order to help Mr. Catesby in his restoration of the shack. Once that is over, you will have to return to your own life and, unfortunately, to Lord Umbridge.*

"I do not precisely know where to begin with the cleaning, however," Henry continued, looking about him with an expression of dismay. "There is just so much dirt and dust that I find I am at quite a loss to know where to start."

"And you are still willing to have my help in this matter?" she asked cautiously, wanting a little reassurance from him. "I am more than willing to do whatever I can to help, but I am still a trifle confused as to whether you truly wish for my company or not."

Henry cleared his throat, coming back to face her. "Of course, Miss Davenport, I would be more than happy for you to help me in putting this place to rights. That is why you are to have your own key so that you can come and go as you please." He looked over her shoulder towards the door, one eyebrow a little raised. "Did you bring a maid with you?"

She shook her head, a little embarrassed. "No, I did not. The less my father knows about where I am, the better."

Henry hesitated for a moment, before giving her a slight shrug. "Very well, Miss Davenport. I will admit to you that I find the whole situation a little untoward but hopefully, with my men around the place, there will be no impropriety."

"Just as long as my father does not find out where I am," Laurie mumbled to herself, catching Mr. Catesby's look of concern as he overheard her. Tossing her head, she walked past him into the kitchen, determined not to let thoughts of her father or Lord Umbridge concern her any longer.

The tea was set out on one countertop that had clearly been washed and cleaned, whereas the rest of the kitchen remained lined with dirt and dust. Laurie smiled to herself, looking over at the teapot and thinking just how much she would appreciate a cup of tea once her work for the afternoon was over.

"There is a well just outside the house, around the back," Henry said, just from behind her, making her start. "And whilst there is no stove to speak of, there is a place to hang a pot over the fire in the main room."

She nodded, suddenly aware of just how close he was to her. Turning to face him, she realized for the first time that he was dressed in nothing but his shirt sleeves, the formal attire she had seen him in on the last two occasions completely gone.

"Thank you, Mr. Catesby," she murmured, looking up into his eyes and seeing just how dark green they were, much darker than her own. His hair was still perfectly in place, in sharp contrast to her own red curls which were constantly falling out of whatever style she wore. Today's tight chignon was still having little effect on her freespirited curls, for even now she could tell that a few of them had sprung free and were dancing around her temples. She had a mad urge to rake her hands through his hair, to dishevel him completely just to see how he would react. But instead, she clasped her hands tightly in her lap, growing hot at such a ridiculous thought.

"I should leave you now," Mr. Catesby said quietly, as though he had seen her thoughts. "Do excuse me, Miss Davenport. Should you need me, I will be outside with my men, seeing to the garden wall and other matters to do with the exterior."

She mumbled her reply by inclining her head, only to raise it and see that he was already gone.

Wincing, Laurie looked away from the sight of him walking towards the door, not wanting to let her eyes linger on him for any length of time. He was so proper, so correct, so formal – which was just what a gentleman ought to be, but she still found him very difficult to make out. She was unsure as to his motivations for asking her to return to the shack and was certainly at even more of a loss to decipher whether or not he truly did wish for her presence here. However, Laurie was determined to continue on regardless. After all, her main goal in coming here was to avoid Lord Umbridge and surely by the time the shack was completed, Lord Umbridge would understand that she was not at all interested in his suit. As for Mr. Catesby…

Laurie bit her lip, frustrated with herself for allowing her heart to quicken when he'd taken her hand, and for noticing just how dark his emerald eyes were. She did not need to consider him in any way and was determined not to eagerly seek his company out for any reason. Besides which, Mr. Catesby was quite obviously a solitary gentleman, looking for nothing more than his own company, his own thoughts, and his own space. There was no sense in pursuing any thought of a man who wanted to live his life alone, now, was there?

Pushing aside her thoughts, Laurie looked all

about her and decided that she would begin with the kitchen, picking up where Mr. Catesby had left off. He had only cleaned one small countertop, but it was a start. Finding a basin already filled with cool, clear water, she dipped the waiting rag that sat next to it. Squeezing the water out of the cloth onto the dirty surface, Laurie let the moisture penetrate the dirt. After a second, she took up the bar of lye soap and began to scrub it through the dirt.

She had very little idea as to what she was doing, given that she was quite unused to doing such menial tasks, but surely it could not be all that difficult? Soap and water got almost everything out, as Miss Stanley had said to her on more than one occasion. Besides which, doing something like this would, at the very least, keep her mind from thinking about Mr. Henry Catesby.

CHAPTER 8

"Miss Davenport!"

Laurie jumped to her feet, suddenly aware that she was covered head to foot with dirt and soot and all other manner of things.

"Mr. Catesby," she hid a growing grin, putting one hand to her hair a little self-consciously. "As you can see, I have been hard at work this morning."

He stared at her, as though both horrified and amused at her appearance.

"But the kitchen is a great deal better, is it not?" she continued when he said nothing. "It is just the floor I am to finish and then I shall be on my way."

"You need not leave immediately, just because I returned."

She blinked, a little surprised, but gave him a quick smile. "Thank you, Mr. Catesby. That is very kind."

He cleared his throat again – a habit of his, she decided, when he was not quite sure what to say or do – then he put his hands behind his back, looking at her thoughtfully.

"My men have been busy in the garden," he relayed with slight hesitance. "The wall is to be repaired soon, and the ground turned. I am not quite sure what to plant in it as yet, but perhaps you might be able to make some suggestions?"

An unconstrained chortle escaped her before she could prevent it, startling Henry. Seeing that she would have to explain, Laurie shook her head and spread her hands wide. "I am afraid I shall disappoint you there, Mr. Catesby. I know very little about flowers or the like, although I am certain Miss Stanley would be able to give me some suggestions."

"Miss Stanley?" he enquired, looking a little calmer. "She is…?"

"My companion," Laurie explained, feeling something on her face itch as she wiped it with the back of her hand. "She will know what will take well and will be thrilled, I am sure, that I am taking such interest in flowers and the like!"

Henry colored and looked away, making Laurie wonder if she had said something untoward. He turned back, a stifled smile still evident, and gestured to her cheek, .

"You have some….dirt there, Miss Davenport."

"Oh."

Now it was her turn to blush. Whilst she knew she was in a dreadful state, the apron and her cap could be easily removed before she returned to the manor house, but smudges on her cheek or forehead would bring questions from Miss Stanley.

"Here," he offered, wringing out what appeared to be a fairly clean cloth from a bowl of water that stood on the countertop and handing it to her.

"Thank you."

She dabbed at her cheek, hoping she was reaching the stain, only for him to sigh and shake his head.

"A little higher, Miss Davenport."

Flushing all the harder, she did as he instructed. Finally, he stepped forward and took the cloth from her hand, grasping her chin gently with the other to tilt her face to one side.

Laurie froze, her stomach turning over on itself as he carefully wiped the dirt from her face, far too aware of just how close he was to her. She had not expected such a strong reaction from within herself, aware that her pulse was racing wildly as his fingers branded her skin.

"There," he said, stepping back and replacing the cloth in the bowl of water. "Now, I was to make some tea, Miss Davenport, which I know may come as a surprise to you given that I am a gentleman. But I should inform you that I am quite used to doing such a thing, given that I live a fairly solitary life."

She caught the twinkle in his eye and the way his lips curved upwards and felt herself smile back at him, her whole body warm all over.

"Might you care for a cup before you depart?" he asked, a little more softly. "I would be glad to ensure you have a little refreshment before you return home."

Nodding, Laurie felt her throat constrict as she tried to speak calmly, despite the hammering of her heart.

"Thank you, Mr. Catesby," she managed to say. "That would be very much appreciated."

Half an hour later Laurie found herself sitting in front of the small fire in the living room, sighing contentedly as she lifted the cup of tea to her lips.

"Does it meet with your approval, Miss Davenport?" Henry asked as he sat down opposite her, the chair groaning as he did so.

She laughed and saw him smile at her in return. "Yes, of course, Mr. Catesby. It is quite wonderful. I thank you." Glancing over at the dirty apron and cap which sat on the floor in a heap, she sighed again and rested her head against the back of the chair. She had done more work in this place these last three mornings than she had ever done in her life. She had struggled at times to keep going, but the sight of the kitchen as it was now made everything worthwhile.

"You have done an excellent job thus far, Miss Davenport," he said gently, as though he could read her thoughts. "It has not been too trying for you, I hope?"

Smiling at him, she shook her head. "I will confess that I am quite unused to cleaning and sweeping, but I find, to my surprise, that I am rather good at it," she replied, with a chuckle. "Although I do not think I have ever slept as well as I have these last few nights!" She smiled to herself as she recalled how astonished the staff had been when she had requested a bath for the third evening running, but she simply could not allow herself to remain as dirty and sticky as she was after a day at the shack.

"And, do you think you will return again tomorrow?" Mr. Catesby asked, quietly, his green eyes fixed on hers. "I know there is a great deal yet to do, but you need not feel that the burden is yours alone."

She tipped her head, regarding him carefully before shaking her head.

"No, Mr. Catesby, I do not feel it is such a burden," she replied, with a soft smile. "I find that I quite enjoy my time here. It is an escape."

To her surprise, he nodded at this sentiment, as though he agreed with her. She did not say anything, despite the curiosity rising deep within her.

"My brother is attempting to encourage me into matrimony," he said, his gaze drifting away from her and towards the flames crackling over the wood in the grate. "I find that I am not particularly inclined, however, to do such a thing."

She nodded slowly, surprised that her heart was filled with sympathy for him.

"He is incredibly persistent," Henry continued, one hand passing across his eyes for a moment. "I know that he is speaking of such a thing out of concern for me, but I have very little intention of doing as he asks."

"And that is why you were so glad to find this place?" she asked, carefully, unable to remain silent any longer. "It has helped you to avoid this ongoing encouragement from your brother?"

His eyes met hers, silence stretching between them for a moment.

Then, he sighed heavily and nodded, his expression a little wry. "It seems we are both attempting to escape from the same thing, Miss Davenport," he said quietly. "Although perhaps going about it in very different ways."

There was something in that moment that Laurie could not quite explain. It seemed as though each of them perhaps understood the other. Whether it was that of a friendship blossoming, she did not know. But, a solidarity was struck up between them as they looked at one another.

Henry shrugged then, his words hesitating momentarily. "Have you any plans for what you shall do if Lord Umbridge continues with his visits, Miss Davenport?"

Tension flooded her body, and she shook her head, reaching to pour herself another cup of tea. "No, I do not know what I shall do," she said, honestly. "However, I continue to hope that my father will come to his senses and allow me the time to find a husband of my own, instead of hoisting Lord Umbridge upon me."

Henry chuckled, his face lighting up and Laurie felt warmth flood her soul.

"Is Lord Umbridge truly such an unfortunate gentleman that you would not even consider him, Miss Davenport?" he asked, his lips curving into a broad smile. "Surely there must be something to endear him to you?"

She laughed and shook her head, the tension

now gone from her. "No, indeed, Mr. Catesby, there is not. He may be rich and titled, but there is no consideration for anyone other than himself. I am simply an adornment to his already wonderful fortune and manor house, and I do not intend to be paraded about on his arm. More so, the idea of having an interesting conversation between us would be utterly lost on him." She shook her head, her lips pursing. "My large dowry is all that attracts Lord Umbridge, that I am certain of. And I do not think that is a good enough reason to propose matrimony, Mr. Catesby, do you?"

Letting her eyes linger on his, she waited for him to respond, then saw something flicker in his gaze. A long exhale left his lips as he shook his head, his whole frame relaxing a little more into the chair. It was as though they were becoming better acquainted and he was not quite sure what to make of it, not quite certain that this was, in fact, something that he wanted from her.

"No, Miss Davenport," he said slowly, his eyes slowly fastened onto hers. "No, I do not think that is a good reason for marriage at all."

"Then we are agreed, Mr. Catesby," she said softly, feeling her pulse begin to quicken as she was caught by the intensity of his gaze. "Marriage should be more than just requirement, more than just expectation or social standing. It should have feeling, have friendship, and a willingness to enter into a lifelong commitment." Drawing in her breath, she smiled at him, aware that his face was a little flushed and having very little idea as to why that might be. "It is good to have someone who finally understands, Mr. Catesby. I thank you for that understanding."

He cleared his throat, pushing one hand through his hair as his eyes darted away from hers. "Not at all, Miss Davenport," he muttered, reaching for the teapot to pour himself another cup. "I am glad to have been of some comfort."

CHAPTER 9

T *en days later*
"Miss Davenport?"

Giving the handle a tug, Henry was surprised to discover that he felt somewhat disappointed that Miss Davenport was not in the shack, which she had affectionately named 'Tumbledown House.' It had been ten days since they had taken tea together. Ten days since he was quite sure that she would not return given the absolute state of her dress, her hands, her face, and even her hair. But, much to his surprise, she had shown great tenacity and fortitude and had returned almost every day to continue with what she had started.

Pulling out his key, he turned it quickly and stepped inside, ensuring that the door was closed tightly behind him. Drawing in a deep breath, he felt the peace he had come to expect settle over his heart as he took a few steps inside, feeling that, somehow here, he was safe.

Of course, Francis had been growing more and more frustrated with not being able to find Henry whenever he came to call, which Henry was able to surmise given the sharply worded notes that continued to come through the door whenever he was not at home, but he did not care. Francis would have to learn sooner or later that Henry had no intention of being dragged into matrimony, whether Francis wished him to or not. On one occasion, Henry had thought about writing to his mother to request her help in calming Francis' supposed determination, but he had then chosen not to do so, thinking that he was more than able to manage his brother himself.

And manage his brother he had, although not in any particularly forcible way. He had simply escaped, making sure to leave the house during the day to come to 'Tumbledown House' and then returning at night, to catch a few hours of sleep before wakening to look at and study the stars.

Francis, he knew, was always busy with estate business and the like in the mornings, which meant that he only had to remove himself from his home by lunchtime, which appeared to be working rather well. His servants were, of course, keeping quiet just as he expected them to do, which meant he had very little to concern him as regarded his brother.

A sigh of contentment left his lips as he wandered into the kitchen, amazed at just how much of a transformation had taken place, all thanks to Miss Davenport's hard work. Of course, there had been some things to fix and some things to replace but, all in all, it was looking much more like a home and less like a ruin that might fall down around his ears at any given moment! His eyes landed on what appeared to be a small covered tray and, lifting the sheet from it, Henry felt his lips pull into a wide smile.

Miss Davenport had been here before him and, as she had done from the first day she had arrived, was showing him great consideration. She had left the tea things out ready for him to make his usual pot, as he had told her he liked to do when he visited, and there was also a small tin of something he was sure would be quite delicious. His smile grew all the more as he lifted the lid, seeing biscuits and some small cakes, which Miss Davenport must have begged from her father's cook. He did not have to look to know that she would have left some fresh well water for him in a covered pot by the fire, all ready for him to heat up when he was ready. She was proving herself to be remarkably kind, even if rather improper.

Setting about lighting the fire, Henry frowned for a moment as he realized what he had just thought about the lady. Improper? That was his first thought when it came to considering Miss Davenport?

Setting the fire alight, Henry sat back on his heels and carefully began to feed it with some larger twigs and branches, before adding a few larger logs, his heart lifting as they began to crackle and burn. Miss Davenport had, only yesterday, watched him keenly as he'd set the fire. She had informed him that she wanted to learn how to do such a thing, which of course, he had found to be both charming and ridiculous in equal measure. She was a lady, was she not? So why should she have need to learn the skill to set a fire?

But nevertheless, he had shown her, and she had watched and asked questions. He had found her mind to be rather keen and had, to his astonishment, enjoyed their discussion. He had been doing his best to accommodate her without truly becoming involved, and yet the discussion he had engaged her in yesterday afternoon had sparked something in him. Something that he was not quite sure he wanted to study further.

Shaking his head to himself, Henry muttered darkly as he rose to his feet, knowing that he could not allow himself to linger on Miss Davenport's beautiful green eyes, or the way that her red curls always seemed to tumble around her shoulders no matter what she did. He did, of course, notice these things and had felt something jolt his heart as he'd watched her, but he had not allowed himself to consider what he had felt. After all, he was spending most of his time avoiding the discussion of matrimony with Francis because he did not wish to become engaged to anyone. Certainly not a red-haired young lady who was one of the most unusual creatures he had ever come across.

Leaving the water to warm, Henry looked around the room with a slight frown. It was still rather dirty, even though Miss Davenport swept the floor every day and had done her best to clean the three chairs that he had been able to salvage from what they had found. Of course, Henry had every intention of bringing decent furniture to 'Tumbledown House' once it was thoroughly cleaned but, for the time being, these would do very well.

Picking up the broom, he thought he might give the floor another do over. As he passed near one of the windows, his ear caught what sounded like someone crying.

Sobs were coming from just outside the shack and, without even having to look, Henry knew precisely who it was. It could only really be one person.

Miss Davenport.

He did not know what to do, moving a little closer to the window so that he had a clear view of outside.

Miss Davenport was sitting on the garden wall, which had only just been recently restored by his men, weeping as though her heart was breaking. Tears were pouring down her cheeks, and she was making no effort to wipe them away, even though a lace handkerchief was in her hand. Her hair was, as usual, falling down around her face. Her back was hunched, her tears falling like the rain as she sobbed, her whole body shaking.

Henry did not know what to do. A lady such as she in distress was a situation he had never been faced with before now. Given that he had very little experience in such matters, Henry felt himself grow tense. After all, even though they had been around one another more than he had anticipated these last many days, he did not know her all that well. More so, he had purposely avoided dropping his guard during their conversations, lest the chance it would deepen their acquaintance. The thought of doing so now left him feeling all the more confused.

He did not know whether to go out to her to speak to her, or whether to leave her alone. Of course, she had come here since it was a place where she could be alone, a place where she might feel the same peace as he did, but whether or not she wanted his company remained to be seen. His heart hammered wildly as he took in her misery once more, suddenly desperate to find a way to console her but having absolutely no idea what to do.

Walking away from the window and towards the door, Henry hesitated for another moment. He knew that if he took another step outside towards her, then their acquaintance, such as it was, could change forever. He would be making the deliberate choice to insert himself into her affairs. Did he really want to do that? Would it not be best for him to just continue as he was, perhaps returning to the kitchen and pretending that he had not seen her outside, should she come in? Then, at least, she could either show him her tears or hide her face until she regained her composure – which would leave the choice of furthering their acquaintance entirely in her hands.

Closing his eyes, Henry battled against the two parts of himself – the one side desperate to help Miss Davenport in her misery, and the other wanting to keep things just as they were. He had spent most of his life doing just as he pleased, living alone without the burden of others around him when he chose, and he had to admit that this was a state of being that he had come to appreciate. To speak to Miss Davenport now would be to endanger that way of living.

That makes you a selfish beast, Henry.

Wincing slightly, Henry heard the whisper of conscience in his mind, aware that he was trying to do what was best for himself as opposed to what was best for Miss Davenport. As much as he tried to convince himself that he did not need to care about Miss Davenport, he could not ignore her distress. He tried to tell himself that their acquaintance would be a short one and therefore, the less he knew her the better, but the sound of her sobs coming towards him continued to pierce his heart.

Setting his jaw, Henry turned back towards the door, put his hand on the door handle and, with a deep breath, pulled it open and strode outside. A cold wind wrapped itself around him, making him shiver. Miss Davenport did not see him at first, too lost in her pain and misery. She gave a visible start when he called her name.

"Oh, Mr. Catesby," she stammered, immediately getting to her feet and wiping her eyes with her handkerchief, turning her face away. "I did not know you were here. I do apologize if I have intruded upon your time here."

He swallowed hard, his heart aching at the sight of her red-rimmed eyes and miserable expression.

"Miss Davenport," he said gently, taking a step towards her. "Come in out of the cold. You will catch a chill if you remain out here." His gaze roved over her as she continued to dab her eyes, clearly attempting to quell her sobs. He realized that she was not wearing one of her old gowns as she had done every time before, but that her walking dress was one of good quality, her shawl thick and warm. Clearly, she had not been expecting to come out here.

"You are not disturbing me, truly," he continued, when she did not move. "Please, Miss Davenport, come inside. I can offer you a fire and a cup of tea, as well as a listening ear, should you require it."

Her pain-filled eyes looked up at him, and Henry felt the swift kick of anguish in his own heart as her lips trembled, evidently finding it difficult to speak without breaking into tears once more.

"Thank you, Mr. Catesby," she eventually managed to whisper, taking his hand with her own. "You are very kind."

His heart jolted as her fingers touched his and, for a moment, he was frozen to the spot. He found himself simply looking at Miss Davenport with a mixture of confusion and surprise at his own reaction to her. Then, as she managed a small, watery smile, he recalled what he was meant to be doing and led her into the house. As they walked into the house together he tried to quell his fear at the impropriety of being alone with an eligible young lady. He told himself that no-one else knew of this place, and that they were not likely to be discovered. He felt her shiver as she stepped into the warmth of 'Tumbledown House,' and Henry allowed the last of his concerns to drift away. Miss Davenport needed him, or at least, needed the house, the tea, and the fire. He need not be concerned about anything other than restoring her in any way he could.

CHAPTER 10

Laurie accepted a cup of tea from Mr. Catesby with a whisper of thanks, now feeling quite mortified on top of her misery. She had not expected Mr. Catesby to be in the shack, given that there were no men outside as she had approached. He had not often been at 'Tumbledown House' alone, and, besides which, she had not brought her key to open the front door. She had not intended to come here but, after the threats from her father, she had only one thought – and that was to run as far away from him and from his home as she could.

In fact, she had not even found Miss Stanley and told her where she was going, even though Laurie was quite sure that her companion would guess where she was. She had to pray that Miss

Stanley would not share this news with Laurie's father, for then the game would be up, and she would be quite done for.

"Might I offer you something to eat?" Mr. Catesby's earnest voice met her ears. She looked up to see him offering her the tin of cakes and biscuits which she had brought earlier that morning during her walk in the woods.

"Thank you," she managed, her voice still trembling as she spoke to him. Picking up a biscuit, she took a small bite but found that she did not really taste it, such was her misery.

Taking a sip of her tea, Laurie felt heat come back into her hands, only just becoming aware of how cold she had been sitting outside on the garden wall. The warmth spread through the rest of her limbs as she took another sip, grateful for Mr. Catesby's kindness.

"Do you wish to talk about whatever it is that is troubling you?" Mr. Catesby asked, perching himself on the edge of the seat opposite her, which made him look more than a little uncomfortable. "I would be glad to listen, although I fear that I will not be able to offer any advice."

She looked back at him, aware that his expression was one of confusion, and yet the eagerness in his voice told her that he was doing his best to help her.

"You are too kind, Mr. Catesby, but I had no intention of crying all over you," she said slowly, as his gaze remained steadily fixed on hers. "I did not think you were here. There were no men about."

He gave her a quick smile, whilst concern still lingered in his eyes. "I thought to come here alone today. There is not much else that needs to be done that I cannot manage myself."

"I see." She did not want to say more, did not want to burden this gentleman who had already done enough for her. He had allowed her to come to his small shack despite his clear unwillingness to share it with anyone else and had even given her a key so that she might come and go as she pleased. The last ten days had been wonderful since she had been able to escape from her father's house whenever she wished. Until this afternoon, she had felt happier than she had in a long time.

There had been freedom from the unrelenting pressure her father had brought to bear in regard to Lord Umbridge. Miss Stanley had done all she could to help, and her father had very little cause to be angry with either Miss Stanley or Laurie. For the two women had simply ensured that, to anyone's better knowledge, Laurie knew nothing of her father's plans with Lord Umbridge, making it so that he could not accuse her of deliberately running away.

All had been going so wonderfully well, that it should perhaps not have surprised her that her father would react so badly.

"Miss Davenport, you are clearly distraught," Mr. Catesby said, breaking into her thoughts. "Might I pour you a little more tea?"

She held her cup out to him mutely, which he took and placed on the small tray before pouring her another cup, adding a small dash of milk. As she accepted it back from him, their fingers brushed gently, and Laurie felt that familiar warmth spread up her arm, making its way into her heart, as it had done before.

"What can I do, Miss Davenport?" Mr. Catesby asked, sounding a little desperate. "You appear to be terribly troubled, and I do wish to help you in whatever way I can."

"You do not need to shoulder my burdens, Mr. Catesby," she replied, hesitantly, not wanting to reject his offer of assistance. "This is nothing to do with you, and I know how much you value your privacy. I will not trouble you with pouring my heart out to you."

He leaned forward, his eyes searching her own. "Truly, I would not consider it a burden, Miss Davenport," he affirmed calmly, appearing to Laurie to be speaking with complete honesty. "Can you not trust me with this?"

She sighed heavily, her heart tearing asunder

once again. "It is to do with Lord Umbridge. And my father, of course." Her voice grew hoarse, and she drew in a few long breaths, determined to keep her composure.

"Yes, I recall that your father was eager for you to wed Lord Umbridge," Mr. Catesby replied, sounding a little relieved that she had said something. "Is that still the case?"

Drawing in a shaky breath, Laurie tried to find a way to explain without turning into a watering pot. Unfortunately, even as she spoke, tears began to flood her vision and she felt the warmth of them on her cheeks.

"My father has betrothed me to Lord Umbridge," she let out, hoarsely. "He has decided that enough is enough, or something like that. He does not wish me to take my time in finding myself a husband and has therefore decided that Lord Umbridge will do me well enough. There is nothing for me to say that will get him to change his mind on the matter."

There was a long silence that lasted to the point where Laurie began to wonder if she had said too much. Then Mr. Catesby cleared his throat once, twice, three times, before leaning forward and refilling his teacup, as though this was a simple conversation between the two of them.

"Is Lord Umbridge a particularly poor choice?" he posed. He casually sipped his tea, and his eyes avoided meeting hers, as if he was giving careful thought to the question. "Is your father not doing the best he can for you?"

A spark of anger shot through Laurie. "My father cares for me, Mr. Catesby, but that does not mean that he knows what is best. Lord Umbridge is *not* the kind of gentleman I wish to bequeath myself to." This was not what she had expected to hear from him, given what he had said about matrimony previously, and his words bit at her already broken heart.

To her horror, Mr. Catesby gave a small shrug. "I doubt that many young ladies get to choose their husbands, Miss Davenport. If the gentleman is wealthy, from a good family and has, at the very least, a decent character, then I cannot see what problems might arise from your match."

She stared at him, her blood turning cold in her veins. Mr. Catesby was not to be sympathetic towards her plight, it seemed. Instead, he was simply quiet and calm, thinking things through on an entirely practical level, instead of allowing any emotion to come through in his words. Apparently, he did not care for her in any way whatsoever and appeared to think that she was out of line to consider herself worthy of having personal choice.

"You think I should marry the gentleman?" she whispered, setting her teacup down carefully with a shaking hand. "Mr. Catesby, it is clear that you think me quite ridiculous being so upset over this. This is not what I expected from you, given our previous discussions!"

He winced just a little, lowering his gaze, and it was as though he had struck an arrow through her heart.

"You think me foolish," she continued, getting up from her chair on unsteady feet. "You think me ridiculous to be crying over this matter?"

He rose, holding out one hand to her as though to stop her from storming from the room. Henry shook his head, "No, I do not think you foolish for crying, Miss Davenport, but I do think that it would be best for you if you looked at this in an entirely different light."

She bit her lip, forcing herself to contain her anger.

"Your father is doing what is best for you. For you cannot remain at home for the rest of your days in the knowledge that, when the time comes for the title to pass on, you will be entirely at the new Viscount's disposal." He lifted his shoulders again, although his dark green eyes were a little wider than before, praying that she would find some way to understand him. "Lord Umbridge is a good match, Miss Davenport, and if I were you, I would simply try to find a way to accept it and move ahead to your wedding."

Shaking her head, Laurie stepped closer to Mr. Catesby, pressing one sharp finger into his chest as she looked up into his eyes. How unfeeling he was! And she had thought him so kind in bringing her into 'Tumbledown House' and making her a cup of tea.

"How dare you!" she hissed, her eyes narrowing, her tears forgotten. "Telling me that I must simply make do, that I must do what my father says without question when you are doing your utmost to avoid the very same situation."

He stared at her, his face suddenly flaming with color. Laurie realized that her hair had, as usual, begun to tumble down over her face. Tucking back an errant curl, she glared at Mr. Catesby all the harder.

"You are telling me that my father knows what is best? That I am to accept this marriage, whilst you are avoiding the very same situation as regards to your brother and his attempts to find you a wife," she continued, harshly. "How dare you suggest that you know what is best for me when you are seeking the very same freedom that I am. Why is it that you believe that you should be able to have the freedom to marry whomever you please, whereas I am forced to marry whatever completely unsuitable gentleman my father chooses for me?"

The question hung in the air, sending sparks

around them both. Laurie could see that Mr. Catesby was struggling to answer as her finger still pressed hard into his chest.

And then, to her utter astonishment, his fingers reached out and touched her hair.

She was frozen to the spot. His fingers were gently tucking back another curl, whilst more fell onto his hand. There was something like bewilderment in his expression. It was as though he had not expected to be doing something as intimate as this, yet couldn't stop himself.

Laurie shivered violently as his fingers brushed her cheek, her hand dropping to her side as she looked up into Mr. Catesby's eyes. She was not quite sure why he had broken his emotionless demeanor and she was entirely unprepared for the way her heart was racing frantically in her chest as a result. His gentle touch was eliciting all kinds of feelings in her that she had never expected, her mouth going dry as he moved a few inches closer to her.

"Miss Davenport," he whispered, his eyes glazing over as he looked at her. "I….." He trailed off, his head lowering as she kept her face tipped towards his.

And then he blinked. Once, twice – swallowed hard and stepped back, his hand dropping to his side.

Laurie stared at him as he looked back at her,

clearly confused and conflicted over what he had done, what he had experienced within himself.

Clearing his throat again, he gestured towards the door. "Do excuse me, Miss Davenport," he said hoarsely, his eyes no longer fixed on her but instead jumping from one place to the next. "I have some work to do back at the house. Do you have the key?"

She felt her heart break all over again and shook her head. A lump arose in her throat and she tried to force it back down. "No, I do not, Mr. Catesby, but let me make matters easier for you. I shall return home to my father and do as you have suggested." Tears stung her eyes as she looked over at him, seeing the way his lips tugged in conflict against saying more to her. "Do excuse me."

Her shoulders slumped as she walked from the room, praying that he might call out her name, that he might beg her to wait so that they could speak a little more…might explore what had just occurred between them – but there came nothing but silence.

Silence that tore her apart as she walked back outside into the cold afternoon air, the door slamming shut behind her.

CHAPTER 11

"Henry?"

Groaning, Henry put his head in his hands and waited for the unwelcome presence of his brother to enter the room. He had no wish to speak to Francis this afternoon, given that he still had Miss Davenport firmly on his mind.

"Do go away," he said, loudly, as the door to his study opened. "I have no wish to be told I am to go here or meet this young lady or that young lady, to be dragged from one place to the next. Nor do I wish for any company to be taken into my house, or to have invitations to soirees thrust into my hands. I am through with this nonsense, Francis. When will you understand that I do not wish to marry?"

"Henry."

Biting back another sigh, Henry lifted his head to see Francis looking at him with a grave expression on his face. A jolt ran through him, suddenly worried that something had happened to either his mother or one of his siblings.

"What is it?" he asked, turning to face Francis a little more. "Is something wrong?"

Francis sighed and sat down heavily.

"Henry, I know about your house in the woods."

Swallowing hard, Henry went cold all over, wondering just how much his brother knew.

"You have loyal staff, yes, but I have an equally loyal steward, who was easily able to find out what you have been doing," Francis continued, sitting down in a chair by the fire. He looked over at Henry, who rose to join him. "Are you trying to hide from me, brother?"

Henry sat down opposite Francis and took his brother in, seeing the concern in Francis' eyes.

"The truth is Francis, when I found that place it was as though a new world had opened itself up to me," he said, quietly. "A place where I can go to be entirely free of your demands – of anyone's demands, in fact." He shrugged, knowing that he would be best telling Francis the truth. "I am aware that it is your property, of course, but I did not think that you would mind, given that you were entirely unaware of its presence."

To Henry's surprise, Francis sighed heavily, shaking his head. He put his head in his hands for a moment, the atmosphere growing thick with tension.

"I have been rather intrusive, have I not?" Francis offered eventually, his head still in his hands. "I have been coming here almost every day, angry that I could not find you."

Henry couldn't help but chuckle, despite the strain in the room. "Yes, Francis, I thought you were rather angry, given the tone of the notes I received from you."

Francis groaned loudly, sitting back in his seat and blowing out a frustrated breath. "I apologize, Henry."

Henry froze in his seat, the smile fading from his face. This was not what he had expected to hear from his brother.

"I was foolish to try and force such a thing onto you," Francis continued. "The truth is, Henry, I have been trying to *encourage* you in the direction of matrimony simply because of my own worries and concerns." He shook his head, his expression a trifle sad. "I feel as though I let our sister Sophia down badly, and so I was determined not to let the same thing happen again. I went overboard, old man, and for that, I apologize."

Henry, being quite taken aback, struggled to get his breath for a moment, before nodding and stretching out his hand to shake Francis'. "Thank you, brother," he said, feeling a heavy burden roll from his shoulders. "To have that freedom is a great blessing."

"And it is a freedom you should have always had," Francis said firmly, shaking Henry's hand. "It is not my place to force you into matrimony with someone you either don't know or particularly care for. If it is one thing I should have learned from Sophia's situation, it is that love should be present if one is to have a joyful marriage. It appears that, in her situation, it has overcome the most difficult of trials."

"Yes, it has," Henry agreed, his mind suddenly filled with Miss Davenport, although he could not explain why. "I know you are concerned for me, Francis, but I assure you that I am more than content on my own."

Francis lifted one eyebrow. "Truly?"

Henry opened his mouth to respond but then shut it again, his throat suddenly closing up tight.

"You are to have that shack, you know," Francis continued, clearly not noticing Henry's inability to answer. "I am having my solicitor draw up the required documents at the moment. You are to have this house and the shack in your own name, Henry, as well as the lands that surround it." He shrugged as Henry's mouth fell open, astonished by his brother's generosity. "I have plenty to attend to myself, Henry. This is as much a gift to me as it is to you."

"Thank you, Francis," Henry breathed, staggered by what his brother had given him. "You are most generous."

Francis shrugged and sat back in his chair. "I trust you, Henry. I trust that what you are spending your time on is worthwhile. I trust that the studies you are making of the stars are going to further mankind's knowledge. But more than that, I respect the fact that you have the freedom to do as you please, without my own intentions being thrown at you every step of the way. Take a wife, or don't, it is not my affair." Francis shot his brother a quick smirk, his eyes dancing. "Although where you will meet such a lady, I cannot think, if you are to spend all of your time between this place and the woods."

Henry tried to laugh in knowing agreement, but found he could not. What his brother had said was resonating with him in a way that he had not expected. Miss Davenport had asked him why he should be chasing his freedom with one hand but, with the other, telling her that she ought to do as her father wanted. Was that fair? Was that right? And why had stating such a thing brought him so much pain?

"Besides which, I must confess that I have my own heart to consider," Francis finished, getting out of his chair and walking to the door. "Unfortunately, I have realized that in focusing all of my efforts on you, I have been ignoring my own heart."

Dragged from his own thoughts, Henry turned astonished eyes onto his elder brother, who was not looking at him but rather out of the window to Henry's left. His expression was one of confusion, his face sporting a rueful smile.

"You care about someone, Francis?" Henry asked, pushing himself out of his chair.

Francis shrugged, his gaze returning to Henry. "I cannot say, old man. It is something I have refused to allow myself to consider thus far, given that I have been entirely fixed on your situation." He sighed, passing a hand over his eyes in evident frustration. "But no longer. I will have to face up to matters of the heart eventually, will I not?"

Not quite sure what to say, Henry simply nodded, watching his brother with astonishment. He had never expected Francis to be so open, so willing to express his own thoughts and feelings, on top of his apology for treating Henry the way he had done.

"I had best return," Francis said, quietly. "Will you join me for dinner tomorrow, Henry?" Catching Henry's sharp glance, Francis chuckled, a gleam in his eye. "No, there will not be anyone else present, I assure you. What do you say?"

Henry nodded, an enthusiastic energy refilling in him. "Thank you, Francis. That would be most enjoyable."

"Good," Francis replied stoutly, clearly relieved to have everything out in the open. "Until tomorrow then, Henry. Good day."

"Good day." Henry waited until the door closed firmly behind Francis before sitting back down heavily in his chair.

He had expected to feel relieved, to feel free and unhindered, but instead, there came a heavy burden lying on his soul. It was a heaviness he could not explain. His forehead lined with frustration as he let out a small exasperation, resting his head back on the chair as he squeezed his eyes shut.

Miss Davenport.

Miss Laurie Davenport would not leave his mind. Again, the memory of what he had said to her came crashing back into his thoughts. He had told her to accept Lord Umbridge, to go on with her life as a young lady ought, whilst he had no intention of allowing anyone, Francis or otherwise, to dictate what he ought to do. Why had he spoken to her so callously? Why had he allowed his head to speak instead of listening to his heart?

Because you are afraid of what you will find there.

Henry groaned aloud again, his heart squeezing with pain. He recalled how he had reached out and touched Miss Davenport's red curls, unable to understand what he was doing or why. The shivers that had spread up his arm had gone to his whole body, and still, he had not moved away from her. Even now, he was caught by the memory of how her green eyes had looked into his. Her beauty had been so close to him that he had been unable to prevent himself from moving yet closer.

His fingers had brushed against her soft skin, sending a shock of warmth straight through him. For goodness sake, he had been about to kiss her! In that moment, he had forced himself to step back from her, realizing with horror what it was he was about to do.

If he had done such a thing as that, then he would have been tying a knot around them both, a knot that would only be strengthened by the inevitable marriage that would come soon after it.

She herself had once said that not every young woman wanted to be married. The flurry of confusing thoughts had been enough to propel him away from her. He had never been one to act on emotion rather than logic, and finding his mind foggy as he shifted the curls away from her face was unfamiliar, and frankly terrifying, territory to him.

Wincing, Henry remembered just how confused, how pained, Miss Davenport had appeared, how tears had sprung back into her eyes as she struggled to regain her composure.

"Why?" he questioned aloud, getting up from his chair and beginning to pace up and down his study. "Why do you not allow yourself to *feel*?"

Francis' words floated back towards him. '*I have refused to allow myself to even consider it.*' That was the truth of the matter. He had not allowed himself to even think about what he was thinking and feeling for Miss Davenport, for fear of what it might mean. He had become so used to his own, solitary existence, and the long-held idea of who he believed himself to be: a resolutely content, academic loner. Then out of nowhere, this Miss Davenport appeared and refused to leave.

He had once longed for the day when he would be at 'Tumbledown House' alone, where he would not have Miss Davenport's presence. Only to recall how disappointed he had been to visit there and discover that she was not within. Was that what he wanted? A life without her? A life where he lived by himself, thinking only of himself and his own desires? Or did he want to let himself explore all that there could be between himself and the beautiful, extraordinary Miss Davenport?

"She is not in any way a lady," he conversed with himself, recalling just how she had struggled to know what flowers they ought to have in the garden. "Nor does she have any of the ordinary skills or talents I would expect from a lady."

He paused, catching sight of his reflection in the mirror.

"But then again, I am not exactly the kind of gentleman society would expect either."

A smile caught his lips, bringing a gleam to his eyes that Henry had never seen before. It was a freedom that he had never before experienced, a lightening of his soul that brought with it a feeling of hope and expectation. Perhaps they were two rebellious souls who were perfectly matched to one another.

He could not allow Miss Davenport to marry Lord Umbridge, not when he knew that she would never be happy with such a man. He did not know whether or not she had any true feelings for him, but he had to hope that, from her earlier reactions, she felt something. When he had touched her hair, she had not moved away, nor had she stepped back when he had almost kissed her. Surely she could not be unmoved, then? Surely he had to have some hope that, deep in her heart, there was the beginning of some kind of fondness towards him?

He swallowed, hard, finding his own feelings – now unleashed – to be rather overwhelming. It was all so new and so unfamiliar that he was struggling to think clearly. Miss Davenport had endured callous words from him, words that he now truly regretted with every part of his being.

"But by now she is betrothed to Lord Umbridge," he now calculated aloud, the smile sliding from his face as he leaned on the window sill and looked out towards the woods. "And a betrothal cannot easily be broken."

Closing his eyes, Henry let out a long breath as a slow-growing tendril of fear began to wrap itself around his heart. He had been foolish enough to send Miss Davenport back to her father and back to Lord Umbridge without any kind of hope that he would aid her in finding a way out. Where was she now? Was she at home, lost in her pain and misery, tears running down her soft cheeks as his heartless, unfeeling words came back to her time and again?

His jaw clenched, his fingers tightening on the window sill as his resolve began to grow steadily.

"I will not lose you, Miss Davenport," he said aloud, as though she were standing before him, hearing every word. "Even if I have to disgrace myself, I will not let you marry Lord Umbridge. You have my word on that."

CHAPTER 12

"Laurie?"

It took Laurie a moment to lift her eyes to Miss Stanley's concerned face, her heart sinking lower as she saw the note in Miss Stanley's hand.

"Is Lord Umbridge to call again?" she asked, dully, her eyes fixed on the letter. "Tell him I have a headache."

Miss Stanley glanced down at the letter and shook her head, folding it up carefully and putting it in her pocket.

"The note is for me," she explained as she did so, coming closer to Laurie. "Do not concern yourself with it, my dear." Bending down, she brushed Laurie's curls from her forehead, her dark eyes alive with worry.

Laurie let out a long breath, feeling her chin quiver as she struggled to maintain her composure. It had been five days since her return from 'Tumbledown House,' five days since she had been sent back with Henry Catesby's bruising words weighing heavily on her mind. Five days since she had realized that he felt something for her, that he was attracted to her, but had chosen to step back and thrust those feelings away.

Her heart broke every time she thought of it and, even now, she felt the tears threaten. How foolish she had been! She had looked up into his face and thought that he meant to kiss her. Worse, she had realized that she *wanted* him to do so, that she would have responded to him at once had he done so. Her heart had burst with a fierce passion, her desire to be in his arms almost overwhelming her – and then he had stepped away, dismissing her from his house.

She could not go back there, not again. Her time in the shack was over. Her time with Mr. Catesby had come to a sudden, abrupt end and that tore her to pieces.

"Laurie, you must listen to me."

Her thoughts shattered as Miss Stanley touched her hand, looking intently into her eyes with such a firmness that Laurie had no other choice but to pay attention.

"I can see that you are in the depths of

despair, my dear," Miss Stanley said, kindly, "and for that, I cannot chide you."

Laurie could do nothing but look back at Miss Stanley, aware that her heart was filled with nothing but wretchedness.

"Lord Umbridge is your father's choice, but not your own," Miss Stanley continued, her lips pulled into an angry line. "You know that he is not right for you, just as I am aware of it. However, your father is still your guardian, and unless something happens, he is not likely to change his mind."

Laurie dabbed at her eyes with her handkerchief, finding Miss Stanley's words anything but comforting. "Why are you telling me all this, Miss Stanley?" she asked, brokenly. "You are doing nothing but adding to my pain."

Miss Stanley gave her a small, sad smile. "It is not my intention to do so, Laurie, but rather to encourage you to find a way to *make* something happen that will change your father's mind."

Staring at Miss Stanley blankly, Laurie could find nothing to say in response, no ideas coming to mind.

"You must be able to think of something," Miss Stanley persisted. "Is there not anyone else you can turn to, Laurie? Someone you perhaps met during all that time you have been in the woods?"

Laurie's shoulders slumped as she looked back at her companion, seeing Miss Stanley's lifted brow.

"You know that I was in the woods with a gentleman," she realized dully. "Well, you can have no hope or expectation there, Miss Stanley. The gentleman will be of no help whatsoever, I can assure you." She did not need to ask how Miss Stanley knew of such a thing, guessing that she had either followed Laurie herself or had sent one of the gardener boys after her. Regardless, it was entirely fruitless to consider Mr. Henry Catesby in this matter. He had made it quite clear he would not help her.

"Might you not go and make your case one more time?" Miss Stanley pressed, sounding a little desperate. "Is it not worth seeking his help again, just in case he has had time to consider, time to change his mind?"

Laurie shook her head, feeling tears trickle down her cheeks. "I do not think I can bear it, Miss Stanley. Not when my heart is…." She trailed off, not able to say more, only for Miss Stanley to take her hand.

"Tell the gentleman that you have come to care for him," she said, her words once more revealing just how much she knew about Laurie. "It may have more of an effect than you know."

"Or he may break my heart twice over,"

Laurie whispered, swallowing the ache in her throat. "It has only been since he turned away from me that I have realized just how much affection my heart has for him. I hate such a feeling, Miss Stanley, and yet it continues to linger."

Miss Stanley squeezed her hand. "Then go and tell him so, Laurie," she said firmly, rising to her feet and drawing Laurie up with her. "Gird yourself with strength and courage and walk back into those woods and tell this gentleman exactly what you have told me." She pressed her hand gently to Laurie's cheek, her expression gentle. "You will come to regret it if you do not, my dear. Trust me in this."

Laurie wanted to sink back into her chair. She wanted to tell Miss Stanley that she could not do as she asked, that she could not find the strength to return to the shack. But instead, she forced her spine straight and kept her mouth closed. Miss Stanley was right. She would come to regret this. One day, she might look back on her life and see the opportunity to escape from Lord Umbridge that she had refused to take.

Despite the trembling in her soul, despite the fear in her heart, she knew that she would do as Miss Stanley had suggested and pour open her heart to Mr. Catesby, whether he wanted to hear her or not. Perhaps, as Miss Stanley had said, he had taken some time to consider his words. Perhaps there *was* just a sliver of hope that she could cling on to, even with the threat of her heart being completely and utterly shattered should he refuse her again.

"You have always been strong and determined," Miss Stanley said softly, taking in Laurie's growing resoluteness. "Prove yourself to be so again, my dear. Tell him everything."

Laurie drew in a long breath, lifting her chin. "I will, Miss Stanley."

Miss Stanley's smile was bright. "Very good, Laurie. I will pray that you will have success."

❦

'TUMBLEDOWN HOUSE' did not look as tumbledown as it had done before. In fact, it looked rather pretty. The garden, whilst still empty of all plants and flowers, was at least neat and tidy, with a small wall around it. The windows shone, as beams of sunlight filtered down from the treetops, and the wind blew a little less chilly than before. It should have brought a smile to Laurie's face, but instead, she felt nothing but despair.

Walking to the door, Laurie felt herself tremble as she put one hand on the doorknob, turning it carefully, only for the door to open. She would not need her key after all. She would not need to sit inside and wait in the hope that Mr. Catesby would appear.

It seemed as though he was already within.

Trying to find the courage that Miss Stanley had told her she would need, Laurie drew in a long breath, set her shoulders and stepped inside, her eyes roving around the room.

"Mr. Catesby?" she called, in a voice that was not as firm as she had hoped. "Mr. Catesby, are you here?"

There was nothing but silence, aside from the cracking and popping of logs that were burning in the grate. A tea tray was set on the table in front of her, and as she walked towards it, Laurie was astonished to discover that there were two cups and saucers, two spoons and one gently steaming teapot. Apparently, Mr. Catesby had been expecting someone.

Caught by a horrible thought, Laurie whirled around to make her escape, suddenly terrified that Mr. Catesby was meeting someone else, someone who might see them together and jump to conclusions. The last thing she wanted was for Mr. Catesby to think she had tried to trap him into matrimony.

"Miss Davenport!"

She halted, her feet pinned to the floor when she heard his voice, closing her eyes tightly as she struggled to keep her expression composed.

"Mr. Catesby," she said evenly, turning around to face him. She was greeted with no sign of surprise, no expression of shock or dismay, but rather a welcoming smile. She could not understand it.

Gesturing toward the tray, she spoke as politely as she could. "I can see that you are expecting someone. I did not mean to intrude."

He tipped his head, regarding her. "Then why are you here?"

She scrambled for a response, relieved when she felt the key in her pocket. "I came to return the key," she said quickly, pulling it out of her pocket and holding it out to him. "Given that I have no need of it any longer, I thought it best to ensure it was returned."

Mr. Catesby said nothing, looking down at the key in her hand for a long moment. Growing frustrated, Laurie jabbed it towards him, her throat beginning to ache with pain at the thought of leaving him.

"Please," she said, brokenly. "Just take it so I can be on my way."

Turning her head away so that he would not see the tears in her eyes, Laurie was astonished when Mr. Catesby's hand touched hers, his fingers wrapping around both the key and her hand.

"No, Miss Davenport," he said gently. "I

cannot let you be on your way. Not when there are so many things I have to say."

Her breath caught in her chest as she turned back to face him, seeing his eyes emote with sorrow.

"I can only apologize for what I said to you when you were here with me last," he continued, not giving her a chance to speak. "My dear Miss Davenport, I was harsh and cruel and entirely unfeeling. I did not allow myself to feel what was going on within me, deciding to return to my usual way of things." Shaking his head, his eyes dropped to their joined hands for a moment. "But I have had a chance to reconsider that now."

She could hardly believe what she was hearing, her heart beating so loudly that she was quite sure he could hear it. This was not what she had expected from him, not what she had thought he would say.

"I have been desperate to see you again, but I could not simply appear at your father's house," he said, his other hand reaching for her free one. "Not when you are engaged to Lord Umbridge. We would not have been able to speak freely there, and so I had to think of a way to have you return here."

Swallowing hard, Laurie blinked furiously as she recalled the note Miss Stanley had received.

"You wrote to Miss Stanley," she realized, her

heart suddenly leaping for joy. "You asked her to convince me to return here."

Henry's smile was tender. "And I am so very glad that she succeeded," he said. "For now I am able to apologize to you, Miss Davenport." Gesturing to the chairs, he led her towards the tea tray by the fire. Laurie felt her heart quicken all the more, her nervous anticipation bubbling to the surface as she looked into his eyes. She could hardly believe what was happening. He had written to Miss Stanley, begging her to ensure that Laurie returned to the shack so that he might apologize for what he had said. Did that mean that he did not think she ought to marry Lord Umbridge any longer? Did that mean that, perhaps, he might admit to feeling *something* for her?

"Miss Davenport – "

"Laurie, please," she interrupted, feeling as though the time for propriety was well past them both.

He smiled at her then, his eyes aglow. "Laurie," he said, with such tenderness that Laurie felt herself almost melt into the chair, such was the depth of feeling he expressed. "Laurie, I do not want you to marry Lord Umbridge."

She nodded slowly, her eyes a little narrowed. "And why is that?"

"Because he does not care for you, nor you for

him," Henry returned, his color a little high. "Whereas I know a gentleman who does care for you, even though it has taken him a good deal of consideration to be able to admit as much, even to himself."

Her throat constricted as he reached for her hand, shifting a little further forward in his seat.

"I am that gentleman," he continued quietly, his eyes roving over her features as though desperate to see her response. "I confess, Laurie, that I have been foolish in almost every which way. I thought that I wanted a life of my own, a life untouched by anyone else, only to discover that the thought of living a life without your presence would be one I could barely consider. Such was the horror of it." His fingers brushed her cheek gently, his eyes warm. "I swore I would not marry, but now I find the idea is becoming more and more welcome with every minute that passes."

Pressing her lips together, Laurie felt her heart heal completely, swelling with a deep and abiding affection that could only really be love.

"Will you forgive me for my foolishness, Laurie?" he asked gently, leaning so close to her that his face was only inches from hers. "Will you allow me to confess the affection that is growing steadily in my heart for you? Will you accept it from me?"

"I – I will, Mr. Catesby," she whispered, her

eyes darting from his eyes to his mouth and back again, hardly able to get her breath. "And I confess to you that my own heart is full of a love for you that I have only just begun to discover."

His face lit up, his hand now gently cupping her chin. "Then might you consider marrying me, Laurie?"

She smiled at him. "I will do more than consider it, Mr. Henry Catesby. I will accept."

He did not wait but pressed his lips to hers, kissing her firmly. Laurie felt caught with passion, her breath gone from her body entirely, as she leaned into him, her heart brimming with happiness.

Only for the door to slam open and a familiar voice to fill the room.

CHAPTER 13

"Lauren, remove yourself from this gentleman at once!"

Henry lifted his head just as Laurie gasped aloud, aware that Viscount Munthorpe, Laurie's father, was standing framed in the doorway. His eyes were wide, his lips trembling with thinly veiled anger and his hands planted firmly on his hips.

"Ah, Lord Munthorpe," Henry said at once, getting to his feet and standing a little in front of Laurie. "I do apologize for the scene you have stumbled upon, but I can assure you, I have every good intention as regards your daughter."

He heard Laurie gasp again, glancing down to see her hand over her mouth, her eyes wide as she looked from him to her father and back again.

Apparently, she had not expected him to speak so calmly to the Viscount but, as far as Henry was concerned, this was all going remarkably well.

"Indeed, Lord Munthorpe, I can assure you that this was all planned," said another voice which came from the kitchen, making both Laurie and Viscount Munthorpe catch their breath. "You see, my brother is deeply in love with your daughter and was unable to find a way to tell her."

Henry grinned as Francis rounded the kitchen doorway, only to stop and lean lazily against the doorframe. His brother had been more than willing to help him in this matter, and Henry could not have been more grateful.

"I – I don't understand," Laurie whispered beside him, her face rather pale. "What is the meaning of this?"

"Yes, what *is* the meaning of this?" Viscount Munthorpe repeated, looking a little less angry and a trifle more confused. "You lured my daughter here, did you?"

Henry shook his head. "No, my lord. Your daughter and I happened to run into each other some weeks ago."

The Viscount snorted disdainfully. "I highly doubt that, Mr. Catesby. My daughter is always in the presence of either myself or her companion, with only a short walk taken alone now and again.

You have used trickery and seduction to lure her here in order to claim her for yourself when I am sure you are well aware she is already betrothed!"

Henry opened his mouth to reply, only for Laurie to step forward, brushing past him as she approached her father.

"Father, you know very well that I have done my best to hide from you whenever Lord Umbridge is about," she said with love, yet confidence. "You need not try to place blame on Mr. Catesby's shoulders in an attempt to secure my reputation."

She looked up at her father as Henry watched. Looking on, he was more proud of her than he could say. She had found that courage, that strength that she needed to stand up to her father in a way she had never done before. To tell him the truth about her feelings for Henry, to state to her father that she would not do as he asked and marry the man he had betrothed her to. This was the woman he loved, the one with fire and determination in her soul that only added to her ever-present beauty.

"I am not the kind of daughter you have wished me to be," Laurie continued, in a quiet voice, "but I cannot change myself in order to suit you. Nor can I marry the gentleman you have chosen for me, no matter how much you might wish it. Lord Umbridge does not care for me, nor

I for him. I do not wish to marry him, father. I wish for a life of happiness, not a life of expectation and duty."

Holding his breath, Henry kept his gaze fixed on Viscount Munthorpe, waiting to see what his reaction might be to Laurie's honesty.

"But it is done, Laurie," Viscount Munthorpe said, slowly, his thick brows knotting together. "You are betrothed."

Laurie shook her head firmly, as Henry felt his anxiety begin to rattle through him.

"I will not marry him, father. You cannot force me to do so."

"You will have nothing from me if you do not abide by my word, Laurie," Viscount Munthorpe replied, in a hard voice. "You know that I will not stand for this incessant refusal to do as you are asked."

"Then she will come to me, and I will give her all that she has asked for – and more," Henry said loudly, stepping closer to Laurie. "If you have not yet noticed, Viscount Munthorpe, I care for your daughter very much. I intend to marry her."

Viscount Munthorpe stared at him for a long moment, his mouth a little ajar.

"And I have accepted his proposal, father," Laurie said, slowly putting one hand on her father's arm. "Do not prevent this by insisting I marry Lord Umbridge, for I will not have it. Is an agreement with that man truly worth ruining the relationship we share, father? For I am your only daughter and you my only parent."

Viscount Munthorpe shook his head, the heel of his hand rubbing his forehead. "It is already agreed," he mumbled, although the fire had gone from his eyes. "Laurie, this is not what I expected of you. Your reputation...."

"Is quite gone," Francis interjected, cheerfully. "For they have been alone together here on more than one occasion and even now were involved in an intimate embrace, which you interrupted, Viscount Munthorpe." He grinned, still apparently enjoying himself. "I am here to ensure that you are aware that I give this marriage my full blessing, and also to inform you that my brother is to retain his own property on my land as well as be given this one in which we now stand, for him and his bride."

He smiled at Laurie, who looked over at Henry with sparkling eyes, her happiness evident. "And so, Viscount Munthorpe, it now stands to you as to whether or not you will allow this marriage to go ahead as everyone here intends, or whether you will insist she marry Lord Umbridge – in which case, she will end up marrying my brother regardless, although with a great deal more scandal."

Henry could barely breathe as Viscount

Munthorpe looked over at him, his jaw clenched. He could not tell what the man was thinking, but by the expression on his face, Henry guessed that he was not particularly pleased with being pushed into a corner by them all. Henry did not care. All he wanted was Laurie's happiness, and this was the only way he had thought of to ensure he got it.

"Very well," Viscount Munthorpe grumbled, eventually. "I shall do what I can to smooth things over with Lord Umbridge, Laurie."

His face split with a smile as Henry watched Laurie thank her father carefully, clearly wanting to throw her arms around him and hug him tightly but restraining herself with the awareness that her father was not particularly pleased with all that had gone on.

"Thank you, Viscount Munthorpe," Henry said with respectful sincerity, stepping forward and holding out his hand. "You have done me a great honor in blessing me with your daughter's hand in marriage. I will do all I can to ensure her happiness."

Viscount Munthorpe looked back at him steadily for a moment, measuring him before sighing and shaking Henry's hand rather weakly. Henry grinned at Laurie, who was looking up at him with shining eyes, wishing that they could be alone for just a few minutes.

"Viscount Munthorpe," came Francis' warm voice. "Come with me for a moment and let us give these two a few minutes alone. In fact, have you seen the outside of this place? I would be glad to show you some of the improvements my brother has made."

Chuckling to himself, Henry wrapped a surreptitious arm around Laurie's waist as Francis, still talking, managed to persuade the Viscount to step outside, leaving them quite alone – if only for a few minutes.

"Oh, Henry," Laurie breathed, turning towards him. "I cannot believe this to be true!"

He touched her cheek gently. "It is true, my love," he replied, softly. "We are to be wed and, should you wish it, we shall make this place our home."

Laughing, she threw her arms around his neck and held him tightly, her joyful tears dampening his cheek. Henry crushed her to him, his own eyes squeezing closed as he struggled to cope with the sheer joy that washed over him.

"I do not quite understand," Laurie continued, as he let her go. "How did my father know where to come?"

Henry beamed at her, his eyes dancing at her confusion. "Miss Stanley played her part very well, I must say," he said, chuckling as her eyes widened. "I asked her to speak to your father once you had left so that he might find us together. Of course, Francis was in the kitchen out of sight – and out of earshot I might add – just to ensure that your father was aware that he too had seen our...embrace, so that it could not be hidden away." His fingers brushed down her cheek, tickled by the red curls that had fallen around her ears. "I wanted to ensure that I would have your hand in marriage by the end of the day," he continued gently. "Francis has given us his blessing, and now your father has done the same – albeit begrudgingly."

Laurie swallowed hard, her smile dimming just a little. "I do hope he will come around in the end," she said softly. "I thought him quite disappointed in me."

Sympathetic to her concern, Henry smiled down at her, attempting to reassure her. "My dear, your father will be more than delighted when his grandchildren are living nearby so that he might dote upon them whenever he wishes."

At that, her eyes brightened, her cheeks flushing red.

"We are going to have a wonderful life together, my love," Henry continued, gently. "I feel as though I have only just begun to know you and that there is so much more for me to discover. I love that you are quite unorthodox, that you are unafraid to try new things or take on new challenges. I admire your tenacity, your courage, your determination. Without you, this place would not be what it is – and I would not be the changed man that you see before you now."

Her smile slowly returned, her hands creeping up around his neck. "You are truly changed, you say?"

"I am," Henry replied, wholeheartedly. "I once thought my life to be a life blessed with solitude, but now I see that I could never go on living without your presence by my side. You have brought such life to my staid, dull existence that I never wish to be parted from you again."

Sighing happily, Laurie threaded her fingers into his hair, her eyes glowing with warmth and affection for him. Henry felt his heart begin to burst with happiness, knowing that one day soon, they would stand in this room as husband and wife.

"And this shall be our escape whenever we wish it," she whispered, her light breath brushing against his cheek. "We can come here to hide from the world."

His mind flared with all the possibilities that lay in his future, and he could not help but tighten his arms around her waist, drawing her even closer than before.

"My world is nothing without you, my love," he breathed, beginning to lower his head. "I cannot be without you. My heart is filled with a love for you that will only get stronger with every day that passes.

"I love you too, Henry," came her sweet reply, her mouth only inches from his. "Swear to me that we will be married by the month's end. I do not think I can wait any longer!"

He chuckled, pressing a light kiss to her lips and hearing her swift intake of breath. "By the month's end," he replied, tenderly. "I promise."

BOOK 6: DILEMMA OF THE EARL'S HEART

BOOK 6

HOUSE OF CATESBY

Dilemma of the Earl's Heart

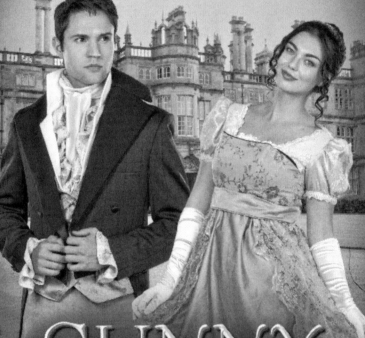

SUNNY BROOKS

FOREWORD

Strength can come in many forms: whether
pursuing the life you've always dreamt of, or
fighting against the life you've been told you are
meant to lead, be true to your own heart,
persevere, and the right path will find a way to
come to you.

- Sunny Brooks

CHAPTER 1

"My dear Francis, what *can* you possibly be thinking of?"

Francis, the new Earl Catesby, sighed heavily as his mother strode into the room. She had removed herself to the Dowager House which was, to his ongoing frustrations, a short distance away from the manor house. It meant that whilst she had her own abode and her own staff, she was still well able to attend the manor house whenever she wished and, somehow, was able to hear all that was going on.

"Good morning, mama," Francis murmured, getting to his feet with an effort. "Should you like a tea tray this morning? Or will you be staying for only a short visit?"

The look on his mother's face told Francis that he had overstepped just a little. Lady Margaret Catesby, the Dowager Countess, was an imposing figure. She had every appearance of elegance, with her carefully set hair only just showing hints of grey. Her refusal to wear a cap often reminded him just how strong a character she was. Her determination to live just as she pleased without the slightest care for what society thought often dug at him. With her sharp grey eyes that could be both stern yet gentle in equal measure, Francis felt himself quail under her steady gaze.

"Francis," his mother said, gently, seating herself opposite him. "I am here because I am concerned for you, that is all."

"You need not be concerned, mama," Francis replied, patiently. "All is well. The estate is doing well. I have begun to study crop rotation for the fields, the tenants are content and hardworking, and I find myself constantly busied by the responsibilities of the title."

"May I remind you, Francis, that your brother continually asked for you to remove yourself from his house, begged you to stop concerning yourself with his affairs, and yet you persisted," came the steady reply.

Francis sighed, shaking his head. "Mama, Henry's happiness was an entirely different matter. He was barely seen, was lost in his work, and seemed to have very little purpose. The sole purpose for my intervention was to ensure that he was not lost in despondency or the like."

One eyebrow slowly lifted, and Francis found himself growing hot with embarrassment. "I am not despondent, mama."

His mother nodded slowly, never once taking her eyes from his. "I can see that, Francis. But when I hear that you intend to find a new housekeeper for apparently no good reason, I find myself concerned! Whatever has come over you?"

Francis sighed inwardly, knowing that he could never explain the true reason to his mother. "Mama, these affairs are my own."

"I am aware of that," his mother said, sharply, "but you are considering yourself only, I think. Has the lady done something to upset you?"

"No, of course not."

"Then what can be your reasons for considering replacing her?"

"Miss Harrington is more than suitable," Francis heard himself admit, despite the fact that he had not intended to say such a thing. "It is simply that I feel that the house could benefit from someone with a little more experience."

This apparently, was the wrong thing to say entirely, for his mother rose to her feet in a flurry of skirts, leaning over his desk ominously.

"Are you suggesting, Francis, that Mrs. Harrington does not run your house well?"

This was not a question that could easily be answered. Francis did not want to lie and to state that yes, his house was in some sort of disarray due to the lady's lack of experience, nor did he want to tell his mother the real reason for his desire to dismiss her from her duties within his house.

"I know that this estate has been run wonderfully, both inside and out," his mother continued, when he said nothing. "I can tell that Mrs. Harrington has been doing an excellent job, Francis. After all, I would not have recommended her to you if I did not think that she would be able to do so with all skill! Why then are you attempting to turn your back on her?"

"I will give her an excellent reference," Francis mumbled trying to find some sort of excuse. "She will not be without work for long."

The dowager glared at him, her lips in a tight line. "You are being much too difficult, Francis. I know that you are not telling me the truth as to why you wish to find a new housekeeper. Therefore, I must question whether or not you are truly being fair to the lady."

Francis spread out his hands. "Mama, Mrs. Harrington is much too young to be a housekeeper." When it had come time to hire a new complement of staff for his estate, so that his mama could take the staff she knew and loved back with her to her new home, he had struggled to know how and what to do. For his mother to suggest a lady named Mrs. Harrington as housekeeper had been, at the time, a wonderful relief. He had heard what his mother had to say about the lady, had read her references, and had sent her an offer of employment before he had even clapped eyes on her. The moment she had appeared at his house, Francis knew he had made a dreadful mistake.

"Does her age or supposed lack of experience have any bearing on the work she is doing now?" his mother asked, clearly unwilling to drop the matter. "Do you find her lazy? Incompetent? Foolish?"

"No!" Francis exclaimed, slamming one hand on the desk as a burst of anger caught him. "No, mama, she is none of these things and yet —"

"And yet you wish to remove from her the safety and security of a position in your home," the dowager replied, with a sad smile. "Do you even consider what such a thing will do to her, Francis? The people who work here, they rely on you in ways you cannot even imagine. They have no home of their own, no money save for the income they earn here. To be let go from a position simply because it is a whim of yours and not because of anything they have failed to do will stain their reputation for a long time."

Biting back another sigh, Francis waited until the anger he felt began to wane. His mother was speaking the truth, and he could not answer to it. There was no particular reason as to why he intended to let the lady go, save for the one thing he was finding more and more difficult with each passing day.

He could not get his housekeeper from his mind.

The unfairness of what he was doing struck him, hard. He *was* considering himself only and never once thinking of what such a decision would do to Mrs. Harrington. He was thinking only of his comfort, his happiness, and his contentment. He did not want to keep thinking of Mrs. Harrington, did not want to even consider her for another moment and yet his heart and mind would not let her go. Therefore, he had come up with the idea of ending her employment here at Catesby House, simply so that he would not have to struggle any longer.

That was entirely wrong of him. Mrs. Harrington had not done anything wrong. She had not failed in her duties, nor been lazy or uncooperative. In fact, his house was running quite well. He had no real complaints. Everything he had told his mother was simply an excuse.

"Francis?"

His mother's voice was gentler now, as though she knew very well what was going on in his mind.

"Yes, mama?" he replied, heavily.

She smiled at him gently, putting her hand on his for a moment. "I do not mean to interfere or upset you, Francis, but I do so want to ensure that you are being a fair and respectful master. You may be the new Earl, but that does not mean that you can simply do as you please without considering the consequences." Her expression grew a little concerned. "I know very well that you *are* that kind of gentleman, which is why I am so surprised to hear such things."

Aware that his mother was only seeking his best, Francis managed a small smile in her direction. "You are quite correct, mama. I was being foolish."

She stepped back and smoothed her skirts, her intentions having clearly been fulfilled. "Indeed you were, Francis. But not any longer, I think."

"No," he grated, hating himself for his thoughts towards Mrs. Harrington and his inability to stop such inappropriate considerations other than to think of removing her completely from his house.

"You will not continue on this path, then?" the dowager asked, pulling on her gloves. "You intend to keep your housekeeper?"

Francis tried to smile. "If it will prevent you from appearing at my door in such a whirlwind, then, yes, mama, I will retain her."

This did not appear to upset the dowager in any way. In fact, she appeared more than satisfied. Nodding to him, she walked to the door, bid him goodbye, and walked out, closing the door softly behind her.

Francis put his forehead on the desk and groaned loudly. Had his mother not heard of his intentions, then he might now be speaking to Mrs. Harrington and informing her that he could no longer give her a position here. Instead, he had agreed to retain her and had, even more than that, allowed his heart to feel the pain and sorrow she would experience should he do precisely that.

His mind was full of her once again, even though it ought not to be. An Earl did not have affection for his housekeeper! A titled gentleman did not think of none other than one of his staff! It was simply not the done thing. Such was his embarrassment that he kept all such feelings to himself, refusing to mention a single word to his mother despite the fact that, had he told her the truth, she might have then encouraged him to remove Mrs. Harrington from his house.

"Or she may have encouraged me in it," Francis muttered darkly to himself, knowing that his mother was a little less bound by the propriety of late. Lifting his head, he rose from his chair and, despite the early hour, poured himself a decent measure of brandy. Today had started off rather badly, and he was not convinced that the remainder of it would go any better.

CHAPTER 2

"Mrs. Harrington?"

Rebecca turned as the dowager walked into the kitchen, immediately curtsying as the rest of the staff followed suit.

"Yes, my lady?" she asked, in a quiet voice.

"Might I have a word with you, Mrs. Harrington?" the dowager said at once, with a kind smile to all of the other staff who were now staring at her as though they could not believe that a Dowager Countess would be below stairs. "I think your parlor will suffice."

Swallowing a lump in her throat, Rebecca nodded and walked quickly towards her own rooms. "But of course, my lady. This way, if you please."

She was aware of the rest of the staff

watching intently, the butler included, as the dowager stepped inside. Glancing back at them, she saw the butler give her a small, encouraging smile and, feeling a small flicker of relief, stepped inside and closed the door.

"Oh, my lady!" she breathed, as the dowager smiled softly at her from across the room. "You need not have come downstairs. I would have gladly come to you, as I have done before."

The dowager waved a hand, seating herself carefully on one of the thin wooden chairs that were, at least, cushioned. "You are tired enough already, and I would not ask you to do such a thing again. I think once a week is more than enough – although you need not call upon me this week if you do not wish it since I am here now."

Rebecca sank into her chair, lacing her fingers in her lap. "Well?"

"Well," the dowager replied, with a warm smile. "I have spoken to Francis – I mean, Lord Catesby – and he will not be ending your employment here. I have had his word on that."

Tears immediately came into Rebecca's eyes. "Truly, Lady Catesby? That is wonderful news," she breathed, blinking rapidly. "I can never thank you enough."

The dowager shook her head, her expression a little grim. "I have not yet ascertained as to the reason for my son's reluctance in keeping you on but have no doubt, I will find it."

Nerves swam through Rebecca's stomach. "You do not think that he suspects that – "

The dowager laughed. "Francis? No, indeed. He has nothing but estate matters to consider. You need not worry, my dear."

Letting out a long breath, Rebecca tried to return her breathing to normal, having been somewhat anxious to hear whether or not Lord Catesby intended to retain her or would let her go, as she had been gently informed by the butler only last week.

"You have no real idea as to why he would wish me to depart from this place?" she asked, the question having dogged her mind ever since she had first heard it from the butler. "I have questioned myself over and over. I have looked at my work and strived to discover where I might be failing, but I cannot see where it is I am going wrong. Lord Catesby, certainly, has never said a word and so I am quite at a loss as to what it might be."

The dowager shook her head, her expression now somewhat thoughtful. "No, my dear, I cannot tell you for I do not know. What I will say is that it has nothing to do with your work or your expertise, for Francis, from his own lips, confessed that he was more than content with you. I cannot tell what it might be." She shook her head again. "But it is not all that long until you can return to your position in society now, is it? How long until you can gain your fortune?"

Swallowing hard, Rebecca tried to smile, but the thought of her late father brought tears to her eyes. "My father's will states that I must be the grand old age of five and twenty before I can possess the fortune in its entirety. If I wed before then, my fortune goes to my husband, as my dowry."

The dowager nodded slowly, her eyes glittering with faint anger. "Your cousin is a wicked man indeed, my dear. I am just glad I was able to provide you with such assistance when you wrote to me and asked for it. Although I still do not understand why you did not wish to reside with me instead of taking on the role of housekeeper – although I confess that you do it very well. I must admit that I find it rather difficult to refer to you as 'Mrs. Harrington' when I know you as Miss Patterson."

Rebecca smiled softly. "I confess, it took me some time also to acknowledge and respond to my change of name! I am glad, however, that you feel I am doing well in my role here."

"Your cousin does not know of your presence here, it would seem," the dowager murmured. "My son has not received any correspondence from him, from what I know. I cannot imagine that he would pursue you all the way here, my dear girl."

A slight shudder shook Rebecca's frame. "With all due respect, my lady, you do not know my cousin. He would try anything in order to get what he wishes. When he did not receive my father's title as he had hoped, given the reappearance of my brother from overseas, he made it more than plain that he would do all he had to in order to gain some kind of wealth. I knew that he would use me against my brother, or my brother against me, in order to achieve his aims. That was why I had to become anonymous."

"And what can be more anonymous than a housekeeper working for a lord of the realm?" the dowager murmured, gently. "I am truly glad that you came to me for aid, my dear. Your mother was a very good friend of mine, and I am honored to be able to assist you."

"And I can only thank you for your generosity," Rebecca replied, quietly. "You have done more for me that I have ever hoped for. I need only wait a few more months until I am of age and can claim my fortune. Then it belongs to me regardless of whether I marry or not."

The dowager frowned. "And do you believe

that your cousin will refrain from chasing you at that time?"

It was a question that had dogged Rebecca's mind for some time. "I must hope so," she said, slowly. "For hope is all I have."

Sighing to herself, the dowager looked back at her steadily for a moment. "I must hope so also, my dear. If it comes to it, however, I know that my son will do what he can to help you. I can well understand your reasons for keeping such things from him at this time, for the less who know the truth of your identity, the better, but do not push Francis from your mind entirely. He may still be able to assist you, in time."

Rebecca, who wanted to do nothing more than get on with her work and have as little notice from the master as possible, tried to smile. "Thank you, dowager. I will, of course, remember what you have said, and I must thank you again for all you have done for me thus far. Had you not been able to offer me such help then my life might be very different from how it is at this present moment."

The dowager nodded, smiled and rose to her feet. "Do be careful, Rebecca," she said, softly. "I know that you have said before that your cousin is a dangerous man. Always be on your guard. Of course, I will keep watch as best I can."

The knot of fear that Rebecca had constantly

been forcing away now returned to her stomach. "I will, Lady Catesby. I thank you."

The dowager held Rebecca's hand for a moment, her expression a little strained. "Very good. Do come and see me next week, if you can."

"Of course," Rebecca replied, knowing that her weekly visits to the dowager always lifted her spirits. "I look forward to it, Lady Catesby."

With a swift goodbye, the dowager was gone, leaving Rebecca alone with her thoughts. Despite the fact she had duties to attend to, Rebecca sat back down in her chair for a moment, her head heavy with thoughts. She did not know why Lord Catesby had thought to remove her as housekeeper and, even though the dowager had assured her that it would not happen and that she was quite safe, the matter still pierced her heart.

She sometimes felt a little guilty over her deception in the face of Lord Catesby's apparent willingness to take her on even though she did not have a good deal of experience. Her references had been quite made up, although the dowager had taken care of those for her. But to be given that freedom had been an opportunity she could not pass up. She had been offered the chance to escape from the fears and worries of living with her brother whilst their unfortunate cousin, the

Honorable Stephen Jefferson, had an extended stay with them.

She could still recall how Stephen had warned her, in no uncertain terms, that she would wed him or it would be all the worse for her brother, Mark, the newly titled Viscount Rapson. That had been the day she had known she needed to leave. Having told her brother some of the story, she had begged him not to look for her until she had come of age, telling him to rid his house of their cousin. How much he had hated letting her go, but he had seen her reasons for it. Having been as good as his word, he had not once tried to contact her, and she had received not so much as a note in the months she had been here.

Sighing heavily, she rose from her chair and made her way back towards the kitchens. There were duties to take care of and, sooner or later, she would have to speak to Lord Catesby about the menus for the week as well as another few matters. For one, they needed to hire some new maids since two had recently accepted a post with Lord Catesby's younger brother, Henry, which now left the Catesby House short.

She hated how flustered she became whenever she spoke to him, although he had never commented on it, of course. Whether it was because he was the master of the house and her now the housekeeper, or because he unsettled her with those sharp blue eyes of his, she could not say. Her awareness of him was always there deep within her, her skin prickling whenever he was nearby. It was ridiculous to have such reactions as these to her employer, and she always fought to keep herself composed whenever she was in the same room as he.

Wondering if that was the reason for his consideration of removing her from his house, Rebecca sighed to herself as she chivvied the maids up the stairs. Perhaps it would be best simply to ask Lord Catesby outright what it was she was doing that caused him so much discontent. It would take a good deal of courage but, mayhap, that would bring an end to her wondering and an end to his dislike of her. She could only try.

CHAPTER 3

"Lord Catesby?"

Francis turned slowly, seeing Mrs. Harrington in the doorway. "Ah, Mrs. Harrington," he said, in a voice that fractured for no particular reason. "Do come in. I thought to ask you about the dinner I am to host on Friday."

She nodded and came a little further inside, standing a little uncertainly in front of the fire.

"Please," he continued, hating that his heart was quickening all the more. "Do sit down, Mrs. Harrington. You need not stand when this will be a prolonged conversation."

To his surprise, she paled at once, seating herself quickly. Her hands were tightly clasped together, her papers set neatly on the table beside her.

"You need not fear me, Mrs. Harrington," he said, slowly, seating himself opposite and ensuring there was a good distance between them.

She nodded, a wane smile on her face. "Of course, my lord. I just hope that I have not displeased you in some way."

The tremor in her voice gave him pause. Looking at her steadily, he realized that mayhap she had found out that he had been considering removing her from her post. His heart dropped to his toes, feeling a weight of guilt settle on his shoulders. Of course, she would have heard of such a thing! It was not as though this house was without rumor and gossip, despite his best attempts to quash such a thing amongst his staff.

"No, indeed, you do an excellent job as housekeeper, Mrs. Harrington," he said, firmly. "I am sorry if you have heard anything other than that." A slight flush made its way up his neck, and into his cheeks and he contained his embarrassment with an effort. "I know the way staff can talk, Mrs. Harrington but I can assure you that your position here is quite safe."

She nodded, her cheeks now a little less pale. "I thank you, my lord."

"Now," he continued, briskly, wanting to move onto more polite conversation. "Might we discuss the menu?"

"Of course, my lord," Mrs. Harrington

murmured, her cheeks now a dusky pink. She began to talk through what the cook had suggested, which included a good number of his favorite dishes. Francis felt himself focusing less on what she said and more on how her beauty caught his attention. She was, as usual, wearing her dark gown which was perfectly pristine. Her long dark hair was tied up in a neat bun with nigh a hair out of place. She ought to be entirely nondescript, entirely unremarkable and for whatever reason, he could not stop himself from looking at her.

Her full lips brought the urge to kiss her senseless, her beautiful blue eyes filled him with longing and a slow-growing affection for the lady. It was as though he wanted to know her better, wanted to have her sit with him and discuss matters of all natures, simply so that he might know her thoughts, know her feelings, know her heart. It was ridiculous indeed, of course, and he knew he ought not to even entertain such feelings, but he was entirely unable to prevent himself from doing so. His heart was calling out for her more and more, which had been the only reason he had thought to dismiss her from his employ.

"Does that satisfy you, my lord?"

With a start, he realized he had not been paying attention to what she had said. Flushing, he reached for the paper in her hand. "May I see it again?"

She handed it to him with an uncertain look in her eyes, her whole body jerking as their fingers brushed. Feeling suddenly alive from the briefest of touches, Francis cleared his throat again and forced his eyes down on to the paper, struggling to focus on her handwriting for a moment.

He caught his breath.

"Goodness, Mrs. Harrington, I did not realize you had such a wonderful script," he commented, taking in the ornate handwriting. "Beautiful."

She blushed, and he smiled at her, glad to see that she no longer appeared quite so uncertain.

"Thank you, my lord," she murmured, dropping her gaze. "You are most kind."

His smile lingered as he let his eyes rest on her for a moment longer before returning to the menu. "Yes, this all looks quite wonderful," he said, finally. "Thank you, Mrs. Harrington."

Reaching for the menu, she took it from him and rose to her feet. "Thank you, Lord Catesby. Is there anything else I can assist you with whilst I am here?"

Hesitating for a moment, Francis nodded. "Might you seat yourself once more, Mrs. Harrington?"

She did as he asked almost at once, her eyes now a little rounded with concern.

"I simply wanted to take the time to apologize to you for the rumors that have circulated about this house. The rumors came from me, I will confess, but it was only a moment of madness."

Blushing furiously, Mrs. Harrington looked away. "You need not explain yourself to me, my lord."

"But I wish to," he replied, fervently. "I should never have thought such a thing. Your work here is impeccable. I have no complaints as regards to that. I wish you to know that, Mrs. Harrington."

Finally, her eyes lifted to his and such was the warmth in her gaze that Francis felt quite lost for words. His breath caught, his body burning with a sudden awareness of just how drawn he was to her. Struggling to regain his composure, he cleared his throat harshly, rising to his feet and seeing her follow suit.

"Thank you, Mrs. Harrington. I must return to my correspondence."

She nodded, inclined her head and retreated towards the door.

"Oh, I quite forgot," Francis called after her, seeing her turn towards him. "For the dinner party on Friday, we are to host an old acquaintance of mine, who wrote to me only yesterday to signal his arrival to the area."

"Of course, my lord." Mrs. Harrington turned back towards the door, only to pause and look back at him. "Might I ask who it is, Lord Catesby? It is simply so that the place settings are in order."

"Lord Rapson," he replied, remembering the gentleman from the time he had spent in London. "Viscount Rapson, you understand. He has only recently gained the title and wishes to seek my advice on some matters as regards his estate." He did not know why he was telling her this but found that, as he looked back at her, she was staring at him with a mixture of horror and fear in her expression. He started towards her, suddenly worried that she was about to collapse, only for her to start, straighten herself and incline her head once more.

"Thank you, my lord," she whispered, her chin trembling slightly as she held onto the door handle with one hand, as though using it to steady herself. "I will ensure that the place is set for him."

Frowning, Francis took a step towards her. "Are you quite all right, Mrs. Harrington? Is something the matter?"

Her smile was tight. "I am quite all right, my lord, I thank you. I just felt a little weak for a moment, but I am quite sure a drink of water will set me to rights. Do excuse me."

She bobbed a quick curtsy and stepped from the room, pulling the door closed behind her. Francis looked at the closed door for some time, his brows furrowing all the more as he considered Mrs. Harrington's strange reaction. Was she unwell? Or was it the mention of Lord Rapson's name that had her behaving so strangely? A sudden, protective urge rose up within him. He felt the strange need to ensure that Mrs. Harrington was kept quite safe from Lord Rapson, even though he knew that the gentleman was well respected and kind.

He had known him before he had gained his title but had never been blessed to meet the rest of the gentleman's family, nor even his father who must have passed away given that he was now Viscount Rapson. His year of mourning must have come to a close were he to be travelling to London and, despite Mrs. Harrington's rather strange reaction to this news, he was quite looking forward to seeing his acquaintance again.

"Why do you consider what it is Mrs. Harrington thinks of it all, anyway?" he muttered to himself, shoving one hand through his brown hair and disordering it completely. "You must stop thinking of her!"

His stern talking to did nothing whatsoever to relieve his considerations of the lady. Instead, for the rest of the day, Francis discovered that, no matter what he did, he could not remove the lady from his thoughts, growing all the more angry with himself at his continued inability to forget her.

CHAPTER 4

The rest of the week dragged slowly. Rebecca found no time to go to the dowager's home in order to tell her this new development that had taken her completely by surprise and, therefore, found herself growing more and more anxious with each day that passed. Her brother had known where she was coming to and had sworn not to say a word to another living soul. He had promised not to so much as write even the shortest of notes, but now here he was, apparently ready to call on Lord Catesby and take dinner with him.

Not only that, but since that information had been told to her, she had now discovered that Lord Catesby had offered her brother an extended stay in Catesby house and that her brother had accepted. She could not understand *why* Mark was to come to Lord Catesby's home now. Why had he suddenly decided to come to the one place where she was meant to be staying hidden. The speculation brought her a good deal of anxiety.

He was not coming to speak to her directly, of course, which was her first reason for concern. She was to remain in her role as housekeeper whilst he was here as Lord Catesby's guest. Why was he still making sure to keep her secret whilst still coming to reside at Lord Catesby's estate?

On top of all of this, she had been keenly aware of just how truly apologetic Lord Catesby had been when he had explained to her she would not be sent away. Even though she knew that it was certainly more than a simple rumor, even though she knew that there was a good deal of truth in the idea that he wanted to remove her from her position for whatever reason, she accepted his apology and the promise that such a thing would not happen. Yet, she was still entirely unsettled. She did not know what to think and struggled to focus entirely on what she was doing. The dinner on Friday consisted simply of the dowager, Mr. Henry Catesby and his wife – Henry being Lord Catesby's brother - and now, her own brother, Viscount Rapson.

Rubbing her eyes, Rebecca tried to focus on what she was doing. Even though she had been in

Lord Catesby's presence many times, she had still forgotten to speak to him about the matter of the maids. They needed to hire two more and whilst the butler was more than happy to secure those they would need, Rebecca still required Lord Catesby's approval. Why she had not yet been able to ask him was quite beyond her. Perhaps it was because she had so much on her mind as regarded her brother that she simply didn't recall.

Quietly entering the library - Lord Catesby's usual haunt come this time of the evening, she rapped quietly on the door but heard no response. Pushing the door open further, she stepped inside but saw no-one. Setting her candle down, she saw that the fire was burning brightly and let the heat wrap around her for a moment, chasing away the dark thoughts she had let spill all through her. The maids had not yet managed to tidy the library, however, since there appeared to be papers everywhere, with a few books stacked haphazardly here and there. She sighed to herself and began to tidy the room, knowing that it was not the maid's fault that such things had been forgotten, not when they were short of staff.

"I did not think such things were your remit, Mrs. Harrington."

An astonished cry fell from her mouth, and she turned on her heel, her heart hammering painfully.

"Oh, Lord Catesby," she breathed, trying to catch her breath. "I must apologize, my lord. I did not see you come in. I will remove myself at once."

He held up one hand, stopping her exit. "Continue with what you were doing, Mrs. Harrington. I will not prevent you."

She saw the easy smile on his face, took in the way his eyes almost glittered in the shadowy light and felt her stomach swirl with a sudden warmth. Her face flushed darkly as she turned her head away, astonished at her own reaction to him. He appeared a little less formal than before, looking at her in such a way that brought with it a shiver of awareness.

You are the housekeeper, she reminded herself, quickly stacking the books one on top of the other before picking them up from the bottom. *You cannot act as though you are a lady of society.*

"Careful, there," Lord Catesby said, his words a little slow, seeming to stretch out across the room. "Here, let me help you. I insist."

She realized then that he had been drinking, given the smell of alcohol on his breath and the way he attempted to help her but, instead, managed to knock into her and push the stack of books from her hands. Closing her eyes, she drew in a long breath and felt herself a little frustrated. For a moment, she had allowed herself to become affected by Lord Catesby's presence, seeing him as a little more relaxed than usual – and now it became apparent as to why that change had occurred. He was in his cups.

"Goodness," Lord Catesby muttered, looking at the books on the floor. "I am something of a fool. Here, Mrs. Harrington, allow me to help you."

"No, please," Rebecca replied hastily, bending to pick up the books so that he would not help. "I am quite able to – ouch!"

Unfortunately for her, Lord Catesby had leaned forward just as she had done and their foreheads had collided. It felt as though she had been hit across the head by a large rock. Stars sparkled in her vision as she rubbed furiously at the growing lump on her forehead, seeing Lord Catesby do the same, albeit with a lesser intensity.

"I am truly sorry," he said, his voice muffled through his shirt sleeve as he rubbed his forehead. "I thought that I was assisting you, Mrs. Harrington."

"I do not require your assistance, Lord Catesby," she replied, as firmly as she could. "Why do you not seat yourself and I will find you something to drink?" Seeing him nod, she let out a small sigh of relief and picked up the books again, despite the ache in her head.

Suddenly, she found herself desperate to be

away from him. At another time would she look into her heart and find out why she was feeling such things for the lord of the manor. A jumble of frustration, irritation, and a growing confusion over the sudden warmth she had felt when he'd smiled at her made her head ache all the more. Setting the books on the shelf, she turned to see Lord Catesby still standing, looking at her with a puzzled frown.

Her heart turned over.

"Might I assist you into a chair, Lord Catesby?" she asked, thinking she ought to, at the very least, pretend to be helpful. "Do you wish for another brandy? Or I could fetch you a tray of coffee if you would prefer it?"

Grunting, he let her help him sit down, his hand catching hers as he did so. When she rose to stand, he did not let it go but rather looked at her for a long time, considering things carefully.

"You are unhappy, I think," he said, patting her hand. "And I think that has a very good deal to do with me."

She shook her head, not quite sure what to make of the heated sensations running up and down her arm as he held her fingers tightly. "I am quite content, my lord."

"But not at peace, Mrs. Harrington," he stated, firmly, his eyes drifting closed for a moment as he tried to look up at her. "You have not found contentment, just as I have not. You are struggling with something." His eyes opened again and the intensity of them burned into her soul all over again. "Pray tell me, what is the matter, Mrs. Harrington? I am quite sure I will be able to help you should you wish to discuss the matter with me."

Rebecca made to dismiss the question outright, only for her to find a moment's pause. There was sincerity in his expression, despite his slightly drunken state and for a second, she found herself desperately longing to tell him everything that was on her heart. It was foolish to even consider it, of course, for she was nothing more than a housekeeper to him and she could not tell what he would do with such information should she tell him.

But despite her fears, the urge was there. It grew steadily as she looked down into his face and felt his fingers grasping hers tightly. He was no longer the calm and collected gentleman who said very little and often appeared to be ill at ease with her, but rather his expression was open, his small smile appearing genuine as he looked up at her waiting for her response.

"You are very kind, Lord Catesby," she said, slowly, "But I feel as though such matters are not for your consideration. You have more than enough to deal with, I am quite sure."

He shook his head firmly, although his eyes took a moment to refocus on her. "No, indeed, Mrs. Harrington, you are quite mistaken. I wish to know what troubles you. I saw it in your face the moment I mentioned Lord Rapson. Is there something wrong with that particular gentleman? Do you truly fear him? Is that it?"

A little unsure as to what to say, she hesitated for a moment, only for Lord Catesby to speak again.

"I cannot remove you from my mind, Mrs. Harrington," he said, hoarsely, his voice and expression now terribly earnest. "Release me from my torture. Tell me what it is that troubles you. I can assure you I will do all I can to aid you in this."

Her smile became sad, her heart slowly dropping down to the floor. "You are very gracious, Lord Catesby, but I am afraid that such matters do not require your input. Lord Rapson, I know nothing of. I believe what you are speaking of was when I was simply feeling a little overwhelmed by all that was to occur. I am so afraid that I shall not have the dinner as perfect as you hope it will be. The additional guest was a little…. surprising, I will admit."

She had not meant to speak too plainly but given just how open Lord Catesby appeared to be at this very moment, she had found the words tripping from her tongue regardless. Blushing furiously, she made to tug her hand from his but found that he held her fast.

"I did not inform you of Lord Rapson's arrival in due time, did I?" Lord Catesby murmured, sounding most apologetic. "Tell me, is cook utterly furious with me? Did she begin to throw flour all over the kitchen in anger? Did you have to dodge a swipe of her rolling pin?"

A little astonished at Lord Catesby's carefree and mirthful comments, Rebecca struggled to keep her face expressionless. "Cook is quite content, my lord, I assure you."

His eyes glinted with humor, his lips curving into a wide grin as he retained hold of her hand. "Are you quite sure, Mrs. Harrington? You did not need to have a glass of wine and a lie down after telling cook the news that there would be one additional guest?"

She could not help but laugh, despite the awkwardness of the situation. Cook was, in fact, known to have a dragon-like temper and could put fear into any man's soul should they anger her, but Rebecca knew that the lady would never once show such a failing to the lord of the house. And yet, the picture he had drawn her with his words made her laugh. It echoed around the room and had the surprising effect of allowing her to look at Lord Catesby in a very different light. It was almost with fondness that she took in his grinning face, his bright blue eyes and disheveled hair. This was a very different Lord Catesby from the gentleman she was used to.

"You are quite remarkable, Mrs. Harrington."

His words cut her laughter dead, seeing something burning in his eyes that both confused and unsettled her.

"I confess that I find you quite…..extraordinary," he continued, his voice now a little thick. "What am I to do with you, Mrs. Harrington?"

She could not breathe. Her chest was tight, her throat constricting as he slowly got to his feet to gaze down into her eyes. The air was crackling with tension, the heat from the fire washing over them both and seeming to set her body alight.

"You impossible, impossible woman," he whispered, tugging her even closer. "Why can I not forget you?"

His lips were brushing hers before she could react. Her body froze stiff, her arms down by her sides as he held her there. What was she doing? Why was *he* doing this? What did he mean that he was unable to forget her?

Slowly, her body began to relax, his lips a little more persistent as he kissed her again. The stiffness left her frame, warmth slowly unfurling in her belly as one of his hands slipped about her waist.

And then the reality of what she was doing crashed over her like an icy wave.

She was kissing Lord Catesby, the gentleman who was both her employer and, in a way, her protector, even though he did not know it. This was not a good situation. He could easily turn around and tell her that he had made a mistake and did not want her to remain here any longer under his roof.

She jerked away from him, one hand pressed to her lips as horror sank into her bones. Was he doing this purposefully, so that he had a reason to ask her to leave? It would not be the first time a gentleman had attempted to press his attentions onto his staff – and more the fool her for allowing herself to become so caught by his advances.

"What are you doing?" she whispered, backing away from him. "Lord Catesby, I –"

His face was flushed, his eyes boring into hers without a single hint of regret within them.

But why would he regret it, if this was his intention all along?

"Excuse me, please," she whispered, turning on her heel and practically running from the room, tears filling her eyes as she stumbled away, torn apart by her own foolishness and regret.

CHAPTER 5

Francis woke on Friday with a blinding headache. It did not dissipate even though he drank copious amounts of coffee and it was only when he was in his study, attempting to read some of the papers that were requiring his attention, that it began to fade.

The throbbing behind his eyes was still painful and, despite the fact that it was a little less agonizing than before, he rang the bell in order to request a cool compress. He was in no fit state to greet his brother and his wife, his mother and now Lord Rapson, for which he had no-one to blame but himself. In his struggle to prevent himself from considering Mrs. Harrington, he had turned in desperation to the one thing he knew would wipe his mind completely – brandy.

Clearly, he had drunk far too much of it. Last evening was almost a blur, although he was quite certain he had spoken to the lady in question at some point. The last thing he had recalled was staggering into the library, not quite sure where he was going or what he was doing. Had Mrs. Harrington been within? Was that when he had seen her?

"Ah, Mrs. Harrington," he mumbled, as she answered the bell pull. "No, it is not more coffee that I require. Might you, in fact, fetch me something cool to put across my brow?"

To his surprise, his housekeeper seemed incredibly ill at ease. She was jittery, moving from foot to foot as though something was terribly wrong. He did not know what to make of this and looked at her through slightly narrowed eyes. "Is something wrong?"

Mrs. Harrington stared at him for a moment, frozen in place with wide eyes. "N – no, my lord," she managed to say with an effort. "It is just that I thought....." Trailing off and with a look of pure relief on her face, she turned from him and made her way back through the door. "I will fetch you something at once."

The minutes ticked by slowly. Francis closed his eyes and tried *not* to think of the lady who had just left his presence, reminding himself that this was how he had managed to get himself into such a sorry state in the first place. How much time he had wasted either chastising himself for thinking of her or allowing his mind to return to her again!

She had such a quiet beauty about her that it almost drew him towards her, almost forcing him to have her near him. They had talked many times but always about nothing of importance – menus, maids, staffing, guests. There was nothing of significance, not really. Of course, for a lord of the realm, that should not make any particular difference. What gentleman *wanted* to talk to those beneath him? And yet, he could not remove the desire from himself. She caught his attention like no other lady before.

Frowning, Francis opened his eyes as a memory tried to make its way into his mind. A memory of Mrs. Harrington standing near him. It began to piece itself together with such slowness that he wanted to scream, feeling it burning in his mind with more fierceness than he had expected. For whatever reason, his heart began to quicken, his stomach knotting itself painfully as he tried to remember.

"Here you are, my lord."

Mrs. Harrington stepped back into the room with a small bowl and a wet cloth.

"I have tried my best to have it as cold as could be," she continued, her feet faltering just a little as she moved towards him. "Where shall I place it?"

A small smile tugged at his mouth, the memory gone altogether. "Here," he said, pointing at his forehead. "Would you mind terribly, Mrs. Harrington? I know I ask a lot of you, but my head is aching terribly, and I fear that if I move, it may fall from my shoulders altogether!"

Her lips quirked but soon returned to the thin, tight expression that she had worn ever since she had come into the room. "Of course, my lord," she murmured, wringing out the cloth carefully so that the remaining water stayed in the bowl. "If you would just lean back in your chair."

The way she moved closer to him had his breath catching. The fragmented memory of last evening began to return to him, and he stared at her, seeing the uncertainty in her eyes and finding that such a look brought him a sense of awareness, as though he should know something.

"Mrs. Harrington," he said, holding up one hand to stop her approach, ignoring the stab of pain right between his eyes. "Did I...?" He trailed off, not quite sure what to say and saw her step back just a little, her cheeks paling.

"I was rather drunk last evening," he continued slowly, seeing her glance away and lick her lips, evidence of her nervousness. "You were present, I think."

A jerky nod.

"Did I treat you terribly?"

All of a sudden, her face was aflame. "Indeed not, my lord. You cannot recall last night, it seems, so I hardly think that it matters."

That was not an answer at all, he realized, growing coldly aware that whilst he had either done or said something he ought not to have done, Mrs. Harrington was not about to tell him what it was. That was the thing with staff. They always were to ignore their employer's less than perfect behavior, even if they had been injured in some way.

Closing his eyes tightly, he let his breath shudder out of him, feeling suddenly lost and a little afraid. "Did I hurt you in some way, Mrs. Harrington?" he asked, hoarsely. "Please, say I did not bring you any kind of injury!" He could see her now, in his mind's eye, looking down at him. What had he been doing? Had he fallen? Had she come to his aid in some way?"

Mrs. Harrington's face was still a delicate shade of pink. "My lord, pray do not ask me any more questions. You did not injure me in any way, I can assure you."

A small wave of relief crashed over him, despite the frustration that he still was quite unaware of what he had done. "Very well, Mrs. Harrington," he muttered, shaking his head at himself. "If you will not tell me and I cannot recall, then it appears we are at an impasse. Whatever behavior I exhibited, however, I must beg for your forgiveness, for I can see that it affected you somewhat."

Mrs. Harrington did not deny this, her eyes darting from here to there before continuing on with her task of laying the cool cloth on his forehead.

The reprieve was immediate. Sighing heavily, he closed his eyes and let the coolness take some of the pain away. "Thank you, Mrs. Harrington," he murmured, lifting his hand and accidentally catching hers with his fingers. He did not jerk away from her, however, even though he knew he ought to. Instead, he lingered for a moment, feeling the softness of her hand and marveling at it, given that she was a housekeeper and not an elegant lady.

It was she who stepped back first. "Of course, my lord," she replied, in a hoarse voice. "Is there anything else I can get you? The staff is all hard at work preparing for this evening, and I am quite sure that everything will go to plan."

He did not open his eyes, feeling the warmth flood his soul at what had been the briefest of touches. "Thank you, Mrs. Harrington. No, there is nothing more. You may go."

Waiting to see if she would respond to him, he was filled with disappointment to hear the door close quietly behind her. It irritated him that he could not recall what he had done, upset him that he had somehow upset Mrs. Harrington, and still the desire to have her in his arms and in his life continued to grow steadfastly.

The ache in his head intensified with such thoughts and so, with a good deal of strength, Francis pushed the lady from his mind. He had to recover quickly so that he would be able to meet his guests. They would soon be here, and he could not exactly be found lying in the study with a cool cloth over his eyes, although silently, Francis vowed not to drink so much brandy again. It had done him no good – and done Mrs. Harrington no good either. Perhaps, with his friend Lord Rapson here, he would be able to forget about Mrs. Harrington entirely, and all would go on as normal, just as he had always intended.

CHAPTER 6

"Mark!"

Rebecca stumbled towards her brother, tears pouring down her cheeks unabated. It had been some months since she had last seen him, but the complete separation had been difficult to bear. She had seen his carriage arrive and had allowed him to see her from a distance, pointing towards the gardens so that he would know where to find her. At last, he was here.

"My dear sister," he said, grasping her hands before holding her close for a moment. "My dear, brave sister. How are you?"

She shook her head, trying to wipe at her eyes with the back of her hand but finding it almost impossible to do so such was the sheer number of them. "I am well, brother. Whatever are you doing here?"

The jut of his jaw had her stomach tensing.

"Our dear cousin has made it plain that he intends to pursue you no matter where you are," Mark replied, darkly. "He wants your fortune, Rebecca. I have offered him a sum of money to stay away from the both of us, but he refused it outright."

Rebecca closed her eyes tightly, refusing to cry over a cruel man's actions. "I see. That was good of you, Mark. You did not need to do so. I am quite safe here I am sure, and it is only a few months until I am of age. I shall have my fortune and will be able to live wherever I please."

To her chagrin, her brother's expression did not change. There was not even a hint of a smile on his face.

"He intends to pursue you regardless of whether or not you have your fortune in hand," he said, slowly. "Wed to him, you will be forced to give up your wealth. You know how the law sees husbands and wives."

Unfortunately, Rebecca did know. She had seen it all too often – a downtrodden, mistreated young wife who was seen as nothing more than her husband's property, to do with as he pleased. To be married to Stephen Jefferson would give him the liberty to treat her in any way he saw fit.

She did not have to imagine what that would involve.

"But why have you come here?" she asked, hoarsely, not understanding the reason for his presence. "I was quite safe here."

He shook his head. "Cousin Jefferson is doing all he can to try and force me to reveal where you are. The last thing he did was attempt to burn down my home."

Her hand flew to her mouth. "A fire?"

"Fortunately, it was put out very quickly," he said, calmly, one hand on her arm. "You need not concern yourself, my dear, the damage was not great. However, I thought it best to avoid the manor house for a time. I need to secrete myself away and, in addition, I needed to warn you about Jefferson's heightened determination. I confess I am quite at a loss as to what to do. I called him to a duel, but he simply laughed and refused to meet me. He does not care about his reputation, of course, for all he wants is you and your money."

"But I will not marry him," Rebecca whispered, her voice not strong enough to speak with any firmness. "I cannot. I will not."

"After seeing what he can do and what he intends to do, I would suggest that you are on your guard, my dear sister," her brother replied, darkly. "Together though, I am certain we can find a way through this. We can find a way to set Jefferson apart from us for good – but I could not think of a way on my own."

Closing her eyes, Rebecca dragged in air, trying to keep her thoughts in careful order. There was so much he had said, so much she would have to try and take in, and yet it was difficult to see past the lurching fear that now filled her.

"We can ask the dowager also," her brother continued, trying to reassure her. "She has been more than helpful already. And," he finished, looking a little awkward. "We ought to tell Lord Catesby also. He may be able to advise us."

"No."

The word shot from her mouth like a speeding bullet. Shaking her head fervently, she shut her mind off from considering what Lord Catesby would do should he discover her deceit.

"Why ever not?" her brother asked, with a frown. "He is a good man, Rebecca. Good and kind-hearted, with a steady character and true moral compass. You need not shirk from him."

She shook her head again. "No," she replied, with as much firmness as she could muster. "Here, I am safe. What if things become worse and all and sundry in this house know the truth of who I am? That will make things all the more difficult for both of us, even for the dowager. Besides, we cannot guess at Lord Catesby's reaction."

Given that she was quite sure he was still attempting to remove her from her position in his house, Rebecca did not want to imagine what he would think or say or do should he find out the truth, not when it was so apparent that he was dissatisfied with her already. Even now, she believed that he wished to get rid of her in whatever way he could, finding herself waiting for him to dismiss her.

Her brother shook his head, clearly disagreeing with her decision. "Very well, my dear sister. If you wish to remain as you are, then I cannot disagree with you. However, if the time comes to tell Lord Catesby the truth, then I will not step back from that."

"If, as you say, our cousin does not yet know of my whereabouts, it is not quite likely that he has followed you here."

At that, her brother shook his head fervently. "When last I saw him, he was blind drunk in the gatehouse by our home. I took the opportunity to leave soon after. The staff knows only that I intend to go to London and have no knowledge of my intentions to come here. I do not think that you need worry, my dear."

A slightly frustrated look crossed his face, as though he had been unsure as to what to do when it came to their cousin and, putting one hand on her shoulder, he dropped his head. "In truth,

Rebecca, I was afraid for my life. I had no
knowledge of how you fared, and the attempt on
my life made me afraid for you." Sighing, he lifted
his head and looked into her eyes. "I will need
your wisdom when it comes to dealing with our
cousin once and for all," he finished, hopelessly.
"Everything else I have tried has failed utterly."

For a fleeting moment, Rebecca recalled what
it had been like to have Lord Catesby kiss her. She
considered if there was anything in his kiss that
could possibly be the answer to their difficulties.
But then she remembered that not only had he
been drunk but that she believed it to be a reason
for him to dismiss her. Why he had not used it as
yet, she could not understand. Thinking to herself
she wondered if either he simply had not recalled
it or that he was holding it carefully in his mind
until a more suitable time – mayhap after his guest
had gone. Whatever the reason, she was still
uncertain around Lord Catesby, despising her own
reaction to him, her body growing warm,
whenever he drew near.

Her brother was looking down at her and,
with an effort, she drew herself back to the
present.

"We will think of something," she said,
carefully, looking up at him and trying to smile
despite the fear in her heart. "I am just glad that
you are safe." He leaned down to hug her again,

and she felt her heart lift just a little. How much she hated that her brother had been forced from his estate, simply to ensure that his life was not in danger from their cousin! She would marry Jefferson if that was what it took to keep her brother safe, but she knew full well that Mark would not allow her to do so. There was a strong bond between them and oft times she was grateful for the kindness and affection of her brother. It was not every lady who had such a sibling, and for that, she was truly grateful.

"I suppose I had best let you go," Rapson murmured, as she stepped back from his embrace. "It will be very strange seeing you as the housekeeper, I think." He took her hands and smiled at her. "Mrs. Harrington, is it?"

"Yes," she replied, with a small chuckle. "It is. Mrs. Harrington took a little time to become used to, but it comes very naturally now. Not that you will see much of me, I do not think."

Her brother frowned. "But I must see you again. How will we speak?"

She bit her lip, hesitating for a moment. "I can sometimes meet in the library. We are short of maids at this present moment, and often I go in there to ensure everything is as it ought to be." She tipped her head, thinking quickly. "Perhaps tomorrow evening, a little after supper?"

He nodded. "Yes, of course."

"It will give me some time to consider the matter of our cousin and attempt to come up with some kind of solution," she said, shaking her head a little. "Thank you, Mark."

Letting go of her hands, they turned together to walk back into the house – only to see a figure coming towards them. Rebecca stiffened at once, seeing it to be Lord Catesby. Had he seen them talking together?

"Ah, Lord Rapson," Lord Catesby said, ignoring Rebecca completely. "I can see you have met our staff." He threw a curious look at Rebecca, who blushed furiously. It was a little strange to see the housekeeper out of doors at this hour.

"I had a few minutes and thought to take a turn outside," she explained, hastily. "I have greeted your guest, of course."

Lord Catesby shrugged. "Of course. Come, Rapson. My brother and his wife have only just now arrived, and I would be glad to introduce you."

Rebecca stayed where she was as her brother and Lord Catesby walked back towards the house, feeling her heart break just a little. It was difficult to be the housekeeper, difficult to remove herself from her former station – particularly now when her brother was here. Consoling herself with the fact that she would soon be able to speak to him again, Rebecca quickly made her way towards the servant's entrance and tried to push the worry about her cousin from her mind. She had the dinner to think of now. The rest she could consider later.

CHAPTER 7

T*hree days later*
Francis was not altogether pleased. There was something very strange going on between his housekeeper and Lord Rapson, although he was not quite sure what it was. When Lord Rapson had first arrived, Francis had come upon his friend walking with Mrs. Harrington, which was in itself somewhat surprising, but even more so to see her smiling up at him. That had irritated him a good deal, although he had dampened such a feeling down.

And then, only last evening, he had heard voices coming from the library and had listened hard at the door, which had been slightly ajar. Having expected his friend to be in the drawing room, which was where he had been going, to hear Lord Rapson and Mrs. Harrington's voices from the library had stunned him. They were talking with a good deal of familiarity although he had been unable to quite make out what had been said. Hearing Lord Rapson state that he would have to return to the drawing room, Francis had torn himself away from the library and sauntered to the drawing room to await his friend, feeling not even the smallest fragment of guilt over listening to what had been a private conversation.

When Lord Rapson had entered the drawing room, he had apologized for being late by stating that he had thought to search for a novel with which he might read in his bedchamber during the early hours of the morning, should he waken. This was not, perhaps, a lie, but there had been no mention of Mrs. Harrington, and Francis had not yet found a way to ask his friend about her.

Frowning hard, Francis rubbed his forehead with the back of his hand, groaning aloud as he saw his mother's carriage pull up the graveled path. She had not been about for a few days since their dinner together and, as much as he hated to admit it, he had rather enjoyed her absence. She had kept Lord Rapson entertained with good conversation over dinner, however, he did have to confess.

He had not recalled that Lord Rapson had known his mother from a prior acquaintance but,

then again, Francis had been forced to admit that
he had no great knowledge of his friend's
acquaintances nor even his family! When his
mother had expressed her sorrow over Lord
Rapson's late father, he had colored hotly,
realizing he had not done such a thing himself –
not that Lord Rapson seemed to mind.

Francis' frown deepened, recalling the rest of
the conversation. He had asked Lord Rapson
what family he still had, and Lord Rapson had
seemed quite ill at ease in answering him. Finally,
he had stated that his mother had passed away
some years ago and that he had a sister, a Miss
Rebecca Armitage. For whatever reason, this had
appeared quite difficult for Lord Rapson to say
and Francis got the distinct impression that the
man did not want to speak of her.

Shrugging to himself as he walked back to his
study table, Francis sat down to look through the
sheaf of papers on his desk that required his
attention but still the matter of his guest and Mrs.
Harrington dogged his mind. Why was it that
Lord Rapson was able to have Mrs. Harrington
laugh and smile within a few moments of meeting
her, whereas he struggled to garner nothing but
fear and anxiety whenever they spoke? Even
though some days had passed since the night he
had been rather drunk, Mrs. Harrington still eyed
him with slight suspicion, as though waiting for

him to do or say something terrible. What made it worse was that Francis found himself longing to take her in his arms and reassure her that everything was quite all right. Worse, he dreamt of placing his lips on hers as she looked up at him, finally able to fulfill his greatest longing.

It was quite ridiculous. He ought not to be so upset over Lord Rapson's ability to ease Mrs. Harrington into conversation and laughter. It was foolish to consider it so deeply. Mrs. Harrington was simply a little ill at ease with him for whatever reason.

His hand curled into a fist, and he thumped the desk. "I must know why that is!"

His words echoed around the room, filling him with a sudden determination that had not been there before. He *would* find out Mrs. Harrington's reasons for behaving as though he was a tiger crouching in the reeds, ready to attack her at any moment. Perhaps then he would be able to press such questions away from his mind.

"Lord Catesby?"

The door opened slowly, and Francis realized that Mrs. Harrington had evidently knocked and had assumed that his loud mutterings to himself were, in fact, a call for her to come in.

Never mind, this could simply be the opportunity for such a conversation.

"Mrs. Harrington, sit down."

She stared at him for a moment, the color leaving her cheeks as he rose to his feet.

"Please," he added, trying to gentle his tone. "I would like speak to you."

Slowly, she shut the door behind her and came to sit down in the seat he indicated by the fire. Her eyes looked up at him with anxiety, faltering a little as he sat down opposite. He noticed that her fingers were almost white as she clasped them together in her lap, evidently frightened about what he was to say. His frustration grew. He had to discover why she was so afraid.

"Mrs. Harrington," he began, in rather more of a harsh tone than he had intended. "Why is it that you appear to be shaking whenever I ask you for a simple conversation?"

Keeping his gaze steady, he watched her closely as she took in his question, although she did not immediately answer it. Instead, something flickered in her blue eyes, her lips pulling tight for a moment.

"I – I am not afraid of you, my lord," she replied, slowly. "I apologize if I have led you to believe such a thing."

This was not the answer he wanted. Rather, this was the answer he had expected for a servant did not ever question the master.

"No, Mrs. Harrington, that is not true," he said, slowly, leaning forward in his chair just a little and seeing her shrink back. "There is something that you are not telling me, and I wish to know what it is. Why are you always so afraid to speak to me? What is it you think I will do?"

To his surprise, two spots of color appeared in her cheeks, and she looked away, her gaze resting on the fire. "You do not intend to let me go then, my lord?" she asked, in something of a flat tone. "From what has occurred, I fully expect you to do so, and I cannot understand why, as yet, you have not done so."

Confused beyond words, Francis took a moment or two to think carefully, letting Mrs. Harrington's words enter his mind and settle there. He had already reassured her, had he not, that he had no intention of removing her from his employment, so why was she still under the impression that he would do so?

"Mrs. Harrington," he replied, softly. "I do not have any plans to remove you from your post. I thought I had made that point clear."

She looked at him disbelievingly. There was no smile of relief on her face, nothing to suggest that she was glad of his words.

"Lord Catesby, if I may speak plainly for a moment, I am well aware that there is a good deal of truth in the supposed rumor that you intended to find another housekeeper and what has clouded my mind for many days is that I do not know *why* you intend such a thing." Her expression grew somewhat frustrated, as well as a little scared. "I cannot tell what it is that I have done to offend you, what I have done to bring you to such a conclusion, but I know that the intention is still within you. Why, only last week, you attempted...." Trailing off, her eyes widened, and she clapped one hand over her mouth, as though she had said too much.

Francis let out a long, slow breath, trying to keep a hold of his temper as he realized that, yet again, he had no understanding of what it was Mrs. Harrington spoke of.

"Mrs. Harrington, I can *assure* you that I have no plans to remove you from your post," he said, firmly, striking the flat of his hand on his knee for added emphasis. "I considered the matter at one time but have discarded it."

"But why?" she asked, softly, her hands now back in her lap. "Why did you consider removing me from my station here?"

It was a question he could not answer, not truthfully at least. As he looked at her, he saw that, for the first time, she looked as confused as he felt. The anxiety was no longer there, the fear was gone completely – and that opened her expression all the more. His heart lifted, filling him with a new appreciation for her. *My goodness, she is beautiful.*

Clearing his throat, he passed one hand over his eyes in order to give him a few more moments with which he could consider his answer. "Mrs. Harrington, the reasons are of little consequence. I —"

"They are not of little consequence to me," she interrupted, showing a good deal more spirit than he had ever seen from her. "Am I failing you in some way, my lord? Or is it simply that you have taken a dislike to me?" Her words were coming faster now, accentuated by anger. "Is that why you tried to shame me? So that I would have a reason to leave of my own accord and, if I did not, you could use that reason to force me out?"

Helplessly, Francis spread his hands. "My dear Mrs. Harrington, I have very little idea of what you are speaking of."

Her mouth closed tightly. "I see. I should be grateful that you have either evidently forgotten or have chosen not to use it against me. I cannot tell which one to believe."

"Why do you think so poorly of me?"

Francis was on his feet in a moment, his anger bursting to life.

"I have not harmed you, I have not shamed you, and yet you speak as though I am some sort of conniving rogue who....." Trailing off, he saw her wide eyes and slowly, so slowly, a memory came back to him.

A memory of the night he had been drunk. A memory that had only been fragments and shards. A memory that told him he had done something altogether foolish.

"Oh....."

Slowly, he sank back down into his chair, seeing Mrs. Harrington watching him with a good deal of astonishment on her face. His cheeks colored at once as he finally remembered what he had done that night. He had not injured her nor brought her to harm, which was a relief, but rather, he had kissed her. Kissed her soundly.

"You remember, then," she stated, bitterly. "Am I to be sent from your house, Lord Catesby?"

Groaning aloud, he put his head in his hands. "No, Mrs. Harrington. No, you shall not be sent away. That was my own foolishness, my own drunken idiocy. There is no blame for you in that unfortunate circumstance."

Daring to send a glance in her direction, Francis was surprised to see that she was blinking back a sudden flurry of tears.

"I am truly sorry, Mrs. Harrington," he said, slowly, meaning every single word. "What a terrible position for you to be in. I can well understand why you have been so troubled. I should never have so much as mentioned to the butler that I was thinking of replacing you. It was my own foolish thoughts, and I deeply regret ever allowing myself to consider it as an appropriate solution.

As for –" he struggled to get the words out, heat creeping up his spine and into his face. "As for kissing you, Mrs. Harrington, I can only apologize again. I should not have done so. This is nothing to do with you, and I would not ever ask you to depart from this house based on my own disgraceful behavior."

Sitting up, he cleared his throat before glancing at her again, seeing tears on her cheeks and felt guilt slam into his heart. "I do not know if you can forgive me, Mrs. Harrington but I do beg it of you. My inhibitions were evidently lowered – if not absent altogether, and so I must have given in to my desires without even realizing them."

If it had not been for Mrs. Harrington's swift intake of breath, Francis might not have realized what it was he had just said. Ice clung to his limbs, making it impossible to move. He stared at Mrs. Harrington, who was looking back at him with utter astonishment.

"I –"

There was nothing he could say to explain what he had meant. Having just told her outright that he had given in to his desire to kiss her, he could not easily explain it away.

"I – I think I should leave you, Lord Catesby," Mrs. Harrington murmured, her face pink and eyes roving around the room in a desperate attempt not to look at him. "Do excuse me."

"Mrs. Harrington."

He had risen to his feet without really knowing why, looking at her directly as she turned back slowly to face him.

"Mrs. Harrington," he said again, slowly beginning to realize what it was he wanted to say and trying to find a way to say it. "I do not want you to think that I am a gentleman intent on seducing his staff simply to satisfy his own fleeting whims." He saw her blush and felt his own cheeks warm, but continued on regardless, determined to speak the truth to her as though, in its own way, it might save him from his embarrassment. "I do not do such things. It is not my way. Rather, I will confess to you that I have been quite unable to get you from my mind ever since you have come to my house."

Her eyes were rounded, staring at him, whilst her mouth hung a little ajar. Evidently, he had astonished her completely.

"I tell you this because it is the truth, Mrs. Harrington," he continued, refusing to shy away from it. "That is the only reason I have attempted to remove you from this house, and it was wrong of me to do so. I do not want you to go simply because of my own struggles. That would be entirely unfair. However, I will confess that I continue to desire to know you better, to spend time in conversation, to talk and laugh and share – but such a desire is quite ridiculous. I am aware of that. I am a lord of the realm, and I would not sully your reputation by forcing my desires on to you. I should not have done so then, and I will not do so again."

Breathing hard, he finished his little speech with a feeling of both relief and a sudden awareness of just how honest he had been with her. He had never said such things aloud but now that they had been spoken, his heart felt a good deal lighter.

Mrs. Harrington, however, was looking entirely stunned – and he could not blame her for such a reaction. She had one hand to her heart, her eyes glistening with sparkling tears and, suddenly, Francis felt himself jolt with fear.

"You will not leave the house because of what I have told you," he said, as though stating a fact rather than asking a question. "You cannot, Mrs. Harrington, that would not be fair." He realized immediately that in saying what he had done, he was practically forcing the lady from his home. That had not been his intention. He had wanted her to understand why he had been so conflicted, but by being so forthright, he could now have opened the door for her to leave of her own volition.

Tears fell onto her cheeks. "Oh, Lord Catesby," she breathed, clearly struggling to get the words from her lips. "You have astonished me entirely. I did not think that you would have such a depth of feeling for one such as I."

She did not look either angry or upset at what he had confessed. In fact, there appeared to be almost a lightness about her, as though what he had said now brought her some kind of relief.

"I will not ruin your reputation or your standing by doing anything I should not," he promised, going against everything that he longed for. "I will remain as I ought, and you can continue your duties regardless of what I have said." A small smile caught his lips, tugging them ruefully. "I did not mean to confess all of this to you, Mrs. Harrington, but I could not bear your distress any longer. I will not have you afraid of me."

She shook her head, her eyes dropping to the floor for a moment. Francis closed his eyes and took in a steadying breath, refusing to let himself reflect on the significance of what had happened that evening in the library. If his memory was correct, Mrs. Harrington had responded to him in her own way. She had not slapped him and run from the room but had grown soft and warm under his embrace. But no, he would not think on this, would not allow himself to consider, to dream. He had said and done enough already.

"Lord Catesby, I think there is something I must tell you," Mrs. Harrington stammered, her cheeks now cooling to a dusky pink. "I –"

The door opened just as she was about to speak, admitting the butler.

"I am terribly sorry, my lord," the butler apologized, ignoring Mrs. Harrington completely. "I knew you were talking to Mrs. Harrington and thought to step in. You have an unexpected visitor."

Francis, rather irritated by such an interruption, sighed heavily and picked up the card from the silver tray. "Who is this gentleman?" he asked, waving the card about. "I do not recognize the name."

The butler lifted one shoulder. "I cannot say, my lord, although he claims to be the cousin of Lord Rapson. Apparently, he is looking for him for I believe there has been some sort of upset back at the estate."

That brought a frown to Francis' face. "Very well," he stated, waving the butler away. "I will see him. Just bring him along here and send for the tea tray."

The butler withdrew, leaving only Mrs. Harrington remaining. Francis turned back to her, expecting for her to continue, only to see her turn puce.

"Mrs. Harrington?"

"Lord Catesby," she whispered, coming towards him and grasping his arm with one hand. "Has the honorable Stephen Jefferson come to see you?"

Astonishment shot through him. "You know the gentleman?"

She swayed slightly, and for a moment, Francis thought she might collapse where she stood. "You must not tell him that Lord Rapson is here," she replied, hoarsely. "Please, my lord, do as I ask. It is for Lord Rapson's safety."

Knowing that he could not delay in order to demand how Mrs. Harrington knew of both Mr. Jefferson and Lord Rapson, Francis put one hand over hers. "I will not pretend to understand, Mrs. Harrington, but you appear to be quite in earnest."

"I am," she pleaded, her eyes boring into his. "He must not know, my lord."

"Very well, very well," he said, softly, although he was entirely unsure as to why she could have asked him such a thing. "Although I will expect an explanation from you as regards this matter forthwith."

She nodded, no smile or even flash of relief

on her face. "Thank you, Lord Catesby. I must go."

Francis watched her leave the room, feeling more confused than ever. Mrs. Harrington had been more receptive to his confession than he had thought and now, it appeared, there was more to her than he had first believed. How did she know Mr. Jefferson? And what did Lord Rapson have to do with it all?

"The honorable Stephen Jefferson, my lord."

Jerking in surprise, he saw the butler standing at the open door, standing to one side to announce Francis' guest.

"Mr. Jefferson," he said at once, hoping the gentleman had not seen his lack of preparation. "Do sit down and tell me at once what it is I can do to assist you."

CHAPTER 8

Rebecca's breathing was ragged as she hurried from one room to the next, desperate to find her brother. Jefferson was here. Mark had to be warned.

How he had found them, she did not know, and she could not believe that it was simply happenstance. Mark had promised her that no-one knew of her whereabouts. He had promised that not even his staff knew that he intended to come to Catesby House, and yet here Jefferson was.

Whilst she had been able to talk with her brother on more than one occasion, she had not been able to come up with any particular solution as to how to remove Jefferson from their lives for good. She had thought they would have more time, that they would be able to talk with the dowager who, as yet, they had been unable to visit together. Angry, frustrated and afraid, she turned into the dining room to find her brother busy finishing a late luncheon.

"Rebecca!" he exclaimed, looking delighted to see her. "Have you come up with something?"

Closing the door tightly, she leaned against it for a moment before shaking her head. "No, Rapson, I have not."

His expression changed at once, evidently seeing her demeanor. "Is something the matter, Rebecca?"

"Jefferson is here."

His knife and fork clattered unceremoniously, on the plate. His face went sheet white as he stared at her, his smile fading at once.

"You told me that your staff knew nothing of this," she said, hoarsely, walking towards him on trembling limbs. "How, then, has he found us both?"

Her brother did not say anything for some moments, his eyes glazing over as he looked at her, clearly thinking about what he had said and who could have told their cousin.

"Jefferson may have found a way to gain entry into the estate," he murmured, eventually. "I never once let him in, and the staff was told to refuse him, but I am quite sure he could have easily wheedled his way in using one of the more impressionable maids. He is, as you know, a particularly persuasive man."

She didn't understand. "But what would that matter? You did not tell any of the staff where you were going."

"But I did keep my correspondence in my study," he admitted, quietly, his gaze faltering as he looked at her. "If he found a way in there, then he might easily have discovered the letter I received back from Lord Catesby welcoming a visit from me."

Her breath caught. "Oh, no, Mark."

He dropped his head. "I should have burned the letter," he lamented regretfully. "But truly, I did not for one moment imagine that he would find a way into the manor house if that is what he has done. I am sorry, Rebecca."

She shook her head. "It is not something you could have anticipated, Rapson. Our cousin is more devious than either of us ever expected."

"But what are we to do?" he asked, hopelessly. "I feel so very useless, Rebecca. I am meant to be protecting you, but without realizing it, I have managed to lead our cousin directly to us." His eyes caught hers, and she was caught by the lack of hope that was within. "I am failing in my duties, Rebecca. I have been unable to protect you, and even now when the danger has loomed even closer, I find myself entirely at a loss."

Rebecca drew in a long breath in an attempt to steady herself. "I have begged Lord Catesby not to say a word about your presence here," she began, seeing a flicker of light in her brother's eyes. "He agreed, I am glad to say, but it will require an explanation from us both." The way Lord Catesby had spoken to her before the news of Jefferson's arrival still warmed her, the sudden anticipation catching her off guard. "I cannot predict what his reaction will be, but I pray that he will be able to help us."

Her brother nodded. "I could send a footman to fetch the dowager also," he murmured quietly. "It is a little discourteous given that we are guests in Lord Catesby's home, but she will need to talk of her part in all of this, especially if we are to convince Catesby to help us."

Rebecca leaned heavily on the table. "I think that would be wise."

She waited quietly whilst her brother called for a footman, dictating a short note which would be taken at once to the dowager. Whilst she waited, her mind turned back to her employer. What Lord Catesby had revealed to her already, only a few minutes beforehand, had quite taken her by surprise – and now she was to reveal something of her own to him.

To hear him speak of affection, of his desire to be close to her and how he could not remove her from his thoughts had forced her to see him in a very different light. Suddenly, his reasons from turning from her, for considering that he ought to remove her from her position and replace her with someone entirely new, all began to make sense. He had been afraid of what he had begun to want, turning away from the overwhelming sense of longing that he had spoken to her of.

A lord of the manor might have whichever of his staff he chose, given that he was of a much higher station than they. But she knew that Lord Catesby was not that kind of man. He was a gentleman.

He had thought to send her away rather than disgrace her or soil her reputation. That spoke of kindness, of consideration and of a strong sense of what was right and what was wrong. Her brother had been correct to state that Lord Catesby was a trustworthy fellow, with a good, strong moral compass. At the time, she had thought that entirely incorrect, believing that Lord Catesby had kissed her in order to ensure that she could not remain in his employ for very much longer, but she had been wrong on that count. Very wrong. Lord Catesby was, all in all, a very good man.

"There we are," her brother muttered,

thrusting one hand into his hair as he began to pace the room in a state of agitation. "The note is sent. The dowager will be here shortly, I hope. Although it will take us some time to explain it all to Lord Catesby, I think."

She gave him a rueful smile. "I do hope that he will not be too angry with me."

"Angry with you?" Rapson repeated, looking astonished. "My dear sister, I am quite sure that Lord Catesby will understand. He will not be angry with you, not when, as I understand, you have been doing such a remarkable job in managing the household."

A small blush crept into her cheeks. "Did he say such a thing?"

"On more than one occasion," her brother said, firmly. "You cannot imagine how proud I was to hear it. You have done remarkably well, Rebecca. I am only sorry I have been unable to do more."

She shook her head and caught his hand, preventing him from walking away again to pace the floor. "You did all that you could, Mark. You even called him out, but he refused to meet your demands. That is hardly your fault." She squeezed his hand gently. "You were willing to put your life on the line for me. Even worse, you have been chased from your home by the crazed attempts of a gentleman desperate to have what he has long desired, despite having no claim to it."

Shaking her head sadly, she looked up at him again. "You and I are both at as much of a loss as the other when it comes to dealing with our cousin. Aside from having him shot, I can see no easy solution to our present difficulties – unless…." She trailed off, an idea sparking in her mind. If she were to marry another, then Jefferson would have not only herself and her brother to contend with, but also her husband. It would mean giving up her fortune to her husband but if she found a good man, then would that be as much of a trial as she feared?

Her mind filled with the face of Lord Catesby. She could not pretend that there was not a small amount of feeling that filled her soul when she thought of him, burning all the brighter now that she knew the real reason for his thoughts of sending her away. He was a good man, was he not? If she gave him her fortune by wedding him, she was quite sure that he would not withhold anything from her that she desired. It was not as though she knew any other particular gentleman, given that she had only just finished her half year of mourning before she had been forced to run from her home.

But, then again, Lord Catesby might not have

any thoughts of matrimony. That was a foolish hope and certainly not one she could cling to.

Letting out a long sigh, she looked up into her brother's anxious face, knowing just how much he wished to help her and just how little they were able to do. "We will think of something, Rapson. I am quite sure we will be able to come up with something, once we have the assistance of the dowager and Lord Catesby."

"I do hope so," he murmured, clearly very despondent. "I have done nothing of use thus far."

She embraced him, trying her best to draw up her courage and strength whilst reassuring him also. He hugged her back, murmuring yet more apologies as frustration radiated from him.

Just as she was about to step back, the door opened, and Lord Catesby stepped inside, stopping dead as he looked at them both, an angry glint in his eye.

CHAPTER 9

"Whatever is the meaning of this?"

Francis knew his voice was loud and held a good deal of anger, but to walk in and see Mrs. Harrington in the arms of Lord Rapson was more than he could tolerate. He had just bared his soul to the lady and, whilst he had not expected her to run to him, he certainly did not think she would then be in the arms of another gentleman! On top of all of this, he had just come from a very confusing conversation with Mr. Jefferson, who had apparently been searching for Lord Rapson in order to inform him about some terrible news which, for whatever reason, he could not divulge to Francis himself.

It had been as though Mr. Jefferson knew that

Lord Rapson was within and had been trying to force Francis to admit it. Francis had not liked the gentleman, and for this reason, finding Mr. Jefferson's sharp hazel eyes and slightly menacing smile a little disconcerting. But, as he had promised to Mrs. Harrington, he had not mentioned a word about Lord Rapson's presence, even though the gentleman had persisted with his questions for some minutes.

"Lord Catesby," Mrs. Harrington stammered, stepping back from Lord Rapson. "Is Mr. Jefferson still here?"

He frowned, finding himself growing angry with her lack of consideration for what he had just stumbled upon. It was as if he did not really know the lady before him. Upon retrospect, he began to question what he really knew of her. He had thought her sweet and kind, gentle and respectable, and yet here she was with her arms around Lord Rapson's neck!"

"I think you need to explain yourself, Mrs. Harrington," he grated, coming a little further into the room and closing the door with a little too much force, making Mrs. Harrington jump. "Whatever are you doing here with Lord Rapson? I did think that something strange was between the two of you, but I never once considered that it could be.....*this*." He emphasized the last word, arching an eyebrow as he regarded her, seeing her flush a deep red.

"Now, see here," Lord Rapson said, firmly, stepping forward. "There's more to this than you understand, Lord Catesby. Don't suggest something foolish."

"Foolish?" Francis exclaimed, waving a hand at Mrs. Harrington, who was now standing a little further away from Lord Rapson. "Do you have any idea what has just passed between myself and the lady? I have told my housekeeper, my *housekeeper*, if you can imagine, that I am half in love with her and that I cannot remove her from my thoughts. I have begged her forgiveness for kissing her and have asked her to remain within this house in her position here, promising not to give in to any of my own desires ever again. And then, some minutes after baring my soul, I walk in to see her standing with you!"

A dark flush burned in his cheeks, his expression growing angry. "Evidently, Mrs. Harrington is not the lady I thought her to be! If you wish, Lord Rapson, I suggest you take Mrs. Harrington with you when you leave. I am quite sure she will make a *warm* companion."

Lord Rapson took a step forward, his face filled with rage – only for Mrs. Harrington to step forward and tug at his arm, begging him not to harm Lord Catesby. Francis' lip curled.

"I do not require your assistance, Mrs. Harrington. In fact, I do not require you at all. Go and collect your things. You are dismissed."

Much to his surprise, Mrs. Harrington did not look either astonished or regretful, as he thought she might. Instead, she looked at him calmly, her hand still on Lord Rapson's arm.

"My dear Lord Catesby," she said, in a clear voice. "You must excuse my brother. He is most protective."

Francis's heart stopped dead. His smirk fell from his lips, replaced with an open-mouthed gape. His eyebrows practically vanished into his hair as he saw Lord Rapson give him a small, apologetic smile. This lady, the lady he had thought of as his housekeeper, the one he had been battling to forget, battling to ignore, was not a servant after all. In fact, she was the daughter of a nobleman and the sister of a viscount!

It was some moments before he could speak and even then, his voice was thin and wispy, his whole body feeling as though it had been filled with ice.

"But – but why?" he asked, hoarsely. "I do not understand."

Mrs. Harrington – or whatever her true name was – shot him an apologetic look. "I had no other choice, Lord Catesby. Your mother was so willing to help that I could not –"

"My *mother?*" Francis repeated, interrupting her. "Do you mean to say that my mother has been aware of this situation for...." He trailed off, recalling just how interested his mother had become in his life of late. "I see," he muttered, feeling as though he were adrift at sea with no way of getting to dry land. "She has been involved in this matter, whatever it be, since the beginning."

"Indeed," Lord Rapson agreed, quietly. "I do apologize, old boy, but I couldn't tell you the truth, for my sister's sake. It was imperative that she remained hidden."

A dull ache began to form between Francis' brows. "Why is that?" he asked, glancing from one to the other. "Is this something to do with Mr. Jefferson?"

"Our cousin," they both said together, making Francis all the more astonished.

"Your cousin who came to call to tell me that he has been eagerly searching for you, Lord Rapson, to tell you of some terrible news," he said, slowly. "Am I to understand that this supposed news is nothing of importance?"

Lord Rapson shook his head. "I think it nothing but a ruse, Lord Catesby," he replied, with a small shrug. "Should we, perhaps, seat ourselves around the table? There is a good deal to explain, and I believe your mother will be joining us shortly." He cleared his throat, glancing away from Francis for a moment, evidence of his embarrassment. "I do apologize, Lord Catesby, but I sent a note and asked her to join us."

Mrs. Harrington smiled tightly. "We could not be sure of your reaction to this news, Lord Catesby. We thought it best she be present also."

Francis felt as if he had woken up in a dream and was able to walk about in it. Nothing seemed to make sense. Mrs. Harrington was not, in fact, a housekeeper of the lower classes, but was a lady of quality. Lord Rapson had not simply come here for a brief stay, but evidently had come to ensure the safety of his sister, for whatever reason. And his mother, the dowager, had apparently facilitated all that was going on without saying a word to him about it.

Why had he not been informed? What possible reason could there be for a young lady of the *ton* to hide in another gentleman's estate? Anything might have occurred that could have brought Mrs. Harrington harm, and he would not have known how to help her.

"May I ask," he said, as he sat down in a chair by the dining table. "What is your real name, Mrs. Harrington?" He looked at her seated across from him, seeing her gentle features and feeling his heart fill with confusion and doubt. Was what he felt for her finally able to come to some sort of conclusion? Was he now able to allow himself such a depth of feeling without chastising himself completely? It should have brought him a sense of happiness, but he felt nothing but bewilderment.

Letting out a small sigh, Mrs. Harrington settled back into her chair, folded her hands in her lap and smiled at him. "I am Miss Rebecca Patterson, my lord. Daughter to the late Viscount Rapson."

He inclined his head almost without thinking. "I am glad to finally make your true acquaintance, my lady."

She flushed a deep, rich red. "I cannot tell if you are teasing me or if you are genuine, my lord, but for my part, I will say that I did not enjoy deceiving you. There was, however, no other way."

Clearing his throat, he took in her sad smile, her burning cheeks and the flash of hope in her eyes. She was praying that he would accept her, he realized, just as she was. Did she not understand that such a sudden change in her circumstances meant that he did not have to continue preventing himself from allowing his heart to fill with her, that he was free of the desperate longing to rid himself of her from his mind?

"Oh, Francis."

Turning his head, Francis saw his mother walk into the room, her face a picture.

"I am terribly sorry you had to find out this

way," she said, with a shake of her head. "But it was all for the best, you understand."

He closed his eyes for a moment, keeping his frustration under control. "So everybody keeps telling me, mama, but as yet I have received very little explanation as to why this was the case." He looked at his friend, Lord Rapson, who was seemingly very interested in the painting hanging on the wall just behind Francis' head. "If anyone cares to start from the beginning, I should very much like an explanation."

"Of course," his mother replied at once, soothingly. "Just let me ring for tea, my dear. It has been a rather trying afternoon for you all, has it not?" Her eyes flickered to Miss Patterson. "I understand your cousin is here?"

It was not Miss Patterson who answered, however, but her brother.

"He is," he replied, heavily. "And I must have made the mistake of thinking him unable to discover where I was headed. Thankfully, Lord Catesby was able to do as my sister requested and give him no information as regarded my presence here. I am sure he is quite well on his way by now."

A slow sense of dread began to fill Francis, starting from his stomach and going all through him. His blood began to roar in his ears, his mouth going dry as he saw Miss Patterson's face fall.

"Oh, no," she breathed, one hand at her heart. "What has occurred, Lord Catesby?"

He tried to clear his throat, tried to appear matter of fact, but the words stuck to his lips.

"Mr. Jefferson is to reside here overnight," he said, with a fair amount of difficulty. "He explained he was to continue on to London come the morrow and it would not have been proper for me to ignore such a matter. Of course, I offered him a room."

For a moment, there was nothing but stunned silence. Francis let his eyes rove around the room, taking in his mother's horrified face, Lord Rapson's astonished expression, and Miss Patterson's fearful gaze.

"What is it I have done?" he asked, feeling the burden of responsibility settle onto his shoulders as he spoke. "What is so terrible about Mr. Jefferson that I ought not to have offered such an invitation?"

Miss Patterson sat a little further forward in her chair, piercing him with a suddenly fierce gaze. "Because, Lord Catesby, he has threatened the lives of both myself and of my brother. Because he is nothing more than a scoundrel and a villain. Because I have spent months hiding from him, only to now find he has discovered us. Is that enough of a reason for you?"

CHAPTER 10

"Lord Catesby?"

It had been some hours since Lord Catesby had discovered the truth about her identity and about Mr. Jefferson and still, the guilt on her shoulders had not yet dissipated, not even slightly. She ought not to have spoken so sharply to the gentleman, to the one man from whom the truth had been hidden. And yet, hearing that he had offered Mr. Jefferson a place to stay had sent both fear and anger through her, and she had spoken from the feelings within her heart.

He half turned. "Mrs. Harrington – I mean, Miss Patterson. Good evening."

She bobbed her curtsy as usual. "I think, given

that I am to remain as your housekeeper for the time being, you ought to refer to me as before."

A rueful smile caught his lips. "Is that so?" he muttered, turning his back on her to walk closer to the fire that was burning in the grate. "I confess I am finding this all very difficult, Miss Patterson. I do not know what to call you, and I certainly think it rather terrible that you are still under the guise of a housekeeper when you ought not to be anything of the sort."

Rebecca gave him a half smile. "It is for the best, Lord Catesby. I am quite sure."

They had discussed the matter at some length that evening, quite uncertain as to what Mr. Jefferson's plans and intentions were. Lord Catesby surmised that the gentleman wished to ensure that the house was, in fact, entirely free of Lord Rapson and so, from that, a plan had been formed. It was by no means a very good plan, for there was a good deal that could go wrong and even the dowager had looked somewhat perturbed. She had suggested that Rebecca and her brother relocate to her smaller home, but Rebecca had not agreed. This was not the way forward. They had to face this together and stop Mr. Jefferson altogether. Running and hiding was no longer something she was willing to continue.

"Mr. Jefferson retired early," Lord Catesby continued, in a flat voice. "I am quite sure he intends to squirrel all through the house once we are all abed and, even if that is not what he has thought to do, I am quite sure that George, the footman, will make certain to put the idea in his head – just as we have intended, of course."

Her stomach turned over, even though she knew this was what had been planned. "I am a little frightened, I confess," she replied, quietly. "I do hope my brother will not be in danger."

Lord Catesby did not smile. "You can trust me," he said, softly. "You know very well that he will not deal with your cousin alone."

"Yes, I know," she said quietly, shutting the door tightly behind her so that it closed with a soft click. "I do trust you, my lord."

Lord Catesby looked at her then, his eyes filled with the flames of the fire. There was a deep intensity to them, a burning that seared her very soul.

"I am sorry," she said, knowing that she had already apologized more than once. "I did not mean to deceive you."

He held up one hand, turning his face away. "Enough, Miss Patterson, I beg you. I have had enough apologies for one day. I hold no anger nor regret in this matter. I can understand why you have run from your cousin and why your brother has felt so helpless. To be facing a man who does not care about his reputation, nor about your own lives, must be difficult indeed."

She nodded and moved away from the door, her body humming with a mixture of anxiety and anticipation. "My brother did all he could, going so far as to call Jefferson out, but my cousin ignored him. I believe he has lost his mind somewhat, growing so obsessive over what he long desires that he will do anything to have it."

"Your fortune," Lord Catesby murmured, looking a little more relaxed. "He would take it by force."

She shook her head slowly, feeling the agony and the fear she had been so used to wrap around her again. "I knew he would use my brother against me and so I left. I thought that if my cousin could not find me and if my brother remained on his estate, then the matter would come to an end. I never imagined that my cousin would make an attempt on my brother's life in order to force him to reveal my whereabouts." Filled with sadness, she closed her eyes to prevent tears from falling. "What else could I do? What could Rapson do? We are at the mercy of a madman."

When she opened her eyes, she found Lord Catesby standing by her, having moved closer to her in seeing her distress. His eyes sought her own, searching her face as he managed a small smile.

"I am here with you now," he assured her, touching her hand with his own. "I know why you did not say a word to me, why you kept your identity a secret from me, but I do wish that you had told me from the very beginning."

Rebecca shook her head. "Your mother was a little unsure as to how you would react," she replied, quietly. "You have been caught up with all manner of estate business, and there have been so many weddings to deal with that even I did not want to bring more of a burden to you. After all, you have nothing whatsoever to do with my family. Why should I bring my difficulties into your life?"

His lips curved gently. "Mayhap because I would have been entirely willing to have helped you," he suggested, his fingers still capturing hers. "From the moment I saw you, Miss Patterson, you burned into my very soul. Had I but known the truth, then I would not have spent all this time berating myself, forcing my heart to forget you, only for it to fill with you all over again."

His breath brushed across her cheek and, for a moment, Rebecca forgot completely about Mr. Jefferson and her very reason for being in the library with Lord Catesby. "I have confused you, I know – and in turn, I suppose, you have confused me, but even with only a few hours consideration, I know that I care for you still, Miss Patterson. I wish to know you better, although I am quite certain that your kind and gentle nature is truly who you are." He glanced around the room at the books before returning his gaze to her. "There are so many things I wish to discuss with you. Miss Patterson, my desire is to know everything I can about you, to allow my heart to feel all it wishes. Can you understand that?"

She swallowed hard, her throat dry. "I – I can, my lord," she replied, hoarsely.

"When I kissed you," he continued, making her face flame with heat, "You did not turn from me, I do not think. If I remember correctly, you remained as you were and allowed me to do so. I distinctly remember you returning my kiss, Miss Patterson."

She closed her eyes tightly, overwhelmed by the awareness of him. "I did not think you would recall such a thing, my lord."

"But I did," he replied, gently. "Might I hope, my lady, that there could be some return to my affections?"

Going quite still, Rebecca looked into his eyes. Her heart and mind were full of a great many swirling emotions and thoughts, all wrapped up in one another and now he was only adding to them.

"My lord," she said slowly, trying her best to put her colliding thoughts into words. "I do not know what to say, nor what to think. You are right to state that I returned your kiss, but I will admit to being rather surprised by my own response." Even now, the touch of his fingers on hers was sending streaks of excitement up into her heart, a heart that was clouded by the knowledge that Mr. Jefferson was not only present in this house but would soon be seeking either herself or her brother. "I do not think that there is a lack of feeling, my lord, but only that it is very slight," she confessed, seeing the light in his eyes begin to fade. "There has been so much happening of late that I do not know what I truly feel about anything."

He touched her face with one finger, sending a shiver straight through her. "And once Mr. Jefferson is dealt with?" he asked, his voice low and warm, wrapping itself around her. "What then, my dear lady? Will you consider your heart again? Might you permit me to court you?"

She smiled at him then, relieved that he understood. "I can promise you, Lord Catesby, that I would be more than delighted to receive your court," she confessed, making his smile widen. "But as to my heart, allow it some time to be free from the fear and the worry that has held it for so long. As you may recall, I accused you of kissing me simply so that you might turn me out of your house!"

Rubbing the back of his neck, Lord Catesby looked at her ruefully from under his brows. "I can understand why," he admitted, quietly. "My goodness, we have both been wrapped in uncertainty and suspicion, have we not, Miss Patterson? Although I will admit a certain relief in being able to speak to you so freely."

Her heart lifted all the more. "I thank you for your consideration of me, Lord Catesby. I would have you know that I am truly appreciative for all you have done for me thus far – and all you will do when it comes to Mr. Jefferson." The reminder that her cousin was within the house sent shivers down her spine, and she stepped away from Lord Catesby for a moment, rubbing her arms as though to ward off a chill. Out of the corner of her eye, she saw the smile fade from Lord Catesby's face, replaced with an almost grim appearance, as though he too had only just recalled why they were in the library. "Ah yes, of course. We are to take on your adversary together, are we not? When did your brother say to be ready?"

"Within the hour, Lord Catesby," she replied, glancing at the grandfather clock in the corner. "Come now, I suppose we must prepare."

Lord Catesby chuckled, his eyes darting to hers and causing her to blush all the more. "I must say, I find that I am rather expectant with this part of my mother's plan, Miss Patterson. What say you?"

She stepped closer to him, the heat from the fire warming her completely. "I find that I am a little anxious, my lord," she replied, her voice a little thin. "What if it is all to go wrong? What if my cousin does not believe you?"

He patted her shoulder before resting his hand there for a moment, running it down her arm so that he might catch her fingers. "He will," he stated, firmly, giving her not even a single moment to disagree. "It will all come out in the end, my dear. You will be safe; your brother will be able to return home, and you shall have your fortune in its entirety when the time comes."

She let out a long, slow breath so as to ensure she remained composed and calm. "I hardly care about that any longer, Lord Catesby. Just so long as my brother is safe, then that is all that matters to me."

This seemed to please him. "Which is just as it should be, Miss Patterson."

CHAPTER 11

"I hear footsteps."

Francis looked down at Miss Patterson and saw her cheeks flush with heat. Her eyes were flickering with both fear and expectation, akin to his own swirling emotions. Believing it to be Mr. Jefferson who was to come into the room, having been prompted by Francis' footman, Francis took Miss Patterson in his arms, holding her tightly against him. Her back was to the door, and he let his hands slip to her waist, her hands linking behind his neck.

Her breath quickened, matching his own. This was both a delight and torture, giving him just what he desired whilst anticipating that he was to be encountered found at any moment. George, Francis' footman, had been told to speak to Mr.

Jefferson about the presence of Lord Rapson within the house, making sure to appear as though he ought not to be speaking so candidly. He was also to mention that he knew Lord Rapson often enjoyed spending his evenings in the library, which was just where Francis intended to be 'discovered' with Miss Patterson.

"Are you quite ready, my dear?" he murmured, seeing her eyes burn with a sudden fire.

"Quite," she whispered, moving all the closer.

He had not intended to kiss her but, much to his surprise, Francis realized that this was precisely what he was going to do. His mother had suggested that he and Miss Patterson stand close to one another, embracing with a tender affection, but had never once suggested that there be anything more than the holding of hands. And yet, somehow, he had lowered his head and captured her lips with his own, forgetting entirely about the reason for their closeness.

"Good gracious, Lord Catesby! I did not know you had a mistress within these four walls!"

Miss Patterson lurched away from Francis at once, and it was only the fact that he held her tightly around the waist that kept her from moving away entirely. The fear in her expression was immediate, and Francis felt his own heart tug with both anger and dread.

"Mr. Jefferson," he said coolly. "I was not expecting you. I thought you had retired for the evening." Francis was relieved to see that Miss Patterson had recalled what she was meant to do and had kept her back to her cousin, refusing to reveal herself to him.

Mr. Jefferson eyed her carefully, before turning his sharp gaze back onto Francis. "I thought to come and fetch a book or two," he explained, lazily. "Couldn't sleep."

"Is that so?" Francis murmured, lifting a brow. "Well, if you will just excuse me for a moment, I ought to –"

"Is this your wife?"

Francis lifted his chin, glaring at Mr. Jefferson's impertinence. "Mr. Jefferson, I hardly think it is of any importance to you whether or not I am wed. These affairs are entirely my own."

This harsh reprimand, however, only appeared to make Mr. Jefferson's interest all the more apparent.

Mr. Jefferson took a step forward. "Of course," he muttered, whilst still casting a sharp eye over the back of Miss Patterson's head. "It was just that we did not dine with anyone else and I did wonder if you had any other guests present."

Francis' eyes glittered. "Again, Mr. Jefferson," he stated, firmly. "None of this is of any importance to you and I would kindly –"

Mr. Jefferson gasped, one hand to his mouth whilst his eyes widened. "Good gracious! Rebecca!"

Miss Patterson, who had half turned her head so that her cousin would be able to make out her profile, drew a little away from Francis, who let one hand slip from her waist, pushing her behind him.

"It *is* you," Mr. Jefferson continued, sounding utterly thrilled. "My, my, my. However, did you end up here?" His dark eyes flickered to Francis and back again whilst a wide grin spread across his face. "Came to him for help, did you?"

Miss Patterson lifted her chin. "I am the housekeeper, Mrs. Harrington."

Mr. Jefferson let out a shout of laughter. "Is that what he calls you, is it? Keeps you here as the housekeeper but makes sure you know *precisely* what your role is – your nightly duties."

Francis' body rippled with anger. "Steady, Mr. Jefferson. That's quite enough."

Mr. Jefferson ignored him, however, seemingly aware that Miss Patterson was in something of a difficult situation.

"My goodness, Rebecca, how unfortunate that you have been discovered! And here I am looking for your brother, only to discover you here! My, my. Your reputation is quite ruined now, you know. What will you do now?"

Miss Patterson stepped away from Francis entirely, crossing her arms across her body in a defensive gesture. "My dear Mr. Jefferson, I care very little about my reputation. I have my fortune, as you know."

Mr. Jefferson chuckled. "And what of your brother and his future, Rebecca? To have a sister so soiled, so defiled – well, that will make his chances of finding a suitable bride almost impossible! No-one will want to align themselves with such a family now, will they? What are the chances for your brother to then find himself a wife and produce the required heir?" His eyes glittered, and he took a small step forward. "Very little, do you not think?"

Francis said nothing, despite the growing urge to step forward and smite the man hard across the face. They had known that Mr. Jefferson would use what he had seen against Miss Patterson, just as he had done. He was immensely proud of Miss Patterson, seeing her standing there with a firm stance and cold, sharp eyes that glared at her cousin. She was not showing him even a modicum of fear, despite the fact that she was probably trembling inside. After all, had he not felt her shudder in his arms but a few moments ago?

She glanced up at him and, for a moment, Mr. Jefferson's smile slipped. Francis knew what he was thinking. Should Francis offer to wed the lady in order to save her reputation, then there would be very few consequences. In fact, Miss Patterson would do her family line the world of good in marrying an earl. This was where he had to step in, where he had to show his disdain for the idea of marrying the lady, even though it was quite the opposite of what he felt.

"I am sorry, Miss Patterson," he grated, his hands curling into fists as he forced himself to steady his resolve. "But you can receive no help from me." Shaking his head, he let his eyes drift away from her, placing an arrogant expression on his face. "After all, a gentleman does not marry their mistress."

A small cry of glee escaped from Mr. Jefferson's throat. "So, you see, Miss Patterson, you can have very little option *but* to do as I have asked," he said, as Francis slowly began to make his way towards the door, feigning disinterest. "What say you to that?"

Francis heard Miss Patterson take in a shuddering breath and felt himself curl with rage. He wanted nothing more than to throw himself at Mr. Jefferson and beat the man until he knew nothing but the welcome arms of unconsciousness, but he had to continue on with this façade. After all, that was what it was, he reminded himself. Play acting. A disguise. A falsehood that would lead to Mr. Jefferson being outsmarted and disgraced.

"Ah, Lord Rapson," he said loudly, pushing the door open to admit Miss Patterson's brother. "I'm afraid I have something to confess to you."

Mr. Jefferson swung around as Lord Rapson stepped inside, his face paling a little as he looked from one gentleman to the other.

"It seems Mr. Jefferson had stumbled upon myself and your sister in a rather…intimate embrace," Francis continued, in a somewhat apologetic tone. "I do apologize for keeping her presence here a secret, but she came to me *begging* for help and urged me not to let a single person know of her whereabouts, not even you." He saw Mr. Jefferson's mouth swing open in surprise. "I know you have been looking for her."

Lord Rapson played his part wonderfully. He let his eyes trail from Miss Patterson to Mr. Jefferson before turning dark, angry eyes onto Francis.

"Do you mean to tell me, Lord Catesby," he said, harshly. "That you have been keeping my sister here all along?"

Francis shrugged. "She has been the housekeeper," he said, truthfully.

"Amongst other things," Mr. Jefferson added at once, putting his hands firmly on his hips. "And unless you want all and sundry to know of what else your dearly loved sister has been up to, you'll hand her over to me, Rapson."

Lord Rapson started as though he had been slapped and it was only with a sharp warning look from Francis that he prevented himself from swinging around and punching Mr. Jefferson hard across the face. Closing his eyes for a moment, Lord Rapson drew in a long, calming breath before turning away from Francis and facing Mr. Jefferson.

"You've been looking for me," he said, slowly. "Why?"

Mr. Jefferson chuckled. "I am not to be outdone, Lord Rapson. I know what I want, and I intend to have it."

Lord Rapson shook his head, putting one hand to his brow. "You want money. I will give it to you."

A sneer crossed Mr. Jefferson's face. "Not enough. I want your sister's fortune – and having her as my bride, and as one of my possessions, will make me more than satisfied." His sneer spread as he looked at Lord Rapson with a hard look in his eyes, ignoring Francis completely. It was as though the man had forgotten that he was even in the room, focusing entirely on Lord Rapson.

"Else," Mr. Jefferson continued, firmly, "everyone in good standing will know of your sister's disgrace. Think of the damage that will do to your good name, to your attempts to secure a bride. Your name will be tainted, your children unable to escape the shame brought on them by *her*." He spat the last word, shooting a glance at Miss Patterson who was still standing tall.

Lord Rapson said nothing for a moment, swaying slightly. "How did you find me, Mr. Jefferson?"

Francis stepped back into the shadows, allowing the scene to play out in front of him. Mr. Jefferson had a gleam in his eye that made him think Miss Patterson had been quite correct to suggest that Mr. Jefferson had gone mad. He appeared almost crazed with the desire to have what he had long sought. He was speaking with such freedom, seemingly so unconcerned at Francis' presence in the room, that Francis felt himself grow tense. There was no certainty about what Mr. Jefferson would do once he discovered that this had all been nothing but a ruse.

Mr. Jefferson chuckled. "One of your maids is very easily persuaded, Rapson. A little bit of attention and she gave me whatever I wanted. *So* sympathetic, truly." Leaning lazily on the back of the chair, he gestured towards Miss Patterson as he spoke. "No-one knew where your sister had gone to, but I soon found out that you had been corresponding with someone of late. Took a little bit of persuading but that stupid maid soon

brought me your last piece of correspondence
with Lord Catesby." Shaking his head with a
touch of wryness about his expression, he looked
at Lord Rapson with a degree of satisfaction.
"Those maids are so easily persuaded and, as I
have said before to you, Rapson, I always get what
I want."

"And you want me."

Mr. Jefferson did not so much as glance at
Miss Patterson. "I want your fortune," he said,
with a small sneer. "You ought to have given it to
me the moment I asked for it. Your father always
promised I was to have something!"

"And you did, did you not?" Lord Rapson
interrupted, darkly. "But it was not enough."

"It is *never* enough!" Mr. Jefferson shouted, his
face suddenly going a dark, blood red. "I was to
have the title! I was to be the heir! And then
suddenly *you* reappeared!" Something flashed in
Mr. Jefferson's hand, and Francis felt his heart stop
dead. This was not something they had ever
considered.

Lord Rapson shook his head slowly. "There
was a misunderstanding, that was all, Jefferson.
News was brought to my father that I had been
taken gravely ill and, of course, a good many
people presumed I had died as often happens. It
was not the case, as you can see." Shaking his
head, Lord Rapson let out a long breath whilst

fixing his cousin with his gaze. "You have no claim to anything, Jefferson."

Mr. Jefferson looked all the more crazed. "I *need* the money, Rapson!" he shouted, clearly growing desperate. "I must have it, else —"

"Else, what?" Lord Rapson interrupted, loudly. "Your creditors will come to your door, to take away all you own? All the money you claim you require is simply due to your own lack of sense, Jefferson. Your vices, your follies, are all your own. You can try to claim my sister to seek her fortune, you can even attempt to kill me in order to gain the title — but it has all come to naught. Indeed, it will not be my sister who is disgraced but rather it will be *you*."

This appeared to be too much for Mr. Jefferson to take. Before Francis could move, he leapt wildly at Lord Rapson. It was as though it all happened slowly, for Francis could not move, could not even speak as he watched Miss Patterson let out a shriek and twist her body to prevent Mr. Jefferson from reaching her brother.

CHAPTER 12

The two bodies fell together with a thump on the carpeted floor, just as the dowager burst into the room. Francis had ordered her to remain outside with the footmen and butler ready for his order but having heard the scream from both Mr. Jefferson and Miss Patterson, had been unable to wait any longer. Francis, finally free of the ice that had filled his limbs, rushed forward with his mother towards Miss Patterson and Mr. Jefferson, who was being dragged to his feet by one furious and terrified Lord Rapson.

"Hold him," Francis ordered, as Mr. Jefferson was thrown towards the footmen and butler. He bent down by Lord Rapson, seeing a dark stain begin to seep through Miss Patterson's gown. His throat ached with fear.

"I am quite all right," Miss Patterson replied, her voice weak. "It is just my arm, that is all. Do help me sit up."

"This was not what we had intended," he whispered, as Lord Rapson tried to help his sister up carefully. "We thought to —"

"Never mind that," the dowager snapped, grasping his arm. "Help her up and seat her here." She turned to the butler, telling him to fetch the doctor at once and ordering hot water, cloths, and bandages. "Goodness me, Miss Patterson, whatever were you thinking?"

Francis, still on his knees, shuffled towards Miss Patterson, looking at her arm with concern. It was bleeding, evidently and he could not tell how deep the wound was.

Lord Rapson pulled a chair over to his sister and sat down heavily, clearly shocked by all that had gone on. He took her free hand and held it tightly, his expression tight. "You did not have to do that, Rebecca. I —"

"I could not let him hurt you," Miss Patterson interrupted, gently, as the dowager carefully pulled the torn sleeve away from Miss Patterson's arm, revealing the wound to her forearm.

Lord Rapson swallowed hard, shaking his head and raking one hand through his hair over and over as he attempted to speak. "You could have been gravely injured, Rebecca."

"But she is not," the dowager replied, practically. "You must have raised your arm in defense of your person as you jumped in front of your brother, Miss Patterson, but I do believe you saved your life by such an action." She smiled at the young lady, clearly relieved and yet upset at what had occurred. "You are quite remarkable, truly."

Francis was utterly relieved to see Miss Patterson manage a small smile, though her face was rather white. She was not going to die, it seemed, and his heart finally broke free of the terrifying worry that had torn through it the moment he had watched Miss Patterson leap in front of Mr. Jefferson's knife.

"What shall I do with him, my lord?"

Slowly, Francis got to his feet, turning to see Mr. Jefferson sitting, white-faced, in his chair. The man had appeared to shrink into it, as though only just realizing what he had done. Anger coursed through him, urging him to move forward and strike the man hard but it was only by sheer force of will that he remained exactly where he was.

"Send for the constabulary," he grated, harshly. "This man made an attempt on the life of Lord Rapson and, in doing so, has gravely injured Miss Patterson, the viscount's sister. In addition, I believe he is very badly in debt and will be wanted by a good many others."

Mr. Jefferson let out a low wail of fear, no longer the arrogant, haughty gentleman who believed he was owed everything.

"And take him below stairs and secure him tightly," Francis finished, as two footmen hauled Mr. Jefferson out of his chair. "You are to stand guard over him until he is taken away. Send the constabulary to me the moment they arrive. We all will have a good deal to say to them, I am quite sure."

Mr. Jefferson whimpered, a pathetic creature now. "Please," he whined, looking at Lord Rapson desperately. "I did not mean – surely, you cannot….it may be the gallows!"

Lord Rapson turned his head away from Mr. Jefferson, clearly disgusted by the fellow. "Take him," he muttered, as the men moved towards the door. "I have nothing more to say to you, Mr. Jefferson."

Finally, the door shut behind the offending gentleman and the occupants of the room gave a collective sigh of relief. Francis felt his legs a little weak and immediately offered them all a brandy, which was accepted, although the dowager insisted on having a tea tray also sent, despite the hour.

"This was not what we had intended, as you

know," Francis murmured, handing Miss Patterson a small brandy. "I was meant to reveal to Mr. Jefferson that this had been nothing more than a ruse. He was meant to realize that he had revealed his hand not only to me but also to my mother waiting outside. Our influence and our threats were meant to be enough to send him away and, if that had not been the case, then I would have settled his debts with his creditors and taken them on myself. That would have been enough, surely, to stop him from –"

"My lord."

Miss Patterson put her good hand on his arm, preventing him from finishing his sentence.

"You need not go over it again, my lord," she said, gently. "What happened was not what any of us expected, I will admit, but we have brought Mr. Jefferson to justice regardless." She glanced down at her bloodied arm, which the dowager was carefully cleaning. "I may have sustained an injury, but I will recover fully, in time, I am quite sure. You need not feel any guilt, my lord. I am glad it is all at an end, and I am glad that I was able to protect my brother."

Lord Rapson shook his head. "I ought to have been the one protecting you, my dear sister."

Francis, who had been unable to take his eyes from Miss Patterson, finding her both extraordinary and utterly wonderful, let out a sigh of relief that took the tension from his limbs. "You were both in danger from a very dangerous man. I know he cannot hurt either of you again and that does bring me a good deal of relief, I will admit."

Miss Patterson smiled at him, wincing just a little as the dowager dabbed at the wound. "Thank you for all you have done, Lord Catesby. I am sorry that I did not come to you from the first. Mayhap I should have done."

The dowager glanced up, her expression a little guilty. "And mayhap I ought not to have encouraged Miss Patterson not to do so, Francis. I thought you too caught up with all other manner of things."

Francis shook his head, a small smile capturing his lips. "Mama, you too need not worry. I think that it has all ended quite well, Miss Patterson's injury aside. I just pray that this may mean that you shall begin to absent yourself from my house and my study a little more?"

His mother laughed, brightening the mood all the more. "Indeed, Francis, I shall. Thank you for your understanding."

At that moment, the door opened, and the butler announced both the doctor and the constabulary had arrived. Both parties clearly willing to answer the summons of an Earl with the greatest of speed.

"I shall leave you with the good doctor,"

Francis murmured, as Lord Rapson got up to speak to the two men from the constabulary. "But I think it best if you remain at Catesby House for some time, in order to recover yourself. What say you?"

Her eyes glowed despite the pain. "You are most kind, my lord."

His smile grew slowly. "I believe we have some things to say to each other, my dear Miss Patterson. Perhaps tomorrow?"

She nodded slowly, her cheeks a little dark. "Tomorrow would suit me very well, Lord Catesby. I thank you."

EPILOGUE

Despite the urging of her brother and the dowager, Rebecca did not wish to remain in her bed for any length of time. She had slept wonderfully well, even though she had refused the doctor's suggestion of laudanum, her thoughts no longer worried over Mr. Jefferson and what he might do next.

She did not regret for a single moment her actions of last evening. She had seen the knife, seen Mr. Jefferson lunge for her brother and had reacted out of instinct. The pain of the knife slicing into her arm had taken her breath from her body, the sheer weight of Mr. Jefferson landing on her as they had fallen to the floor adding even more to her distress, but within the hour, everything had seemed to be a good deal brighter. Her arm had been cleaned and dressed, her brother and Lord Catesby had talked to the constabulary about all that had occurred, and she and the dowager had sunk back into their chairs and drank a nice hot cup of tea, finally free of it all.

"Do stop worrying, Mark," she muttered, seeing her brother hesitate in the doorway of the drawing room. "I am not an invalid. My arm is already improving. You see?" She lifted it and attempted to wave at him, only for a stab of pain to shoot through her. Wincing, she set it down gently in her lap, seeing Mark's concerned expression.

"Are you sure you are quite all right?" he asked, gently, coming to sit by her. "After last evening, I thought you might be quite overcome with exhaustion."

She smiled into his anxious face. "I feel quite free," she replied, quietly. "My heart is glad; my mind is filled with nothing but delight. I do not have to worry about Jefferson any longer. He can never come near us, never attempt to hurt either one of us ever again."

Her brother nodded, his expression a little rueful. "Indeed. Although I shall have to find out which maid it was that was so willing to tell Mr.

Jefferson such details and to go through my personal things in order to give him the information he required."

Rebecca nodded her expression a little sad. "Foolish girl. I do not believe she had any true understanding of what she was doing."

"Regardless, I will have to send her away," Mark said, firmly. "No references, nothing. I will not have such disrespect shown to me."

Understanding, Rebecca patted his shoulder gently. "I know, Mark. Now, why do you not go in search of a good book for me to read since I am supposed to be resting?"

He chuckled and got to his feet. "You really do not wish to be fussed over now, do you?"

"No," Rebecca said, sternly. "I do not. Now, off with you."

Her brother laughed and quit the room, promising to be back in a few minutes with at least four books for her to choose from. Rebecca laughed softly and closed her eyes to enjoy the peace for a moment – only for a gentle hand to touch her shoulder.

Jumping, she opened her eyes expecting to see her brother had sneaked back in to again ensure she was all right, only to see Lord Catesby looking down at her. His expression was one of tenderness, sending a flurry of warmth all through her.

"My dear lady," he murmured, quietly. "Might I sit with you for a moment?"

Her throat was suddenly dry. "But of course, Lord Catesby," she replied, in a voice that did not sound like her own. So much had changed over the last two days, so much had developed within her own heart, that she felt almost nervous to be alone with him.

Sitting down next to her, Lord Catesby glanced at her arm. "How are you this afternoon, my dear?"

Smiling at his caring expression, she looked into his eyes and found him looking back at her with a soft smile on his face. "I am doing very well, I thank you," she replied, her eyes drifting to his lips for a moment as a flush went straight through her. "You have been quite wonderful, Lord Catesby, truly."

"No." He picked up her good hand and brought it to his lips, placing a kiss to the back of it. Sparks shot through her.

"You are wonderful, Miss Patterson."

"Rebecca," she found herself saying, suddenly desperate to have such an intimacy from his lips. Lips she had already kissed a good many times. "Please, do call me Rebecca."

The delight in his eyes glowed. "Rebecca," he murmured, softly. "I did say to you last evening that I had a good many things to say to you, but now that I am with you, I find my heart filled with one single desire that eclipses all other."

Swallowing, her stomach filled with butterflies. "If it is that you wish to court me, then I will gladly accept," she replied, her voice barely audible. "I believe I have already made my affection for you more than evident."

He chuckled softly. "I believe I too have done the very same," he replied, his hand now holding hers tightly. "And yet now that you are to remain here until you have recovered, I find the idea of letting you return to your brother's home almost torture. It pains me to think of you leaving my side, not when we have experienced so very much." Smiling at her still, he drew in a breath and ran his fingers down the curve of her cheek, forcing her to catch her breath. "I would rather it, Rebecca, that you would never leave."

Her heart burst from her chest, soaring towards the skies. It was as though, with the departure of Mr. Jefferson from her life, that she could finally see what it was that she wanted, what it was she desired. This gentleman here, the one who had clearly loved her for so long despite his determination not to do so, was becoming more and more to her with each passing minute. Her emotions were stirred every time he came into the room, every time his lips pressed to hers. She did not want to leave, she realized, but that would mean....

"I would have you as my wife, Rebecca," Lord Catesby finished, quietly. "If you wish it, you can reside with my mother until the time passes for your fortune to become your own. I know that is important to you and I would never ask you to wed me before that time."

She shook her head immediately, and the light faded from his eyes. He thought she was refusing him when the opposite was quite true. "My dear Lord Catesby," she replied, leaning a little closer to him. "My fortune matters not. It is no longer what I think of, no longer what I fear I must protect. My heart has begun to call for you. You asked me to trust you, and that is what I am doing. I know you will treat me with all kindness, with all care, and therefore my fortune matters not a jot."

His eyes widened for a moment before his lips tugged into a smile. "Does that mean, then, that you will marry me, Rebecca?" he asked, hope filling his expression. "Will you be my bride? My heart has been filled with none but you since the first day I saw you. No longer do I have to hide my heart and ignore my feelings. They are all for you, my dear lady. I love you with every part of my being."

Wishing she could fling herself into his arms,

Rebecca contented herself with pressing his hand tightly with her own. "I love you in return, Lord Catesby. I will be your bride. I will be your wife. And I will love you every day of my life."

BOOK 7: THE SCANDALOUS DOWAGER COUNTESS

BOOK 7

HOUSE OF CATESBY

The Scandalous Dowager Countess

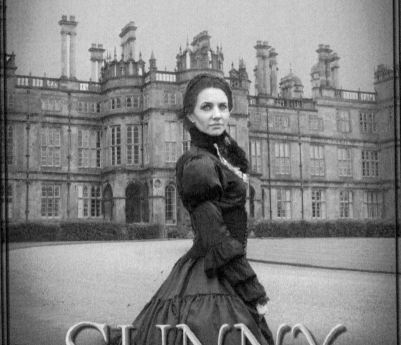

SUNNY BROOKS

FOREWORD

Never let it be said that the young have all the fun.
Let's embrace life at every age, after every setback,
during every chapter of our lives!

Live your best life and know that you deserve to
be happy and loved.

From my heart to yours!

- Sunny Brooks

CHAPTER 1

Lady Margaret Catesby, wife to the late Earl Catesby, looked around with a satisfactory air. She was to go to London and, having spent the last six years in this quite wonderful and yet often lonely house, she was looking forward to a little more excitement.

"Mama," her daughter, Emily, said in a slightly unconvinced tone. "Are you quite sure about all of this?" She frowned at her mother's smile, clearly not as delighted as she that Margaret was to go to town.

"Yes, yes, I am quite certain," Margaret replied, patting her daughter's shoulder. "Believe me, each of my children in turn has done their best to convince me that I ought to remain here in the dower house, but I feel as though I deserve a little more enjoyment from life." Seeing Emily's startled look, Margaret regretted her quick words. "That is not to say that I do not greatly enjoy your visits, Emily, dear, and especially now that you have such a beautiful son of your own, but almost everyone else is so very far away." She smiled sadly, hoping that her daughter would understand.

"Francis and Henry do not live more than a few miles from here!" Emily protested at once. "You cannot mean to tell me that you live too far for you to visit whenever you wish?!"

Margaret laughed, knowing that Emily was quite right. "No, indeed, that is not at all what I am suggesting. However, what I am trying to say is…" Sighing, she took her daughter's hand, knowing that she would have to be truthful. "My dear girl, when one's children marry, then it is quite right for their lives to move on in a very different way from one's own. I know that I am always welcome to see Francis and Rebecca, and indeed, to call upon Henry and Laurie, but I am also keenly aware that they all require the space and time to enjoy their own lives together. It would not do for me to intrude too much, although I know they are all most generous in their willingness to see me at any time and for however long I wish it." She smiled, seeing Emily's shoulders soften, a sign that she was beginning to understand. "Besides, almost everyone is with child—or has just had a baby! That is a great adjustment, although I will be glad to visit you when your time comes."

Emily flushed bright red, her eyes widening as she stared at her mother. "How did you know?"

Margaret laughed. "Because, my dear girl, I have borne six children and am well aware of how one looks and feels near the very beginning. I have not seen you this pale and tired since you were first told you were carrying Joseph." She was referring to Emily and Thomas' son and heir who, at almost four years of age, was precocious and utterly charming. Thomas had taken him outside to the gardens for a time, so that Emily and Margaret might have a chance to talk, although Margaret was still suspicious that Emily was trying to convince her to remain at home.

"You are very insightful, Mama," Emily admitted with a small sigh. "The truth is, I have been feeling quite terrible these last few weeks, although I have had a ravenous hunger."

Margaret lifted an eyebrow. "I felt the very same way when I was carrying your brothers." She saw Emily's face pale but patted her hand gently. "There is always the chance of twins, my dear girl, but it is nothing to fear. As I said, regardless of whether it is one babe or two, I shall be with you should you need me, just as I have been for everyone else thus far." A small smile crept over her face as she recollected just how many brows she had mopped, how many hands she had held, and how many baby cries she had wept over. She now had six grandchildren, starting with Joseph, who had been swiftly followed by Matthew, the son of Charles and Abigail. Thereafter had come the birth of Hugh, son to Helena and Richard. Charles and Abigail had then delighted her further with a daughter of their own, whom they had named after Margaret. Sophie and David had been blessed with twins, Sarah and William, and now both Laurie and Rebecca were soon to go into confinement. It appeared that Emily would not long be behind them.

It was all so very wonderful, and yet Margaret had been unable to remove from herself the desire to return to London, to reacquaint herself with some of her old friends. For so many years of her life, her time had been entirely taken up with her children and her husband, whereas now she had time to do whatever she wished. Of course, her children and grandchildren were a joy and a delight to her almost constantly, but that still did not take away from the small stab of loneliness that would attack her most evenings—a loneliness that seemed to be growing steadily.

"Very well, Mama," Emily said with a sigh, breaking through Margaret's thoughts. "If you must go to London, then I see that I shall not be able to prevent you."

Margaret chuckled, patting her daughter's hand. "You have learned of your mother's stubbornness very quickly, I see. I promise I shall not be long in town. A month or two, and then I shall return home." She smiled as her daughter frowned, evidently thinking that two months was much too long for Margaret to be away. "Laurie and Rebecca may need me then."

Emily nodded, although she said nothing more by way of trying to convince Margaret to change her mind. "When do you leave?"

"Tomorrow," Margaret replied, looking about her bedchamber and finding things to be quite satisfactory. "The maids have packed everything I will require and Francis has been very kind in allowing me to stay in the townhouse there."

Emily snorted in a most unladylike fashion. "*Allowing* you, Mama? It is your townhouse as much as his, which he is well aware of. Although I hardly think he agreed to it so easily, given that he is not entirely content with you leaving."

Margaret laughed, rose to her feet, and walked to the door. "Indeed, he was not. However, your brother knows me well enough to understand that I will not allow my mind to be altered by mere pleas."

"Just as I have learned," Emily mumbled

darkly, taking her mother's arm. "Well, then, shall we take tea together since I shall not see you for some time?"

"Of course," Margaret replied warmly, thinking that she would dearly like to talk of other things instead of her trip to London. "And I must remember to promise Joseph that I will bring something wonderful back for him from London. What do you think he would like?"

Managing to successfully move Emily onto another topic of conversation, Margaret let out a small sigh of relief as Emily began to come up with suggestions of what Margaret might buy for her grandson. This trip to London seemed to have caused more trouble than it was worth, given that each and every one of her children did not seem to want her to go.

But, then again, they could not understand what it was like to lose one's husband, to feel the world you had known and come to love now crashing down around your feet. They could not understand the loneliness and pain that came with a life lived alone, instead of a life shared with someone else, and for that, she did not begrudge them.

Six years, she thought to herself, as she walked towards the drawing room with Emily still chatting by her side. *Six years I have been without him.*

Six years since he left for a place I cannot yet follow him to.
Six years of living alone.

Silently, Margaret wondered if that would ever change, or if this was the life she was destined to lead for the rest of her days here on this earth.

CHAPTER 2

Heading towards London seemed to bring Margaret nothing but painful memories, which was something she had not expected. Having spent a good deal of time in London over the course of her life, she had not expected this trip to become something more agonizing than enjoyable.

She could remember all the times she had joined her husband and children in their carriage —although they had required to take two of them in later years—as they had driven towards London for the Season. She could even remember being in London as a debutante herself, never once thinking that she would be wed by the end of it.

A stab of pain brought both a small smile to

her face and a tear to her eye. She had been so young to marry, only just out and enjoying her first Season at the tender age of seventeen, never thinking that she would find herself a suitable husband during her first year. The second year, her mother had reassured her, would be much more likely. She was simply to enjoy herself that first year. She was to make acquaintances, dance, converse and spend as much time as she could savoring every single indulgence.

And then, her father had introduced her to Joseph, the new Earl Catesby.

Even now, the memory of their first meeting had never left her. He had appeared so severe, his thick, dark eyebrows burrowing over his eyes, his mouth set into a thin line as he had surveyed her. She had disliked him intensely, comparing him to Lord Blackford, who had been showing her a particular interest of late, and finding Earl Catesby to be falling quite short. It did not help matters that the earl appeared to be a good deal older than she, and that he seemed quiet, gruff and quite stern in his character. She later learned, through conversation with her acquaintances, that the earl did not often make an appearance in London and certainly had not ever sought an introduction to a debutante. Everyone had thought that he found London society to be as dull and staid as they found him, but now that he had been given the title, perhaps, they had considered, he realized that he now needed a wife and a child whom he might make his heir.

Margaret had prayed that she would not be sought out to be his bride.

But it had not been her choice to make. Within a fortnight, she had discovered herself to be betrothed to Earl Catesby, even though she did not know him at all. They had been introduced, and had conversed on only two prior occasions, but apparently that had been enough for the earl. Her father had been delighted with the match, her mother singing the earl's praises, whilst Margaret had withered silently within. Lord Blackford had stated his congratulations with a look of sadness in his eyes, and she had wanted desperately to explain that it had not been her choice but that of her parents, but nothing had come to her lips.

And so, within the month, she had been married. The earl had not said a good deal to her on their wedding day, although he had been kind and gentle during his visit to her bed. What a shock it had been to discover she was soon expecting a child! She had felt almost a child herself, hardly prepared to be both a wife and mother—and yet the babe had arrived a month before her eighteenth birthday.

From that day on, Joseph had changed from a gruff, severe gentleman into a man she barely recognized. It was as though holding the child in his arms had made him soften completely, breaking apart the hard, coarse shell that he had built up around him. He had become tender in his affections, to the point that Margaret had found herself falling in love with him and he with her. The difference in ages between them—a matter of almost sixteen years—no longer seemed to hold any particular importance. She had loved him for the man he was.

And thus arrived the rest of their children, with Francis as the eldest, followed by Emily, then the twins, Charles and Henry, Sophia and finally, Helena. She had birthed six children in eight years, which meant that by the age of six and twenty, she had well established her husband's household. With each child, Joseph had become even more loving, even more compassionate and caring, spending as much time as he could with his children and refusing to send them to boarding school at seven years of age, insisting that a tutor would do for his children until they were older.

He had been proven correct. Francis has grown up to be wise, kind and considerate, much like his father, and was doing marvelously well as the new Earl Catesby. Margaret was quite sure that his father's influence was the reason for Francis' good heart, just as she believed was the case for the rest of her children.

She could see Joseph's influence everywhere, making her miss him almost every day that passed. It had been six years since he had died, leaving her alone in the world with six unmarried children—the youngest of them not yet eighteen —and all the grief and pain that came with losing the husband she had loved so very dearly.

But now, that grief had loosened its grip on the house of Catesby. Every single one of her children had married, finding love and affection with their chosen partners, and she could not have been more contented for each of them. The children borne thus far brought her so much joy that, at times, she could barely contain her happiness, but still underneath it all, had been a yearning for a life of her own.

The dower house was warm and comfortable, but it did not have the companionship that she had always found in Joseph. It was not, of course, that she was going to London in the hope of finding herself another husband, which, at the age of almost one and fifty, was quite ridiculous, but more that she hoped she might find good company there. Perhaps some of her old acquaintances might have returned for the Season, possibly with children of their own whom they would need to accompany, which would give Margaret the opportunity to reacquaint herself with them all. Mayhap, in time, they would come to visit her, perhaps with a few having an extended stay at the dower house. That was the hope, at least.

Margaret smiled to herself, her head resting back against the squabs as the driver called to her that they were only a few hours away from London. The last three days of travelling had wearied her but she was looking forward to being in town again. How much would have changed? Would anyone be there who might remember her?

A quiet laugh escaped her as she closed her eyes. Her son, Charles, his wife, Abigail, and their two children, Matthew and baby Margaret, also resided in London and she was quite sure that she would often be invited to spend time in their home —most likely so that Charles could report back to his siblings on how their mother was doing, although Margaret did not intend to give all that much away. This was to be her time and she did not feel the need to share the details of what she did with anyone, least of all, her son!

"Stop there!"

A gasp ripped from Margaret's mouth as the carriage suddenly came to a shuddering stop. The sound of horses' hooves caught her ears, making her press her hand against her heart as she realized what was happening.

"Open that door!"

Margaret wanted to scream, looking out of

the window and seeing a figure dressed all in black, sitting astride a black stallion. He had a grey neckcloth tied over his face so that only his sharp, dark eyes could be seen.

"No, I cannot!" the driver shouted, refusing to leave his seat. "That be my mistress and you will not touch her!"

The horseman waved his pistol menacingly. "Would you prefer to be shot or shall I run you through?"

Knowing that it was not just her driver who was at risk of losing his life, but the other servants who accompanied her, including the maid who was still sound asleep in the opposite corner of the carriage, Margaret held her breath. She did not want anyone to be hurt but the way this fellow was talking, she feared that she soon might have an injured—if not dead—servant on her hands.

"That is quite enough."

Throwing open the carriage door, Margaret summoned all her courage and rose to her feet, looking at the man directly. "You will not harm anyone here."

The man dressed all in black looked back at her with an almost baleful gaze. "If you give me what I wish, then I have no need to harm anyone."

Margaret shook her head, growing angry despite her fear. "None of what I own is yours to take," she said clearly, despite the urgent whispering of her maid behind her, who had apparently woken up on hearing Margaret's loud voice. "You are attempting to rob me."

The man chuckled darkly, sending a tremor through Margaret's body. "Some of us must make a living in any way we can, my lady," he said, with a small inclination of his head. "I apologize for the interruption to your journey, but for me, it is quite necessary."

She glared at him. "What is it you want, sir?"

He shrugged. "I do not mind particularly. Whatever it is of value that you can give me, my lady. Gold, coins, jewels." He examined her with a calculating eye. "That necklace you wear, and mayhap the ring on your finger. That would be enough to secure you safe passage."

Anger burned in her chest. "No," she replied, her heart suddenly beating wildly. "I will not give you my ring, but my pendant you may have without question."

A ripple of harsh laughter wafted towards her. "You cannot believe that you are able to bargain with me, my lady."

"I will not give you my ring," she repeated, without wavering. "I have gold, coins and jewels as you can see here." She lifted her pendant from her throat as it sparkled in the sunshine. "But the ring is mine."

The man slid from his horse, his pistol held loosely in one hand.

"I think, my dear lady," he said, his voice now somewhat quiet and gentle, as though he were speaking to a friend, "that I shall have to take your ring, given that it is so very precious to you." He tipped his head, his dark eyes sending a shudder through her. "It must be priceless if you cling onto it so, although, of course, I will take the rest." He held out his hand and she, somewhat unwillingly, gave him her ruby pendant and the small reticule she had in the carriage.

"The ring," he demanded, holding out his hand. "At once."

Despite the fear clamoring in her heart at his nearness, Margaret lifted her chin and looked him steadily in the eye. "This ring will not bring you any great price," she stated with as much conviction as she could. "It is not the worth of it that matters, sir. It is my wedding ring. The one my late husband gave to me on the day I became his wife."

The fellow snorted, evidently refusing to believe her.

"I will not take it off, nor will I give it to you," she continued, ignoring him. "The only way you will have it is if you pry it from my cold, dead fingers."

The man's eyes narrowed, and Margaret

wished she could see his expression for she could not guess what he was thinking. Her spirit threatened to wilt within her but she remained strong with an effort, silently praying that he would give her a reprieve.

"What is your name?" the man asked after a moment, his head tilting slightly as though he might see her better.

"Lady Catesby," she replied, wondering what difference it would make if he knew her name. "My husband was the late Earl Catesby. This ring was his gift and, for the love of him and for the dear memories I have of him, I will not give it to you."

Silence fell. It was as though every living thing was waiting to see what would happen next, although Margaret was quite sure the man could hear the frantic beating of her heart.

Then, much to her astonishment, the man turned away. Walking back towards his horse, he thrust the jewels into one of the saddle bags and then mounted his horse. With a jaunty tip of his hand, he turned the horse around and rode away, leaving her standing, utterly shocked, as she watched him disappear down the road.

CHAPTER 3

Margaret was nervous.

Returning to London had been a good deal more trying than she had expected. First of all, she had been held up by the scoundrel on the black horse, who had taken her reticule and her ruby pendant, although, at least, he had not insisted upon taking her ring also. Thereafter, she had only just settled herself in her town house when Charles had called upon her, although he had not taken Abigail and his children with him. She had been forced to recount what had occurred and Charles had been quite horrified, especially when she had told him that the stranger had asked for her name. He had been quite certain that, in doing so, she had managed to bring down a good deal more trouble on her head, for what was to stop the fellow from finding her in London and robbing from her again? He had tried to insist that she come and live with them all, but Margaret had refused, thinking Charles a little too dramatic. She lived here with her staff, did she not? And the butler was not about to let in any man from the street, simply because he claimed an acquaintance with her, surely? She had managed to convince Charles that she was quite all right and could very easily be left alone, and, eventually, her son had relented, although he had made her promise she would join them for dinner two days hence. It had been Margaret's joy to accept, for she had been very much looking forward to seeing Abigail and the children again.

After a restful night, she had received her first invitation, which was quite remarkable given that not many knew she was in London. She had opened it to discover that she was invited to a small gathering at Lord and Lady Drake's home, which Margaret was quite sure would involve cards, songs and other delightful forms of entertainment. It was the first event she had attended in some time and therefore spent a good many hours ensuring that she looked quite the part.

Her lady's maid had done quite well, but even though she knew that her gown was fine and her hair done wonderfully—albeit more liberally streaked with white than she liked—her stomach was twisting itself in knots as the carriage began to approach the Drakes' home. Lady Drake had been Miss Heatherstone, from what she remembered, and had been enjoying her second year in society. She had become engaged to Viscount Drake whilst Margaret had been getting her head around the fact that she was to become a countess, and that was the last time they had been in one another's company, although Margaret had written to her from time to time. It was kind of Lady Drake to invite Margaret to her little soiree, though Margaret was still rather unsure as to how the lady knew she was in town.

"Here we are, my lady."

The footman opened the carriage door and held out his hand towards her, which Margaret grasped quickly, feeling the need to steady herself. Was she truly this anxious about returning to the society that she had once loved? She felt almost like she had stepped back into her debutante days, when she struggled with both a growing excitement and a nervous fear. What if she said something out of turn? What if she did not recognize someone who knew her? What would the *beau monde* think of her then?

"Thank you," she murmured as the footman closed the carriage door behind her. Taking in a deep breath, she pressed one hand lightly against her stomach as she walked towards the house, wishing she did not feel as nervous as she did. She was no longer a debutante, she was almost to be esteemed by those young ladies given her age and experience, but that thought did not bring her any sort of relief. Suddenly, she became more aware of her aloneness than she was before, her heart aching over the lack of her husband's arm offered to her. Joseph was not here with her. He never would be again.

Tears sprang to her eyes as she climbed the stone steps, forcing herself to blink them back rapidly as she put a bright smile on her face. It would not do to break into weeping at this very moment, for she would surely have to mention her late husband a good many times over the course of this evening. Many would express their sympathy and pass on their condolences at her sad loss and she could not allow herself to lose her composure.

"My dear Lady Catesby!"

Lady Drake, older yet still quite recognizable, had evidently been waiting for Margaret's arrival, for she greeted Margaret with such warmth and fervor that Margaret immediately felt her spirits lift.

"Lady Drake," she began, as her old friend clasped Margaret's hands. "It is very kind of you to invite me."

"Oh, please, you need not thank me!" Lady Drake exclaimed, her once blonde hair now white, although her blue eyes were still as alive as ever. "You cannot know how glad I was to hear of your return to London." She smiled at Margaret's questioning look. "My husband is acquainted with your son and they often meet in Whites. That is how I discovered it."

Margaret smiled. "I see," she replied, truly glad over this lovely welcome. "I confess that I was a little anxious about returning to London, but I do hope it will be a wonderful few weeks."

Lady Drake nodded understandingly. "It can be difficult to return when one is no longer a debutante!" she replied with a quick smile. "But it is also quite delightful. The debutantes for this Season are quite lovely, and it is interesting to see who might court whom. Already there have been whispers about possible matches!"

Margaret did not find this particularly interesting but did not want to say so.

"Of course, there are a good many of our acquaintances from our debutante days here now," Lady Drake continued, as a few more guests gathered to wait behind Margaret so that they might greet their host and hostess. "Most with their own daughters, you understand, but I am quite sure you will recognize a few. You will not be without friends tonight, my dear Lady Catesby."

"No, I think not," Margaret replied, feeling a good deal more reassurance. "Thank you, Lady Drake. I shall leave you to your other guests now, of course."

"Until later." Lady Drake pressed Margaret's hands, bestowed on her another smile and left her to greet Lord Drake before Margaret removed to the drawing room.

The house was large and the drawing room itself wonderfully ornate. There were at least twenty-five other guests there already, spread out across the room in small groups that were caught up in conversation and evident merriment. Margaret did not immediately recognize anyone, despite Lady Drake's promises, and so wandered slowly towards a quieter corner of the room, allowing herself to slide in amongst the shadows and nestle there. The darkness covered her quite well as she let her gaze rove over the other guests.

"That is Lady Johnston," she murmured to herself, recognizing someone she knew. "And I would think that to be Lord Mulford."

"And you would find yourself quite correct in that," said a voice nearby, making Margaret jump violently. A flush hit her cheeks as she kept her eyes away from the gentleman who had spoken so quietly, his figure hidden in the dark next to her. She had not realized that anyone was nearby, else she would not have spoken aloud.

"Forgive me, you must think me terribly rude to be eavesdropping," the voice continued quickly. "It is just that you came to join me here first, although I do not think you saw me hiding here."

"No, sir," she agreed, still not looking at him. "No, I did not."

The man chuckled softly but Margaret did not react. "That does not matter. My apology still stands. I ought not to have overheard, or if I did, I ought not to have commented."

"Not if we are not acquainted, sir, then no," she stated, lifting her chin and praying that the gentleman would not see her as a willing widow, as she knew was the reputation of many rich widows here in London. She was not about to chase after any gentleman's affections, physical or otherwise, for that was not her intention in coming to London. "And I do not recall ever being introduced." Shooting him a quick glance from under her brow, she took the gentleman in, a little surprised that he was older than she had expected. He had a strong jaw, however, with broad shoulders that showed no sign of bowing, and was a good head taller than she. His eyes were alive with good humor, although she could not make out their color as they stood together in the shadows. His face was not heavily lined, although his hair was somewhat grey and a little thinning near the temples. For a moment, Margaret had the impression that she had been wrong to state that they were not already acquainted, believing that they did know one another, but then the thought was pushed away as the man smiled at her. No, she did not know him.

"You are quite right," the gentleman said eventually with a small smile as she turned her head away. "You must inform me of at least one name here that might introduce us properly, for I fully intend to make your acquaintance before the evening is over."

Margaret arched an eyebrow, a little unused to the gentleman's almost flirtatious way of speaking, and certainly very surprised at the compliment. At her age, she had not expected to ever receive such compliments again and was a little unsure as to whether or not she appreciated such things.

"You must be acquainted with our host, that I can be certain of," the gentleman continued when she did not reply, smiling at her when she glanced over her shoulder at him. "But surely you must know a few others here, unless you are hiding in the shadows because you do *not* know many at all and must be introduced?" The sly note in his voice sent a wave of heat all through her, starting from her toes and making its way up to her cheeks. It was not from embarrassment nor a reaction to his voice, but rather it came from anger. Anger that he was attempting to persuade her to find a way to have her introduced to him, when she had not made any such suggestions. It was as though he expected her to want to become acquainted with him without ever considering that she was doing quite well without his company. Besides which, suggesting that she was somehow afraid of being introduced, or was worried that she would be lonely and without company, was a suggestion she could not quite accept in good humor—most likely because there was an iota of truth in his words and she was not inclined towards revealing that to anyone.

"If you will excuse me, sir," she murmured, aware that her face was burning and praying that, as she stepped back into the crowd of guests, no one would be aware of it.

"Pray, wait!" the gentleman exclaimed, moving quickly towards her. "We must be introduced!"

Margaret spun on her heel to face him, lifting her chin and pinning the gentleman with a fierce, unrelenting gaze. She was not inclined towards this fellow at all, whether he wished to be acquainted with her or not. His manner was leaning towards rudeness, his flirtations unwelcome and his urge to become introduced doing nothing more than pushing her away.

"I think, sir, that there is no great need for us to be introduced at all," she stated, finding the courage she needed to speak to him quite plainly. She was no debutante and did not need to find herself a husband, so she did not need to be terribly careful over what she said and how she spoke. She was quite able to speak her mind and was inclined to do just that. "I have a good many acquaintances here already." Seeing a twinkle in his eye only sent another burst of anger shooting through her heart. "I was taking a moment, that was all. You need not think that I am some poor, lonely creature who requires your help, for I assure you that I need no such thing." Seeing the gleam fade from his eyes sent a swirl of warmth through her, allowing her a small sense of triumph. "Now, *if* you will excuse me, I must go speak to Lady Crawford." Choosing not to curtsy nor show any sign of deference or respect, Margaret made her way through the throng of guests and left the rather rude gentleman behind her, aware that his eyes were fixed to her back as she walked away. He had not expected her to speak so, she was quite sure, but that did not matter to her. There came such a sense of freedom in being the older widow that she found herself quite reveling in it, a smile nipping at the corners of her mouth as she made her way towards Lady Crawford.

Lady Crawford, at least, knew at once who Margaret was, for they had been reacquainted only a few years ago, when Margaret had last been in London with one or two of her daughters. She was somewhat thicker than Margaret remembered her, although her smile was almost jolly as she greeted Margaret. The lady's rounded cheeks were bright red, her eyes sparkling with the delight of being part of London society once more. Margaret recalled just how much Lady Crawford enjoyed being in town, often complaining bitterly to Margaret that it was much too short a time for her liking and bemoaning the fact that she would soon have to return to her husband's estate in Cheshire.

Margaret had never felt the same way, although it was quite obvious to her that Lady Crawford was in raptures at being back in town, which did make Margaret smile.

"Oh my! Lady Catesby! How wonderful to see you!" Lady Crawford grasped Margaret's hands tightly. "I am truly delighted." She smiled broadly as Margaret murmured something in the same vein. "Are you here in town with your children?"

Margaret shook her head. "No, I am not, although Charles is here in town with his family, of course." Seeing Lady Crawford's interest, she smiled hesitantly and tried to explain herself. "I thought to come to London to reacquaint myself with my friends and to have a few weeks of enjoyment," she clarified as Lady Crawford nodded excitedly. "I have so many wonderful things at home, of course, but I do miss my old friends, such as you, Lady Crawford."

"And I have missed you also," Lady Crawford said emphatically, catching Margaret's hand and pressing it again. "My goodness, it seems an age since we were debutantes ourselves here in London!"

Having only been vaguely aware of Lady Crawford—or Miss Merriweather, as she had been at the time—during Margaret's debutante days, Margaret could only smile and nod, knowing that she and Lady Crawford had become friends during the years that had followed their marriages. "And yet here we are again," she murmured with a small smile as she looked out at the other guests.

Lady Crawford leaned in conspiratorially. "You are not here to find yourself another husband, are you?" Seeing Margaret's shocked look, she giggled as though she were a schoolgirl and not an older lady of quality. "A gentleman caller or two, then?" she asked, making Margaret catch her breath with horror. "You think me rude to speak so plainly, but you would not be the first widow to come to London in search of such things. And given who you were speaking with, I cannot think that—"

"I have been speaking to no one save our host and hostess!" Margaret exclaimed, looking around quickly to ensure that no one had overheard Lady Crawford speak. "Goodness me, Edith, you must ensure not to speak so."

Lady Crawford, who had long ago encouraged Margaret to call her by her Christian name, such was the depth of their friendship, laughed again and patted her friend's arm. "You need not worry, no one will think the worse of you for conversing with that fellow. He is almost always here in London during the Season, although he has never taken an interest in anyone in particular, I must say. No, he has never married but does tend to ensure he knows and is acquainted with almost every single lady here in London! Right from the very youngest debutante to the oldest, most refined lady of quality." She smiled, the corner of her eyes crinkling. "He is, of course, much too flirtatious for my liking, although I can understand why *some* of our set find him so charming." Her lips quirked. "It is not often that a lady of our years is engaged in flirtatious conversation!"

Slowly, Margaret realized who Lady Crawford was talking about. "The gentleman you saw me talking to is a gentleman I am not acquainted with," she confessed as Lady Crawford chuckled. "I was informing him of such a thing and that was all that was said."

"Oh, but you *are* acquainted with him!" Lady Crawford protested with a gleam of mischief in her eye. "Although I must say, I am very surprised that you do not know him, given that he has almost always been here in London during the summer months. But, then again, you were always very much inclined to focus all your attentions on your daughters and that is quite understandable."

Growing a little frustrated with Lady Crawford's evasiveness, Margaret closed her eyes and settled her inner irritation. "Edith," she said evenly, "who is he?"

Lady Crawford grinned as Margaret opened her eyes. "You do not remember him, Margaret? Why, that is the gentleman whose heart you broke into pieces the day you became engaged to Lord Catesby."

Margaret felt shock ripple through her, her face going pale as ice began to form down her spine, sending shivers across her skin. "That cannot be."

"But it is," Lady Crawford insisted, evidently enjoying herself enormously. "That is Lord

Percival Blackford." She eyed Margaret for another moment, her smile still spreading. "So, you see, my dear friend, you *are*, in fact, already acquainted with him. And I do not think that he has ever been able to forget you."

CHAPTER 4

O ver the course of the following week, Margaret had done all she could to avoid conversing or even meeting Lord Blackford again. Lady Crawford's explanation of who the gentleman was had quite shocked her and she had been unable to compose herself fully for some minutes that night, but thereafter she had become quite determined to ignore the fellow completely. She did not like Lady Crawford's comment that Lord Blackford had been unable to forget Margaret, nor did she think it wise to seek out an acquaintance with him, for he was not at all the sort of gentleman she wished to consider a friend. He was much too flirtatious, she had decided. Much too easy in his manner, much too confident. She did not like the way he had spoken to her.

And yet, she had been quite unable to forget him. Every time she had gone to a ball, a soiree or even a walk in the park, Margaret had found herself always on her guard, her eyes searching for any sign of him. It was as if, in trying to avoid him and thereby evade any further introductions, she was placing him firmly in her thoughts.

How very different he was to Joseph. He was, of course, a good deal younger than Joseph would have been, had he still lived, for from what she could remember, Lord Blackford was only a few years older than she, whereas Joseph had been close to sixteen years older. Not that such a difference in years had mattered to her, for she had loved him completely regardless.

Her eyes began to burn. She did not like having her heart and mind filled with another man, even though her heart was anxious rather than eager to see Lord Blackford again. She had always had Joseph settled there, although she did not think of him as often as she once had, putting that down to the fact that she was so caught up with her children and grandchildren, who brought her such joy that she could not linger on her grief.

And yet, now, she was struggling to think of anything else.

"You are being quite ridiculous," she told her

reflection, surveying herself with slightly narrowed eyes. She had never considered herself beautiful, although she was glad that her grey eyes were still bright and not dull, as she had feared might come with age. Her hair was long and thick, which meant that the maid had no trouble in putting it into a most respectable yet fashionable style, although Margaret did, on occasion, mourn the loss of her light brown tresses which Joseph had always found so wonderful. She was not grey there, for her hair had decided to turn white, albeit very slowly. At the same time, Margaret considered, it did give her an appearance of respectability for, as Lady Crawford had suggested the last time they had taken tea together, it was now their role to appear as proper and as refined as they could, for the sake of the young debutantes who would be looking towards them for guidance. Margaret had not quite believed her, only for Lady Crawford to point out just how many young ladies were watching them both as they conversed at the ball thrown by Lord Hastings only two days ago. Margaret had realized then that Lady Crawford knew a great deal more about society than she did, feeling almost a little lost as she attempted to make her way through the *beau monde*.

At least society is still inclined towards the theatre, she thought to herself, rising to her feet and making her way towards the door in preparation for Lady Crawford's arrival. *I will not have to worry about Lord Blackford there, at least!*

Lord Blackford, regardless of whether or not he would be at the theatre, would not be able to attempt to speak to her, nor would she have to avoid him. Her only danger would be during the intermission, when there was the opportunity for conversation and the like. She would have to make sure that she was quite caught up with someone else, even if it was Lady Crawford herself. Lady Crawford had been very good at ensuring Margaret had been introduced—or, sometimes, reacquainted—with other members of the *ton*, although she had insisted that Margaret always tell the story of the thief that had stopped the carriage as she had come into London. Margaret had wanted to forget it entirely but had not yet been able to, given just how much delight Lady Crawford seemed to gain each and every time Margaret told the story.

"My lady?"

Margaret turned to the butler, who had just now come into the room. "Yes? Is Lady Crawford here?"

"She sends her apologies."

An unfamiliar voice filled the room, as the butler was forced to step out of the way of a gentleman who walked directly into the room without being invited.

"She has asked me to accompany you to the theatre tonight, in her place."

Margaret's stomach tightened, looking into the face of the one man she had been trying to avoid. What had Lady Crawford done?

"Lord Blackford," she stated coolly.

Chuckling, he bowed deeply. "I see that you have recalled me at last," he declared, making her flush with embarrassment. "Although we have not yet been formally reintroduced, which I must beg your pardon for."

She lifted her chin, no smile on her lips. "Pray, what is wrong with Lady Crawford? And why was I not informed of it?"

He smiled, the lines by his eyes thickening for just a moment. "I was visiting with Lord Crawford," he began to explain, spreading his hands as though to evidence his innocence in all of this. "His estate is but a few miles away from my own and we have been discussing the merits of crop rotation—but I digress." Clearing his throat, he put his hands behind his back and smiled at her. "Lady Crawford happened upon us, for she had been in search of her husband to inform him that she was not feeling quite the thing and was, therefore, worried about what she ought to do as regards the theatre this evening. I queried what she meant and she informed me that she was to come for you this evening so that you might enjoy a little Shakespeare together." His eyes twinkled, although Margaret felt nothing but irritation. "Naturally, I could not help but offer my assistance, given just how troubled she was. I did not want her to make herself any more unwell and therefore insisted that she remain at home to rest and allow me to accompany you." He shrugged, as though this was all the explanation she would need. "And so, here I am, Lady Catesby."

She struggled to think of an adequate response, finding the idea of going to the theatre with Lord Blackford to be most unwelcome. "I do not want to trouble you, Lord Blackford. I am quite content to remain at home this evening."

"But I am not," Lord Blackford countered easily. "I do so like a little Shakespeare and Lady Crawford informs me that it is something of a favorite of yours." He took a few steps towards her, his eyes now a little pleading. "You need not remain at home just because Lady Crawford is unwell."

"It would not be seemly," she replied, knowing that a good many rumors might begin from such a thing. "I could not."

To her surprise, Lord Blackford laughed, although it was not cruel by any means. "My dear

Lady Catesby, have you not yet learned that society does not consider widows in the same way that it considers debutantes? You need not worry about your reputation or such things over a simple trip to the theatre! No one will think the less of you for it."

Margaret shook her head. "Regardless, *I* would not feel at ease."

Lord Blackford was incredibly persistent. "And why is that?" he asked, his voice dropping to a more gentle tone. "Am I truly that terrible, Lady Catesby?" Seeing her faint blush, he nodded as though he knew precisely what was going on in her thoughts. "Yes, I have been aware that you have been doing all you can to avoid me, Lady Catesby. Why is that, might I ask? Did I make such an unfavourable impression upon you that you cannot bear to speak to me?"

Refusing to be cowed by such questions, Margaret looked back at Lord Blackford without malice or embarrassment. "Indeed," she said plainly. "I found you rather forward, Lord Blackford."

This did not seem to insult him. "Yes, I think that I am," he agreed. "That is why you find me here, seeking to accompany you to the theatre, instead of leaving you to spend the evening at home, in your own company. Perhaps a better gentleman than me would have stayed away, would not have offered his help, given just how obvious your dislike of me is, but I am not that way inclined."

Something stabbed at her heart. Was it guilt? "I do not dislike you, Lord Blackford," she replied slowly, wondering if she was, in fact, being a little unfair towards him. "It is more that I am uncertain as to whether such a connection would be beneficial. I am not, in any way, seeking a courtship nor an agreement from any gentleman here in town." She felt heat climb up her spine and crawl into her face, but she did not allow her gaze to drop from his. He had to know precisely what it was she was saying.

Lord Blackford inclined his head. "I quite understand," he said quietly, his eyes slowly lifting back to hers. "I apologize, Lady Catesby, if I was overly familiar the first time we met. I confess that I recognized you almost at once." He smiled gently. "The years may have gone by but you are still the same."

She waved a hand, hating that she was blushing, and at her age, too! It was quite ridiculous. "You can spare me your compliments, Lord Blackford, for I fear that I cannot return them given that I did not immediately recollect you."

He chuckled, and much to her surprise, Margaret found herself smiling. Perhaps they could, in fact, enjoy one another's company, just so long as he ceased his flirtations and his compliments. She had made herself quite plain, had she not? She could continue to be firm with him if it was required, making him see that she would not accept any such nonsense from him.

"You are more sharp-tongued than I remember, however!" Lord Blackford laughed, shaking his head. "Although there is a greater strength within you than before. I am glad of that."

Her heart twisted. "My parents arranged my marriage, as you know, Lord Blackford. As a debutante, it was quite impossible to turn against their wishes." A smile crept over her face at the memory. "Although now, I confess that I am very glad that they chose my husband so well."

Lord Blackford remained silent, although his eyes were shadowed.

"I cared for my husband very much," Margaret continued, as though she had to give some sort of explanation to Lord Blackford. "He was quite wonderful in almost every way. I miss him terribly."

Lord Blackford cleared his throat, his voice now a little gruff. "How long since he passed, if you do not mind me asking?"

She shook her head. "Not at all." Her voice was thin with pain. "It has been six years since we buried Joseph, six years since my son, Francis, took the title. And yet, sometimes, it feels as though it were only yesterday."

Lord Blackford nodded, his expression becoming wretched. "I quite understand the pain, Lady Catesby."

Her eyes narrowed, sending him a sharp glance as she recalled that Lady Crawford had told her Lord Blackford had never married.

"I see that you do not understand," he said softly. "It may not be the long, firmly established connection such as you had with Lord Catesby, but I, too, lost someone who had become very dear to me. I lost her only a short time after we had wed. Five months only." His eyes darkened with memories and Margaret felt her heart swell with sympathy. She knew he was not lying, for she could see the same pain in his expression that she constantly carried with her.

"I am sorry," she said, surprised to find that she no longer felt so disinclined towards him. It was as though this sharing of their pain had allowed her to feel some sort of kinship with him, bringing down the walls between them. "When was this?"

Lord Blackford's laugh was harsh, biting the air between them. "It was only two years after you wed Lord Catesby," he said with a shrug, as though such a thing was quite ridiculous. "So a good many years ago—and yet the pain still lingers. I do not think that it will ever completely leave me."

"No," Margaret agreed, a little taken aback at just how open Lord Blackford was being, when they were only just reacquainted. "And perhaps that is how it is meant to be, Lord Blackford. We remember them, do we not? They have helped to form the person we are today and one cannot simply forget all that has gone before."

"Indeed." Lord Blackford's voice was gruff, his eyes now looking away from hers. Margaret swallowed the lump in her throat as she allowed her mind to drift back towards Joseph, finding both the joy and the pain that came with her memories.

With an effort, she put a small smile on her face, brushing aside her sadness. "Well, then, Lord Blackford, shall we go to the theatre? I should not like to miss the first act."

Lord Blackford's head shot up, his expression one of complete astonishment. "You intend to allow me to accompany you there?"

"I do," Margaret replied, praying that she was not making a mistake in doing so. "Although I will not stand for any flirtations or the like, Lord Blackford. And I have my own box."

A broad smile began to spread across Lord Blackford's face, chasing away the darkness that had lingered in his eyes. "I quite understand," he stated with a small bow. "Thank you for allowing me such a privilege, Lady Catesby, I—"

"That is precisely what I mean, Lord Blackford," Margaret interrupted, walking past him towards the door. "No such nonsense, if you please. I do not hold with frilly compliments, not at my age." She smiled to herself as Lord Blackford hurried after her, feeling quite in control and finding that she rather enjoyed being able to speak her mind without fear of the consequences. "Do come along, sir."

Lord Blackford hurried after her, making Margaret smile quietly to herself. She was quite able to ensure that her acquaintance with Lord Blackford was seen by the *ton* as nothing more than that—a simple acquaintance. She would speak sharply if she had to and would not allow any such flirtations to escape from his mouth. If he persisted, then it would be quite easy to simply bring an end to their acquaintance, for it did not matter a fig to her whom she spent time with during the Season here in London.

Although, she considered, as she climbed into the carriage, there was that sudden connection between them now, which she had not expected. It had come from Lord Blackford's openness, his willingness to allow her to see his loss and the pain that came with it. That had brought an understanding between them, she thought, managing a small smile in his direction as Lord Blackford came to sit down opposite. Perhaps she had been foolish in her attempts to avoid him. Perhaps this might be the beginnings of a friendship.

"Lady Crawford will be quite delighted that I have managed to persuade you," Lord Blackford said lightly, as the carriage drew away from the house. "Although I will, of course, tell her that I did nothing of the sort and that you were fully convinced in your own mind regardless of what I said or did."

Despite herself, Margaret laughed. "Indeed, Lord Blackford, I expect you to say just that. Lady Crawford knows me well enough to understand that I will not be pushed and pressed in one particular direction any longer."

Lord Blackford's smile did not quite reach his eyes, his gaze becoming almost contemplative as he looked back at her. "Indeed you will not," he murmured, as though this was something new to consider. "You are quite changed from the girl I once knew, Lady Catesby."

"We all change, Lord Blackford," she replied, wondering why she suddenly felt quite so anxious. Her stomach had tightened, her breathing had quickened and she was suddenly a good deal more aware of his presence. "I cannot believe that all change is a bad thing either."

"It is not, of course," he agreed quickly. "And certainly not in your case, Lady Catesby. I think you quite remarkable, more than I have ever done before."

CHAPTER 5

"Tell me, what of your children?"

A little surprised that Lord Blackford would show any such interest in her life, as well as the fact that she had not known he was aware of her family, Margaret stared at the gentleman for a moment, nonplussed.

Lord Blackford chuckled. "I am not as ill-mannered as all that, Lady Catesby," he commented, as though he had known what she was thinking. "Yes, I am aware that your son has taken on the title of his father and that he is recently married. I am also aware that you have four—or is it five?—other children."

"Five," Margaret replied faintly, barely aware of the buzz of conversation from the other theatre-goers around them. "Charles remains here in town."

"Ah yes, of course," Lord Blackford murmured, his eyes alight. "I am acquainted with him, I think, although I gather he finds his time quite taken up with his occupation and his family."

"Indeed," Margaret agreed, managing to find her voice again amidst her surprise. "They have two children."

Lord Blackford smiled, his expression kind. "Then you are a grandmama twice over, Lady Catesby. How wonderful for you and for the children."

A little unsure whether this was one of the compliments she had warned Lord Blackford against, Margaret studied the man's expression and decided that he was being both genuine and kind. Her mind went back to when they had first met, which seemed so long ago now. Lord Blackford had appeared to be quite wonderful in her eyes, for he had not been brusque nor overly flirtatious, but had good conversation and, from her limited experience at the time, had seemed quite eager to hear what she had to say. He had not lost that trait, it seemed, although he certainly had become more carefree with his compliments. Silently, Margaret wondered why he had never chosen to marry again, given that his first marriage had been so long ago and of such a short duration.

"Grandchildren are a blessing most wonderful," Lord Blackford continued softly, his head turned away from her and now looking towards the stage, as though he were speaking to himself.

"I have six grandchildren," Margaret murmured quietly. "And they are all quite adorable, although one or two can be something of a trial at times."

Lord Blackford's eyes twinkled as he looked back at her. "As children are inclined to be," he said, as though he knew what he spoke of, although she could not understand where such knowledge came from. After all, he had only been married to his first wife for five months, had he not? And he had not mentioned any children.

"You—you do not have any children?" she asked haltingly, not wanting to appear rude or improper in any way. "It is just that the way you speak of them makes me believe that you—"

"Should you care for some refreshment?" Lord Blackford was on his feet, her question torn from her lips and flung into the air before she had even had a chance to finish speaking. "Goodness, how rude of me to sit here conversing when the time is fast slipping away from us! What should you like, Lady Catesby? Champagne?"

"That would be sufficient," Margaret uttered, terribly surprised at how brusquely he had thrown her question aside and changed the subject. "I thank you."

Lord Blackford was gone from the box in a moment, leaving Margaret sitting quite still, her shock mounting with every second. Evidently, there was something Lord Blackford did not wish to talk about with her and she was quite willing to remain silent on such a matter, but the way in which he had ended the conversation had rubbed at her angrily. She felt almost bruised, quietly chastising herself for being quite so forward with her questions. An acquaintance long forgotten could not simply be brought back to life again with only a few hours spent together!

"Mama!"

Jumping in surprise, Margaret turned to see her son, Charles, enter the box with his wife, Abigail, on his arm.

"Goodness!" Margaret exclaimed, a glad smile on her face as she rose to greet them both. "I did not know you would be in attendance this evening."

"Nor did we know you were here," Charles replied with a chuckle. "It was Abigail who spotted you from our box." Something dark flickered in his eyes. "Who was it you were sitting with, Mama?"

"Oh, that is Lord Blackford, an acquaintance from when I was a debutante," Margaret answered with a quick smile, refusing to allow her son any sway over who she chose to spend her time with. "It has been quite wonderful to spend so much time here in London with those that I consider to be my friends, both from years ago and more recently."

Abigail smiled, pressing Margaret's arm and making her quite aware that she, at least, had nothing of concern in her mind when it came to Margaret sitting with Lord Blackford. "I am glad for you, Margaret," Abigail smiled, sitting down in one of the chairs near to where Margaret stood. "Have you nothing to drink? Charles will go and fetch you something, if you wish." She gestured for Margaret to sit down, evidently eager to speak to her.

"Lord Blackford has gone in search of something," Margaret replied, a little lamely, as she saw her son's gaze flicker yet again.

"Then, in that case, I require something," Abigail said briskly, looking pointedly at her husband. "Champagne?"

Charles rolled his eyes. "We have both just—"

"Yes, but I am so very hot," Abigail said with a small smile in Margaret's direction. "If you would, Charles, I would be very much obliged."

Charles sighed heavily, although Margaret saw

the smile in his eyes as he reached for his wife's hand. Dropping a kiss to the back of her hand, he bowed grandly as though they were just being introduced.

"Anything for my fair lady," he said, with a broad grin that made Abigail blush. "Do excuse me."

Margaret watched fondly as Charles left the box, knowing that he adored his wife and finding her heart swelling with happiness for them both. Abigail was a strong-willed woman, much like Margaret herself had become, but she brought out the best in Charles. She was loving, kind and yet absolutely firm in her decisions. Margaret thought the world of her.

"Now," Abigail began, tilting her head. "I think, Margaret, that there is something I must tell you so that you are not left entirely unawares."

A stone dropped into Margaret's stomach, sending her into a whirlwind of anxiety.

"Do not fret so," Abigail laughed kindly, reaching to take Margaret's gloved hand. "It is not at all to do with you but more of the company you keep."

Margaret's eyes widened. "Is it something to do with Lord Blackford?"

Slowly, Abigail nodded.

Margaret's stomach tightened. She could feel

herself growing tense, her breathing a little ragged as she watched Abigail carefully.

"You know very well how rumors and things go in London," Abigail said gently. "And it may very well be nothing, but the rumor is that Lord Blackford's estate is not doing particularly well at all. In fact, some say that he is quite poor and is therefore looking for a rich widow or even a lady with a large dowry that he might marry." Her eyes grew keen as she leaned forward to look directly into Margaret's eyes. "You must understand that I am not accusing you of caring for Lord Blackford in any way, for I have only just seen you in his company this evening, but you must be on your guard."

Margaret's breath left her all in a rush, relief pouring into every part of her. "Oh, is that all? You are quite mistaken, my dear girl. I am not in any way inclined towards Lord Blackford in that sense. We have only just picked up our acquaintance this very evening!"

Abigail nodded although she did not appear to be entirely convinced. "It is no crime if you begin to care for someone new," she said slowly, evidently choosing her words with care so that she would not offend Margaret. "I know that you love your husband still, but to care for another soul does not mean that your love for him grows cold."

It was Margaret who went cold at this, a

trickle of ice making its way down her back. "This is not something you can speak of with any certainty, Abigail," she said, as kindly as she could. "You have no experience of it."

Abigail did not seem to take offence, a small smile catching the corner of her lips. "I have experience of love," she said gently. "I know that I loved my first child so dearly that I was quite afraid that I could not love another in the same way. Of course," she continued, her smile softening, "I found myself to be quite mistaken in that. I love both my children with such a fierceness that at times, it quite takes my breath away. Loving one does not stop me from loving the other."

Margaret swallowed.

"I am aware that this is not the same as what you have endured, Margaret, and I know that you have said you came to London with the express intention of seeking out your old friends simply to bring that part of your life back again, and that is, of course, wonderful. However, if you should find yourself considering something new, then I do hope you will not fear it, that you will not turn from it. None of us will think the worse of you."

A harsh laugh escaped Margaret's lips before she could stop it. "I hardly think that is so, Abigail," she said darkly. "I know my children. I saw my son's expression when he mentioned who it was I was sitting with this evening. You cannot truly believe that my children will not consider me foolish, if not betraying their father, if I were to even *consider*—"

Abigail had taken both of Margaret's hands in her own, her expression determined.

"Margaret," she said firmly, interrupting her. "Stop. Your children love you. *I* love you. Charles may find the idea of your happiness with another to be quite unsettling, but that does not mean that he will not be glad for you should that situation ever arise. No, they will not think ill of you. They will not think you a betrayer and nor should you think of yourself in such a way. I cannot tell you how glad I was to see you talking with Lord Blackford in such a way that brought a smile to your face and a lightness to your eyes. Do not shun that, Margaret, not out of fear, at least."

Margaret realized that the ache in her throat had been building slowly, to the point that the pain was sending tears to her eyes. She looked back at her daughter-in-law, wondering when the girl had become so wise. It was not that simply conversing with Lord Blackford had brought back any sort of feelings of affection or the like, for she could not simply forget the years of love and devotion she had spent with Joseph, but rather that she had found herself enjoying his company and his conversation but had been chiding herself inwardly for doing so. Abigail was correct to state that she had been shunning the idea of continuing her acquaintance with Lord Blackford, for she had no intention of spending any further time with him. Why had that been, she wondered? Was it because she was afraid of what might come of it? Or was it because she had quite set herself against the idea of ever considering another gentleman ever again? Was she truly determined to live out the rest of her life as a widow, even though the opportunity for companionship and even affection might be open to her?

"You will think about what I have had to say?" Abigail pressed gently, seeing the other theatre-goers quickly arriving back to take their seats again.

"Yes," Margaret replied, her voice hoarse with the strength of her emotion. "I will."

Abigail gave her a warm smile, and her eyes twinkled. "And do not worry about Charles, I will be able to talk him into accepting almost anything!" she laughed, and Margaret could not help but smile in return, chasing away the tears that still threatened.

"I am sure you will," she agreed, just as Charles and Lord Blackford reappeared in the box. "Thank you, Abigail."

Her daughter-in-law pressed her hands again before letting them go, urging her husband to return to their box with haste so that they would not miss the second half. She greeted Lord Blackford kindly, but then took her leave, almost dragging Charles along with her.

"My, my," Lord Blackford murmured, handing Margaret a glass. "Your son does not appear to like my presence here with you, Lady Catesby." He frowned as he sat down again. "I would not like to bring you any sort of trouble, of course, so if you would prefer, I can easily find somewhere else to seat myself for the duration of the performance."

Margaret, recalling what Abigail had said, shook her head. "You must forgive my son," she said with a fond smile. "He is, I think, a little perturbed to see his mother in London for the Season, simply to enjoy myself. He is much more used to me being at the dower house, making calls or inviting my family to stay." She took a sip of her champagne, her mind working furiously. There was so much going on within her that she could not quite sort everything out, although she was certainly not concerned with Charles' behavior. Whether he liked or disliked Lord Blackford was not of particular importance. What *did* matter was just how much *she* was enjoying Lord Blackford's company.

Lord Blackford cleared his throat, suddenly appearing to feel a little awkward. "Then, might I ask if you would care to accompany me for a short walk through Hyde Park tomorrow? Or St. James' park, if you prefer? I have been assured that it will be quite a fine day."

Margaret considered this for a moment, her stomach twisting this way and that. Lord Blackford was looking at her from under lidded eyes, appearing almost boy-like in his nervous anticipation of her answer. His gaze was darting this way and that, his feet shuffling uncomfortably on the floor of the box as his lined brow furrowed all the more. She could not leave him in such a state, struggling to find her answer.

"Yes," she found herself saying, surprising them both, it seemed. Lord Blackford's eyes widened slightly as he looked at her, making Margaret laugh.

"My goodness, Lord Blackford, this cannot be the first time a lady has accepted an invitation from you, surely?" she smiled, as he let out a breath of relief. "You look quite done in."

He shrugged, his eyes twinkling, the deep furrows gone from above his eyes. "I thought you would be quite set against me, Lady Catesby."

"I thought I would be also," she stated truthfully. "But it seems that my first impression was, perhaps, incorrect."

Lord Blackford looked both gratified and relieved. "That is generous of you to say," he said, although his eyes darted away from hers for a moment as though he were hiding something from her. "Shall we say tomorrow afternoon? A little before the fashionable hour?"

"A good time *before* the fashionable hour, if you please," Margaret replied with feeling. She did not want to be caught strutting about the park at her age, for the idea of it had never really enticed her. "I would much prefer a quieter walk, Lord Blackford."

He grinned at her, evidently pleased with this answer. "Then a quieter walk it shall be," he said with alacrity. "I am looking forward to it already."

CHAPTER 6

Margaret smiled as Lord Blackford offered her his arm, feeling somewhat awkward as she accepted it hesitantly. This was now the fifth outing they had enjoyed together since that night at the theatre, but she was still rather uncertain about it all. She could not get Joseph out of her mind at times, fearing that he was almost looking down from above, disapprovingly. She had no particular feelings of affection for Lord Blackford, she told herself repeatedly, every time she felt such a way. She simply enjoyed his company, his conversation and the way he could make her laugh at a moment's notice. She would return to the dower house at the end of next month, leaving her filled with such happy memories of her time in London.

"You still are a little uncertain around me, Lady Catesby," Lord Blackford commented, a little dryly, as his eyes caught hers. "Why is that, I wonder?"

She shook her head. "I am not uncertain," she refuted immediately. "You are quite mistaken there, Lord Blackford."

"Am I?" he queried, making her laugh. "I cannot allow you to disagree with me without evidence, surely? I offer you my arm quite regularly and every time, there is a moment or two of hesitation before you accept." His brow lifted, although no smile caught his lips. "That must speak of uncertainty, surely."

Seeing the seriousness in his expression, Margaret allowed herself to speak honestly and openly. "I am glad of your acquaintance, Lord Blackford, truly. I was wrong, as I have admitted before, to shun you as I first did. Lady Crawford should be thanked, I suppose, for choosing to have a dreadful headache that night of the ball!" She was disappointed that he did not even chuckle at this comment, realizing that he was truly in a very serious frame. "I confess to you, Lord Blackford, that I am constantly on my guard, wondering what the rest of the *beau monde* must think."

Lord Blackford frowned. "But that should not matter, Lady Catesby. You are a widow, with means of your own and a wonderful reputation.

No one speaks ill of you, no one would even dream of remarking on anything you choose to do, unless, of course, it was quite scandalous. I might add that accepting my arm is by no means scandalous, Lady Catesby, in case there was any confusion there."

This last sentence was spoken with such sharpness and irony that for a moment, Margaret was quite taken aback and did not know what to say. Lord Blackford's expression was darker than she had ever seen it before with all trace of joviality and good humour gone.

"I apologize," she said slowly, not quite able to look at him. "I apologize if you think I have wronged you in some way by my hesitation, Lord Blackford. It was not intentional, of course. This is all quite new to me in so many ways, even though I was once here as a debutante." Her heart ached suddenly and she felt the urge to step away from Lord Blackford, to drop her hand from his arm—but with an effort, she remained exactly where she was. "To be here again in society as a widow, and not as either a debutante or a married lady chaperoning her daughters, has been something that I have struggled with, Lord Blackford."

He sighed heavily, rubbing one hand over his eyes, appearing suddenly a good deal older than she had ever seen him before. His face almost drooped, the lines in his forehead and beside his eyes seeming to grow heavier as he sighed again.

"You are much too good, Lady Catesby," he grated, not looking at her. "It is I who must apologize. I have not considered things from your perspective, of course. I can see that now." There was a moment or two of silence as they walked, leaving Margaret with the feeling that Lord Blackford was not yet finished speaking. She was correct in her assumption.

Lord Blackford stopped walking, dropping her hand from his arm as he turned to face her.

"I must apologize, Lady Catesby," he said heavily, his eyes still fixed on the ground by her feet. "I have been rude and that is quite uncalled for. You have every right to do exactly as you wish, regardless of what I should want."

Margaret felt her heart quicken at his words, silently wondering what it was, exactly, that Lord Blackford wanted from her.

"I apologize," he said again, finally looking into her eyes. "I have had some news that has brought me some pain and I have let that come out on you."

Margaret raised her eyebrows, a little surprised at his confession. Lord Blackford was not the sort of gentleman to speak about himself a great deal, she had come to realize, for he did not often speak of his life, his family, his estate or the like. She had been forced to draw him out when she could, finding him to be something of a challenge which, Margaret had to admit to herself, she had found almost enjoyable. Here, now, stood another opportunity for her to do just that.

"If you wish, Lord Blackford, you are welcome to share your news with me," she suggested, as calmly as she could. "You are, of course, quite within your rights *not* to do so, but I would state that such pains shared with another can often bring about a good deal of relief."

Lord Blackford smiled sadly. "You have found that to be the case, have you?"

"I have indeed," she stated quietly. "My children and I shared our grief with each other over the loss of Joseph, and that helped us comfort one another." Silently, she wondered if he had never told anyone about his own grief and pain when it had come to the loss of his first wife, considering that he might have carried—and continued to carry it—entirely on his own.

Lord Blackford ran one hand over his eyes. "Then I shall speak to you," he said aloud, as though confirming the idea to himself. "Although might we continue to walk?"

His eyes were filled with worry and she nodded at once. "But of course."

For some minutes, they walked in silence. Margaret's heart was beating a little more quickly than usual, worrying about what it was that troubled Lord Blackford so much.

"Did I ever tell you that I have a son?"

Margaret caught her breath, stumbling just a little as she struggled to take in what she had heard.

"I take it I have not told you this before," Lord Blackford continued, a touch of humour in his voice. "No, I have not. That is not surprising. His presence is not particularly well known amongst society. In fact, it has never been well known amongst society, for I have made sure to keep it that way."

Margaret struggled to know what to say, both astonished and confused. Had not Lord Blackford stated that he had lost his wife at only five months after their marriage?

"His mother died giving life to him," Lord Blackford continued, as if he had been able to see where her thoughts were directed. "The pain that came with such an event... well, I cannot tell you of it for there are not words to describe what I endured," he finished thickly.

"Indeed, I quite understand," Margaret said softly, wondering how such a young man as Lord Blackford had been could have endured the loss of a wife and the birth of a son at the same time. The emotions that would have torn at him must have been fierce and unrelenting.

"For a long time, I did not want anything to do with the child," Lord Blackford admitted darkly, not looking at her. "I blamed him, I suppose. The wet nurse had full charge of him, then the nurse thereafter. It was not until he was three years of age that I finally began to spend some time with him." A harsh laugh poured from him. "The regret that came to me at that moment has never quite left me. I should never have blamed the boy, I realized. What had I missed in turning away from him at such a young age?"

Margaret placed her free hand on his arm, unable to prevent herself from wanting to encourage him in some way. "The boy would not have been old enough to know that you were absent from the first few months of his life," she said gently. "And you spent time with him thereafter, did you not?"

"As much as I could," Lord Blackford stated firmly. "I am more proud of him than I can say."

Margaret smiled at this, recognizing the pride of a father over his son. Joseph had often spoken that way of his own children.

"He is not yet wed but does not wish to come to town and find a bride," Lord Blackford said with a half-smile. "He has been courting Lady Crawford's youngest daughter, given that our estates are close enough to one another." He chuckled at her astonished expression. "Lady

Crawford has not been forthcoming about this, I presume? I quite understand. I think she hopes that her daughter will forget about Theodore soon enough." His hazel eyes flickered with good humour. "I doubt it, however. Theodore is singular in his affections towards Miss Catherine."

"Theodore?" Margaret asked gently. "That is your son's name?"

"The Honorable Theodore Hornby," Lord Blackford smiled, although his face was still somewhat shadowed. "Yes, that is his name. He is gone to the continent, to see what is left of my holdings. However, I have had news that they are just as unprofitable as ever." His face fell, the frustration evident. "I have done all I can for my son, but I cannot give him an unprofitable estate."

Frowning, Margaret came to a stop. "Your estate is unprofitable? Surely, that cannot be? You told me only a last week that you were speaking to Lord Crawford about your crops and the like."

Lord Blackford looked wary, as though he were a rabbit about to be snapped at by a wily fox. "I spent so many years leaving it to wilt and ruin," he said slowly, "that the estate has never quite recovered."

"You left your estate?"

"Yes," Lord Blackford said harshly, turning away from her. "When my wife died, everything became meaningless. I left my estate, turned my tenants out and spent every moment I could in London, doing whatever I could to forget the grief and the pain." He closed his eyes, his head hanging low in apparent hopelessness. "What else could I do? And then, when I came to my senses and spent some time with my child, my only son and heir, a little light began to come back into my life."

"I am glad to hear it," Margaret said slowly. "But as for your estate—"

"I did not return to it until my son was almost six years of age," Lord Blackford interrupted miserably. "The tenants' houses were almost entirely ruined, the fields waterlogged. The money I should have spent on it all, I had thrown away in my grief."

"I see," Margaret said quietly, wondering just how difficult life had been for Lord Blackford, shouldering all of his grief and responsibilities alone. She did not think ill of him for having reacted in such a way to the death of his wife, for pain such as that almost seemed impossible to bear at times.

"It has taken years of work to restore the estate to what it should be," Lord Blackford finished, his eyes haunted as he looked back at her. "I have kept my trials to myself, not wanting anyone to see my struggle, not wanting to shame my son, but I am leaving him with such a small fortune that I am almost ashamed of it." His eyes closed tightly, his voice jarring. "What sort of father am I that would leave my son and heir with the consequences of my own actions?"

Margaret did not know what to do. Lord Blackford had never spoken to her with such openness before, for she felt as though he were bearing his very soul to her, revealing the deep wounds and scars that lay within him. She wanted to find something of comfort to say, wanted to be able to bring him some relief and reassurance, but no words came to her mind.

"He does not think little of me," Lord Blackford whispered, his eyes still closed. "But he ought to. He does not know it all."

"I know that he will be certain that you love him," Margaret said, feeling entirely inadequate. "You have made that clear and I know that that is one thing a child will always seek from their parents."

Lord Blackford smiled sadly, opened his eyes and looked at her. "You are much too good for my acquaintance, Margaret," he said gratefully, the sound of her Christian name on his lips sending a shiver down her spine. "You do not know me at all and yet you speak with such kindness."

She managed a small smile, wondering at the quickening of her heart and the urge to draw him close to her to bring him comfort and relief. Why did she have such a yearning to do such a thing? It would be most improper and certainly ought not to be something she was allowing herself to consider.

"I am here as your friend," she told him. "I am here if you wish to speak of the things that trouble you. You know that I can understand your grief and your pain, do you not?"

"Yes." His hand reached for hers and she gave it willingly, her heart suddenly fluttering as his fingers intertwined with her own. "Yes, I know that, Margaret. You have always had such a generous and kind heart."

She could not speak, her mouth going suddenly dry as she looked up into Lord Blackford's face and found his eyes fixed on hers, burning with such an intensity that she wanted to look away but could not. Pressing her lips together and ignoring the butterflies that were pouring into her stomach, making her feel as though she were a foolish girl accepting her first attentions from a gentleman, she tried to smile and speak calmly.

"I am glad to be considered your friend," she said, reminding herself that this, after all, was everything she had wanted to pursue with Lord Blackford. "I am sorry for what has occurred with your holdings but I am quite sure that, no matter what it is you are able to present to your son when he comes to claim the title, he will not consider what it is you have burdened him with, but rather all you have done to ensure he has everything that you have been able to give him." She was not even sure that her words made sense but, to her relief, Lord Blackford smiled, a heavy sigh escaping him.

"I think you must be an angel, Margaret," he said quietly, his expression warm as he studied her, his hand still holding hers. "An angel sent to comfort me in my hour of need." Something flickered through his gaze, a pain that she could not quite make out. "Thank you."

She smiled and gently tugged her hand free, refusing to allow herself to consider what was going on within her own heart, not when it confused her so. "But of course, Lord Blackford," she said, turning towards the path again. "Now, shall we continue to walk? We must be quick if we want to avoid the fashionable hour."

He laughed, breaking the air of sadness that had seemed to settle over them both. "And we cannot allow ourselves to be caught up in that now, can we, Lady Catesby?" he commented with a broad smile. "Although what say you to a short visit to the bookshop as we return back to the house?"

She smiled at him, knowing that he was doing so just because she had expressed a love of reading to him earlier in the week. His thoughtfulness did not go unappreciated. "I think that quite a wonderful idea," she said, looking up at him.

"Then might I offer you my arm again, Lady Catesby?" he asked with a playful smile.

"Of course," she laughed, accepting it at once without even the smallest flicker of hesitation. Something had grown and blossomed between them both this afternoon, something that brought her a good deal of contentment and yet a good many questions with it. Questions that she was going to have to consider the very first moment she was alone.

CHAPTER 7

This was to be her first hosted soiree since she had come to London, and Margaret could not help but feel both nervous and excited. She had invited only a few guests, with Charles and Abigail amongst them, as well as Lord and Lady Crawford. She had not hesitated to invite Lord Blackford, who had promised eagerly to attend, and Margaret had found herself almost glowing with the excitement of it all.

Taking one last look at herself in the mirror that hung above the drawing room fireplace, Margaret smoothed down her gown and told herself that she had no need to feel so anxious. It was not as though there was anything that could go wrong this particular evening, for she had both refreshments and entertainment already prepared.

So why did she feel so terribly anxious?

Her mind immediately went to Lord Blackford, recalling how, earlier that week, he had talked so openly about his son—the son she had never known he'd had. One question had lingered in her mind and she had allowed herself to consider it once she had returned home: If the baby had been born after only five months of wedlock, then that meant that the child had been conceived beforehand. It was quite scandalous, of course, but now that they were decades past such a time, it no longer seemed to carry quite as much weight. Perhaps that was why Lord Blackford had chosen to keep the news of his son fairly quiet. She was glad that he had both an heir and a family, although she was sorrowful that he had lost his wife at such a difficult time.

The way Lord Blackford had been so open with her, the way he had chosen to reveal his deepest wounds to her, had had an impact upon her heart that she still could not easily explain. It terrified her, though she had forced herself to consider it all as rationally as she could. Abigail's words came to mind over and over again, helping her to remember that she was not betraying Joseph by beginning to have a gentle affection for another gentleman. She still loved Joseph desperately, still grieved for him and had him in her thoughts every day, but there was the beginning of something new growing in her heart. Something for Lord Blackford.

Margaret did not know whether or not she welcomed such feelings, still confused over all that she felt and wondering what this could mean for the rest of her life. Would her children react as Abigail had suggested, not holding such a thing against her but rather being glad for her happiness? It might not come immediately, she realized, sitting down rather heavily in a chair by the fire, but perhaps they would learn to accept such a situation.

"What situation?" she muttered aloud, pressing one hand to her forehead in order to rid herself of such ridiculous thoughts. Lord Blackford had not made any advances towards her and she had certainly not done so towards him. They were, as she had said to him herself, very good friends, and for that, she was truly glad.

But it was a friendship she did not want to lose. To return to the dower house now, to turn her back on society, on London and even on Lord Blackford seemed quite impossible. He had become part of her every day and to return to a life where he was not present brought her a sense of pain that she could not easily remove from herself.

"Oh, Joseph," she said aloud, as though he could hear her. "Am I doing you wrong?"

The scratch came at the door, making her jump with fright, only to realize that it was the first of her guests arriving.

"Lady Crawford, my lady," the butler said grandly, as Lady Crawford stepped into the room, looking resplendent in a dark red gown.

"My dear Edith," Margaret greeted her. "Thank you for coming. Where is your husband?"

Lady Crawford waved a hand. "He was lingering over his cravat so I came without him. The blessings of having been long married—one does not have to wait for one's husband! One can simply tell him that the carriage will return for him and his cravat in a few short minutes." She chuckled as Margaret laughed, shaking her head. "He is becoming quite ridiculous in his old age, I'm afraid."

"Oh, do not say that," Margaret sighed heavily. "I do not feel old and yet my appearance tells me that I grow older every day."

"Nonsense," Lady Crawford proclaimed with a good deal of firmness. "You look quite wonderful, Margaret. Indeed, I believe you have looked all the better these last few weeks." She smiled, a knowing look on her face. "Yes, I am referring to Lord Blackford, my dear. I am not ashamed to speak directly."

"Lord Blackford and I are friends," Margaret

insisted, not allowing her friend to make any sort of accusation. "That is all."

Lady Crawford's expression gentled. "And is that all you wish for him to be, Margaret, my dear? You cannot tell me that you have not found his company to be anything less than enjoyable."

Margaret hesitated. "He is a kind man, yes."

"And I have not seen him spend so much time with any one lady in all my years in London society," Lady Crawford added, sending a blush to Margaret's cheeks. "There, you see!" She grinned triumphantly. "I knew you had something of an affection for him."

Groaning, Margaret prayed silently that her friend would not continue to speak so openly when the other guests arrived. "My dear Edith, you must not be ridiculous. I am in my sixth decade and am no longer a debutante."

Lady Crawford snorted. "I hardly think age is of any particular concern when matters of the heart are involved, Margaret. If you have any sort of affection for Lord Blackford, then I suggest you pursue it."

Margaret shook her head, her confusion mounting. "I loved my husband."

Lady Crawford's eyes filled with sympathy almost immediately. "I know that, my dear friend," she said, reaching for Margaret's hand and pressing it gently. "But you do not need to spend the rest of your life in abject sorrow simply because you are widowed. You loved your husband, yes, and you love him still—but that does not mean you cannot find happiness with another."

"It is not as simple as it might seem," Margaret said heavily. "How can feeling such a small amount of affection for a gentleman feel as though I am being condemned for doing so at the same time?"

Lady Crawford took both of Margaret's hands in her own. "Because you are a loyal creature," she said gently. "You are devoted and unselfish. Your torment is your own self battling against what it feels. You may let yourself feel, Margaret, my dear, without allowing the guilt or the worry to take hold. It may take some time, of course, and there will undoubtably be moments when you will think yourself quite lost, but you must not hold yourself back. There is no shame in taking a hold of one's future and finding a little light where there was once only darkness."

Margaret swallowed hard, feeling tears threaten. Her friend spoke with such compassion and consideration that it was as though she had looked into Margaret's heart and was tugging out her concerns one at a time.

"Now, do not begin to weep, for it is most unseemly for ladies of our age and standing,"

Lady Crawford said, a good deal more briskly. "For if you begin, then I shall have no other choice but to join you in your tears, and then what shall your other guests think?"

Reaching for her friend, and unheeding as to whether or not her gown would become crinkled, Margaret hugged Edith tightly, battling her tears as she did so.

"You are quite wonderful, Edith," she said hoarsely. "I do not know what I should have done without you."

Lady Crawford smiled and squeezed Margaret's hand before letting it go. "You are quite welcome, my dear," she replied kindly. "I only want to see you happy and if Lord Blackford is the one to bring that to you, then I can have nothing but praise for him."

Margaret laughed. "I hear his son is courting your youngest daughter."

"Yes," Lady Crawford stated with no smile on her face. "Catherine, who would not even come to London for the season! I had to send her to my sister's in order to assure the girl that I would not force her to find another."

"And is Lord Blackford's son not a good match?" Margaret enquired, wondering why Lady Crawford had not warmed to him. "Even though Catherine must be quite devoted to him."

Lady Crawford laughed and rolled her eyes.

"They are both very strange creatures, in their own way," she said with a small shrug. "Neither wishing to go to town, to dance and acquaint themselves with a good many others. No, you are quite right to say that there is nothing wrong with Hornby, it is more that I wanted to make sure that Catherine was quite certain about her feelings for the gentleman. I thought if she came to town, she might be swept off her feet by an earl or some such thing, instead of a mere viscount... but then again, she is the daughter of a viscount and I confess that I can be somewhat ridiculous about these things." Margaret laughed, aware that Lady Crawford had always loved London and the society that came with it. It must be very unusual for her to have a daughter that rebuffed the very things Lady Crawford loved.

"Ah, here is Lord Crawford," Lady Crawford exclaimed as the door opened again to reveal her husband with his perfectly tied cravat. "And your son. How wonderful." She smiled at Margaret, who felt a sudden swirl of butterflies in her stomach as she waited with anticipation for Lord Blackford to arrive. "This is going to be a wonderful evening, I am quite sure of it."

SOME HOURS LATER, Margaret had to admit that she was somewhat disheartened. The evening had gone wonderfully well, just as Lady Crawford had predicted, and her guests had seemed to enjoy the refreshments and the entertainment. Now, a good few were sitting to play cards of some sort, whilst others were still deep in conversation, enjoying the champagne that the footmen continued to serve.

But Lord Blackford had not appeared.

Margaret smiled tightly as her son drew near.

"This has been a lovely evening, Mama," Charles said, smiling at her. "You were not nervous, I hope?"

"No, not at all," Margaret lied, knowing that she could not tell her son that she had been anxious about Lord Blackford's arrival. "I think it has been most enjoyable."

Charles' smile faded. "You have not enjoyed it yourself?"

She put a bright smile on her face. "Of course I have, Charles!" she exclaimed, pressing his arm. "I confess that I was somewhat anxious over my first social event without your father being here, but I am delighted it has gone so well."

A shadow crossed Charles' face. "I thought you might be thinking of him, Mama."

"I am," she admitted quietly. "But not in the way that you might think, Charles."

Her son looked at her, a steadiness in his gaze that told her he already knew what it was she was going to say.

"I will always love your father, Charles," Margaret began, her hand still on his arm. "But I confess that I have begun to find a new happiness with another."

Charles did not so much as blink, although his eyes flickered with something akin to worry or concern. "With Lord Blackford, then."

"This does not surprise you."

Charles shook his head. "No, it does not," he said slowly. "I have spoken to Abigail about this previously and she has a remarkably different view from my own, I confess. I will not pretend that I do not find the idea difficult, Mama, but I must admit to my own selfishness with such a view." He smiled at her, his expression no longer troubled. "I cannot imagine what it must be like to have lived so long with so many of us around you, and then to start life alone in the dower house. There is nothing to hold against you if you choose to pursue happiness with Lord Blackford, Mama. You will have no complaints nor murmurs of disapproval from me."

Margaret let out a long breath of relief, only just realizing just how troubled she had been over her son's reaction to such news. "That means a very great deal to me, Charles. I want you to be assured that I will never stop loving your father, for he blessed my life in more ways than I think I can ever express. But I confess that it can be lonely to live in the way you have described, more lonely than I think I realized before I came to London. I have so many joys in my life, but I cannot pretend that I do not long for a companion to share my days." She smiled as Abigail came to join them, not afraid to speak openly to them both. "I cannot promise that Lord Blackford is to be that companion, but there is the start of something growing between us that I am still trying to comprehend!" Laughing gently, she shook her head as a slow sense of contentment filled her. "Your reassurance means the world to me, Charles. As does yours, Abigail."

Abigail took her husband's arm. "I am glad you have both had the opportunity to talk. Now, I think Miss Graham is willing to finish this evening with a few songs, Margaret, if you would like her to take her seat at the pianoforte?"

Margaret smiled. "That sounds wonderful, thank you."

CHAPTER 8

Margaret did not rise early the following morning, finding herself quite at her leisure. She was rather tired after a very late evening, although she was truly delighted with just how well the occasion had gone. The only thing that troubled her now was just why Lord Blackford had not appeared.

Resting in bed, with her breakfast tray at her elbow and her recent novel on the table beside her, Margaret let out a small sigh of contentment, trying not to allow her mind to linger on why Lord Blackford had been absent. She felt a good deal more at peace over what she had begun to feel for the gentleman, given her discussion with first Lady Crawford and then her son and daughter-in-law. She knew that she did not need to fear this affection that was growing within her heart, for it did not take away from the love she still had for her late husband and, from what Charles had said, would not make her family distressed in any way. Yes, it might take her children some time to accept that she was being courted by Lord Blackford—if he were to ask her, that is—but they would come to approve of it soon enough.

"You are most ridiculous, Margaret," she said aloud, reaching for her cup of tea. "The gentleman has not yet even made mention of such a thing as courtship!" A small smile lingered on her face as she considered this, aware that all they had been doing of late, with their many outings and time spent together, might well be considered a courtship by any other person aware of their continuing acquaintance! Mayhap Lord Blackford was less than inclined towards considering a possible courtship with her because of how firm she had been at the beginning of their acquaintance. She would have to find a way to reassure him that she did not feel that way any longer.

Of course, there was always the chance that Lord Blackford was not disposed towards her in such a way as she hoped, but given how he had been with her, Margaret was not inclined to believe that. There had been those long glances, the vulnerability of his heart towards her own, as well as the laughter and good conversation they had shared. Their friendship did not show any sign of diminishing and it was this that gave Margaret hope. Lord Blackford wanted to call upon her, wanted to remain in her company for a good deal of time each day—aside from the fact that he had not shown up at her soiree last evening.

Biting her lip, her brow furrowing as she let her mind drift onto that particular matter again, Margaret shook her head to herself and let out her breath slowly, aware of the tension that was filling her. She had no need to be concerned. Lord Blackford had, most likely, become caught up in something of importance and would write to her very soon with his apologies, if he did not call upon her instead. There was nothing to be anxious about.

"My lady?"

Just as Margaret had settled her mind, the bedchamber door flew open and, much to her surprise, the maid hurried in with a note in her hand.

"Goodness, whatever is the matter?" Margaret exclaimed as the maid bobbed a curtsy and handed her a note. "There is no need to come bursting into the room in such a way, surely!"

"I was told it was a matter of great urgency,

my lady," the maid replied, looking as though she were about to burst into tears. "Should I remain here with you, in case you have need of me?"

Margaret frowned, then nodded. "Very well." Looking at the letter, she turned it over to examine the seal but found none there. It was tied with a bit of ribbon and not sealed as she would expect of a letter from any of her children, which was something of a relief.

Pulling aside the ribbon, she unfolded the letter and began to read.

Her heart seemed to stop in her chest.

'Lady Catesby, my master has asked me to send for you. He is in need of aid and states that he can trust you. If you might spare the time to call just as soon as you can, Lord Blackford would be most appreciative.'

There was no signature on the note to tell her who had written it, but it was quite apparent to Margaret that this had come from one of Lord Blackford's staff, although what had occurred that would require her help, she could not say.

The maid had picked up the breakfast tray and had set it aside, leaving Margaret free to throw back the covers and swing her legs over the side.

"I must dress at once," she said, no longer irritated with the maid. "You were quite right to bring that to me at once. It is of the greatest urgency."

"There is a carriage waiting for you, my lady," the maid whispered as she hurried to help Margaret into her things. "The footman who brought the note is below."

Margaret said nothing, her heart pounding wildly. She had very little idea as to what had occurred with Lord Blackford, but the fact that he had his servant write the note instead of writing it himself did not bode well for him. She had to get to him at once.

Hurrying the maid to dress her hair into a simple chignon, Margaret sat quietly for a moment and looked at her reflection in the mirror. She looked pale and weary, her eyes wide with apparent fright and a slight tremble about her lips. There was no doubt in her mind now. She was afraid for Lord Blackford.

ARRIVING at Lord Blackford's home seemed to take an inordinate amount of time, making Margaret more and more fractious with each minute that passed. Finally, the carriage door was opened and she stepped out into the street, before hurrying up the stone steps that led to Lord Blackford's front door.

It opened for her at once, the butler appearing just to her left as she walked inside.

"Thank you, my lady," he said, bowing slowly. "Might I take your things?"

Margaret found herself almost throwing her hat and gloves at the butler, growing desperate to seek out Lord Blackford. "What has happened?" she asked hoarsely. "Where is he?"

The butler cleared his throat as the footman closed the door behind her. "He is in the study, my lady," he said, beginning to walk away from her. "If you will just come with me."

She did not hesitate but hurried after him, her heart beating so frantically that she could barely catch her breath.

"In here, my lady," the butler said, opening the door. "Shall I send up some tea? Although mayhap you will need something stronger."

"Both," came Lord Blackford's voice from inside the room, flooding Margaret with such relief that she almost collapsed where she stood. "And some more hot water and bandages, if you please."

Walking into the room on unsteady legs, Margaret tried to make out where Lord Blackford sat, wondering why the drapes were still closed on what was a quite lovely summer morning.

"I must have some light," she said, bumping into something solid. "Do you mind?"

Lord Blackford let out a heavy sigh. "I suppose I

shall have to allow it," he said in a voice that rasped with either pain or irritation. "Thank you for coming, Margaret. I did not know who else to turn to. This is the first time such a thing has occurred and I doubt it will be the last, should I choose to continue. Not that I think I will, however."

The depth of pain in his voice had her practically rushing towards the drapes, doing her best to avoid the heavy oak table and then the chair that seemed to deliberately be in her way. Pulling them back, she fastened them quickly and then turned to look at Lord Blackford.

He was sitting, slumped, in a chair by the fire, which only had a few glowing embers remaining. He was in his shirt sleeves, with a large red stain covering the top of his right arm.

Margaret caught her breath.

"Yes, it is as you see," Lord Blackford said heavily. "I have been shot." His eyes met hers, a rueful smile twisting his lips as he kept his agony hidden behind his eyes. "Twice, in fact. The other one has nicked my ribs, although it is nothing more than a flesh wound. This one," he indicated his right arm, "has the bullet still embedded in my flesh, I fear. You can understand why I was unable to write to you myself, I think."

Margaret was, by this point, leaning heavily on the oak table, trying to draw in enough breath to stop her head from spinning. She was quite overcome with what she saw and had heard from Lord Blackford. He had been shot? On two occasions? It was almost impossible to take in.

"I know this is all most awkward," Lord Blackford said in a gentler voice. "And I know I shall have to explain to you why such a thing has occurred, but for the moment, I must have this bullet taken from my arm so that I might sew it up and bind it thereafter."

"Then a surgeon," Margaret breathed, closing her eyes tightly. "You require a surgeon."

"No." Lord Blackford's voice was sharp. "I cannot. They are prone to talking about what they have seen and what they have done and I will not allow them to endanger me... even though, I confess, I would most likely deserve any punishment that came my way."

Margaret looked at him, confused, trying to keep her eyes averted from the large bloodstain that covered Lord Blackford's shirt. "Punishment?"

Lord Blackford cleared his throat and, for the first time, Margaret realized just how pale he was. "As I said, my dear lady, I will explain it to you all much later but I cannot do so now. This arm of mine is a more pressing matter and I fear that my staff will not be of much use. I have only told a few of them what has occurred—the butler, housekeeper, maid and footman—and I pray that they will be able to keep what has occurred secret, known only to themselves. However, I am well aware that this may be wishful thinking on my part. After all, that is what London runs on, is it not? Rumor. Gossip. Intrigue." He shrugged. "Your presence, however, could prevent such a thing. I will not need to send for a doctor or a surgeon if you are able to assist me."

Margaret closed her eyes, rubbing her forehead with the back of her hand. "I do not understand, Lord Blackford."

"Here." He held out his hand to her and, unwillingly, she went towards him, thinking quietly to herself that this was not at all what she had expected and that she certainly had no skill when it came to doctoring! She wondered why he had not sent for the doctor, her eyes taking in the stain on his shirt which still appeared to be wet with blood. The injury had not stopped bleeding, then.

"Margaret, I know that I ask a great deal of you, but might you be able to help me in this matter?" Lord Blackford asked, his voice serious and his eyes filled with desperation. "I promise that I shall tell you everything you wish thereafter, and I shall not be at all angry if you should choose to turn your back on me."

This sounded rather ominous but Margaret knew she could not refuse. "I do not know what it is I am to do," she said, her voice shaking. "What if I hurt you further?"

Lord Blackford managed a tight, hard smile. "Most likely, you will, but it will be worth it given that the bullet will then be removed from its resting place. You need not fear, Margaret, I will tell you exactly what to do and when. You are not inclined to fainting, I hope?"

"I have not fainted yet," Margaret replied with a small sense of pride. "In all my years, I have never once swooned or anything so ridiculous."

Lord Blackford nodded, his face contorted with pain. "Then I hope this will not be the first time," he said with a sigh. "Now, you will need the whisky and that knife that I have set on the table. Bring them both to me. The butler will bring more bandages very soon, but we have no need of them as yet." He managed to smile, his hand tightening on hers. "Thank you, Margaret."

She nodded, her anxiety rising too high for her to either speak or smile back at him.

"You will do wonderfully, I am sure."

HALF AN HOUR LATER, Margaret was doing her very best not to cast up her accounts in the middle of Lord Blackford's study. The bullet was resting safely on the floor somewhere and she was now attempting to sew up the wound, which she found more trying than anything she had done before.

Lord Blackford had looked away as she had begun, having already let out a yelp of pain when she had been forced to delve into the bullet wound with the knife, in an attempt to find the bullet. She was sweating all over, feeling hot and ill at ease as she pushed the needle through the edge of the wound and pulled it as tightly closed as she dared.

Lord Blackford let out a hiss.

"It is almost over," she said quickly, attempting to be encouraging. "You need not worry."

"Splash it all liberally with whisky when you are finished," Lord Blackford instructed. "Do not worry about wasting it, for it is suggested that such a thing will prevent infection."

She did not question this but accepted it as she had done with everything else. Finishing the stitching, she filled a small glass with a mouthful of whisky and poured it down over the wound. Lord Blackford cried out, his face screwed up tightly with the pain of it.

"Again," he said, through gritted teeth. "Do not fear hurting me, Margaret. This is for my own good."

Margaret made to do so, only to pour herself a second, smaller measure in another glass which she then picked up and threw back, allowing the heat and the smoke of the whisky to ignite her very being, capturing her breath and bringing her fresh wakefulness and awareness. She then did as Lord Blackford had instructed, until, finally, he allowed her to bandage his arm.

His ruined shirt was soon on the flames as the butler helped Lord Blackford change into a fresh shirt, whilst Margaret kept her back turned. Her mind was filled with questions, her worry growing steadily. What was it Lord Blackford had been doing?

CHAPTER 9

"You cannot know how much I wish to keep the truth from you," Lord Blackford murmured once the butler had quit the room and Margaret had seated herself opposite him, a tea tray to her right. "I have been considering this matter ever since I first knew you had arrived back in town."

Margaret tried her best to remain completely silent, despite the many questions that came to her lips, burning her lips and tongue as she left them unspoken. Her stomach was knotting, her heart beating wildly as she looked at Lord Blackford, wondering what it was that he had to say to her. Why had he wanted to keep this from her? Was it something so terrible that she would not be able to forgive him?

Lord Blackford sighed heavily, his face haggard. His eyes were heavy, with deep shadows beneath them. His forehead was wrinkled, his brow furrowed. Whatever it was he had to say, it was bringing him a great deal of distress.

"I will tell you this, Margaret, although I cannot expect you to believe me, that I have only ridden out on three occasions. Yours was my second attempt and I have done nothing with the things I took."

"Took?" Margaret repeated, not understanding him. "I do not know what you mean."

Lord Blackford closed his eyes and ran a hand over his face, before looking at her directly.

"The day you came to London," he said slowly. "What was it that occurred?"

Margaret frowned, wondering what he meant. "I came by carriage."

"Out on the road," he said, leaning forward in his chair. "Do you recall? Lady Crawford insisted you tell it on multiple occasions."

Margaret's eyes widened. "You mean, the rogue who stopped my carriage and threatened to shoot my men?" she asked, her heart slowing as she realized what Lord Blackford was saying. "The man who did not take my wedding ring from me but took gold, coins and a ruby pendant?" That had not meant much to her, she had to admit, for she had been so very relieved that she had been allowed to keep her wedding ring that she had not thought twice about the pendant or the money.

Lord Blackford nodded. "Yes, that is what I mean, Margaret. That rogue, that man who stood in your path and threatened to shoot your men—that man was I."

Margaret stared at him, her breath gone from her chest. Her world began to tip sideways, a loud buzzing in her ears as she fought to keep herself from fainting. This could not be so. Lord Blackford could not have been the man who had stolen from her in such a terrible way.

"I did not do anything with your coins or your pendant," Lord Blackford continued, his head dropping so low that his chin almost rested on his chest. "They are in a locked drawer in the table." One hand reached out and pointed to the large oak table behind her but Margaret did not look at it. "I should never have taken them."

Margaret rose unsteadily to her feet, surprising Lord Blackford entirely.

"You are not leaving me?" he asked, suddenly sounding quite desperate. "I know I have done terrible things but there is more for me to say, Margaret. I want to explain."

She shook her head, holding out one hand to him in order to silence him. "Pray, give me a moment, Lord Blackford."

She walked towards where she had left her glass of whisky, praying that she would not collapse before she reached it, such was the shock coursing through her. Lifting it to her lips, she threw back the rest of the whisky in one smooth motion, letting the fire bring life back to her veins.

Setting it down, Margaret drew in her breath and pressed one hand firmly against her stomach in an attempt to calm herself.

"My pendant," she said, turning around to face Lord Blackford, who was staring into the flames in abject misery. "Where is it?"

Lord Blackford closed his eyes. "The key is in the lock," he said, gesturing towards the table. "I have thought of returning it to you on so many occasions but I found I could not, not when you would wonder why I had such a thing in my possession."

Margaret ignored this, walked around the table and found the small drawer that Lord Blackford had been talking about. Turning the key, she opened the drawer and found not only her ruby necklace, with a few gold coins scattered underneath it, but also a ring or two, pearl earrings and what appeared to be a rather large emerald.

Lord Blackford was a thief.

He must have seen the look in her eyes for as she came back to join him—reluctant as she was to hear his excuses for becoming a vagabond—his face fell and his expression grew desperate.

"When I came upon your carriage, Margaret, I did not know what to do," Lord Blackford said urgently. "I saw myself as if for the first time, saw the depths of what I had allowed myself to become."

Margaret, realizing that she had not said anything as yet, took in a steadying breath, settled her shoulders and looked at Lord Blackford with as much calmness in her expression as she could. "You stole from me."

Lord Blackford did not argue with this. "Yes."

"You threatened to shoot my men."

"Yes."

"You would have done so?"

Lord Blackford shook his head firmly. "NO, indeed, I would not. My pistol would not have fired, even if I had wished it. I am not that sort of gentleman, Margaret. Surely you must know that."

Margaret shook her head slowly, sadness seeping into her every pore. "I do not know what to think, Lord Blackford. I have spent so many days trying to work out what it is I feel for you but now I fear that all that time has been nothing more than wasted, for the man I believed you to be is not, in fact, the man you truly are."

"But it *is*," Lord Blackford exclaimed, leaning

forward and then wincing as his arm pained him. "I did not want to become such a rogue as all that, and yet in my desperation, I felt I had no other choice."

Margaret wanted to tell him that this was poppycock, that there was no good reason for anyone to turn to a life of crime, but there was something in Lord Blackford's eyes that made her hesitate. Did she not owe it to him to allow him an explanation? After all, he had been most kind and generous to her, as her friend, over these last weeks.

Looking down at the ruby pendant in her hand, Margaret sighed heavily, her shoulders slumping. This was all so very foolish. She had been battling with her feelings for Lord Blackford, relived that she had finally come to a decision that she was both glad and relieved about, only to discover that Lord Blackford was not the gentleman she thought him to be. Her mind went back to that day she had been travelling to London—had he not struck fear into her heart? Had she not been afraid for her servants?

And yet, had he not allowed her to keep her wedding ring? Had he not shown her kindness in that? Yes, he had taken what was not his, but she had not given the pendant nor the coins any more thought since they had been taken. They were not of particular importance to her—but to Lord Blackford, they had obviously meant a good deal.

"Why did you steal from me, Lord Blackford?" she asked solemnly. "What could be your reason for doing so?"

Lord Blackford's eyes drove into hers. "My son," he stated quietly. "It has been an attempt to rectify my estate for my son."

Something dropped into Margaret's stomach. "What do you mean?"

Lord Blackford sighed and ran one hand through his greying hair, evidence of just how difficult he was finding such explanations. His eyes turned away from hers, towards the fire that burned beside him.

"As you know, I have made a rather unfortunate mess of my estate," he began slowly. "At the death of my wife, I lost myself for some years. I have been trying to bring my estate back to its full capacity since then, have been trying to regain some of the wealth I did not care about at the time." He sighed, shaking his head. "My son wants to marry Catherine, Lady Crawford's daughter. It was this news that made me consider what it was I could do in order to add to my coffers, feeling almost desperate in my attempts to do so. That is why I chose to steal from those who have a good deal already." His eyes slid back towards hers, a deep sadness lingering in them. "It was foolish and ridiculous, yes. It was also wrong, but such was my desperation that I threw all that to the side." A small, wry smile caught his lips. "The first time I was fairly successful, for the rest of that box is what I took from the unfortunate inhabitants of the first carriage." He shook his head. "I wrestled with what I had done for some weeks, only to convince myself that not only could I do it again, but that I could slowly begin to accumulate wealth for my son and his future. And then, I encountered you."

Margaret let out her breath, not realizing she had been holding it. That was why the gentleman had ridden away when he had asked her what her name was. He had recognized her and had been filled with such horror that he could not have lingered.

"I was so very ashamed of myself, Margaret," Lord Blackford continued, his voice thick with emotion. "I was doing all I could to be callous and detached and yet when you spoke of your ring and your husband, I could feel my own heart crying out in understanding. How could I take such a precious thing from you?" His eyes caught hers and Margaret found that she could not look away. "But I told myself that a thief such as I was trying to be would be cruel and hard of heart, and so I tried not to allow my emotions to hold sway over me. In the depths of my mind, I felt as though I knew who you were, which was what brought me to ask your name. When you told me, I felt as if I were about to fall through the ground in shock, my heart beating wildly with both fright and disgust at myself." Shaking his head, he rubbed his forehead with the back of his hand. "I have been so afraid that you would recognize me."

"And that is why you wanted to spend time with me?" Margaret asked, finding, to her horror, that tears were beginning to pool in her eyes.

"No! No!" Lord Blackford was on his feet in a moment, his arm forgotten as he flung himself towards her, on his knees before her as though he were a desperate man looking for a reprieve. "I told myself, Margaret, that I should stay away from you, but I could not. You have become so very dear to me that this burden only increased in weight with every passing moment."

She sniffed and pulled out her handkerchief, dabbing delicately at her eyes. Her heart was breaking and she did not know what to do about the pain.

"I have wanted to tell you that I feel more for you than I had ever expected to, but I could not allow those words to pass my lips while I carry this weight with me," Lord Blackford explained, his eyes wide and his expression pained. "It is all my own fault, of course, and I do not even attempt to pass the burden onto any other. This was my own choice, my own responsibility and my own foolishness."

Margaret wiped her eyes and looked at him. "And yet it did not stop you from attempting to do so again," she pointed out, looking at his arm. "You were shot."

Lord Blackford hung his head. "I will never do so again," he said hoarsely. "That is enough. I have been foolish long enough."

A short, heavy silence rose between them.

"But why?" Margaret asked, trying her best not to cry. "Why would you do such a thing when you know that it is both wrong and unwise? Why did you go out again?"

"Because of news of my holdings," Lord Blackford muttered, his shoulders slumped as he knelt before her. "It is all borne from desperation, from fearing that my crops will not yield as much as they ought, that I shall have to take more money from my accounts in order to improve the estate. Money that my son shall have to struggle with when it comes time for him to take the title." His eyes darkened and he looked away. "I wish to goodness that I had never allowed my grief to drive me to such foolishness," he finished, looking for all the world as though he had quite given up on ever regaining her trust or her understanding again. "But it did. I behaved in a most selfish and irresponsible manner and even now, years later, I am bearing the consequences of what I have done."

Margaret closed her eyes, almost battling against the wave of sympathy that threatened to crash over her. Lord Blackford had admitted that he had been wrong to do as he had done, had confessed to his reasons for doing so and had told her the entirety of what he had done without hesitation—although she knew he had been keeping it from her since they had first met. She found that she wanted to understand, that she wanted to express to him that she knew why he had behaved in such a way and that she did not hold his actions against him, but found that she could do no such thing. Not yet. The shock of his revelations had been too much.

"I think I must leave you," she said softly, trying to rise to her feet without brushing against him. "I do hope your arm recovers quickly, Lord Blackford."

Lord Blackford did not look up, evidently having expected or simply accepting that this was the course of action she had chosen to take.

"I will write to you very soon," she promised, making him glance up at her. "This is not the end of our acquaintance, Lord Blackford, but I must do some thinking."

He nodded, eventually pushing himself from his knees to a standing position, although his body remained hunched over, his guilt and shame evident.

"Know that everything I have said to you, Margaret, is the truth," he said without looking at her. "If I had any hope of your acceptance, I would press you for your agreement to let me court you, but I know that what I have done would not allow for such a thing. I quite understand, of course. I am just glad that you know the truth now."

Her heart ached terribly but Margaret said nothing, one hand pressed against her chest as though she might prevent the pain from increasing.

"I have enjoyed every moment in your company, Margaret," Lord Blackford continued, his head still bowed low. "This has been one of the most delightful seasons I have ever had, and that is all down to you. Your company, your conversation, your generous heart has called out to me and I have reveled in all of it. Whether or not you choose to continue our acquaintance— and I would not blame you if you do not—I have been glad to know you again, Margaret, after all these years. You have brought light back into my dark existence. I have found happiness—and love —growing within my heart."

Margaret caught her breath, her whole body

alive with a sudden, fierce joy that she could not quite explain.

"I know you must go and I will not beg you to stay," Lord Blackford finished, turning away from her. "I am grateful for this opportunity to share my heart and my disgrace with you. It has freed me in a way I did not expect. My apologies are heartfelt, Margaret. I should never have done such things, neither to you nor to the others I stole from. I swear I shall do so no more."

Margaret nodded, closed her eyes and forced herself to draw in a steadying breath. She was battling against her own desire to fling all that he had done aside and run to him, to confess that her own heart had found an affection for him that she had not expected either, but the pain of what he had done still lingered in her mind. Opening the door, she looked back at him for another moment, but found that his back was still towards her. Without another word, she slipped out the door and walked towards the entrance of the house, leaving Lord Blackford behind.

EPILOGUE

Margaret had not slept.

Instead, she had spent the night tossing and turning, her mind filled with questions and her heart both joyful and despondent in equal measure.

She could not forget Lord Blackford's confession of both his wrongdoing and his love for her. They battled against each other, making her struggle to understand what it was she felt and what it was she wanted to do.

One thing was quite certain, however. She did *not* want her acquaintance with Lord Blackford to come to an end, no matter what he had done. He had reignited her heart in a way she had never thought would ever occur again. Yes, she still grappled with what she felt for Lord Blackford and the deep love for her late husband that ran through her, but slowly she was beginning to find a way for them both to run alongside each other in contentment and understanding. She loved Joseph still, but she was beginning to love Lord Blackford also.

She loved a man who was a thief.

Closing her eyes, Margaret rubbed at her forehead, aware that she had deep shadows smudging underneath her eyes. Breakfast had not been particularly appetizing and now, even though she had barely eaten anything, she was still not hungry for the tea tray that had been set before her. There was a small arrangement of various sweets, but none caught her interest. How could she eat when she was in such confusion?

Pouring herself a cup of tea and praying that it would calm her somewhat, Margaret stirred it carefully before sitting back down in her seat by the small fire. The day was rather dull and not particularly warm, adding to her feelings of discontent. Looking into the flames, Margaret questioned whether or not she could understand *why* Lord Blackford had chosen to behave in such a brutish manner... and to her surprise, found that she could.

She knew all too well what grief was like. She knew how it troubled one's soul, to the point that it seemed to be all that one could feel. The misery, the pain, the distress that came with it almost every waking minute could drive anyone to distraction—and Lord Blackford had dealt with it in a way that had brought ongoing consequences. He had, as he had said, been trying to rectify that for decades, but the damage he had done had obviously been severe. Trying to heal those wounds, financial or otherwise, was quite honorable, although using theft and robbery to do so was not something she could accept. At least, on that point he had admitted as such and had only done so on three occasions—with one of those occasions being her own. If he could return the jewels to their respective owners, then that would be the start of a way to make amends, would it not?

Sipping her tea, Margaret let a sigh shake her frame, aware of just how much he had been offering her by confessing the truth about his feelings. He loved her, which was something equally extraordinary and frightening. She had not expected such feelings from him, although she could now understand why he had not spoken to her of them before. Now that he was free of his burden of guilt, he had been able to tell her the truth about his heart—and she had found herself drawn to him with such desperation that she had almost wanted to fling herself into his arms right there and then.

"Is that what you will do now, then, Margaret? "she asked herself aloud, a frown creasing her brow. "Will you go to him? Or will you return home?"

Home. That word did not bring her the joy she had thought would come with it, realizing that she would be quite alone once more, although her family would soon ensure that she was kept busy, of course. But there would not be the pleasant conversation after dinner, the laughs and smiles at the breakfast table that she had once enjoyed with Joseph and now found herself longing for again. If she turned her back on Lord Blackford, if she chose to tell him that she could not forgive this nor allow her understanding to show him any sort of compassion, then she would be resigning herself to a life without his company.

Her stomach twisted, just as a knock came at the door.

"Yes?"

The butler cleared his throat. "My lady, Lord Blackford has arrived. He says he will not stay if you do not wish it, but he has come to take his leave of you."

Margaret blinked, her heart quickening dramatically. "To take his leave?"

"Yes, my lady," the butler repeated, his face stoic. "That is what he said."

Margaret got to her feet, her tea forgotten. "Send him in at once."

She began to pace up and down in front of the fire, her fingers twisting together as she held her hands in front of her. Take his leave? What did that mean? Was Lord Blackford leaving London?

Another scratch at the door. Margaret forced herself to stand still, her eyes fixed on the door as it opened.

Lord Blackford stepped inside, his eyes only lingering on her face for a moment before they dropped to the floor. "Thank you for seeing me, Margaret. I was not sure you would and I am—"

"Are you leaving?" Margaret asked, interrupting him. "Are you leaving town?"

Lord Blackford nodded, his eyes heavy with grief. "I think it best," he stated quietly, pulling out a small parcel from his pocket. "This is yours, I think." He made to hand it to her, only to pull his hand back and set the package on a table, as though he did not want to touch her. "It is what I took from you, Margaret. I have sent the Egertons their own monies back also, although they will not know who has sent it, of course."

Relief flooded her heart. "That is wonderful, Lord Blackford."

A wry smile pulled at his lips, his eyes finally lingering on her face. "It is the end," he said slowly. "The end of my foolishness. I have made amends, I have paid for my actions." He gestured to his arm. "And now I think I must return home, where I can oversee all that goes on at my estate. I must make it as profitable as I can for my son."

Her heart sank to the floor. "You are leaving?"

"I think I must," Lord Blackford replied, turning away towards the door. "Although I will be sorry to leave you behind."

Margaret shook her head, her stomach roiling as she took a few steps towards him. "Wait. Lord Blackford, please."

Slowly, Lord Blackford turned back to face her, his expression confused.

"I do not want you to go," she told him, lifting her chin. "In fact, I do not think I can allow you to do so."

Lord Blackford frowned, confusion etching itself across his expression. "You cannot let me go?"

"No, Lord Blackford, I do not think I can," Margaret replied, her mouth going dry as she saw the look in his eyes. "I have spent a good many hours considering what it is you have said, letting myself think over what has occurred and what the future might hold should I either refuse to continue our acquaintance or allow myself to forget everything that has happened." She saw his eyes flare, a glimmer of hope appearing within them. "If anyone can understand the part that grief has played in your actions, Lord Blackford, then it is I."

Lord Blackford let out a long breath, shaking his head in apparent disbelief. "You cannot think that what I did was right."

"No, indeed!" she exclaimed, a small smile on her face. "It was quite wrong, but you have confessed it to me and have returned what is mine." Her hand was trembling as she settled it on his arm, the enormity of what she was doing coming home to her as she looked up into his face. "I cannot forget all that we have shared, Lord Blackford. You have become quite dear to me, although I confess that I have been struggling with what I feel."

Lord Blackford did not move, as though to either move or speak would prevent her from saying more.

"I love Joseph," Margaret continued, her voice hitching as she thought of her dear husband, who had been so wonderful to her during their marriage. "Even though he is gone, I love him still. And yet, within my heart, I have felt the beginnings of a second love. A love for you, Lord Blackford."

Lord Blackford swallowed hard, his face seeming to pale as he placed his hand over hers. "You make me feel as though I am a young gentleman again, seeking to claim the hand of the most beautiful creature he has ever set his eyes upon," he murmured, his tender words bringing a light to her soul. "I have not felt such things for years."

"Nor I," Margaret admitted. "Joseph has been buried almost seven years now, and I have found my life to be both wonderful and lonely in equal measure. I came to London in the hope of pursuing old friendships, never thinking that I would find my heart lost to another." She smiled up at him, taking in his lined face, his hazel eyes that were still vibrant and filled with light. "I do not want you to leave London, Lord Blackford, not unless you intend on taking me with you."

She laughed as his brows shot up towards his hairline, aware that she had been more than obvious about what she expected their future to be.

"You cannot mean it, Margaret," Lord Blackford whispered, evidently overcome with what she was offering him. "Not after what I have done."

Margaret placed one hand on Lord Blackford's chest, the other still holding his hand. They were closer than they had ever been before and yet she felt no guilt or awkwardness about it. This felt right, as if this was where she had meant to be ever since she had returned to London.

"I do not intend to think of what has passed any longer, Lord Blackford," she replied truthfully. "You have made amends, you have told me the truth and I have chosen to accept it, forgive it and set it aside. My heart will not allow me to forget the love that has begun to grow within it. To separate myself from you now would only bring me pain and struggle, and I have had quite enough of such things, I think." She smiled as he nodded, his eyes fixed on her own. She knew that he understood everything she was saying. "I have wealth, Lord Blackford. Wealth enough to share with your estate so that your son will have a good future with his wife."

Lord Blackford framed her face with his hands, his eyes searching hers. "I would not marry you for your wealth, Margaret."

"Then what would you marry me for?" she asked, her heart beating wildly with all that she felt.

"For love," Lord Blackford said, his expression gentling as her hands ran over his shoulders to twine around the back of his neck. "I confess this to you now, Margaret. I love you desperately. Terribly so. I love you more than I think I can ever express."

Margaret smiled up at him, knowing that this was the beginning of something truly wonderful, something she had never expected to occur at this stage of her life. She had found a new love with Lord Blackford, a love that she knew would only continue to grow with every day they spent together.

"And I love you, Blackford," she murmured as he began to lower his head, his hands falling to her waist so that he might hold her close as he kissed her. She leaned into him, her fears and her doubts falling aside as she gave her heart to the man who had lost so much, who understood her grief and who, ultimately, had come to be more precious to her than she had ever expected.

THE END

ALSO BY SUNNY BROOKS

I truly hope you enjoyed experiencing love & mystery with the Catesby family!

Would you like the journey to continue?

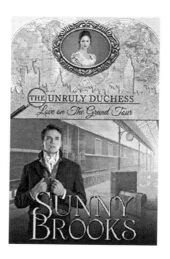

Enjoy my next series, starring the Catesby's American-bred cousin, Lady Cecelia, as she journeys to England on an epic adventure.

The Unruly Duchess books are available now!

Cheers! Sunny

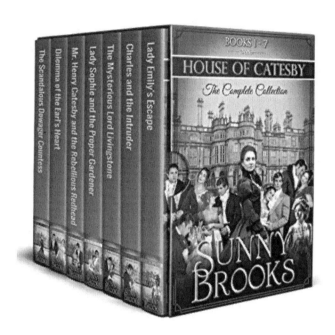

Book 5: Mr. Henry Catesby and the Rebellious Redhead

Book 6: Dilemma of the Earl's Heart

Bonus Book 7: The Scandalous Dowager Countess

The Unruly Duchess (series)

The Unruly Duchess trilogy stars the Catesby's American-bred cousin, Lady Cecelia, as she journeys to England on a life-changing adventure.

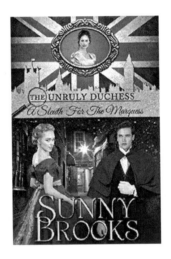

Book 1: Love on The Grand Tour

Book 2: A Sleuth for the Marquess

Book 3: Married to the Duke: A Royal Wedding Mystery

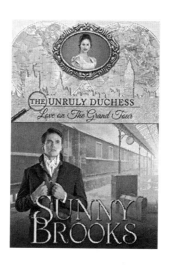

WHAT REVIEWERS ARE SAYING ABOUT SUNNY BROOKS:

Fantastic! If you love this genre this is **a must read.**

After the death of the Earl this family does what it must with strength of will. **The author has developed them so well you will feel as if you have known them for a long time.** Great job. I highly recommend this collection. **I know I will re-read these stories many times.**

Sweet love, forbidden love and second chance love as each of the family members find their own happy ever after.

I completely loved this set of books. Each book is lovely in its own way, but **they are all truly special.**

A suspenseful collection of Regency romances.

Reminiscent of **Downton Abbey**...an enjoyable way to pass the time on a cold winter's day.

I had read the first six books and been delighted by them, but Book 7 with **the adventures of the 50-year-old widow Lady Margaret Catesby is heavenly.**

Sweet clean romances with a bit of drama and a lot of chemistry. Nice storylines and plots. Likeable characters. **Captivating from start to finish.** I like the mix of mystery, suspense, drama, danger, villains and romance. **It kept me on the edge.**

Very well done, Sunny!!! BRAVA!!!

ABOUT THE AUTHOR

Sunny Brooks may seem mild-mannered, but she secretly craves the dramatic! For years she worked in the theater, producing period plays and productions on everything from scrappy little stages to sold-out amphitheaters. Through it all she found that one thing stays the same: a great story is always compelling, regardless of budget, production quality, or costumes.

Sunny now brings those stories of inspiration, suspense, heartache, redemption, strength and overcoming adversity to an even wider audience through her books.

With a true love and devotion to story-telling, she aspires to bring her readers on a journey culminating in happiness and hope.

When she is not writing she tries desperately to master the art of baking pies, and spends a whole lot of time reading (you guessed it) romantic novels!

To find out about more great books visit:
www.LoveLightFaith.com